PUBLISHING
PRESENTS

VS.

EDITED BY DAWN CANO

READ ORDER

334 (9)	20	134	346 (15)	314
58	82	170	118	32
68	220	188	250 (16)	93
301	388	202	152	361
414 (10)	400 (12)	232	266	
		288 (14)	424	

VS.
US vs UK Horror

First Published in 2016

VS is copyright © Dawn Cano 2016
Copyright of each story belongs to its listed author.

Compiled by Dawn Cano.

Edited by Dawn Cano.
Proofed by Duncan Ralston.

Published by Shadow Work Publishing.

Cover design by Michael Bray.
Interior design by Daniel Marc Chant.

ISBN: 978-0995242364

DEDICATED
TO THE ANIMALS.

CONTENTS

PRE FIGHT HYPE

US FOREWORD
ZACHARY WALTERS
THE EYES OF MADNESS

VS

UK FOREWORD
JIM MCLEOD
GINGERNUTS OF HORROR

US FOREWORD
ZACHARY WALTERS
THE EYES OF MADNESS

Americans.

We are a brash, fickle bunch. Oftentimes we are egotistical, confrontational, heart strong. We can be swift to overreact and leisure about seeing issues from another point of view. Anxious to rally the troops against authority or any perceived threat to or belief system at the risk of overlooking actual threats to our way of life. We idolize celebrities a bit more than we should, role models and legitimate heroes a bit less, but hey, nobody is perfect... although Americans are pretty damn close.

Do we apologize? Rarely. Apologies are like cryptids, many people claim to have seen one but nobody has concrete proof. We are more likely to take offense that you're not completely on board with our individual, varied, views.

I goof, somewhat. What the above says to me is that American's are passionate. The specifics of that passion can be heartfelt and sincere, it can also be vapid and

selfish. But passionate nonetheless. We place what we love on a pedestal and sing its praises while placing what we hate in the flames, dragging it amongst the coals. Fueled by pure emotion.

I myself am passionate about dark fiction. And what I thirst for is the unnerving discomfort, the grisliest of bloodshed, and the bleakest of shadows. As a young lad I cut my teeth on American horror & dark fiction. My earliest nightmares were directly affected by the honey laced poison of Clive Barker.... wait a minute. I mean the labyrinthine landscapes of Ramsey Campbell... hold on. Mary Shelley and Dennis Wheatly's classical prose and landscapes... fuck.

In actuality Charles L. Grant ruled my bookshelf for a long time with his Oxrun Station series of tales, a landmark of quiet horror fiction. Robert R. McCammon's *Boys Life* & Dan Simmons's *Summer of Night* taught me that there could be a lot of depth and deep personal connection to dark fiction. A few Ray Bradbury yarns, *The Halloween Tree* and *Something Wicked This Way Comes*, get frequent rereads. And let us not forget drunk Uncle Stevie (now sober Uncle Stevie) whose mesmerizing novel *IT* opened the door to what horror fiction could achieve. *IT* touches on so many of my deep-seated personal fears that I can honestly say that I think of it daily. Stephen King taught us all about excess, taught us about the fragility of life, all the while tearing down the wall and making horror a household genre. Dark fiction is what I live for and I'll wave its flag, sing its praises, until my last breath.

Which brings us to *VS.*, a Rumble-in-the-Jungle of dark works. American and UK authors butting heads in a match-up for the ages. Place your bets and crack that spine, folks. This beast is sure to please. I have a personal stake in a few of these battles as I see many names I recognize, a couple of authors I'd consider favorites. On the other side of the coin, there are some who will be first time reads for me, which is always exciting.

Publicly, I'll place my wager on the American side, all day long. And I'll be glad to buy you all a drink with my winnings. Where my loyalties truly lie? Well, I'll keep that close to the vest, for now.

I know a guy, an important guy, an authority on dark fiction. You don't know him but believe me when I say that he knows what he's talking about. He believes this is one of the most profound anthologies in dark fiction history. He also says the Americans TRUMP the UK blokes. Hands down. So there you go.

I bet you though I was going to say 'Merica.

- Zakk is a big dumb animal,
Ex Libris the Eyes of Madness

UK FOREWORD
JIM MCLEOD

When Dawn asked me to write the introduction to *VS.*, I thought, "Let's do a serious discussion about the differences between Great Britain and the US." Then I sobered up and thought, "No chance. Let's do a discussion on why Great Britain is better than the US."

Now before all of you from the US start banging your fists against the table, demanding that I get sent an orange jumpsuit and a free ticket to that resort in Cuba, calm down, take a chill pill and listen to why I am right.

Language:

1. Pants. What the hell are pants? It's *trousers.* Pants are either what you wear underneath your trousers, or what we use to describe your complete lack of understanding of the English language. Notice how it's THE ENGLISH language, not THE AMERICAN Language. There is a reason for that. You Americans, and Canadians as well, have a bastardised version of The Queen's language. There are loads of other examples. Let me give you one more.

2. A Sidewalk. What does that even mean? Is there a

"central walk," and "slightly off the middle walk?" No, it's PAVEMENT.

This brings us to your food, and in particular, your chocolate. Seriously, America, you need to stop eating that brown crap you think is chocolate. It's bad enough that it exists over there, but you then have the cheek to buy out one of our chocolate making companies and mess about with our cream eggs. To those of us with a sweet tooth, that is an act of war. If you want to eat your vile stuff, then fine, go and do it in a corner, away from the rest of the world, but keep your dirty ape paws off our stuff. And what is your obsession with adding peanut butter to chocolate? Who even eats this stuff on its own? You do realise that peanut butter is made by harvesting squirrel shit, don't you? It's true. I saw a video on YouTube once.

Chips. Chips? What are you on about? They are crisps. Chips are chunky bits of potato, deep fried in lard or drippings. I won't even recognise British chips that are fried in some oil. If it isn't the thickness of an adult's thumb and dripping in the remains of some poor cow, then it isn't a chip.

Let's talk politicians:

To be fair, we both have our fair share of nasty, unethical politicians. And sometimes, the scumbags have worked together; the love affair between Blair and Bush was one of the sickest and most twisted things ever to walk the face of the planet. Until, that is, you crazy fools thought Trump was a good idea. This vile excuse for a human being is surely the spawn of Satan in human form. At least our cretinous politicians have an air of tomfoolery about them. While Boris Johnson may be just as nasty as Trump, at least we get a laugh at his bumbling attempts at being a politician.

Music:

Yes, you gave us blues, country and thrash metal. But, you also gave us Miley Cyrus, modern country and hair metal. For every Johnny Cash, there are a hundred Luke

Bryans and Kenny Chesneys. For every Anthrax there are unlimited Bon Jovis, Motley Crues and Poisons. Look at what we gave you: The Beatles, The Stones, The Clash, Iron Maiden, The Specials, Pink Floyd, I could go on and on. Hell, even our terrible singers have a purpose. Where would we be without all those Rickrolls? I'll tell you where we would be—we would be in a much duller world.

Sport:

We have rugby; you have American football - a game that seems to last for decades, where your sportsmen are too scared to get hurt or to damage their pretty boy faces, so they have to wear more armour and padding than even a Knight of The Crusades would feel comfortable wearing. Look at our rugby players. At most, we wear a gumshield and a nut guard. And that's only because British dental hygiene is so bad, we need to protect our crooked and broken teeth from even more damage.

You have baseball; we have cricket. Both are inherently mind-numbing sports that can last for days, but at least we use our game as an excuse to have afternoon tea and eye up the vicar's wife. You use it as an excuse to fill stadiums with hot dog scoffing and weak-as-piss beer drinking layabouts.

I could go on and on, and if you get me drunk enough, I will, but you really should be reading the stories in this excellent anthology, where British and American authors do battle to see who is the best. Dawn has assembled a great roster of writers, even if half of them are American. With the likes of Kit Power, Rich Hawkins, Lex Jones, Thomas S Flowers and Duncan Ralston (see you even have to bring in a Canadian, of all things), this anthology is going to be a great read, and remember it's all for charity, so please, once you have read this book, leave a review on Amazon, tell your friends, and spread the word.

Jim "Ginger Nuts" Mcleod,
The Gingernuts of Horror

ROUND ONE

THE YARD SALE
JOHN LEDGER

VS

LINE DANCING AT HACK HOUSE
JIM GOFORTH

THE YARD SALE
JOHN LEDGER

I.

Every neighborhood has that strange family that people are afraid of. Here on Kennedy Street, in Marinville, Pennsylvania, that honor went to the Hughes family. Becky, or Kitty, as her friends called her, was the head of their clan. Her two sons, Jim and Tony were complete opposites. Jim was tall with long blonde hair and a beard. He was the serious, smart one of her children. Tony was short and bald, covered in tattoos, and loved his death metal. That was the only thing the brothers had in common, their love for loud music.

Becky's daughter, Dani, was the bad one. All of her children were adults themselves now, but Dani had been a problem since day one. She was the baby, and Becky almost died giving birth to her. She was in labor for seventy-four hours and had to have her thyroid gland removed afterwards. From that point on, it was one problem after another with Dani as she got older. By the

age of seven, she had already started torturing animals and setting fires for fun. Becky realized her boys were no angels, constantly getting into trouble and getting kicked out of school, but Dani was evil and enjoyed hurting people. Now, Becky was nearing sixty-years old, and her family had formed quite a lucrative business over the years.

She sat in the living room with her boyfriend, Lex, as her children showed up, ready for their next job. Dani headed straight for the fridge, opened a beer and downed half of it immediately. Tony sat down in the recliner and lit up a cigarette, and Jim remained standing, awaiting his mother's orders.

"Now that you're all here, we can begin. The job needs done tonight. We got a special request from a repeat customer. And he pays well, so don't fuck it up."

"Who's the repeat customer?" Tony asked.

"You don't need to know that. You three don't meet the customers. That's my gig," Lex chimed in.

"Fuck you, Lex," Tony mumbled, flicking ashes all over the place.

"Watch the damn carpet, you jackass!" Becky yelled, as she stood up and handed a photograph and a piece of paper with an address on it to Jim.

"Let me see," Dani said, making her way over to her big brothers. "Oh, she's hot. Check her out Tony."

"Holy shit, you ain't kidding!" Tony started howling like a wolf. "We're gonna have some fun with her."

"No, you're not. None of you. You do the job and that's it," Becky ordered.

"Yes, mother," Tony and Dani replied in unison.

"Jim, I'm counting on you to keep these two in line." Becky kissed him on his cheek.

"Who's gonna keep him in line?" Lex laughed, scooping popcorn from a bowl in his lap, feeding his face as he surfed through the channels on the television. Jim turned the TV off and faced the couch.

"Don't worry, mother. I can handle it. And fuck off,

Lex."

"Fuck you, asshole," Lex yelled, jumping up from the couch, spilling popcorn on the floor. Tony was out of the recliner and at his brother's side in a second. Dani already had a switchblade in her hand as she moved closer to Lex.

"Knock it off, knock it off right now. All of you. You three, get the hell out and do your job. And you, you jackass, clean up this fucking mess." Becky stormed off to the kitchen to get a drink as her children exited the house quietly. Lex cleaned up his mess, mumbling to himself the whole time.

"I hear you in there, ya damn fool," Becky reminded him. "I'm not done with you yet. We got plenty of time til they get back. So, when you're done making my room look nice and clean, you can bring your skinny little ass up to my bedroom cause I got some more work for you to do."

"Yes, dear. I'll be right up."

"Oh, I know you will," Becky laughed, as she made her way upstairs. It was going to be a long night for Lex.

II.

They took Jim's van and it was past midnight when they showed up at the address. The house was a nice ranch home and there was only to be one person inside: their target, a woman named Meghan. As they parked across the street though, they noticed two cars in the driveway.

"Is somebody else here?" Tony asked from the backseat.

"How the fuck should we know? Maybe the bitch has two cars. She's obviously a rich little cunt." Dani laughed. She was excited. She only wished that she could truly do whatever she wanted to the woman inside.

"Alright, let's go." Jim opened the door and started walking towards the house. Dani and Tony followed suit, rushing to catch up to him. They both had their knives in hand while their brother carried the bag. They made their

way around the side of the house and hopped a fence to get into the backyard. Jim stopped and looked around in all directions. After he was sure the coast was clear, he addressed his siblings quietly.

"Okay. Here's the masks. Put em' on." Jim reached into the bag and pulled out three ski masks. Dani and Tony both crouched, setting their blades down momentarily as they covered their faces. Jim joined them and put the bag on his back. All three of them were wearing black and carrying blades, ready to work.

"Let's do this shit." Jim said, as they headed towards the patio door.

III.

Meghan was happy not to be spending another Friday night alone. Kit was just the company she needed. He didn't try to hit on her, and he didn't make her feel bad about herself. Sure, he was a guy, but he was just a friend, and that's what she needed more than anything right now. Meghan was well aware that she was a gorgeous, twenty-five year old with no financial problems in sight. But that was only thanks to her father leaving her everything when he died. Meghan had accomplished nothing with her life other than one failed relationship after another and mastering the art of loneliness.

Tonight, though, she was perfectly content staying in with her friend, Kit, and watching his favorite movie, *Robocop*. He rambled on about stuff that she didn't understand while they drank wine, and that was fine with her. He was happy and full of energy and it made her happy. A little too happy actually, she realized. Meghan was feeling the alcohol and noticed that she started thinking about Kit making love to her. She excused herself to the kitchen in order to clear her head. More wine was the last thing she needed, but she had to be alone for a minute. The thoughts of Kit undressing her quickly

vanished as she entered the kitchen. Meghan dropped her glass as she saw them, walking right in through the patio door.

"Don't move a muscle, bitch!" Dani yelled, approaching Meghan with a knife pointed at her chest. Meghan was scared to death as she stood there defenseless in front of the three intruders. Jim took the bag off his back and set it on a counter, opening it as he rummaged around before finally pulling out a hood and a pair of handcuffs.

"What's going on here?" Kit cried out, running into the kitchen. He was immediately silenced by Tony coming up behind him and putting his blade up to his throat.

"Please don't hurt us," Meghan cried. "Take whatever you want, but just leave us alone."

"Shut up," Dani snapped, as she slapped Meghan hard across the face. "We're not gonna hurt you. Somebody paid good money for your sweet little ass."

"What do we do with him?" Tony asked, looking at his brother Jim who shrugged his shoulders and simply responded, "Kill him."

Kit's throat being sliced open was the last thing Meghan saw before a hood was placed over her head. She cried even louder as they placed the handcuffs around her wrists. Jim looked at Dani as he spoke. "Watch her while we load the van. Then we go."

"Oh, I'll watch her, alright," Dani laughed, as her brothers headed off further into the house to collect any valuables worth selling. As soon as they were out of sight, Dani decided to have some fun with Meghan. "You sure are a pretty little thing, aren't you? I hate bitches like you. How about we take a look and see what's so special about you. I already saw your face and I gotta admit you're just as hot as some of those bitches in Hollywood. Let's see what you got going on under here though." Dani sliced Meghan's blouse open and roughly yanked her bra down until one of her breasts was exposed. Meghan was terrified.

She didn't try to fight back, she didn't say a word. She just kept crying.

"Well, look at that. You're just about fucking perfect, aren't you? I sure wish my tits looked like that." Dani pinched Meghan's nipple with her free hand until she cried out in pain, begging her to stop. Dani stopped and laughed, but she was far from done yet.

"Turn around and lean over the counter now," Dani ordered. Meghan listened because she was afraid not to as the maniac behind her began reaching up under her skirt. She grabbed a hold of Meghan's ass before using the knife again to cut her panties off of her. "Now, I'm really gonna have some fun with you, bitch."

"What are you doing?" Jim yelled, as he and Tony came back into the kitchen to find the woman bent over the counter, with Dani about a second away from sticking the handle end of her knife inside of her.

"I was just gonna have some fun. You two were taking too long."

"The van is loaded. Let's go," he replied.

Meghan was led outside, unable to see, hands cuffed behind her back, her breast hanging out and her panties left behind. They tossed her into the van, and the next thing she knew, she was on her way to a destination unknown. She had a feeling things were about to get much worse, and she was right.

IV.

When Meghan woke up, she was still blindfolded. She wasn't handcuffed anymore, but her current situation wasn't any better. She was in a standing position, but her hands were now tied above her with ropes connected to something. To make matters worse, she was now completely naked. She had no clue where she was, but the thoughts of Kit being murdered came racing back through her mind as she began crying again. Before she had a

chance to think about anything else, a voice interrupted her.

"Oh, don't start that shit. They told me you were a crybaby when they brought you back, but I ain't gonna put up with that shit."

Meghan immediately noticed this voice was different than that of any of the three intruders in her house, and that realization frightened her even more.

"I bet you're wondering where you are and who I am, aren't you?"

"Yes. Please, just let me go, I won't tell anybody. I have money, I can pay you."

Lex laughed. "Quit your begging, it ain't gonna get you nowhere. I'm the guy that gets to watch you until the person that paid for you comes to pick you up."

"Paid for me for what? What are they going to do with me?"

"Honey, I don't know, and I don't give a shit. You're nothing more than merchandise to me. And you're bought and paid for. In the meantime though, we're gonna have us some fun, just you and me."

Lex walked up to her and took the hood off her head as she finally got to see for the first time in several hours. She noticed she was in a garage, and sure enough her hands were tied to a beam above her head. The man in front of her wore a ski mask like his cohorts, only he had no shirt on and a pair of blue jeans.

"You are one hot piece of ass, that's for sure. I don't know if you're worth the money that was paid for you, but hey, it's not my money. Now, you see, I was told I'm not allowed to touch you and God knows if my woman found out my ass would be out on the street. But guess what, I don't see her or anyone else here to stop me. Do you?"

"No," was all Meghan said as she stared at the man, noticing his multiple tattoos.

"That's a good girl. You're learning quickly." Lex took off his jeans and underwear, and Meghan couldn't help but

notice that he was more than ready to go. She knew exactly what was about to happen and there wasn't a thing she could do to stop it.

"Now, I promise this won't hurt much. Or maybe it will? Just in case you're a screamer though we gotta take care of that. Open wide."

Meghan had to fight back the urge to vomit as Lex shoved his underwear in her mouth as a gag. He disappeared behind her, and a few seconds later he was inside her, grunting and thrusting as he raped her. He came inside of her, leaving the gag in her mouth as he sat down and lit up a cigarette, smiling at her. This cycle continued several times throughout the night until he finally wore himself out and Meghan cried herself to sleep.

V.

"Okay, Meghan, so the last time we had a session we left off at the man raping you in what you thought was a garage. Would you like to continue from there?"

"I don't think it was a garage, Dr. Hickman, I know it was a garage. I said I thought it was at the time. Now, I know it was."

"Okay, so you know it was a garage. You can call me Kyle, by the way. I want you to think of me as a friend instead of a physician, Meghan."

"Okay, Dr. Kyle." She smiled, as she leaned back on the leather couch. "I hope you have a lot of time cause I've got plenty to talk about."

"We have all the time in the world. I get paid by the hour, so we're in no hurry here."

"And I can tell you whatever I want and it stays between us?"

"Absolutely. Your secrets are safe here."

"Well then, Kyle, whenever you want to press the little red button there, I can get started."

"I'm ready when you are." Doctor Hickman pressed

record, and the session was underway.

"Okay. Well as I said before, my name is Meghan Oliver. I'm twenty-seven-years old and I live here in Marinville, Pennsylvania with my two year old son Russel."

"Let me stop you there. I don't want you to tell me anything that you're not comfortable talking about, but we can skip the introductions. I have all of that from our last session. If you would like to continue where we left off last time, that's up to you. You can talk about whatever you desire."

"Okay, so after the garage. That's what you want to know right?"

"I want to know whatever you want me to know. Whatever you feel the need to discuss. Can I ask you a question about Russel?"

"My son? Sure, what do you want to ask me?"

"Well, this may be a hard question. Who is the father Meghan, do you know?"

"I don't know. Maybe the guy from the garage, maybe not? I guess I should continue my story."

"Only if you want to. But if you do, yes, what happened after you fell asleep in the garage?"

"Okay, after the garage. Well, the next time I woke up I was still naked. I was in a bed this time, and I wasn't blindfolded or tied up but I still couldn't move. I was obviously drugged somehow. I could see but I couldn't move my head or anything else for that matter. Later on, I would come to discover that apparently the man who purchased me was named Daniel and he bought me as a birthday present for his bisexual boyfriend, Rich. I'll spare you the details because I can do without reliving the incident myself. Let's just say I was raped again, several times by this Rich guy, while his boyfriend Daniel pleasured himself in the corner as he cheered his lover on. When they were done with me, they blindfolded me and loaded me into some sort of vehicle before dropping me off on the side of the road like a piece of trash. Once I

could finally move, I took the blindfold off to discover I was literally in my own front yard. So there you have it, Doc, the father of my child could be the scumbag from the garage or the other guy. I'll never know now, though."

"And that's the end of the story? Why do I sense there's more to tell me, Meghan?"

"Oh, because there is. I gotta ask again, Kyle, you sure I can tell you anything here?"

"Absolutely. Like I said, anything you say here in this room stays between us."

"Okay, well that was two years ago, but that's not the end of my story."

"Alright, continue if you want to. If not I understand. We can wait til our next session if that's better for you. I realize you already shared a lot of information with me today that's tough for you to talk about."

"I don't think there will be a next session, so I should probably just get it all out now. I'm healed. I feel better. I just need to tell somebody what I did. Do you understand that, Kyle?"

"What you did? I think I understand, but either way, continue if you wish."

"Not too long ago, about a month before the first time we spoke, I took care of all my problems."

"How did you take care of them, Meghan?"

"I was taking Russel out for a walk in his stroller and I came across a yard sale. I didn't think anything of it at first until I saw him. The man that raped me from the garage. Of course I didn't ever see his face, but I recognized the tattoos immediately and I knew it was him. I looked around and saw a garage behind the corner house and my suspicions were confirmed. I didn't even hesitate at that point, I knew this was the place I was first held captive. I took Russel home immediately and called my mother, asking her to watch him for a while. I told her I had something important to take care of."

"Okay, then what happened, Meghan?"

"Well, after the home invasion and the multiple rapes, I bought a gun. I headed straight back to the house and knocked right on the front door. I got lucky too, they were all home. One of the men opened the door and I pointed my gun in his face, letting myself in. Once I got inside the house, I had a little talk with the old lady and her family. Long story short, I discovered the three that kidnapped me were her kids, and the fucker that raped me was her boyfriend."

"What happened after that, Meghan?"

"I made them give me the address to the house of the gay couple that bought me and then I led them out to the garage. That's where I took care of shit."

"What do you mean by 'took care of shit?'"

"You sure I can tell you anything? Absolutely anything?"

"Absolutely, but only if you want to."

"Okay, well, first I made the brothers tie the old woman's boyfriend up. Just like they did to me, with his arms hanging above his head. Then I shot both of the brothers in the face."

"You shot them?"

"Yes, I shot them. Should I continue?"

"Yes. I'm sorry, Meghan. Please continue."

"Next, I made the daughter take the rapist's pants off and shove his underwear in his mouth. Just in case he was a screamer. You know? Then I made her take her pants off and handed her a knife. She was confused and scared, so I had to explain to her what to do. I made her stick the handle inside herself and told her to stand behind the rapist. After I warned him that this might hurt a little bit, I made her fuck him in the ass with the knife. I watched for a while as the old woman screamed and cried. It was beautiful at first, but then I got bored, so, I shot both of them. I would've shot the old bitch too, but when I turned to face her, she was already laying on the floor, clutching her chest. She had a heart attack, I guess? I'm not sure, but

I checked and the old hag was dead."

"So, you killed four people?"

"No. I killed six people. After I made sure they were all dead, I loaded up my car with a couple cans of gasoline and headed off to the gay couple's house. I didn't waste any time there. I made sure they were both home and I torched the place. Once it was up in flames, I drove off and headed home. That's the end of my story."

"That's quite a lot to take in, Meghan. I believe we should stop for today and continue next time."

Meghan glared at Dr. Hickman. "I told you, there won't be a next time." She stood up and headed for the door. "I have one more thing to take care of now to clear my conscience. But you won't be hearing from me again. Goodbye, Kyle."

Meghan left the office before Dr. Hickman could say a word and headed straight to her vehicle. She opened the trunk and grabbed a couple cans of gasoline. Ten minutes later, she was driving away with the doctor's office in flames behind her. Headed home to her son, free from all her demons.

LINE DANCING AT HACK HOUSE
JIM GOFORTH

Draw the Line or Cross the Line.

At first, it was just a game. No, not even really a game. A discussion. An exchange of ideas. An exploration into taboo realms, wondering just how far people would be willing to go when faced with certain situations or scenarios. Where their moral limits existed. Where would they draw the line, and when would they cross the line?

The premise was ridiculously simple.

Initially, eight of them comprised the group—four boys and four girls—which made the concept work perfectly. Four would ask the questions, four would answer, then roles would be reversed. No questions could be doubled up. No passing on questions, no avoiding them; quite simply, either draw the line or cross the line.

Steal from those close to you.

Inject heroin if you knew you wouldn't overdose.

Cheat on your partner.

All these and far more formed the basis of the game, many more which probed deeper into the unique psyches of the participants, delved into the corners of their minds, trying to drag whatever darkness might lurk in there out to be laid bare.

Some of the responses surprised all the members, even those who willingly announced they'd elect to cross the line, and others were not surprising in the least. It was evident there were still plenty of taboos and things most of them just wouldn't do, nor be drawn into admitting they would cross those lines.

Nonetheless, it was all in fun. They weren't hurting anybody, they weren't putting dangerous or illegal things into practice, they were just pushing the boundaries and exploring the darkest corners of each other's minds. Essentially a bastardised version of truth or dare, albeit light on the dare side of things.

That all changed when Sienna joined their little ensemble.

Not only did her arrival alter the whole dynamic of what was a neatly balanced, and mostly innocuous pursuit, it changed everything.

As soon as Sienna Mia joined the Line Dancers, David knew nothing was going to be the same ever again. And he was right.

De facto leader Aleshia recruited her, and up until that point was the group's driving force, right down to coining the lame moniker for them, but once Sienna was on-board, she became the one who called all the shots.

And the Game became so much more than it had ever been before.

Alongside Aleshia and David, the Line Dancers were Brett, Anna, Jeremy, Monica, Simone and Stan, and few of them were overjoyed about Aleshia drafting the unbalanced Sienna into the mix, but apparently, the whole

concept of Draw the Line/Cross the Line had become stale and needed a shake-up. They were all too comfortable in it, they'd run out of ideas and were just rehashing old notions.

Few were prepared for what Sienna would bring.

"For a start, it's not even a game what you do, it involves no risk. It's nothing but a tired discussion where you just sit around asking each other questions, trying to figure out what you would or wouldn't do in any given circumstances." Sienna poured scorn on the whole notion. "Sure, it might get edgy, racy, make you uncomfortable, or surprised by what's in each other's minds, but at the end of the day, it's just a safe little debate. A faux charade of Truth or Dare, without the dare involved. So if I'm going to be in, the rules are gonna change. To my rules."

Sienna's rules were simple. In fact there were only two rules.

No more would it be just a discussion-based event. No more safe sitting back and vowing they'd definitely cross the line. No. Under Sienna's reign, they had to act on it.

Given the nature of some taboo topics broached in the past, the Line Dancers were predictably loathe to cross that line themselves, where mere talking became action, where fantasies or dark desires became reality, but Sienna's manipulation was both subtle and smart.

She started them off with small, innocent things, deeds with little risk to them, but enough to blast euphoria and adrenalin through the participants who actually admitted they'd cross the line and then successfully did so.

Yet with the safety blanket of saying and not doing, having been stripped away by Sienna's rule, more often than not the Line Dancers elected to draw the line.

Which is where the second rule came into play.

If a member drew the line on three consecutive occasions, they were then presented with a situation where they'd have no other choice but to cross the line. Whatever

it was. Or be permanently expelled from the whole group and ostracised.

"Tonight, we're upping the stakes. We're going big," Sienna gazed with derision and amusement at her assembled acolytes—and they were hers of course, Aleshia was no true leader. If she had her way, the Game would still be the same mundane back and forth, a faux charade. Unlike what Sienna brought to the table, enriching all of their boring lives. "The last few weeks, all the lines you've crossed really haven't been anything we wouldn't all have willingly crossed years ago as kids. Sure, it's been fun, but really, dine and dashes, stealing things, breaking up people's relationships, they're hardly cutting edge. They've been the warm-up. Time to take things up a notch or ten. To the next level."

As Sienna's words washed over the collective, they all exchanged glances. Looks of consternation and apprehension chased curiosity and measures of downright fear over countenances. Several of the Line Dancers shifted uncomfortably.

"But first..." Sienna clapped her hands and the sudden burst of noise, sounding amplified in the tense silence, made some of them jump with alarm, descending into nervous laughter. "Drinks!"

David wasn't sure what expression he was wearing outwardly, but if it reflected the butterfly flutter of nerves residing in the pit of his stomach, then he guessed he must be looking pretty apprehensive. Nor was he sure whether imbibing in drinks would alleviate that feeling.

They'd always engaged in a couple of drinks while they played the Game, even before Cyclone Sienna's arrival, but then it was only some beers, and maybe a little wine.

Sienna didn't fuck around with that. She brought spirits, plied them with hard liquor, had them downing shots.

David knew it was to loosen up inhibitions, break down walls, make them susceptible to engage in risky behaviour and receptive to the possibility of crossing lines they mightn't otherwise consider.

All the same, he'd never been much of a drinker before, and now he was regularly smashed, as were the rest of the Line Dancers.

Doing some of the things they'd already done had been dicey enough whilst partially inebriated, so he shuddered to think of the potential danger or risk involved with whatever shenanigans Sienna had in mind now.

As alcohol started flowing, Sienna organised the sides for questions and answers by way of a simple coin toss. With the balance of equal numbers now disrupted, that meant one person would be able to avoid being involved each round, so they were designated drinks provider for the others.

David was surprised when Sienna didn't immediately nominate herself as the first individual to distribute alcohol, and watch proceedings with malicious amusement, but instead threw her hat in the ring to play. His nerves didn't subside at all when the coin came up heads for her, meaning she'd be on the side asking questions and he'd be on the other.

Fortunately, she didn't target him. She went straight for Aleshia, and with the first question fired, David realised with a cold blast of fear that Sienna wasn't fucking around when she declared they were going hardcore.

All those trivial lines they'd previously crossed, everything done up until this point, faded into indistinct kiddie pursuits, childish little larks.

"You're going to take a straight razor and slice off Brett's balls while you're in the middle of giving him a blowjob," Sienna directed at Aleshia. "Are you going to draw the line or cross the line?"

"Jesus!" Aleshia erupted in an exclamation blending both shock and revulsion, rocking back in her chair.

At the same time, Brett, another of the questioners, sitting right next to Sienna, released his own gasp of horrified astonishment and his grip on his bourbon glass. It slipped from his fingers, smashing on the floor, but the ensuing alcohol and glass shower was almost an afterthought to Sienna's query.

"Draw the line or cross the line?"

"Jesus fucking Christ!" Aleshia looked appalled, but David couldn't tell if it was the idea of sucking Brett's dick, chopping off his nuts or a combination of both, which was responsible for that. "Draw the fucking line! On all counts. For a start, I'd never be giving Brett a blowjob."

"Okay, then." Sienna threw back her shot of tequila and gestured to designated bartender, Monica, for another.

"Dodged a bullet there, Brettster," Stan said with a nervous giggle, and David guessed he didn't mean about getting a hummer from Aleshia.

"You're up next, Brett. Fire away. And remember, we're not playing the kiddie version anymore."

Still looking shaken, but gradually regaining his composure with the knowledge none of his friends would realistically cross that line where they'd have the blade of a razor at his scrotum, Brett requested a refill before slowly scrutinising the others waiting to be asked. Simone, Jeremy and David.

"David," Brett suddenly spoke and David's heart jumped with a painful kick in his chest. It was inevitable he was going to be in the firing line sooner or later, but he'd kind of been hoping for later. Much later.

"You're going to kill your neighbour's dog. Draw the line or cross the line?"

After the initial question posed by Sienna, nothing else seemed shocking, but Brett's query still slugged David like a physical blow. He knew Brett had attempted to conjure up something to appease Sienna, and judging from the barely perceptible nod she gave, it seemed to suit her.

David's neighbour had a dog. A Pomeranian. A

yappy, vicious little beast with a penchant for incessant barking and a mouthful of needle teeth. Constant threat to the mailman, passing schoolchildren, religious door-knockers and just about everybody in between.

Many times David had wished death on the midget canine devil, most of those coming in more recent weeks following Sienna's alcohol-fuelled Line Dancer sessions. Trying to navigate a hellatious hangover and snatch some sleep while a high-pitched jackhammer bark bored holes through his skull tended to conjure up caninicide contemplations. But actually killing the furred fiend himself?

David tried to picture himself doing so and found it impossible. As much as he detested that persistent bark spiking a power-drill into his brain, he just couldn't envision doing something akin to firing up an actual power-drill and putting it through that animal's brain.

"Draw the line." David shook his head, shaking away images of canine dismemberment from his thoughts. "I'd draw the line there."

"Pussy," Brett snorted, shooting a sideways look at Sienna to see if she shared that opinion. Her expression, blending disappointment with scorn, suggested she did.

And so it went. Back and forth, switching positions and roles.

The relatively innocuous overtones that existed in the Game's infancy, back when the Line Dancers first formed, were long gone.

The mildly daring, the slight dalliances with taboo, the potentially uncomfortable scenarios, were ground into dust by Sienna's incarnation of the Game.

And the vast majority of the collective, fuelled on alcohol and goaded by Sienna, fed into this and breathed dangerous life into it.

There was no gentle prodding or probing in their queries, no light-hearted fun; they were increasingly darker and malicious, perverted, overtly sexual, violent, downright

grotesque.

Fuck your sister.

Bust in on your parents having sex and jerk off to them.

Kidnap those passing schoolchildren and mail them home piece by piece.

Invite the religious doorknockers in to be tied up and tortured in the basement.

Finally, David found himself the last member on the questioning side. With Sienna the last to ask on the other side.

He acknowledged how much he'd drunk over the course of the evening, but found he didn't feel as intoxicated as he should have. Instead he felt supercharged with nerves and fear, generated by the dark, demented turn the Game had taken, which hummed violently within him as he gazed at the group's new spearhead.

The words were out of his mouth before he'd given it much thought, his tongue betraying him before he could carefully word something clever.

"You're going to strip off and get naked in front of everybody here. Draw the line or cross the line?"

She didn't immediately answer. Instead, she delivered one of her customary derisive snorts, which he wasn't sure meant she took his lame attempt at being edgy as nothing more than a pathetic bid to ogle naked females, or something else.

Then she stood up in a rush, kicking her chair backwards.

A sardonic grin crawled across her face as she shucked off the open leather jacket she'd been wearing over a dark button-up top, and let it slide down her slim arms to drop on the floor behind her. She effected a deliberately ponderous sway as her fingers trailed up her body and began to undo the buttons of that blouse.

Another stunned silence—not the first of the evening—descended on the congregation as they realised what Sienna's response to David's half-assed Game

question was.

Necks craned, chairs were shifted around to get a better view as Sienna wriggled free of her top and wasted little time discarding her bra as well.

Her breasts, though not large, were perfectly formed, and stiff nipples jutted from the middle of dark circles of areolae, pointing at David like mocking fingertips.

Gasps of shock and disbelief jostled with loud whistles and cheers of approval, but it was all background noise to David as he stared transfixed. Her skirt followed, slipped down smooth thighs and kicked away. She shed her matching thong panties without preamble, then spun them around a forefinger in a lazy circle, before flinging them at David.

Caught somewhere between flinching and instinctively reaching out to catch them, he ended up having them hit him in the face and glance off his cheek, falling in his lap.

Sienna sat her naked ass back on her chair. Parting her thighs wide and placing a hand between them, she spread herself open, the mocking smile never falling from her countenance.

"Cross the line," she smirked. "Unlike all you pussies, who've drawn the line every fucking time tonight. And just in case it's escaped your attentions, you've all drawn the line *three times* in succession."

David's head was elsewhere, fixated on her shameless nudity and almost absent-minded masturbation, kicking himself for not having the stones to have pushed the envelope even further with her, when the ramifications of her final statement kicked in.

All of them failed to cross the line at least once.

One thing remained a constant fear for all the Line Dancers. The possibility of being ostracised and banished from the group. For all of them, that was all they had. They were misfits, outcasts, pariahs who didn't belong

anywhere else. It was what they all had in common, what instigated them to band together and create their own circle of friends in the first place. Without it, they had nothing and nobody, and no other clique would ever take them in.

It was why they remained steadfastly loyal to the credo of the group, even as the risks and elements of danger amplified, ramping up under Sienna's helm.

This time though, Sienna's ultimatums were off the charts crazy, to the point where thinking they had to remain with the Line Dancers would itself be off the charts crazy. Especially in David's case. As usual though, Sienna had an ace up her sleeve, one that trumped the whole banishment threat.

Now, here they all were bound for a single destination, where, Sienna proposed, all their line crossing could easily occur. And David, despite the devastating ultimatum posed to him right at the end of Sienna's enforced stipulations on all of them for failing to cross a single line, was present too. In a state of shock. Numb.

"No option to draw the line here, you know the rules. You knew them before you all elected to draw the line at everything you were presented. So now, whatever you get, is what you do. You all know the price for failure to comply; we agreed on this right from the start. We signed. In blood.

"So, let's get to it, the night's a-wasting. Aleshia, you're up first. What you're going to do…is break into a house."

The terrified spark of alarm blooming on Aleshia's face as Sienna pinned her in the spotlight first vanished completely under a wash of utter relief. Breaking into a house was fucked up, make no mistake, particularly an occupied one, but compared to the tidal wave of perversion and depravity flooding over the line queries earlier, that shit sounded like a walk in the park. Closely watching Sienna's visage crawling with gleeful malice,

David knew it wasn't that simple. There had to be more to it.

"Not just any house though," Sienna dropped the punchline. "You have to break into The Hack House. And stay in there. The rest of you, except David and Brett, your Crossing Line duties are pretty straightforward. All you have to do is make sure Aleshia stays in that house, no matter what. Whatever it takes, she doesn't get out. That means you're able to go into the house too and use whatever means keeps her from leaving. Pretty simple, hey?"

The relief that drenched Aleshia was now evident on the rest of their faces, swamping them in shaky gales of laughter and exhalations of stunned reprieve. Not so with Aleshia. The terror swam back over her countenance, blanching it white.

The Hack House wasn't just an ordinary house. It was a legend, an abomination soaked in bloody history. Though it was an abandoned abode and had been ever since the hideous deeds which etched its name in notoriety around not just the town, but countrywide, breaking into an occupied family home with gun-toting residents sounded like a more inviting prospect than broaching the walls of this domain.

Everybody knew the Hack House, or as it was originally more commonly known, The Morgan Residence, number 69 Continental Drive. Over a decade ago, back when all members of the Line Dancers were mere primary school-aged children, Dale Morgan and his wife Elaine befriended down-on-his-luck transient John Pomone and eventually invited him to stay with them, along with his young daughter.

Formerly an award-winning novelist, Pomone went into a tailspin after an acrimonious separation from his wife. Though he managed to retain the family house and custody of his adolescent daughter, Pomone refused to remain residing in the place, choosing instead to become a

nomad, a wandering vagrant of no fixed address, with his child in tow. Too elusive and ghostlike to be apprehended by the authorities for his erratic lifestyle choices and questionable methods of keeping his daughter sheltered, he drifted around until the chance encounter with the Morgans.

Originally wary, Pomone accepted their offer to take up residence with them, acknowledging the stability it would bring his daughter and for a while, they were all essentially one big happy family together.

Until the night Pomone inexplicably and systematically slaughtered the entire Morgan household as they lay interred in sleep. Armed with an assemblage of tools garnered from Dale's workshed, and kitchen implements, Pomone hacked, slashed, sliced and diced through the two Morgan parents, their children, Elaine's elderly mother and the live-in nanny.

There was no pattern followed, no specific modus operandi adhered to in the killings. It seemed more like some insane murderous experiment where the vast array of items used to mutilate and massacre were tested out for their killing capacities. Kitchen knives left bodies with so many stab wounds, facial recognition was impossible, pickaxes cleaved skulls and sprayed blood and brain matter in ridiculously high arcing patterns up walls. Garden shears mutilated genitals, scissors punctured eyeballs, and blades of all varieties sawed through limbs until the whole abode ran red with blood. Reports of Pomone cannibalising sections of his victims flesh were prolific, but remained unconfirmed.

Allegedly, the blood-drenched killer was shot dead in the front yard as police swarmed and surrounded the premises, his catatonic daughter-who was said to have followed him from room to room as he butchered the Morgans rushed away into psychiatric care.

What actually happened over the night, and primarily the tail-end of it, became clouded and vague, with few

43

substantial details ever making it into press, but the grotesque nature of the reprehensible crimes and the location itself became legendary. Depending on who was telling the story, the Hack House was either heavily haunted by the Morgan clan, returned as vengeful poltergeists angry at their good natures allowing a psychopath to undo them all, or it wasn't Pomone at all who was shot by police, but instead one of the Morgan's adult sons, and Pomone himself still remained in the house, putting his vagabond skills to good use to remain undetected.

In any case, the place was abandoned, with no estate agent looking to move on it and nobody game to reside there. It became nothing more than a squat for undesirables at best, or a place left to its own devices, a location for all and sundry to avoid. And like everybody else, up until now, the Line Dancers had managed to avoid it.

"Come on, you're telling me after all this time you've been doing this Line Dancers thing you've never contemplated anything to do with that fucked up place?" Sienna was astounded the group hadn't ever involved the notorious spot in their hometown in their Game. "Goes to show just how goddamn lame your whole interpretation of Draw the Line, Cross the Line is. Would've thought a lunatic cutting up a bunch of idiots would've been just the place you could've held your events. If any of you had any spine. Fortunately for you, I'm running this show now and everything that happens tonight happens at Hack House. All wrapped up in one convenient location."

"And us?" Brett challenged belligerently, buoyed by alcohol and the fact that all of them so far, bar Aleshia, were tasked with Crossing Lines not near as horrific as they'd been dreading. "You mentioned me and David not having to keep Aleshia in the house?"

David could have punched him right in the face. Why the fuck would he even bring it to light? Should have let it

be; maybe Sienna herself was intoxicated enough to have forgotten that part. Though he didn't really think so.

"Well, if we're going to pay homage to that sick fuck at Hack House in a roundabout way with tonight's Game, may as well toss in a little meat eating. So as for you Brett, you're going to eat some raw meat. Of my choosing."

"Is that it?" Brett looked incredulous, unable to contain a smirk of triumph. He almost pushed it further still, questioning whether Sienna had gone soft and lost her edge, but drunk or otherwise, he knew when to leave well enough alone.

"That's it. Don't start patting yourself on the back just yet. You might be eating the meat of David's neighbour's dog, so just cool your jets."

An icy freeze of fear clenched David in a tight grip. He knew Sienna wasn't about to make him go ahead and kill that damn dog, since repeating questions already posed or tasks already accomplished prior was a rule established before Sienna's reign, and one she'd kept in place, but still…

His ultimatum was coming next and somehow, he didn't think he was skating by as easily as the others.

"First, before you get your assignment, David," Sienna said. "One other thing. Just in case anybody considers pussying out of anything, I've been preparing some insurance during our last few expeditions. I've recorded everything you've all done. Fuck up and try and back out of this shit tonight and everybody sees everything you've done. *Everything.* Yeah, some of it's been tame, but there are things you've all done you don't want anybody finding out about, correct? Want it to stay that way? Then you'll tow the line."

Another Sienna word-bomb exploded amongst them, sending shockwaves of disbelief and panic rippling through everybody. Searching looks were exchanged, each member trying to gauge whether it was possible she'd done what she claimed or if she was bluffing. Though Sienna

wasn't producing anything to corroborate it, few were really willing to call her bluff. Like she stated, the majority of lines they'd crossed hadn't been things that would see them locked up in jail for a lifetime, but there was some dodgy shit done which could greatly impact on their various futures, both near and far.

"And David, in keeping with Hack House themes, well, I've a special line to cross just for you. Tonight, you're going to kill somebody."

Number 69 Continental Avenue, AKA Hack House, wasn't in too bad a condition considering the years of abandonment it had withstood. Structurally, it was still sound. Bar a couple of windows, busted by shiftless neighbourhood kids, everything was in place, and even the lurid graffiti once adorning outer walls was faded to the point of shadowy scribble. It wasn't entirely disused, considering the occasional transient would temporarily use it as a squat, caring little about the ghastly history, or rambunctious teenagers would gather up their pluck to use it for a site to garner some illicit thrills, but they were far and few in between.

The last house on the left, it had a park on one side, also long fallen into disuse, and a similarly vacant abode on the other. This end of the street where Hack House hunkered may as well have been a ghost street. Nobody wanted to be here and those who ever came into this orbit, whether by choice or accident, usually didn't want to stay long.

It should have been knocked down long ago; nobody wanted to own it, rent it, live anywhere near it. As it was, it just sat there…abandoned. Building up more legend and feeding on horrific lore.

It didn't really look like anything more than a vacant house that needed some serious lawn-mowing, tree-trimming and garden work. But to David, it looked fucking terrifying.

It obviously looked that way to Aleshia too as she was bundled out of the car, escorted by Monica and Stan right up the weed-infested front path, to the low verandah and the door.

"You two can stay there too," Sienna commanded. "Right outside that door. She won't be getting out that way."

Stan and Monica exchanged uneasy glances, clearly intent on seeing Aleshia inside before high-tailing back to the park where the others loitered in dark tree shadows. They said nothing though, merely remained in apprehensive thrall on the old porch.

"The rest of you, circle out around the place. Watch the back door, windows, wherever it's likely a terrified bitch would flee through. That's all you have to do, unless she makes a run for it. Pretty fucking simple, hey?"

Those tasked with that, did so, not keen to be close to the forbidding building, but eager to acquiesce with what seemed like pretty simple line crosses, at least in comparison with that horror handed down to others. David and Brett both hesitated, lingering in the shadows, unsure of their positions here.

Given that Sienna wasn't yanking anybody's crank about making Aleshia enter Hack House and stay inside, with forcible prevention from exiting on the cards, David wasn't sure whether his ominous line-crossing ultimatum was genuine or if she was just testing to see how far she could push this shit. He sure as hell hoped it was the latter, because the alternative didn't bear thinking about. At all. Shit, he couldn't even contemplate deep-sixing his neighbour's yappy mutt, let alone anything more heinous…

"What are you fuckers waiting for? Go on and watch the fun too. No point skulking in the dark, hiding like bitches. You have a date with destiny too."

Screams sliced through the night like an air raid siren. High-pitched, blood-curdling. Issuing from inside the dark

house.

The hair on the back of David's neck stood up; his bowels felt like they were constricting, ice water taking up residence in his veins.

"What the fuck?" Brett whispered hoarsely.

"Showtime," Sienna exulted, the sadistic grin of glee visible on her face even with shadows pooling over it.

"Are we just going to stand out...?"

"Yes," Sienna interrupted David harshly. "You know the rules. She stays in there. No matter what."

More screams lanced the formerly uneasy quiescence, rippling with unadulterated terror. They pierced David like knife blades, searing into him. He couldn't sit here doing nothing.

"Fuck this! You said the rest of them had to keep her from getting out. Didn't say shit about me or Brett going in to get her out!"

David moved, bursting out from the cluster of trees, and sprinted for the house.

Sienna's enraged voice chased after him in a strident banshee wail.

"Don't you dare! You'll be sorry!"

David didn't doubt that. Shit, he was already sorry. Sorry he was here in the first place. Sorry he'd ever entangled himself with the Line Dancers concept. Better to be nobody with no one than to be spiralling down into this nightmare Sienna managed to warp it into.

He didn't stop running though. He charged through knee-high grass, feeling like he was treading water, angling towards the back of the residence, certain that door was closer than the front where Monica and Stan were standing guard. He wasn't thinking of much more than getting in and to Aleshia; he didn't allow himself to get caught up considering what hell might be waiting inside.

With his focus on the house and nothing else, his breath punching out in sharp, raspy bursts, he didn't see the rush of movement from his right side. He felt it

though, barrelling into him like a speeding train and smashing him down into the tangled mess of grass. A hefty weight dropped atop him as he was rolled onto his back and the splash of moonlight above let him see Jeremy swinging astride him, ready to plant a fist in his face.

"Fuck are you doing, David? You're not messing this up. You know the rules! I fucked a damn hooker last week, I crossed that line and my girlfriend cannot find out about that! You aren't gonna fuck this up!"

Another scream skittered through the air, a petrified sound that set David's nerves on edge. He felt the fear in that desperate shriek, humming like a palpable thing.

"Are you serious, Jer? You're going to stand by and do nothing? Fuck Sienna, fuck this damn Game!"

The clenched fist came down in a flash. It rocked him; he hadn't been expecting Jeremy to follow through with the implied threat of violence. Sienna's craziness was infecting them all. Jeremy was the kind of guy who'd walk away from any fight, any time. He wasn't the guy to start swinging like Mike Tyson at a piñata party.

David tasted blood in his mouth; felt a gash in the inside of his cheek where his teeth cracked together and sheared into flesh. He wasn't wasting time playing fair here; he didn't have it. He threw himself backwards along the grassy ground until he was just about clear and kicked his feet up square into Jeremy's balls. The guy squealed like a pig on a date with the abattoir and keeled over on his side.

Not sticking around to see what else happened, or whether Sienna and Brett were on his tail too, David got up and hauled ass for the house. Whoever was supposed to be remaining vigilant at the back door wasn't there, or was just inside, so he thundered right in. He expected it to be pitch black, but moonlight spilled through an assortment of windows, throwing plenty of erratic visibility inside.

Aleshia hadn't made it past than the lounge room, if

indeed she'd ever planned to venture farther than that. She was sprawled on her back on a threadbare carpeted floor, pinned down, kicking and screaming as a great dark bulk of a figure tore with furious hands at her clothing, removing pieces of it in a violent frenzy.

Skidding to a halt, David froze, suddenly unsure of what to do now that he was here.

"You wanna be the fucking hero, David?" Sienna's mocking voice rang in his ears from behind. She and Brett had entered the house too. "Here's your chance. There's a filthy fucking hobo trying to rape Aleshia. Cross your line, pussy. Kill him."

Heart kicking in his chest, blood pounding in his ears, David just stared, transfixed with horror.

"Do it, softcock!" Sienna screamed.

The dark mass assaulting Aleshia was either a giant or swathed in layers of clothing. If it was the latter, then he'd be well-advised to remove his own clothing first, but whatever the case, David's sudden bravado in charging in had tapered away to jackshit right about now.

"Do something!" Simone screamed and David realised that most, if not all, of the Line Dancers had now converged inside Hack House.

"Nah," Stan spoke and his voice was full of lecherous malice. "I'd rather watch."

Everything felt as though it had slowed down, like time was moving in a sluggish mire around David. He heard the other girls screaming, chiming in a hellish crescendo with Aleshia, uncharacteristic perverted comments from the guys. Sienna's mocking screech.

"Do it, pussy! If you can't kill a filthy rapist hobo, who are you gonna kill? One of your friends?"

Then her ranting tirade segued into something else, a scorn-laden expulsion of disgust and finality.

"Fuck it." Amidst the soundtrack of chaos, a new sound issued. A sharp, flat crack that reverberated in the room, bouncing off the walls.

The frenetic figure tearing at Aleshia's clothing and exposed flesh pitched forward as though they'd been struck with an invisible baseball bat, a puff of blood splashing from the head. As the mass slumped atop Aleshia, which didn't extinguish her screams any, Monica, Anna and Simone rushed from their respective positions, and Sienna stepped forward, holding a handgun aloft. Before the other girls arrived, she stood over the slouched hobo and pulled the trigger twice more, punching bullets into the already bloodied cranium, spraying more arcs of gore and ruined brain matter slop up in the air.

With assistance, Aleshia wriggled out from beneath the gory-headed corpse, her hysterical shrieks unabated. She was virtually nude now, her bare breasts heaving and splattered with blood.

"Brett," Sienna barked. "You're up. See that chest of drawers in the corner? There's a knife in the top one. Get it. You're eating raw meat now."

"What?"

"Do it! Jeremy, Stan…roll this fucker over. Let's see if he had a boner. Brett's gonna cut it off and chow down on raw hobo cock."

"I'm not…"

The nose of the gun lined up on Brett's face. Unhinged glee glinted in Sienna's eyes, something dark and deadly lurking behind that.

"Yes, you are. Or you're next to get your skull realigned."

For David it all still seemed to be slowed down and surreal, like treading water in molasses. He watched Brett stumble towards the drawer, produce a knife and drop to his knees alongside the slaughtered vagrant, his face an anguished mask. Sienna followed him, jamming the gun against his temple, forcing him and the blade of the knife down.

The would-be rapist did have an erection, present even in death, at least for now, and it protruded from the

51

folds of filthy coats, short and stubby, but hard nonetheless.

"Cut it off. And eat. Cross the line, Brett."

Though he wanted to, David couldn't tear his eyes away from the gruesome spectacle as Brett's trembling hands worked the blade against the stumpy organ, sawing and hacking clumsily at it. A geyser of blood spurted, dousing his face and hands. David thought the penis would have been lopped right off with one slice, but it seemed a little more difficult to achieve that than expected.

Pervy Stan lost his libido and his dinner. He bent double and ejected a bilious stream of vomit, predominantly alcohol. Then he staggered away and started for the front door.

"Fuck this, I'm out..."

"The hell you are!" Sienna yanked the gun away from Brett's temple as he finally managed to remove the penis and fumble the bloodslick, slippery piece towards his mouth, and shot Stan twice in the back. It was a broad target and he wasn't moving fast, but it was still a remarkable feat to have him, dropped on his face floundering and choking on vomit and blood, and the barrel of the gun jammed back against Brett's head, before anyone fathomed what exactly happened.

Renewed screams created a new tableau of terror. The girls slumped to the floor alongside Aleshia who now seemed oblivious to her own nudity. David wasn't oblivious to it at all; her breasts were far bigger than Sienna's had been and thrust blood-covered nipples out, stiff with fear rather than arousal. Nonetheless, there were no stirrings of lust or anything remotely connected to that in him as he stared, using them as some kind of focus to keep his eyes off the rest of the horror swarming around him.

"Why are you doing this?" Monica screamed.

"Why?" Sienna mimicked, swinging the gun away to jab towards the quartet of traumatised women. "I'll tell you

why. For a start, my name isn't Sienna Mia. I can't believe none of you nerd, brainiac, bookworm whatevers can't figure out a simple anagram. I am exactly what the doctors said I was. *I Am Insane.* My name's Tamara Pomone. I know every inch of this house right here because I was with my father the night he diced those simpletons, and let me tell you, I wasn't an unwilling spectator. I learned plenty then and I loved it, and I swore as soon as I got let out of the nuthouse I was going to add a pile of more bodies to the Hack House total. You fucking losers with your silly little game pretty much fell over yourselves to sign up for that."

She pulled the trigger again, almost nonchalantly, as if she wasn't even thinking about it. The ensuing bullet chewed through Simone's face, splatting blood against the adjacent wall even as the girl's head jerked backwards.

Jeremy went for the gun, in an awkward lunge.

By some preternatural psychopath sixth-sense, Sienna knew he was coming. She sidestepped and he slipped in the bloody quagmire pooling around the cock-chomping Brett. As he sprawled, he knocked the knife and the uneaten portion of penis Brett was gagging on away, skittering the bloody-bladed weapon across the gory floor. Sienna shot him in the back of the head.

David didn't see what damage a bullet punching through the back of a skull from close range might do because he was watching the knife. As it ceased its slide across the floor. At his feet.

Then he was holding it, bloody handle sticky in his shaky grip.

Sienna was turning around when he ripped her throat open with it, bathing himself in a sudden crimson shower. Even the blossom of shock in her eyes didn't overwhelm the insanity dwelling there, and if he wasn't mistaken, he saw a grin twitch at the corner of her lips, an expression of malicious triumph and satisfaction appear before she stumbled backwards and away, dropping down to join the

tangle of bodies now littering the floor.

"And David, in keeping with Hack House themes, well I've a special line to cross just for you. Tonight, you're going to kill somebody."

ROUND ONE WINNER

LINE DANCING AT HACK HOUSE
JIM GOFORTH

ROUND TWO

DEATHDAY WISHES
TONEYE EYENOT

VS

THE THROBBING IN THURMAN
T. S. WOOLARD

DEATHDAY WISHES
TONEYE EYENOT

Have you ever taken pause in your mundane lives to contemplate your impending Deathday? Imagined, perhaps, that you knew the precise day-hour-moment that your life will expire into Death's embrace? How would our lives be, if we knew when we were to die? One could imagine a world gone mad, until our species had been reduced to small, sparsely scattered tribes around the globe. A survival of the fittest scenario, in an ever-diminishing quest for self-preservation. I mean…we all want to prolong the inevitable, right? Paranoia would be the dominant emotion, as people are caught in a vicious vortex, a downward spiral of catch-22. You see your Death waiting patiently for you at journey's end, and as your time draws nearer, you are absorbed along with everybody else into the mass of obsessed suspicion.

Death walks in many guises. Death may even walk in your shoes. You could be driving your car, lose concentration for a moment, and inadvertently take the life

of a child chasing a ball out into the street. The child knows its Death is nigh but may lack the skill or proper comprehension of the matter, and then Death steps in to take the prize. Nevertheless, the parents might also know the time of their offspring's Death, as children are prone to speak what's on their little minds. Particularly on subject matter of such finality. Would they not be extra vigilant in that final hour? Of course, they would be right there, not allowing their child either from side nor sight. Death however, is always up for a challenge, easily providing the necessary distraction to snatch this prize from their grasp.

Thankfully, it is not within the normal capacity of humanity to know such ominous detail. *Normal*, I did say, however. There are a small few around the globe, who have this terrible foresight. There's the case of Dylan Bantram, for instance. Born in 1982, Dylan is due to die at 3:57:24 pm, Friday, April 4, 2019. This is something Dylan has known instinctively, for as long as he can remember. Though the thought is relegated for the most part to his subconscious; as the years race by much faster than Dylan would prefer, the herald of his impending doom is beginning to push its way into the fore, taking up residence in his everyday thoughts. After a mere thirty four years on this earth, he only has three years, four months, twenty seven days and thirty minutes exactly until the bell's final toll.

Dylan has always been more than a touch irritable. Recently though, with the heavy burden weighing on his unconscious mind, his impatience is beginning to pose a problem for him when out in public. He has gradually distanced himself from lifelong friends and barely keeps contact with his family. Dylan obsesses constantly over just who it is that could be instrumental in his demise. It could be friend, foe, stranger or dear old Uncle Joe. Dylan Bantram drives himself mad on an hourly basis with all the possibilities that present themselves to his troubled mind.

Many times, Dylan has contemplated the unthinkable.

To cheat Death is out of the question – he knows this in his heart, but what if he was to beat Death to the punch and take his own life before the appointed expiration date? Now, that would be something to laugh about in his premature grave. Pacing around the self-imposed prison which is his house, Dylan thinks of ways to kill himself. He's a bright fellow with a vivid imagination, and some of his ideas are spectacular to say the least. A lot of them will require him to leave the house though, and he's not sure if he's quite ready for that yet. His agoraphobia and high levels of anxiety prevent him from being able to carry out some of his more inventive ideas. He would prefer a painless death really, like maybe a heroin overdose or an obscene overindulgence of alcohol and sleeping pills—but hey, if you're gonna go out on your own volition, why not do it in style?

Standing in his kitchen, he absent-mindedly goes through the motion of running a blunt butter knife across his wrist. The contemplations of suicide are now a prevalent aspect of his thinking. He comes to the realisation that death by misadventure is pretty much out of the question for the next few years, and this gives him a new found confidence to venture beyond the relative safety of his house, in search of an inventive way to kill himself and subsequently spit in the face of Death.

Opening the front door and stepping out onto the porch, a rush of apprehension makes him pause, but only for a moment. Taking a deep breath, Dylan steps confidently onto his weedy, overgrown lawn and heads for the street. He has no idea where he is going, just anywhere that may give him some form of inspiration to carry out his morbid plan. The overcast sky and slightly chilled breeze adds to the dour mood that permeates his mind, as he wanders aimlessly along the footpath towards the heart of town.

He is bemused at the oblivious nature of the people he passes in the street. Not a care in the world shows on

their faces. Well, not entirely. Of course, they all carry around the everyday worries of living, but the fear of Death seems absent from their thoughts and this just pisses Dylan off considerably. He wishes he didn't have this terrible foresight and burns with furious envy at the rest of humanity. Berating himself for his distracted mind, Dylan returns his ponderings back to the ominous task at hand. Where and how? Behind him, several feet away, and over his left shoulder, Death follows, chuckling quietly. *Not today, Dylan…not today.*

As he gets closer to the centre of town, the streets gradually become more populated. Dylan starts to feel that dreaded anxiety build in his chest: *people*. He has become so accustomed to his own company, the mere thought of people invading his personal space, let alone the actual sight of them up ahead, causes him to falter in his progress. Shortness of breath and a fine layer of sweat oozing from every pore accompany his racing mind. *Fuck this*, he thinks, seriously considering just turning back in a run to the sanctuary of his home. He's come this far though, much further than he has in several months. He's out here with a specific purpose this time as well—in the middle of the day and not in the relative quiet of the late evening, when he would normally venture out to get groceries or smokes. No, this time, Dylan Bantram is on a mission. Today, he will cheat Death, or so he has himself convinced. With an increasing volume of traffic on the road, he abandons his plan to be inventive in his demise, suddenly stepping from the footpath.

Molly Tannenbaum is late. Her daughter has finished school for the day and will be waiting out front to be picked up. Neither Molly nor Dylan realise it, but Death has played a hand in Dylan's impromptu decision to leave the house, insidiously so. Reaching for her phone, she plans to call her little girl and let her know she will be there within minutes. She fumbles with the phone, juggling it one-handed before dropping it to the floor on the

passenger side. Cursing her clumsiness, Molly unclips her seatbelt and quickly reaches for her phone, taking quick glances back up to the road ahead of her. As her hand closes around her phone, she looks up just in time to see some sad-looking idiot walk right out in front of her.

In a fit of panic, she drops the phone again, gripping the wheel and slamming on the brakes, swerving wildly to miss the surprise pedestrian. Molly's life flashes before her eyes, to be replaced with a fast approaching bus shelter on the opposite side of the road. The last thing Molly Tannenbaum feels is her face shattering the glass of her windscreen as she rockets from her seat, clearing the hood of her car to smash bodily into the steel frame of the mangled bus shelter. Death has claimed its prize.

Dylan stands in shock at the tragedy he has just caused. A mix of anger and adrenaline courses violently through his veins at his thwarted attempt to cheat Death. His moment of disappointment is disturbed by the screech of brakes, followed by the deafening sound of metal on metal. Not only has he caused the death of his targeted motorist, the *accident* has caused several cars behind to brake suddenly and collide with each other in a three-car pileup. He doesn't stick around to see if there are any more fatalities at the site of his botched first suicide attempt. Dylan absconds as fast as his feet can carry him, Death following close behind.

One failure down, and already, Dylan suspects Death is playing with him. His stomach in his chest and his heart in his throat, he slows his abrupt getaway to a laboured walk. So unfit, after spending so much time moping around indoors, the brief run itself nearly kills him. Maybe running himself to death is an option, but no. That would require far too much effort, and he is of an inherently lazy character. Dylan ducks down a narrow laneway and stops to catch his breath. A few paces away, he spots a broken liquor bottle littering the path. Although there are people walking by in the street, the laneway is deserted. Dylan

walks over to the mess of broken glass and squats down in contemplation. He could open himself up and bleed out in minutes, but not here. Someone was sure to see him from the road, and come to his aid. He picks up the bottle neck and begins moving further down the lane.

The anxiety begins to take hold again and Dylan stops to lean against the seven foot cyclone fence running the length of the laneway down one side. He slowly slides himself down the springy wire into a squat, bottle neck dangling loosely in his hand, and rests his head on his knees. Taking slow, deliberate breaths, he waits for the distressing sensation to pass, unaware that he is just about to have company. He lets his empty hand flop forward in front of him, raising his head slightly to gaze at the jumble of veins down the inside of his forearm. This is it. Uninterrupted and free to carry out the deed, Dylan begins to mentally go through the motion of opening his arm from wrist to elbow.

The burning tickle of bile enters his throat at the thought of the pain he is about to put himself through. His eyes shift to the dirty, broken glass in his other hand, and he hesitates before bringing one of the sharp points to the soft flesh of his wrist. He exhales a slow, shuddering breath and presses into the flesh slightly, feeling the hot prick and then the pop of the first layer of skin. His nerves get the better of him and he pulls away. Now that he has the power of his own life and death in his hands, the fear of imminent and intense pain stifles his resolve. Part of him wants to just submit to Death and wait his turn, and he struggles momentarily with the belligerent side of him which refuses to be a victim to circumstances beyond his control. He reasons with his acquiescent self that he can in no way bear to continue this depressing existence for the next three and a half years, only to have it end without his say so. Again, he brings the jagged glass to his wrist. Again, he pauses at the unnerving intrusion.

So caught up in the intensity of the moment, Dylan is

oblivious to the two hoodlums meandering through the laneway. The cacophony of thoughts, screaming to be heard above one another in the rattling cage of Dylan's mind, drowns out the voice of the instigating thug...

"A cutter, ay? Do it. Do it, you fuckin' wimp."

These people are ghosts; apparitions beyond his awareness. Dylan has strayed from the reality of the world around him, lost in the realm of his conflicting intent to the point of shutting out the world entirely. Although they stand over him, in his mind, they are not there at all. Not there, that is, until they attack. He is shocked out of his reverie by a solid boot to his ribs, followed by another, then another. They don't stop kicking him as he keels over and curls up, attempting unsuccessfully to cover himself from their merciless assault. A sudden and violently painful ring silences the voices in his head and brings Dylan fully back into the moment. Dizzied and battered as the two continue to lay the boot in, finally Dylan snaps. He lashes out with the bottleneck and connects with the calf of an incoming leg. He sees them now, and he most definitely hears the sickening sound of tearing flesh, followed by a high-pitched yelp of pain.

Anger rises in Dylan's chest, incensed at the actions of these two lowlife hoons distracting him from his purpose; thinking themselves above him in any way. Death discriminates not, and as fate would have it, today Death treads surely in the shoes of Dylan Bantram.

In taking pause due to the unexpected retaliation, the two thugs aren't ready for what comes next. Dylan uncurls from his prone position on the littered ground and rolls towards the assailants, lashing out wildly with the glass. The already injured party bears the brunt of his enraged strike, the sharp glass splintering into a new wound as the bottle stabs deep into the thigh of the same leg. A vicious punch descends between Dylan's shoulder blades, delivered by the uninjured foe, but to very little effect. The adrenaline screaming through Dylan now rendering him

near impervious, he lunges with the bottle to stab into the side of the second thug. His mate, down and bleeding profusely from his leg, the cowardly goon deserts him, holding his side and half running back towards the street.

Dylan leaps to his feet, as though he hadn't just undergone a savage beating, and towers over the fallen thug, whose demeanour has gone from that of a threatening bully, to a whimpering slug. His pleading goes unheeded and the darkness in Dylan's gaze terrifies him. As Dylan advances and the thug scampers in pained retreat across the ground, Death smiles warmly over Dylan's shoulder. His rage subsides and is replaced with a cold intent as a sinister leer creeps across his visage. His suicidal thoughts pushed now to the back of his mind, Dylan becomes consumed with the aspiration to end this pernicious cunt's life. His movements, at first slow and deliberate, accentuate the inevitability of the assailant-turned-victim's fate. Dylan relishes the terror playing on the downed thug's face. He is no longer himself, but a manifestation of evil as the darkness plunges his soul into unfathomable depths.

As though a charge jolts through him, Dylan's slow, menacing advance transforms into a sudden, frenzied maelstrom of stabs and slashes as he falls upon the man with a guttural scream. The ripping sounds of glass on flesh mingle sickly with the howls of Dylan's homicidal rage and the screams of terror and pain issuing from his victim. His *friend* stops further down the lane, turning to see the horrific murder taking place, his own wound soaking through his shirt and staining his jeans. After several stunned moments, he turns again and resumes his cowardly retreat.

Drenched in the blood of his victim, Dylan rises achingly to his feet. The savage kicking he has just endured now bringing its results to prominence as the adrenaline subsides and the red fog in his vision clears. He stumbles backwards to fall against the cyclone fence, doubles over

and empties his stomach on the ground. His day is getting worse and more tragic by the minute. Dylan stares at the puddle of spew, saliva still drooling steadily from his gaping mouth as he struggles to breathe. What began in his mind as a good idea suddenly loses all appeal, and Dylan decides he should abandon this quest before more people die through his foolish attempts. With a grimace of pain, he straightens himself up and, nursing his cracked, bruised ribs, limps down the laneway, away from the road entrance.

The blood staining his hands, arms and clothing now caked and dry, Dylan looks down at himself and shudders. He was never a violent person; more just a misanthropic loner who preferred a respectable distance between himself and the next person. What he has just done is far from characteristic. Dylan has now become a murderer. He tries to rationalise it in his mind as he limps along a backstreet in the direction of home. It was by no means a pre-meditated act, he had simply reacted at first, and then something took over.

The police will be looking for him. First, the massive accident he had caused, resulting in at least one gruesome death, maybe more, and now a truly violent murder as well as an assault to add to the charges. There has been no shortage of witnesses either. Many people saw him flee the scene of the car accident, and the person he stabbed in the side had made his escape, no doubt headed straight to either a hospital or police station. Dylan Bantram is now in some serious trouble. *No more fucking around*, he decides. As soon as he gets home, he will be heading straight for the bathroom cabinet and taking a razor to his jugular. There will be no mishaps then. No turning back after the fatal slice and no interference from Death, who he is now convinced is stalking, thwarting and taunting him in his attempts.

Once again, Dylan is lost in his reverie. Oblivious to his surroundings and deep in tortured contemplation, he

continues his hobbled journey towards home. Only two streets away now and he can end things once and for all. The thought dominates his very being, drowning out any other consideration. Crossing the street, the deafening screech of tyres causes him to look up from his shambling feet, but a moment too late. The bus driver had seen him but didn't expect him to turn suddenly into the path of his vehicle, and although he instinctively slammed his brakes, there was simply no time or safe distance to stop in time.

Dylan's attempts to move are in vain. He can feel nothing but a strong throb in his skull and an uncomfortable intrusion travelling from between his lips to down his throat. He can hear a steady beeping sound and several voices amidst bustling activity. His vision is drastically blurred. All he can see is shadows intermittently disturbing an otherwise harsh, bright light. It takes him several confused minutes to realise he is in a hospital. Several minutes more to realise he is paralysed from the neck down. His vision blurs even more so as the tears of realisation fill his eyes and begin to slink down the sides of his face, tickling his ears.

Death chuckles softly and departs.

THE THROBBING IN THURMAN
T. S. WOOLARD

"Mother of God!" screamed Jonesy with both hands clamped on each of his ass cheeks. Blood splotched his dingy tighty-whiteys, and his face contorted in a painful mask. "It's up in my ass!"

Thurman looked at his friend, trying to grasp the situation. He was certain he or Jonesy, or even both, had smoked way too much weed before passing out earlier that night.

"What the hell are you talking about, and where are your pants?" chuckled Thurman. His friend's agony failed to register in his doped up mind.

"It's in my ass, Thurman, and it's going deeper!" he yelled.

"What is?" Thurman began the overwhelming motions of trying to stand, but Jonesy was already sprinting out of the giant double doors of the old church

Thurman lived in.

When Thurman reached the stone steps that led to the parking lot, Jonesy was on all fours in the gravel. He shrieked as he arched his back and pushed with all his might to rid his body of whatever it was attacking his virgin anus.

"Help me, bro. Please, help me," Jonesy pled.

"What the fuck do you want me to do about it?" Thurman said. Indignant was the understatement of the century.

"Get it out of me!" Jonesy rested his forehead on the gravel and cradled his belly in his arms. "It's killn' me. It's tearin' shit apart in there!"

"I know damn well I ain't fucking with it, then. It'll just have to kill your ass."

And, as if on cue, it did.

Guts and bodily fluid erupted from Jonesy's abdomen in a grayed-red flood with chunks of organs. His body went limp and collapsed on top of the juicy pile.

Thurman squinted at what he thought he saw. It couldn't be real, just couldn't be, but he swore he saw a small, neon green penis hopping on two balls from the carnage of what used to be his drug dealer and best friend. Even in the muck blanketing the rock-hard tally-whacker, the green pulsed with an otherworldly glow.

As he backed away from the advancing male appendage, Thurman tripped on the steps. He turned over and crawled, like a baby, over the threshold. Sliding like some trained assassin in a blockbuster movie, he twisted on to his side and kicked the door shut just in time to see the dildo-monster dive for his ass. The door popped, and the head of the dick slammed right into it.

"What the—"

"Fuck!" Sally screamed behind him. She held her tummy like she was pregnant.

"Oh, Jesus. You too?" whined Thurman.

"It's trying to kil—" began Sally. Then a tiny green

69

cock shot from her mouth with a tail of spit and blood, like an X-rated comet of death.

"Holy shit!" Thurman was beyond shouting now. As he watched Sally—just another call up on a Saturday night skank—collapse to the floor, it dawned on him, in a matter of minutes, two of his high school friends died in gruesome, unimaginable ways.

The new penis approached him. This one acted more cautious. It studied Thurman, tentative, not wanting to pounce too quickly.

When it stood about three feet away, Thurman dove at it, grabbing the thing around the shaft. A singeing acidic burn blistered his palm. Instead of a fleshy, soft feel to it, the glowing rod seemed to be metallic.

"Oww, shit!" Thurman flung the little bastard from him. He retreated from it, as the dick gathered its bearings, his head smacked against the door. The slightly bigger, more bloodthirsty dick began banging on the other side of door again.

The small penis cornered Thurman in the crevice between the door and wall. He searched for something, anything, to help him.

Beside him, a two-gallon metal pail sat on the floor, which he used to catch the water from the leaking church's roof. Thurman grabbed it and tossed the cold water on his stalker, hoping to blind it or stun it long enough to stand and beat the shit out of it with the bucket.

Before he had the chance, however, the cock went flaccid and fell over, like a wilted flower. If it hadn't killed his favorite booty call and burned the hell out of his hand, Thurman may have pitied it, as it folded in on itself, sizzling in the water.

So that was it; he needed to cause shrinkage. Then the little intrusive shits would lose their rigidness, and, with it, their desire for penetration.

How many were there, though? Thurman had seen two and deflated one. That couldn't be all. And where did

they come from? He needed to work fast and think faster, far faster than his cloudy mind allowed at the time.

While he ran through the church, gathering up some things he wanted to carry with him—clean underwear, a bag of Doritos, the leftover donuts in the box he and Jonesy picked up earlier, and a couple of joints—an idea struck him. He could go to his parents' house. The water tower for the town stood in their backyard. Since it was dead in the middle of winter, the water would be frigid and perfect to inflict shrinkage.

If he had a phone, and they didn't think he was ape-shit crazy, Thurman could probably get the Fire Department to help. Being the great-great grandchild of the founders of the town had its perks. However, being named Thurman Thurman wasn't one of them.

His family's surname was the same as that of the town. Most of his relatives, distant included, had enough sense to avoid the repetition, but his parents thought there would be no better way to honor their heritage than to give the name of the town to match it. So he was Thurman Thurman, from the town of Thurman. Sometimes he hated his own existence, and the shit-eating alien pricks weren't making him think otherwise.

When Thurman fled to his car, the Jonesy-raping dildo-monster was nowhere to be found. Ever vigilant, Thurman held the pail of icy water at the ready, prepared for anything that may happen.

At the top of his lungs, he screamed as he ran across the gravel parking lot, like it was a scene from a mafia movie. Somewhere in his mind, "My Maria" played in his fallen friend's honor.

A vision torn from a horror movie played out in from of him, though. As he drove to his parent's house, massacred corpses, with rips down their middles, or rectums split wide open like a cartoon demon's mouth, littered the streets and sidewalks downtown. Sometimes, one of the fated ran out in the road, in front of Thurman's

car. They pleaded with him to run them over. He obliged every last request.

By the time he reached his destination, the right headlight had been ripped from the grill of his little Honda, which happened when he splattered Old Man Cummings all over the front of the cheap, used bookstore in the cinder block strip mall on Main Street. Old Man Cummings weighed three-hundred and fifty pounds, easy, and he lived in the apartments behind the ancient strip mall. He lived on disability and food stamps, and was never late with his rent. Thurman thought to himself how mad his parent's would be when they found out he killed one of their best tenants.

Thurman hopped from the car without turning it off. He grabbed the joints, the donuts, and the pail, which surprisingly still contained water, and started for the door.

Mr. Thurman, Thurman's father, busted from the house. Mrs. Thurman trailed behind him in a granny gown and hairnet.

"Lord, have mercy on my ole bowels," cried Mr. Thurman. He, too, had the telltale signs little green dick death upon him, clutching his swollen gut and bleeding from the asshole.

"What's the matter, honey?" Mrs. Thurman yelled over her husband's pleas for divine intervention. "You reckon it was that chicken? I thought I cooked it enough, but—"

Mr. Thurman ignored her and squatted in the driveway.

"Don't do that here!" protested Mrs. Thurman. "Have you lost every bit of your raising over a stomachache?"

"Shut the hell up, Thelma. Something's tearing my innards all to damn pieces."

"Well, I never…."

Thurman grabbed his mother by the arm and dragged her to the water tower in the backyard. He heard his dad's yelling turn into high-pitched squeals of pain. The man's

wailing was interrupted by the familiar liquid explosion that accompanied the alien penis killings.

"What just happened to your daddy, and why are you jerking me around like a baby doll?" Thelma asked.

"He died, and I'm trying to keep us from the same fate. Stop fighting me and come on."

Thelma's face showed the shock of her son's matter-of-fact delivery of the news his father had died. "How can you say that? Maybe he just got a hold of something bad."

"More like something bad got a hold of him. Now, get your old ass up that ladder, or I'm leaving you here."

She stared at her disrespectful son. All his life, he had been a disappointment. He laid up in the old church they used before building a new one for the town, smoking dope, listening to that shit he called Grunge music. His only fodder was three-day-old pizza. Welfare whores were his favorite type of woman, and he wore the same old ripped blue jeans and faded flannel shirts for days at the time. But Thelma drew the line at being talked to like one of his old high school buddies.

"Watch your mouth when you talk to me, you little asshole."

"Fine. If you wanna live, meet me at the top." Thurman had no time to argue, and began climbing the metal ladder. He clutched the rungs with one hand and the donuts and pale of water in the other.

When he was about a quarter of the way up, a woman began moaning beneath him. Terrified as he was that he would find his mother being attacked by the dildo-monsters, he looked over his shoulder to see Mrs. Wilson, his parent's crazy, cat lady neighbor, whimpering before his mother. And just like he knew the old fool would, his mother tried to help her.

"Oh, dear. What's the matter with you?" Thelma rubbed Mrs. Wilson's arm while she bent over weeping. "Is there anything I can do?"

"Get up here. Now!" Thurman's voice boomed in the

flat bottom of the backyard. His mom even flinched at his command.

"But, Josephine—"

"Is a dead bitch," Thurman cut across her. "Now come on."

As he said the last word, every bit of Mrs. Wilson's insides plummeted from her agape anus. Her shriek was one that would frighten a banshee.

Thelma seemed convinced to listen to her son now, as she galloped up the ladder with the agility of an Olympic hurdler. She caught up to him before he climbed another rung. Her wheezes were gales of a hurricane in Thurman's stressed ears.

To make matters worse, the dildo-monsters were growing more violent. Mrs. Wilson's death was by far the most horrible he'd seen thus far. Her organs were little more than a darkened chunky salsa in the grassy earth. Thurman's stomach turned, and he wondered why the hell the donuts were so important. He let the box go, fluttering by his mom's head like a paper airplane with a broken wing.

The green death dick that killed Mrs. Wilson sprang from the ground higher than Thurman could've ever imagined. It clung to Thelma's meaty thigh, causing her to lose what little cool she still possessed.

Thurman mule-kicked his mother right in the chest without a second thought.

She slammed into the ground with enough force to knock all the air from her lungs and break her hand. A fresh yelp of suffering entered the backyard.

The terroristic reproductive organ scurried up Thelma's leg. It could taste its next victim already, mere inches away.

A wave of cold water rolled over it, and it shriveled into near nothingness. All of its hunger, its desire, went with its insanely strong erection. It finally winked away into a minute radioactive deposit.

Thurman held the empty bucket in his hand, watching as, in the distance, the same green glow of the cocks of demise came from a mound on the hill behind the water tower. The earthen lump looked like trash or mud in the dark, but he could see the dildo-monsters breaking through the surface, like worms coming from the ground after a summer rain storm.

Thinking fast, Thurman jumped from the ladder, landing on his feet beyond his mother, and tucked and rolled the impact through his body. His knees still clonked, but his fall wasn't nearly as bad as his mother's.

He ran to the shelter his father and he built as a teen, jutting from the side of the barn. Tucked under it was his father's old, red tractor. Just like Thurman had hoped, the rotary mower was attached to the back.

Slowly, the tractor came to life, spitting a thick cloud of black smoke from the rusted stack that smelled like burnt machine oil. Thurman wasted no time popping the clutch and making a beeline for the water tower.

He pulled next to the tower and backed the rotary mower into its leg. Showers of sparks flew from the metal on metal contact. An awkward, teeth-grinding metallic twisting whined, and the tractor's engine bogged down when the resistance was too much for the horsepower.

After what felt like hours, the tower's leg broke from its grounded brace. It began weeble-wobbling, but it wouldn't fall on its own.

Thurman drove to the other side and rammed the tractor into it. Everything crunched—the leg, the front end of the tractor, and Thurman's bones, but the water tower crashed down in front of the green glowing pile.

A flush of ice-cold water cascaded from the hole in the top and the crack in the side of the container the fall caused. The glow in the center of the pile faded away, and all of the Martian manhood impostors in it shrunk to nothing. The pile slid into a lagoon on the backside of the hill.

In the days following, news crews from the bigger surrounding cities traveled to the town of Thurman to report on the gory, mass deaths from the tainted drinking water source. Thurman tried to explain the truth, but soon learned the lie was easier to tell. He even said the contaminated water was what corroded the water tower, causing the leg to give way from the weight of the container.

Coroners said they'd never seen anything like it before. There wasn't enough left of any person to bury or send home to their families. In an agreement with all the deceased's relatives, they incinerated all the bodies, hoping to kill the bacteria responsible for all the deaths in the first place. Thurman and his mother rebuilt the town to be better than it ever was before the hellish events of that night.

The alien ship housed some quite strange extraterrestrials. They originated from the bowels of Uranus, deep inside the thick, gaseous surface the Earthlings knew of. The aliens had long, spindly bodies, like twigs, but their heads looked like perfectly circumcised penises. At the top, there was even a slit, but it was a gill for them to breathe through.

The captain of the ship had been having problems with one of his crew. He'd go missing from time to time, and they'd find him hunched over in the bathroom, jerking off furiously. Xynah, the problem crewman, had a major thing for the ship's nurse, Shirley. She wouldn't give him the time of day, but that didn't stop his fantasies.

"Xynah," called Captin Rufarious, "are you in there whacking your meat again?" He heard a startled banging behind the door of the cabin's bathroom. "Get your ass out here. You need to know something."

Rufarious waited a moment, and an embarrassed looking Xynah emerged. "Yes, Captain?"

"We've been watching the earth news in the control

room, and guess what? That shitty little hick town we dumped the waste tank in had a huge attack on its people. One guy said little green penises ass raped everyone to death."

"Oh, no." Xynah shook his head.

"Yeah, that's right. Now half of their world is screaming government cover up. Because of this, the Americans and Russians are all up my ass today, luckily not in the same way."

"I'm sorry, Captain."

"Shut up, and stop jacking off in the toilet. You're sperm doesn't give life; it destroys it."

ROUND TWO
WINNER

DEATHDAY WISHES
TONEYE EYENOT

ROUND THREE

NOT KANSAS ANYMORE
GLENN ROLFE

VS

BONE AND BREAD
LEX H. JONES

NOT KANSAS ANYMORE
GLENN ROLFE

Summer in Kansas, Maine changed with the arrival of the bats, which descended on our small town in mid-May. On May 20, Veronica Talbot's body was found down by Hazard Lake. It was a closed casket funeral. After two freshman burnouts named Derrick Quimby and Brice Lerrette turned up dead behind the backstop at Pedro Field, it was then most of us gave into the idea of staying in after dark.

A curfew went into effect immediately. On the news, they were telling us we had a murderer in our town. In the halls between classes, we were talking about vampires.

No more kids went missing before the end of school, but summer vacation was a fertile ground for hooliganism and shenanigans. It wasn't long before the rebels cast their multi-sided die and wound up on the six o'clock news. The brutal deaths of Jenna Martson, Bobby Jean Horner, Kevin Schaffer, and Ben Roy sealed our town's fate. Nothing would be the same.

The ravaged bodies of the four future seniors were picked out of the trees in the woods by the lake. I heard Bobby Colby, one of dad's friends, say their heads were fished out of the lake.

The Kansas curfew started at six, even though the bats didn't take to the skies until well after eight, but at that point, the adults were still looking for a man. Parents wouldn't let kids out of the yard, even in the daytime. Trips to the store were only okayed if an adult was chaperoning us. Phone calls were our main source of communication. Summer was just beginning, but it may as well have been canceled.

On July 1, just after nine at night, Officer Kenneth Tibbett drove into a group of cars on Main Street. Dad and I were coming home from dropping mom off at the hospital where she worked as a nurse. He refused to let her drive in or home alone. Officer Tibbett was still alive when my dad pulled over and hauled him from the police cruiser. Dad ordered me to stay put. I scooted over to the driver's side and was hanging out the window when I saw why Officer Tibbett's had an accident. There was still enough bruised daylight clinging to the sky to see the blood everywhere. It looked like a bear had tried to chew his face off. There were flaps of skin and tangles of mangled flesh dangling from the horrid wounds. When dad pulled him to the street, I saw that Officer Tibbett's arm was also missing from about halfway down his bicep.

Dad stayed with him until the ambulance arrived. I watched my father lean in close, like he was trying to catch a whisper. On the ride home, I asked my dad what happened and if Officer Tibbett had said anything. My dad wouldn't say. He looked like he wanted to throw up. He looked *scared*. Mom called an hour later to tell us that Officer Tibbett died on the twenty minute drive to Jefferson Memorial Hospital.

I snuck down to the living room that night well after midnight and caught my father, an empty liquor bottle at

his feet, holding himself up with the front door mumbling on about Pedro Field and someone being dead. *"A man keeps his secrets at the bottom of his drink."* That was a nugget of wisdom he told me when he gave me my first beer last summer. I had just turned fifteen and mom would have killed us if she found out (she never did). He said grandpa had done the same with him, and his father before him. It was a Truman tradition. Watching him now leaning into the door, I knew he tried to drown whatever secret he'd caught from Officer Tibbett.

I sat down and on the top of the stairs and listened to him ramble as he tottered like a weed in the breeze.

"no…mnsssserrrrss…nnnooo… mmonnnssssseerrs…"

I thought he was saying *no answers*. My skin crawled when I realized it was *no monsters*.

I left him in a pile at the door and hid in my room. It seemed like hours before my eyelids dropped. I fell asleep with the light on, staring at the full moon shining through my window. I turned my Kindle on and put on the *Guardians of the Galaxy* soundtrack to bury the midnight song of the bats screeching outside. In my dreams, a werewolf howled across the lake.

I woke up before seven. At some point in the night, my dad found his way to the couch. I got dressed and hurried out. Mom worked overnights at the hospital and had been staying with Aunt Rita when she got out. Dad didn't want her riding home tired, especially since the killings started. I figured I had a good three to four hours before dad woke up to go get her. It was stupid, but I had to see for myself.

In his drunken state, my dad had muttered three things: *Pedro Field, dead*, and *no monsters*.

If Officer Tibbett killed something, the thing that mauled him, ultimately to death, should still be there.

The sunlight never felt as cold as it did when I reached Pedro Field. The humidity was just beginning to

creep into the morning air, but rivets of cold sweat traced my spine at the sight of the backstop. Crimson splotches stained through the freshly painted wood. Brice Lerrette had been one of my best friends in grade school. Gazing at what was left of him reminded me of the report I did on Hiroshima last year for Mrs. Tines. It was about how the outlines of people were singed into walls where they stood before the bomb hit.

I laid my bike behind the set of bleachers closest to me and stepped onto the field. Mount Thompson climbed to the sky just beyond the trees. I hadn't been here since my older cousin Rick took a line drive to the head after pitching to Craig Sheehan in the Coral County All-Star game. Craig's now playing AA ball in Indiana; Rick, who was in a coma for two months, is still trying to remember who he is.

The vacant field gave me the chills. If Officer Tibbett killed something here, I was going to have to look for it. I walked out to where the trees started behind right field. When I reached the fence, I caught a whiff of something rotten. Then I saw the blood splattered down the hand painted Pedro Field sign that hung from the fence. My gaze drifted to the trees. I should have turned around and gotten the hell out of there, but a voice was urging me forward, inviting me to carry on.

I was over the fence and into the forest before I knew what I was doing. A dead animal carcass lay about ten yards in. It looked like a big dog, what was left of it— bones and fur, tattered and torn. In a strange daze, I continued into the woods.

Sweat soaked my t-shirt as the ground started to incline. My stomach growled. I had no idea how long I walked, but I came to a stream, with Mount Thompson rising up on the other side.

Impossible. I would have had to walk for hours.

I looked up and saw that the sun was overhead. It was around lunchtime, or close to it. I crossed the stream

and worked my way through the trees until they thinned out. Just up ahead, I saw the mouth of a cave. This is where I was going. I could feel it in my bones.

Standing just inside the opening, I could feel the air within chilling the sweat on my skin. There was a smell I couldn't identify wafting out, but it was wet and damp, like my Uncle Leo's dirt basement in the spring, only there was something unpleasant beneath it.

"Help me...."

The small, feminine voice drifted out from the darkness.

"Hello?" I called.

Ten or fifteen steps in, my eyes began to adjust to the shadows. Using my hand along the cold, wet walls, I pushed on. Whoever was in here needed me.

"Hello?" I said.

"Help me."

The voice was closer, less feminine.

The path curved to the right. Step by careful step, I continued. A dim light began to grow as I rounded a corner. Two slim streaks of sunlight peeked through the rocks above the small chamber before me. A twitching shape sat huddled against the wall farthest from the twin sunbeams.

I could *hear* the twitches and realized what they were—the bats. Before I could decide what to do, they took flight, up from their shadowy perch. They funneled upward, and I could hear them screeching and flapping above me, but my gaze was locked on the form they'd flown from. I watched it rise.

Cold laughter slipped past a mouth full of gleaming white teeth. A man—a vampire. I turned and ran. It whispered something behind me. The bats went berserk and chased me. I couldn't see and bumped into the cave walls. Blood trickled down from a cut above my eye. The bats whizzed past my head, some of them clipping me on their way by, like a swarm of fury bullets. I stumbled and

fell, covering my head with my arms as they came back around. After the last one passed me, I put my hands on the hard ground, got to my feet, and ran straight into the creature. Strong fingers grasped my throat; gravity failed me as my feet left the earth. We were floating backwards, back to the chamber. I could barely make out the egg shape of its head, but could feel the hair or fur on its wrists as I held on tight in an effort to breathe.

Returned to the only inkling of light in the cave, I caught a glimpse of it. Pale flesh held the two yellowy eyes, its mouth filled with a gang of pointy teeth, patches of dark fur covered parts of its chest and arms.

The smell of spoiled meat hit my nose as it leaned forward; its rough, wet tongue lapped the cut above my eyebrow.

It let go of me and began hissing.

I fell hard to the ground as it stumbled to the cave wall. A horrible shrieking noise erupted from it. The bats swooped back down. I covered up, but they didn't want me. They began to blanket the vampire. Not waiting to see what happened next, I ran.

The shriek followed me out, but the bats did not. I burst into the sunlight and kept going. Across the stream and through the trees, I ran not quite knowing where I was heading just trying to put as much distance between myself and the cave as I could.

My mind and body numb, I eventually stumbled out to a road, it could have been the Bachman Road, or maybe Route 3. I followed it East keeping the sun behind me. I could hear a motor coming down the road. My father's Ford pick-up sidled up next to me.

Their gratefulness for my being alive beat out their anger for my act of defiance and stupidity. My mother held me in her arms the entire ride home. After she took care of the cut on my head and the five nicks on my neck, I was sent to my room. I cranked up my fan, shut my shades, and lay

on my bed. I draped my arm across my eyes. Exhausted, I faded fast. The vampire's yellow eyes followed me down.

When I awoke, my room was in complete darkness. Thunder boomed outside, rain attacked the window like a thousand hungry critters that wanted in. I got up and tried the light. No power. Opening my bedroom door, I called out to my parents. I had no idea what time it was. They could be in bed already. No, my mom had work tonight; dad would have woken me up to go with them. I couldn't have slept that long.

There was candlelight coming from downstairs.

"Mom? Dad?"

The front door was wide open. I tiptoed down the steps, started to close the door, and noticed the headlights to my dad's truck were on in the driveway. Then, I saw two silhouettes inside the cab.

I hurried out into the storm and found my parents staring blanks into the windshield. Then I heard the bats. I opened the driver's side door. My father didn't flinch. I tried shaking him, but he didn't move. I waved my hand in front of his eyes; nothing. He was in some sort of trance. Mom too.

Lightning flashed and it was there. At the front of the garage stood the creature, the vampire. It didn't look like Dracula or one of the Lost Boys. Its lean, furry body, yellow eyes, hungry mouth, and egg-shaped head were something from a nightmare.

The monster hissed and I tried to hold my bladder under control.

"Come to me."

The order was not spoken aloud, still, I heard it just the same.

I shut my eyelids tight, shook my head, and turned for the house. Opening my eyes, my rain-soaked bangs hanging in my eyes, I ran as hard and fast as I could for the candlelit doorway.

Sinister laughter roared through my head. I jumped

over the three steps to the porch, flung my body through the door, and slammed it behind me. The voice in my head fell silent. My back against the door, I tried my best to control my breathing. I'd been prone to hyperventilating as a little kid. Mom said it was when my allergies mixed with my anxiety I would go into these fits. I was definitely seconds away from having a fit now.

The vampire had called to me, seen me, and now, was here to finish me off like Brice, like Officer Betts, and the rest of them. I wondered if my parents stood a chance. Did it want them? Or had it only come for me? I might be Mom and Dad's only hope.

Clenching and unclenching my fists, my breathing steadied. I moved to the living room window that looked out upon the dooryard. The headlights to Dad's truck died. A shadow darted from the vehicle to the porch and disappeared. I stepped back and heard the knock at the door.

Movie vampires couldn't come in unless invited. I prayed the same held true for this thing.

"What do you want?" I shouted. I tried to keep the fear from my voice, but the question came out in a wobbly bark.

My knees buckled as the voice returned inside my head.

"Open up and let me in."

I leaned against the wall for support. I needed silver—no, a stake.

"I will not harm you. Open the door and let me in."

I steadied myself and surveyed the room. The coffee table legs. I charged across the room, jumping into the air and coming down hard with my heel atop the table. It collapsed as I tumbled down after it. I grabbed my foot. The pain was excruciating. I hoped it wasn't broken.

I rolled onto my knees and swept my hand across the debris. Both table legs at this end had snapped off. One broke free from the screws and was still a solid block at

the end. The other had splintered in just the way I was looking for. I grabbed the stake and began to climb to my feet. The smell of smoke hit me.

My mom's hazelnut candle had rolled to the couch and set Nan Laurie's afghan on fire.

"Colton…" my mother said. She was behind the door with the thing. It was making her speak.

"Colton, open the door for mommy."

The afghan had now set the cheap couch material on fire. The door knob jiggled. My attention was being tugged back and forth. They weren't supposed to like fire either right? Or was that just Frankenstein? I was mixing them all up.

The door knob made a faint click; my barrier swung inward, smacking against the wall.

"Colton?"

Wind, somewhat cool and humid, blew in. I gripped the makeshift stake and stood my ground as the flames continued to build behind me. Smoke choked the room like fog among the tombstones.

I didn't have time to think it.

"Come in and get me," I said. My mother's body was shoved aside, her head connected with the door frame making a loud, wet smack before she slumped to the welcome mat.

The creature stepped across the threshold. I gripped the table leg tight between my hands and raised it over my head even as the smoke began to take over the room. Visibility dropped exponentially as the vampire came for me. In an ultimate moment of blind faith, I swung the spike toward where I'd imagine the monster would be. I came up with nothing, but tumbled forward and flung myself out the door.

It screeched in the smoky room. On my knees, I tucked the table leg under my arm, grabbed my mother and dragged her to the edge of the porch, pulled her down the stairs, and laid her on the lawn as I watched our house

burn.

The rain petered, now barely a mist. I stood firm next to my unconscious mother, armed and ready for the thing's next attack. I strained my itchy eyes gazing into the smoke and flames billowing out the door. Windows shattered, wood crackled, but nothing exited the growing pyre.

Then, I heard them.

The bats shrieking, a brigade of wings against the wind, as they descended upon me. I turned and was forced to cover my head as they pummeled me into the dirt. Small, flapping bullets hit me like a thunderous rain. After a few seconds that seemed to last forever, they gathered above and left me curled up in a fetal position.

When I opened my eyes, the creature stood before me, the fence of sharp fangs highlighting its awful grin.

"Leave us alone...please..." I begged.

"Too late, my little pest." It spoke aloud for the first time, carrying a slightly southern accent. "I have come. And death is all that follows."

It stepped over me, its yellow eyes beckoning me, sucking me in. Swimming through my thoughts... seducing my will. Through the haze, I felt the makeshift stake beneath me. I tried my best to think of nothing as I snuck the leg behind my back.

The vampire's long fingers traced my face, a long nail scraped a line beneath my jaw. I felt the burn as it cut into my flesh, and coolness of the night air as it touched the blood that trickled out. The monster lifted me from the ground, with its thumbnail sticking me under the chin. It yanked its hand back and hissed as it had done before when we were in the cave.

My moment arrived.

While it leered at its own hand, I swung the stake above my head, my hands like a vice of steel, and brought it down with every ounce of life in my body.

I saw its yellow eyes go wide as the stake found its

mark sinking into the monster's chest like a sword through the heart of a decayed tree. The sound that burst from its mouth hit my ears like a sudden blast of the loudest rock-n-roll band in the world. Everything that followed happened so fast.

I fell backwards and watched as the monster imploded before the inferno devouring my house. Watching the vampire squirm and collapse in upon itself was like the time lapse video of a decaying carcass we'd been shown in science class. The bats swooped in, attempting a rescue, but they were too late...I hoped. They flew off into the night sky, silent for once.

I held my neck trying to stanch the blood flow. A wave of lightheadedness threatened to take me away, but I fought to stay here. My mother stirred.

"Colt? Heather?" My father climbed out of his truck and rushed to my side.

"I didn't mean to...to burn..."

"Shhh, son, don't worry about that right now."

My vision blurred. The fiery background swirled as I finally lost out to a dream.

By the time the school year rolled around, life in Kansas had returned to a more black and white version of its former self. The monster had come and gone along with the bats. I was scheduled for my second round of chemo in a few weeks. Turned out I had cancer and didn't know it. The trip to the hospital following my battle with the vampire turned out to be a lifesaver in so many ways. In a bizarre twist of fate, despite the deaths it had caused in our community, I feel grateful for the monster's place in my life.

No, this isn't the same Kansas anymore, and I'm not the same kid I used to be, either. Sometimes the darkness changes us in ways that only few of us will ever truly understand. I often find myself gazing into the night sky, wondering, and waiting.

BONE AND BREAD
LEX H. JONES

Julia stood beneath the bus shelter, keeping her back to the plexi-glass rear to take best advantage of the shallow covering overhead. The rain had come on quite suddenly during her shift, and the complete failure of the forecaster to mention it that morning had meant she was without an umbrella. She didn't entirely blame the forecaster, of course. The weather had been strange lately, it was hard to keep up. Those lightning strikes around the fracking site had been particularly unusual, but the government bodies concerned had assured the locals that it all perfectly normal. Nothing to worry about.

The lack of umbrella was accompanied by a lack of proper outerwear, meaning Julia's pale blue nurse uniform was outwardly visible beneath a thin white cardigan. Her NHS ID card hung round her neck on a lanyard, replacing the clip-on plastic card that she had repeatedly lost. Thirty-three years old, five years a nurse, and six clip-on cards lost. She assumed that had to be some sort of record.

Against her chest she currently clutched a large box of corn flakes, shielding it against the rain because, assuming it would still be dry as it was on her evening break, she hadn't bothered to ask for a plastic carrier bag.

A quick glance at her watch showed that it was now 10:25 pm. The bus was ten minutes late. Julia sighed to herself. A late bus was hardly a rarity, but she was always curious how they could be late at this time of night? No traffic, no rush hour queues coming out of the city centre. Just one of life's little mysteries, she supposed. Julia leaned forward slightly, looking down the poorly-lit road to see if there was any sign of the bus. The street lamps were mostly covered by overgrowing trees on both sides of the road, giving the appearance of looking into a dark tunnel. This would only make the bus easier to see, though, as it approached from out of the damp darkness.

A noise to Julia's rear left caught her ear suddenly, silent as the bus stop otherwise was. It came from the rows of trees at her back, which seemed to go much deeper in the dark than she knew they actually did with the benefit of daylight. She heard what sounded like a squeal of a fox, then some branches breaking, followed by something running away through the undergrowth. Just animals doing what they do at night, she told herself, but still the noise was discomforting. She allowed herself another glance back to check for any oncoming bus, and then returned her gaze to the woods.

A man staggered out of the treeline, stumbling slightly and propping himself up on a twisted walking stick that looked like a tree branch. He left the wood looking back over his shoulder a few times, and then staggered around the path to the bus shelter. Stopping directly under the street lamp at its side, he then sat on the floor with his back to the post. He rested his head against the post and closed his eyes. Julia shook her head slightly. She'd never been a drinker or a party girl, so had no real frame of reference for those that would find themselves in the

middle of the woods after a few too many.

Despite her assumption that he was just resting off the worst of a heavy night's drinking, Julia found herself glancing back at the man repeatedly to make sure he wasn't injured. It was hard to tell, given that he was wearing what appeared to be a black combat vest over a dark grey shirt, black cargo trousers and thick black boots. He must have been paintballing, Julia assumed. She couldn't see any obvious injuries, but it was doubtful she would see any blood over all the black anyway. Not without a closer inspection. The man was still breathing, but Julia still found herself contemplating going over to him and asking if he was alright.

The sound of the bus braking as it pulled in to the bus stop startled her, and she was grateful that the driver knew to stop here for her every night, else he might have gone right past. Adding to her relief was the fact that the man in the black combat fatigues slowly got to his feet at the sight of the bus, and slowly made his way to the door behind Julia. He was alright, she thought. Just drunk, like she suspected.

"Evening, Nurse Ratchet." The driver smiled as Julia boarded and showed her travel pass.

"Gets funnier every night, Simon." She smirked, walking to the back of the bus and taking a seat.

She watched as the man stumbled down the aisle, leaning on each seat as he went by, before his legs nearly gave out and he almost fell into one. The bus set off, and Julia put her headphones in and relaxed. The journey back to Low Green village was about half an hour or so from here, so she would have enough time to listen to a few songs and forget the day's stress before she got home.

The first song on her "relax" playlist went by without incident, but halfway through the second track she caught sight of her fellow passenger, who had now slumped sideways so badly that he looked set to fall out into the aisle at any moment. Julia rolled her eyes, then quickly

hopped off her chair and went quickly down the aisle towards him, before gently sliding him back upwards. He groaned slightly and opened his eyes, and as she crouched next to him she got a better look. Dark hair shaved military-style round the back and sides, but square and short on top. Dark stubble around his mouth and lower jaw, his eyes dark brown.

"Are you alright?" Julia asked.

"Hm? Fine, fine, just need rest," he grunted, sounding every bit the drunk for whom forming words was a challenge. He wasn't aggressive though, Julia appreciated that. With all the drunks that came through A&E at the weekend night shifts, pawing at her and shouting, it was nice to have a polite one.

"OK, well my name's Julia, I'm a nurse, and I'm just sitting a few rows behind you, okay?"

He nodded and then closed his eyes. Still breathing, just passed out. Around twenty minutes later, Julia's stop came up and she got off the bus clutching her large box of corn flakes and saying goodnight to Simon. The route back to her modest house took her down a dark pathway on the edge of the village, boarded by some woodland and beyond that miles of open fields and hills. Julia's music was playing in her ears, affecting her senses to the degree that she failed to notice that she wasn't the only one to alight the bus at her usual stop.

It was when she was within sight of her house, the only one occupied in a row of three newly-constructed residences at the edge of the old village, that she caught sight of somebody following her in the corner of her eye. She didn't glance around to see who it was, but instead subtly increased her pace until she was at her front door, unlocking it as quickly as she could and then closing it behind her. Julia caught her breath, locked the door and then took her corn flakes to the kitchen and turned the kettle on whilst she was there. As she poured the water into a waiting cup, she heard a knock at the door.

Her heart caught in her throat. Nobody would come to the door at this time for anything good. Perhaps she should just ignore it? Another knock, more like a bang this time, and repeated for longer. Whoever was at the door wasn't likely to go away. Julia contemplated taking a steak knife with her to answer the door, like she'd seen them do in films. But no, that was stupid. This wasn't a film, she wasn't some girl living in a ghetto. This was a small village in the north of rural England. The worst crime that happened here was local youths painting graffiti on a bus shelter. Besides, her father was a police officer, and he always said you should never carry a knife unless you're prepared to use it, and understand the consequences of that. Julia knew that there was no chance she would use a knife, so decided against taking one with her to the door.

"Who is it?" she said, fairly sure that she already knew based on the black-clad outline silhouetted through the frosted glass pattern.

"I need to come in. I have to help you." The voice was less slurred now.

"I'm fine, thank you. Are you the man from the bus? I can get you an ambulance if you need help."

"It's not me that needs help. Please, can I come in?"

"I don't think so. Please, just go away, I don't want to have to call the police." Julia knew that it was something of an empty threat. There wasn't a station for miles. If this man wanted to get inside, he'd be finished doing whatever he wanted to do before the police arrived.

"I'm not going to hurt you, I promise. I just need to talk to you. You're not safe."

"The only person making me feel not safe right now is you," Julia said firmly.

"Look at your left foot for me. Please. Just check the sole of your shoe, is their blood?"

"What are you talking about?" Julia asked, but raised her white-soled Converse trainer and checked anyway. It was stained red.

"Is there blood? I was bleeding on the bus, onto the floor. I think you trod in it, but need to be sure."

"There's some on my shoe, but it doesn't matter. Why on earth have you followed me just for..."

Julia didn't finish the statement before the door was forced open, forcing her to take a few steps back to avoid being struck by it. The black-clad man staggered in, still propping himself up with his curious walking cane. He raised his free hand and held it before him in a 'stop' gesture.

"It's alright, I'm not here to hurt you. I know how this looks, but I just need to...to..." and with that his eyes rolled upwards into his head, and he fell face first onto the floor.

Julia stood and stared at the unconscious man for a few moments, biting her thumb nail and running through the various options of what to do next. Calling the police was obvious, but as a nurse she couldn't ignore the widening pool of blood that was starting to form beneath the man. She'd taken an oath, a duty of care, and as far as she was concerned that applied to everyone.

Roughly half an hour later the man's eyes opened to find he was laying on a double bed, his hands fastened with handcuffs above his head to the iron frame. He looked down at himself and saw that his black combat vest had been removed, as had the shirt underneath. The deep wounds on his chest had been cleaned and stitched up, and he didn't feel as much pain.

"I did what I could," came Julia's voice, whom he now realised was stood at the side of the bed. "But if you move too much you're going to pop those stitches."

"I'm sorry if I scared you." He groaned. "My name's Lucas."

"Well, Lucas, you should know that the police are on their way." This wasn't a lie, except that it was specifically her father that she'd called. He was closer than the station and Julia knew he was in semi-retirement these days.

Rarely left the station, and didn't work the night shift, meaning he'd be home.

"You need to listen to me before they arrive, because I doubt the coppers will give me time to explain."

"Alright, you say whatever you have to say. It's not getting you out of those handcuffs."

"Should I even ask why you have these?" he smirked.

"You're in no position to be making jokes."

"You're right, sorry. And thank you, for patching me up. I meant what I said before, I didn't mean to scare you."

"Then why follow me home?"

"I wasn't. At least not at first. I just needed to get away, so I got the first bus that arrived. I had no interest in you personally, but then you stepped in my blood. I barely registered it at first, but noticed when you got off the bus and left footprints down the aisle. I had to follow you then."

"Why? Is this some cult thing?"

"What? No, nothing like that. They know my blood, know its scent. And now that's scent is on you."

"Who knows your scent? Is someone hunting you with dogs or something?"

"No, not exactly."

"Then what?"

"The things that caused those wounds you saw."

"They looked like knife wounds to me."

"No, they didn't." Lucas looked into Julia's eyes and saw that he was right. She didn't think they looked like knife wounds at all.

"Alright, I'll indulge you. What did that to you?" Julia replied, shifting uncomfortably under his gaze.

"We call them Remnants."

"Is that some sort of animal? Are you a hunter?"

"In a manner of speaking. Remnants are almost human, to look at. That's how they hide so well, but for the ones who go through the change, they have to leave humanity behind and hide in the dark. Those are the ones

I hunt. They have claws, teeth, strength. I'm used to facing a couple at a time. Tonight there were at least ten. That isn't normal. In fact it just plain ain't right."

Julia looked at him with the stare of somebody that had just listened to several minutes of madness.

"You're trying to tell me that vampires are real?"

"What? No, I didn't say anything about vampires."

"Then what are these things?"

"The children of giants."

"Giants?"

"Yes. But they're probably not what you're imagining. They're not just big men like you see in movies. They're huge, but they barely look human. They're twisted abominations, deformed progeny of two races that shouldn't have bred."

"And what races were those?" Julia asked with a raised eyebrow, deciding to indulge this conversation a little longer.

"One of them was man. The other is…complicated. In fact we're not even sure. The stories tell us what we're supposed to believe, but how much can you ever believe from stories?"

"I'm not sure I believe any of the one you're telling," said Julia, rubbing her tired eyes with her thumb and forefinger. "But I believe that you believe it. Which is what I'm going to tell the police when they arrive, so they get you help rather than just throwing you in a cell."

"Any police that come here are going to die. If you let me out I may be able to prevent that."

"You're not going anywhere, so get comfortable." Julia walked over to where she had placed Lucas' removed combat vest and held it up. In the light she could see it was coated with something, almost like dried glue. "What is this? Some kind liquid explosive? Was this going to be a suicide vest?"

"Of course not, for fuck's sake!" Lucas rolled his eyes and banged his head back against the pillow in dismay.

"It's just a Kevlar vest, which usually helps against their claws, but these ones were stronger so it didn't. And that coating you're looking at is the sap from Ash trees. It helps to repel them. But again, it didn't work tonight."

"You don't have guns, or knives?" she smirked.

"I did. Lost them. Now, I just have that stick." He nodded towards the bizarre walking cane.

"That's a weapon?"

"It's Ash again, burns them if they touch it. It's like a big police baton, I suppose. Perhaps not the most practical weapon but like I said, I lost everything else tonight."

"This is certainly a well-thought-out delusion you've come up with," Julia acknowledged, replacing the vest on the floor. As she did, something dropped out of a small pocket on the right side. It looked almost like a coin, a dark rusted metal colour. When she lifted it, it appeared to be made of a central disc, surrounded by two larger rings, like a gyroscope.

"That's a warning beacon." Lucas answered before she even asked. "If the first ring starts to spin, it means the Remnants are close."

"And what if the middle bit starts to spin?"

"That hasn't happened for a thousand years at least, you don't need to worry about it."

"I'm not worried about any of this, I'm just worried about you. I'm starting to believe you don't actually mean me any harm, but I don't understand how you can have gone this far into a fantasy. I didn't do psychiatry; I almost wish I did."

Julia walked over to the far wall and sat down, holding the gyroscopic disc in her hand and toying it as she took a deep breath. She was tired, but she daren't let herself fall asleep with him here. It wasn't even an option. Keep talking, don't let him see you're exhausted, she thought. Dad will be here soon.

"So you're a nurse, huh?" asked Lucas.

"They teach you detective work in this secret

organisation too, I see." Julia frowned, pointing at her uniform.

"My point is, you're a good person. It's for people like you that we do what we do. Actually that's not true, we do it for everyone. Even the arseholes. But knowing that people like you are kept safe by it makes it worthwhile."

"I'm very grateful," she replied, heavy on the sarcasm.

Lucas nodded and laughed slightly, then said: "Can I ask you a question?"

"Sure." Julia decided it was best to keep the conversation going.

"Have you ever been the victim of crime?"

"No."

"But you know that crime exists, right?"

"Of course."

"Right. But there's people out there; police, armies, government officials, surveillance teams, doing what they do to minimise the number of people who become victims of crime. They can't stop it all, but they do what they do well enough that some people, like you, never fall prey to it. And that's both at home and larger scale, with terrorism and things like that, would you agree?"

"Sure, what's your point?"

"My point is, there's a war being fought, of sorts, to keep you safe. And it's mostly fought in the shadows by people willing to do things that you're not, with skills and training and equipment that you don't fully understand. You're willing to believe that when it comes to crime and terrorism, so why not with the stuff I'm telling you?"

"Because you're telling me about monsters, Lucas," she replied as though talking to a child.

"What is a monster, Julia?"

"In the literal sense, rather than figuratively? I suppose you'd say it's a creature that science hasn't identified and can't explain. Like Nessie, or Bigfoot, or werewolves."

"Exactly. Science hasn't explained it yet, because the

102

right people don't know about it. They used to have something called the Kraken on that little list of monsters you just gave me. They don't anymore. Now they call it the Colossal Squid, and it's in science books about oceanic life. An actual name for an actual creature, because hundreds of years after sailors talked about seeing these things, science finally caught up and realized: holy shit, they're real!"

"You make a good argument. But the sea is the sea. It's so vast, it's easy to imagine there'd be things down there that we've never seen. You're talking about humanoid creatures that live on land. Near villages, in England, apparently!"

"They're not mindless animals. They're smart, some of them even lived as humans before their genes triggered off in them. They know how to hide, Julia."

"You should sell this to the horror channel. They'd snatch your hands off for…" Julia stopped speaking when she felt something moving in her palm. She looked down and opened her hand, and saw that the ring inside the gyroscopic coin had started to spin. Slowly at first, but gaining in momentum with each rotation.

"Shit. Julia they're coming."

"I don't understand. How are you making it do this?" she asked, feeling herself starting to panic despite everything.

"I'm not doing anything, that just means they're getting close. They can smell my blood, track it. They remember the blood of their enemies, just like the stories say about their ancestors. Fee Fi Fo Fum, remember that?"

"This is bullshit, this is just bullshit." Julia shook her head, getting to her feet.

"Lock your doors and windows, right now. Please, I am fucking begging you. For your sake, not mine."

Julia agreed there was no harm in that, so quickly went round and made sure the doors and windows were closed and locked. The last one she checked was the kitchen, where the glass French doors opened onto her

garden. She was sure this was locked but thought she'd check anyway; better safe than sorry. As she got close to the door, the sensor outside tripped the outside light, and the garden was suddenly illuminated. Standing there directly in front of the glass, inches from her face and separated only by the double glazed doors, was a figure.

Julia screamed and fell backwards, losing her footing as she tried to step back. Looking up at the figure through the glass, Julia thought it looked human, until her eyes fixed on it better. The eyes were bulbous and milky, like a deep sea fish. The teeth reminded her of fish too, dozens of razors too long for the mouth, tearing through the lips at weird angles. The skin was pale blue and patchy, with the hair wiry and thin. The man-like thing raised its right hand and scratched down the pane with five needle-like claws, then grinned. Julia screamed as it punched through the glass.

"Julia, let me out for fuck's sake!" Lucas roared from the bedroom.

She wasn't arguing this time. Running as fast as she could, closing every door behind her, Julia went straight back to the bedroom and immediately set about unlocking the handcuffs that bound Lucas.

"Oh, god, oh shit it's in my house. It's coming."

"Stay here. Close this door. Do not open it until I say otherwise," Lucas instructed, taking his crooked stick and walking out into the hall.

Julia did as Lucas asked and closed the door behind him, holding it closed with the weight of her body but also trying to hear through the door what might be happening beyond. She heard Lucas shout something, and then a roar-like noise accompanied by a hiss responded. There was a ruckus, something breaking, and then Lucas grunting loudly as the creature howled. Finally, it all went silent, and Julia heard somebody lumbering back up the stairs, slowly taking one step at a time.

"Lucas?" Julia asked quietly, fearing the answer.

"It's me, you can open it."

Julia let out a sigh of relief and opened the door, then gasped when she saw Lucas. He was now covered in blood, but she knew it wasn't his own. In his hands he held the remainder of his crooked cane, broken into two sharp pieces now and dripping with red.

"I had to improvise." Lucas shrugged. "Needed something sharp. That stick was designed as a bludgeon, but I don't really have the energy for that tonight."

"Is it dead?"

"Not quite." Lucas wiped some blood from his eyes. "I need to talk to it. They're more likely to answer me when they're at death's door. And I thought you might want to listen."

"Why would I want to listen?" said Julia, surprised how the statement came out almost like laughter.

"Because you're on the cusp of thinking I'm not completely mental, and I'd like to finish that off, if possible."

With that, Lucas reaffirmed his grip on the wooden stakes, and went back out into the hallway. He ventured down the stairs, and Julia followed. She saw the blood before she saw the creature; a growing pool of it coming into the downstairs hallway from the open kitchen door. Peering over Lucas' shoulder as he entered, she saw that same humanoid creature that had stood outside her French doors, now sat with its back to the washing machine, its head lolled forwards with blood pouring from various wounds on its face and body.

"Rise and shine, beautiful," said Lucas, poking the still creature with the stake as he stood over it.

The creature's head darted quickly upwards and it hissed like a serpent, causing Julia to stagger back and almost lose her footing on the blood pool.

"Keeping me alive for sport, hunter?" the creature rasped. Julia found herself surprised that it could talk, despite the fact that it so closely resembled a human being.

105

"Nah, not tonight. I'll finish you off quickly once you've answered some questions for me," Lucas replied.

"Why should I agree to that, scum?"

"Because I think you want to tell me," Lucas suggested. "So let's have it; why were there so many of you tonight?"

"The awakening has gathered us in greater numbers, human pig."

"Awakening?"

"A line has been crossed. The humans dig too deep with their machines, desperate for gas to light their world of noise and fire."

"What machines, what are you talking about?"

"They've been fracking in those fields just beyond the village. I took part in a protest against it, but of course they didn't listen," Julia explained, nervously biting her nails.

"They have awoken the great ones. They stir and rise again to walk amongst you. The time has come."

"Are you talking about the Watchers?" Lucas asked, swallowing a very visible lump in his throat.

The pale creature grinned, showing its ear-to-ear smile filled with piranha teeth.

"That's not possible." Lucas shook his head.

"Fee fi fo fum." The creature hissed, leaning slightly left to look around Lucas and make eye contact with Julia. "Your bones will make wonderful bread."

With that, Lucas jammed the stake into the creature's throat, and left it there until its subsequent thrashing and gurgling stopped. Satisfied it was dead, he withdrew the stake and took Julia away by the arm.

"I don't understand what's going on," she said, forcing herself to remain as far away from hysterical breakdown as she could.

"Then I'll tell you. A story, yeah? Help you make sense of this."

Julia nodded, breathing into her hands.

"I'd say put the kettle on but that means walking back

106

over that thing and neither of us wants that."

The two of them walked into the living room and sat down, Julia either not noticing or not caring that they had now tracked bloody footprints onto her cream carpet. Lucas sat on the brown leather armchair and placed his gyroscopic coin on the coffee table, still once again. Julia took the couch opposite.

"I'm sorry you got dragged into this." Lucas sighed. "All you did was try to help me. And now you're in the middle of this shite."

"Only myself to blame then, right?" she laughed nervously.

"No, don't think like that. This is nobody's fault but mine, I should have been more careful. But anyway, I need to explain to you what's going on, and fast. I won't dally over this or dance around the facts for you, so listen and just accept what I'm telling you."

"I'll try." Julia nodded, acknowledging to herself that she was more open to it after what she'd just seen lying dead in her kitchen.

"Thousands of years ago, the human race was visited by creatures that defy scientific explanation. Call them aliens, demons, fallen angels, visitors from another dimension. We don't have an exact answer for that, but what we do know is that some of them mated with human women. The result were enormous, horrific creatures that feasted on human flesh. Most myths and legends about Giants were based on these things. We call them Watchers. They're even mentioned in some versions of the old Testament.

"The demons, or aliens or whatever that bore them long since left, but their progeny stayed behind and caused havoc for centuries. Until one day, atmospheric changes wiped them out. Some say it was a great flood, like the Bible, others say it was a general change in temperature or climate. Either way, they disappeared pretty quickly. But not before they started bloodlines of their own. And their

children looked more human, better able to hide. And their grandchildren more so, and with each generation they got better and better at hiding amongst us until we get to the modern day.

"Somewhere along the line, a group of men got together to start fighting back against these creatures, which we call Remnants. Like the one dead in your kitchen right now. We've always believed that the Watcher themselves were long since extinct, but now that handsome chap in the next room says otherwise."

"Do you believe him?" asked Julia, deciding to just let herself go along with the story rather than risk having to think about it too much right now.

"I don't know. See that coin?" Said Lucas, pointing at the gyroscopic disc. "The middle never spins unless it detects a Watcher. That's not happened in our entire history as an organisation. We added that feature out of paranoia more than anything. It hasn't spun tonight, not the middle. But I'm watching it really fucking closely, I don't mind admitting it."

"What sort of signs would there be, if these giant things were really waking up? Raining blood, sheep eating other sheep, that kind of thing?"

"Nothing like that, but some myths say they could affect the weather. Lightning storms, that kind of thing. Have you had anything like…." Julia's face answered Lucas' question for him. "Oh shit, this is really happening."

"Can you stop it?"

"I don't know. Everything we've ever done was to fight back the Remnants. We didn't even think the Watchers still existed."

Julia's phone rang, and for a moment she just stared into space, confused at who might be calling this late. Then realisation hit her and she grabbed the phone from her dressing table and answered it.

"Dad!"

"I'm nearly there, my love. Had to take a detour. A

few trees must have been blown down, they're all over the road. Strangest thing though, rain's picking up, but I didn't notice any wind. Are you alright, anyway?"

"I'm fine, Dad, but listen...oh god, this is so crazy..."

"Is he the police officer?" Lucas asked, to which she nodded. "He needs to go back home, now! They recognise authority figures, they see them as soldiers. Whether or not there's a Watcher out there, the Remnants will swarm him."

"Who is that?" asked Julia's father. "Is that the man? Is he handcuffed like I told you?"

"Dad listen to me, you need to turn back. Go home, don't come here. It's not safe."

"That's why I'm coming sweetheart, just relax, I can almost see your road."

"No Dad! You have to turn back, please just listen to me!"

"I'm not going anywhere, I don't know what's going on but...bloody Hell, what is that?" Julia's father exclaimed down the line.

"Dad!" Julia screamed, fearing the worst.

"There's something coming out of the trees. It's huge, it...oh god. Oh, god, what is it?" he yelled, before being drowned out by a monstrous roar, followed by the sound of metal crunching and being torn apart. Metal, and then flesh and bone, and then silence.

"Dad! Dad!" Julia kept screaming into the phone until Lucas forcibly took it from her, at which point she fell to the floor and sobbed uncontrollably.

Lucas sighed and put a hand on her shoulder, then immediately ran back down to the kitchen. Julia could hear him banging around through the drawers, and when he came back upstairs he was carrying various knives.

"Look, I'm sorry about your old man. I don't know what I can say. But we need to move."

"Move where?" Julia said weakly, not even raising her gaze from the floor.

"Your Dad said he was nearly here. And they got him. That means they're coming, so we can't be here."

"Where would we go?"

"Just away, far as we can. Do you have any ash trees round here? We can use the sap, coat these knives, and that'll at least give us a fighting chance."

"There's ash trees in the wood that surrounds the fields."

"Good, then we coat the knives and keep moving. I'm going to call my people and alert them, see if we can get picked up. But we can't risk staying here."

Julia nodded silently and Lucas helped her to her feet, then handed her a large knife. He placed the remaining three in his belt, then put his shirt and combat vest back on. He grabbed the gyroscopic disc and placed in a hidden pocket inside the vest, then took hold of the two wooden makeshift stakes, handing one to Julia. He then took out his mobile phone and dialled, as he carefully led Julia out of the house.

"We'll head to the tree line, just stay close to me."

"Are you calling them?" Julia asked, gripping the knife and stake in her hands.

"I'm trying but there's no signal. At all."

"Try mine." Julia took her phone from her breast pocket and handed it to Lucas.

"No signal."

"But I just spoke to my…" the final word caught in her throat and wouldn't come out.

"Atmospheric interference," Lucas said quietly, his eyes darting around the dark street. "Like the lightning storms. They're close. *It's* close."

Lucas grabbed Julia by the arm and set off into a run down the street, then turning off into a woodland path that began with a gap between an ancient dry stone wall. The sky was cloudy, full of sudden rain, and little moonlight got through. Lucas was used to operating in the dark, but visibility in the wood was terrible. It was wet,

cold, pitch black.

"Keep close, do not get separated from me," Lucas instructed.

The woods grew thicker, deeper and darker, and louder. Hissing, squealing sounds surrounded the pair as they ran. Behind them, in front, all around. From the trees, from the undergrowth. Lucas had never heard so many at once. Shadows circled them, and then one darted forwards and slashed Lucas across the face. He shielded Julia with his body, then swung out with the knife. The blade broke on the pale blue flesh of the Remnant. Julia saw this, and then caught sight of the ash trees at her back. Breaking free of Lucas' grasp, she ran to the tree and ran the blade up and down the bark, desperately coating it in any sap she could find as Lucas grappled with the Remnant.

"Get off him!" she screamed, plunging the sticky blade into the creature's eye. It howled, a horrid sound that Julia could imagine shattering glass, and then ran away with the blade still stuck in its head.

"Thanks," said Lucas, wiping the blood from his eyes. He took another blade from his belt and handed it to Julia. "We need to coat this fast, or..."

He stopped speaking at the sight that now greeted him. More Remnants than he could count had now surrounded them, braying and howling into the darkness. A complete blockade in a full circle, and they were in the middle of it.

"Stay behind me," Lucas instructed, raising his wooden stake and gripping Julia's hand. He kept moving in a circle, not keeping his back to any of the creatures for too long. "Just stay behind me."

He had no plan beyond 'fight to the death,' which wasn't even a strong option with a civilian to protect. He had no right to make that choice for her. She was his to protect, that was the job. Escape, then. Flight not fight. But escape how? Hope alighted briefly when a gap appeared in the braying crowd, a parting of the writhing

pale creatures which Lucas immediately decided to run through. This, despite the fact that he was acutely aware of the movement occurring inside his vest pocket. The disc was spinning and pulsing in a way it never had before. The middle section was rotating, he knew it without even looking at it. Still holding Julia's hand, he set off running, straight towards the gap that had suddenly appeared, stopping only when he saw why the creatures had parted.

"Oh, fuck," Lucas exclaimed as the twenty-foot tall monstrosity pushed towards them through the trees.

Its footfalls shook the ground, crushing its Remnant offspring beneath its feet should they fail to move in time. Lucas and Julia stared up at the thing in horror, their minds struggling to accept it. Julia remembered the horrifically deformed foetuses in jars that she had seen in her studies. One arm longer than the other, hideous growths all over the body, translucent skin with pulsing organs visible through it along with misshapen bone. The Watcher that loomed over them was all of these things and more; teeth like needles pushing out through its own cheeks. Broken lumps like half-formed would-be wings pushing out of the flesh of its back. One great swollen eye too big for the socket and another small and wincing, unlikely to be able to see.

"Julia, just..."

Whatever Lucas sentence was going to be, he didn't finish it. The oversized right arm of the Watcher swung down, its palm wide open, and mashed Lucas into the ground like a child squashing an egg. In a burst of organs and bone, he was gone. Julia stood motionless, unable to even scream as Lucas's blood sprayed her face. The Watcher turned to her, and something like a smile crossed its lips before Julia passed out.

The crunching sound that greeted Julia's ears when she awoke reminded her of being at work. On those occasions where bones had to be reset or rib cages cracked open, the

sound was something like this. Except she wasn't in a brightly lit hospital, but somewhere dark and smelling of earth. As her eyes adjusted to the light, she realised she was in a cave. Sitting up, she looked around and could see metal constructs pushing into the ground all about her. Fracking equipment; metal siphons pushing down to suck the life from the ground.

"Fee, fi, fo fum." A deep guttural voice filled the cave, followed by what Julia took as a sinister chuckle.

There was another noise too, a scratching noise of stone on stone. Julia looked around slowly, fearful to turn, and saw the source of both noises. The Watcher was sat before a large stone bowl, grinding bones and flesh with a large stone tool giving the appearance that he was working a gigantic mortar and pestle. The contents of the bowl had been alive once, and Julia feared to look too closely in case she saw anything she recognised. Black military gear. A police uniform.

Turning away from the nightmarish sight and covering her mouth to stifle a scream, Julia looked deeper into the cave. Shadows moved there. Lots of them, slowly rising as though stirring from a great sleep. Large shadows, like the Watcher. Some of them bigger, their shape even less humanoid.

The Watcher grinding in his bowl rose to his feet and approached Julia, each footfall echoing more than the last. She closed her eyes tightly and found herself praying. Prayer gave way to screaming when the Watcher grabbed hold of her and grunted a single word:

"Bread."

ROUND THREE
WINNER

BONE AND BREAD
LEX H. JONES

ROUND FOUR

DOORKNOB DAVEY AND THE WINDOW WATCHERS
DAVID OWAIN HUGHES

VS

FAMILIAR SCENTS
JONATHAN EDWARD ONDRASHEK

DOORKNOB DAVEY AND THE WINDOW WATCHERS
DAVID OWAIN HUGHES

He gave the door another hard thump with his fist, causing the small brass knocker to rattle. He looked up at the glass in the top of the door, and saw the hallway light burst to life.

"Thank fuck for that!" he muttered, huddling as close to the door as he could, trying to get out of the wind and rain.

"You're late, Geoff!" his sister said, when she opened the door to greet him. "And you reek of whisky!"

"Well, gee, Gina—it's so nice to see you, too. I'm doing you a favour here, not the other way around."

"Yeah, great. Thanks," she said, rolling her eyes.

"Besides, you know how much those fucking brats of yours love their uncle Geoff!" he said, hiccuping a few times.

She stood there in her bra and panties and stared at

him.

"Are you going to invite me in, or are you going to let me freeze my fucking titties off?!" he snapped. Geoff could feel rain water trickle off the end of his nose.

"You're a drunken cunt who shouldn't be allowed near children..."

"And you're a dirty whore who shouldn't be allowed to bear children! You should have had your reproductive bits ripped out of you at birth, slut!"

She went to slap him, but he caught her arm and shoved her backwards. He loomed over her. Rain water dripped off him and splashed against her cleavage. "One of these days, I'm going to break your neck like a fucking chicken's, Gina. *Snap*, just like that," he whispered, and then looked down at her tits. "Dancing or whoring tonight? It's got to be one or the other!" He smiled at her, and then belched.

She snatched her arm back and spat in his face. "It's work, either way, you bastard!"

"Whatever helps you sleep at night! Now, where are those little shits of yours?!"

"You're an insufferable piece of shit," she screeched, giving him another crack across his whiskery face before turning her back on him and marching upstairs. "If I had someone else to call to look after the girls, I would."

He pushed himself off the wall and staggered into the living room where his nieces were playing – Rosie, twelve and Stephanie, ten. Geoff scoffed as he watched the girls play Monopoly and dropped himself into a nearby chair. He then removed his flask from the inside pocket of his old leather coat, which creaked and squeaked as he moved.

The girls giggled.

Geoff removed his cigarettes, took one out of the box, and popped it into his mouth.

Before he could light it, Gina was screaming from upstairs.

"You better not be fucking smoking down there!"

119

He smiled, and then lit his Marlboro. "Fuck you, bitch."

The girls stopped giggling and went back to their game.

"Is that slaggy, no-good-sister of yours still doing the phone sex gig?!" Rosie and Stephanie looked at him, with the latter poking her tongue out at him. Geoff laughed. "You're a little cunt, just like your mother!" he told Stephanie, who smiled at him.

"Yes, Geoff," Rosie said. "Susan is still…talking on the phone with men."

"A family of sluts!" he uttered to himself, then tutted. "You pair should have been drowned at birth," he giggled. He took a large swallow from his flask, followed by a drag on his cig.

"And you should have your balls cut off!" Rosie said, scrunching her face up at him.

"Ha! You tiny pricks. Where is Susan?!"

"She's in her room," Rosie said.

"Just above me, right?"

"Uh-huh," she said.

"Mmm," he grunted, and then grabbed his cock. *For a sixteen-year-old, she's one mighty fine piece of meat!* he thought. *I've had a thing for her for a while now, and she's at the right age for plucking…*

"I don't know why mum doesn't just ask Susie to look after us!" Stephanie whispered to Rosie.

"What did you say?!" Geoff said, giving Stephanie a slap on her cheek.

"Ow, you bastard! I'm telling my mother."

"What's going on down there?!" Gina screamed. "I can't leave you fuckers alone for five minutes."

Geoff laughed, drank and smoked.

The girls continued to play.

"One of these days, Doorknob Davey and the Window Watchers are going to come for you pair, your sister and your mother. Davey and his posse just love dirty,

120

naughty little bitches like you lot. And when they do come, I'll let them rip you up and take away what's left!" he sneered, before draining the last of his flask and taking another drag on his Marlboro.

"Doorknob Davey and the Window Watchers?!" Rosie said, erupting in laughter which caused Stephanie to do the same. "You're a loser and a drunk, Geoff!"

"Oh, am I really?! Well, you don't know as much as you think you do, child." He pulled his lips back with a scornful look, exposing his yellow, smoke-stained teeth. A few were chipped and broken, others were wonky.

"Loser, loser, loser!" Rosie taunted.

"In that case, you don't want to hear about Davey and his gang then? About what you should do if he ever comes rattling your doorknob at the dead of night…!"

Rosie gasped.

"I do…" Stephanie said. Slowly, she turned her head towards Geoff. "Will you tell us?"

He took one final drag on his cigarette, licked his palm, and then stubbed it. Before enlightening the girls, he withdrew another Marlboro and lit it.

"So, you want to know about the legend that is Doorknob Davey and the Window Watchers?!"

Stephanie nodded.

Rosie scoffed. "We're not in the mood for some child's story!"

"I am!" Stephanie said, smiling. Her pigtails bobbed.

"Come on then, let's hear your stupid, made up bullshit!" Rosie said.

Geoff glared at her and then settled back into his chair. "Doorknob Davey and the Window Watchers were a metal band who performed back in the eighties. They formed in the late seventies and could have been megastars. They could have gone the distance, but they were cut down in their prime. You see, Davey, who was the lead singer and the one who put the band together, drove himself and the rest of his band member's crazy,

after a heavy night of drinking and playing LPs backwards..."

Rosie laughed, "Are you fucking kidding us?!"

"It's true! Certain LPs had subliminal messages when played backwards. It's said that this was the reason the band gave up their musical talent and hit the road."

"Oo, scary! What did they do, play a bunch of gigs out on the motorways?" Rosie said, poking her tongue out at Geoff.

Stephanie laughed.

"Actually, no! They went on a five-year killing spree, which was brought to an end when the band were captured and placed in a high-security nuthouse."

"Get lost!" Rosie yelled. "You're full of shit, just like mum says."

"Okay, if you don't believe me, but they were held right here, in this town."

Rosie's mouth flapped.

Stephanie looked away.

"Not so fucking brave now, are you!" Geoff said. "That's right, they were a Welsh metal band, and were put away in Castell Hirwaun."

"No," Rosie said, her voice shaky.

"Oh, yes. And they would still be there now, had they not escaped some four or five years ago. Some people say the group live wild in the hills and, every now and then, someone hears the screech of a guitar or the crash of a drum in the still of the night..."

"You're lying!" Stephanie said.

"I'm so not. The streets run red with the blood they have spilled, girls, and there's nothing more they like than the blood of dirty, filthy little whores like that of the ones who live in this house!" he yelled, and then laughed like a madman.

"Shut up!" Rosie said.

"There's four of them in the band. You have Davey, the ringleader and vocalist; Jon "Needle Sticks"

Ondrashek—the drummer; Peter "Skull-Fuck" Wonder—the bassist; and Dawn "The Texan Torturer" Cano on six-string. Remember the band Kiss? Well, Davey and his crew also used to wear black and white make up, but not like Gene Simmons and his boys. Oh, no. The Doorknob and the Watchers' make-up made their faces look like they were skeletons."

"Stop it! You're starting to scare Stephanie!" Rosie said.

"No, he isn't – you're the one pissing in your panties," Stephanie said. "Why was the drummer called Needle Sticks?" she asked him.

He smiled. "That's a good question, and it's one I'm only too happy to answer. You see, old Needle Sticks liked to file the end of his drumsticks down to sharp points, until they resembled stakes. He used to do this before he and the rest of the band turned loopy. But, once he'd lost his marbles he used to take those pointy drumsticks of his and poke the eyes out of small children. Yeah, he'd dig them out and eat them. Just chew them up like they were balls of chewing gum…Every seen an eyeball pop? It's disgusting. All yellow, yoke-like fluid bursts out."

"Oh, God…I think I'm going to be sick!" Rosie said.

"When the eyes were gone, Skull-Fuck would come along and deposit a hot load of love muck into the cavities. They didn't call him Skull-Fuck for nothing!"

"He would do it to…*children*?!"

"Yes. He'd also do it to men, women and family pets. He didn't give a fuck!"

"That's enough!" Rosie said.

"What about the woman…?"

"*Phew*, the Texan Torturer? I'm not sure you want to know about…"

"Tell me!" Stephanie pushed.

"The Texan, being the lead guitarist, would use the strings of her B.C Rich to torture her victims. She would wrap it around the dicks of her male captives and slowly,

but painfully, emasculate them. It's said that she wore a necklace of chopped cocks!" he said, laughing.

"Mum!" Rosie yelled. "Mum!"

"Shut up!" Geoff said. "You said you didn't believe a word…"

"You're sick!"

"You know what else the Texan Torturer would do?!"

"*What*?!" Stephanie gasped.

Geoff smiled. "She likes to wrap her strings around the nipples and tits of women, and then cut them off. Yeah, the Torturer likes to hear her prey scream and beg for their lives. She also likes to watch them bleed out, or choke on their tongues!"

"They sound pretty awesome!"

"I'm not sure you would think that, little lady, if they turned up at your door."

"My God, don't get dragged into his bull, Steph! If there had ever been people like that, we would have know about them. Especially if they were on the run…"

"But that's the thing, the government covered up their escape, Rosie. Castell Hirwaun is on its last legs as we speak, due to escapes in the past – it doesn't need any fresh headaches. If the place does incur any more trouble, then the government will be forced to close it down and I'm sure the private owner wouldn't want that!" Geoff said, smiling and blowing smoke in the girls' faces.

A thump from above caused him to look up at the ceiling. As the girls spoke among themselves at his feet, Geoff tuned them out. He pricked his ears and squinted. Faintly, he heard Susan's voice – she was on the phone.

"Would you like to know what I'm wearing…"

What a dirty, disgusting little whore! he thought, smiling. *It would be much better if she was down here where I could hear her better. But if that was the case, she would be free to look after her sister, and I wouldn't be here to hear her at all…*

"I'm wearing a negligee, with no panties or bra…"

Oh, God…I wonder if that's true? She's probably lying

124

around in old joggers and a jumper…

"My pussy is completely…"

"Geoff, Geoff!" Rosie yelled in his face. "Tell her you're making that shit up. She'll have nightmares otherwise. Come on, she's only ten!"

"Get out of my space, bitch!" he said, startled and dropping his cigarette onto his lap. "Ah, shit…" he screamed, slapping his hands against the ash and crushing the glowing end of the Marlboro. "Christ, girl. I could have gone up in flames."

"Yeah, or burnt down the only tree in your fores…" Stephanie muttered, then giggled.

Rosie laughed.

"And no, it's not a lie. It's all true."

More thumps from above.

He looked up.

God, what I wouldn't give…

"But it can't be true!"

"Look, you little shit, I told you it is! You want proof. Here," he said, reaching into the inside pocket of his coat and pulling out his wallet. When he opened it, he withdrew a ticket stub. "August '84 – I saw them live in Cardiff."

"Let me see!" Stephanie said, snatching the ticket from her uncle's hand.

"You can't read," Rosie said, taking it from her. "Okay, this proves nothing."

"It shows the band exists! Not only that, it was an all access area ticket – I met the band backstage."

"Oh, *wow!*" Stephanie said.

"*Pft*, please. I ain't falling for this mumbo-jumbo," Rosie said.

"Well, you looked pretty scared earlier," Geoff said.

"Yeah, well…"

Geoff smiled, pulled another Marlboro from his box and lit it. "Go and play for a bit. It won't be long before your mother goes. Scram!"

When the girls returned to their game of Monopoly

once again, Geoff went back to listening and daydreaming. Looking up, he blocked out the noise around him and homed in on Susan's voice.

He failed to spot Rosie pick up her iPad.

The floors and walls are so thin…

"Bet you'd like to be here right now, wouldn't you. Touching me. Kissing me…*fucking* me!" he heard Susan say.

*Oh, God…*he groaned internally, then instinctively grabbed his stiffy.

"I'm touching my tits for you."

He'd seen her tits. They were magnificent for her sixteen years – they were small, pert and tight. *The nipples were so pink…How badly I'd wanted to suck one into my mouth.*

Geoff felt pre-come drizzle into his pants.

A shiver slithered down his back.

Maybe she's not wearing joggers. Maybe she has her little orange shorts on – the ones she likes to wear to the gym; the ones that show the under curves of her arse.

He put his fist into his mouth and bit down.

"I've found them!" Rosie screamed, jumping to her feet. This brought Geoff out of his dream-like trance. "It says here that they were a band but they disappeared some ten years ago. That they were feared dead!"

"I knew you were talking shit!" Stephanie said.

"Okay, okay! So I lied."

"Arsehole!" Rosie said.

"Hey, I only lied about them still being out there. Or did I…?!" he said, grinning.

"How can they be – they were 'feared dead' a decade ago!"

"*Pft*, that's just a cover up."

"Whatever!" Rosie said.

Then he heard footsteps on the stairs – his heart caught in his throat.

Susan…

"You brats make sure you listen to your bum of an

uncle!" Gina said as she reached the bottom step.

Geoff got off the couch and made his way into the kitchen. There, he opened the fridge and pulled out a beer. After popping the top off, he went back into the living room and clapped eyes on his sister.

She was wearing next to nothing.

He drank her in.

She wore suede fuck me boots, which were bright pink, matching her lipstick.

The dress she wore barely covered her arse and snatch, with the front exposing her cleavage. Her make-up was thick. Her hair long, black and curly — it flanked her pretty face.

"Off shagging, then?!" Geoff said, laughing.

"In front of the kids?!" she asked. "Really? You fucking dickhead!"

"Like you're one to talk!" he said, taking a swig of beer. "Susan going to be on the phone all night?!" he asked, wiggling his eyebrows.

Gina slowly turned to him. "Yes!"

"Pity."

Gina walked up to him and slapped him across the face. "You stay away from her, you hear? I've seen how you look at her…"

"Slap me again and they're going to find your body in a gravel pit!" he told her, getting close to her face. His spittle plastered her chin and forehead.

"You're disgusting!" Turning her back on him, Gina bent over and gave her girls a kiss goodbye. "Remember, no later than ten to bed!" she told them whilst pointing a threatening finger in their direction. "I'll see you both in the morning…"

Her words derailed as she turned to face Geoff.

"What?" he asked. "You know I always drink out of the bottle!"

"I'm not looking at you, Geoff. I was wondering what the hell that noise was?!"

"What noise?!"

"That fucking noise!"

Geoff listened with intent. At that moment, he heard Susan panting and groaning.

"Well, that would be your dirty whore of a sixteen-year-old talking filth and having an orgasm over the phone to strange men!"

"I'm not talking about Susan, you bastard! I'm talking about *that* noise!"

As he opened his mouth to talk, Geoff heard it. It sounded like scratching.

"Fingernails on glass?!" he uttered, scrunching his eyes.

"Girls, turn the TV off," Gina instructed.

The four of them stood there and listened, waiting for the sound to come again. It did.

"It does sound like someone is scraping the front window!" Geoff said.

"It's probably a branch," Gina said. "Right, girls, I'm off." And with that, Gina headed out and down the passageway to the front door.

Geoff followed close behind and watched as Gina disengaged the locks.

"Don't go out there…!" he whispered.

"I don't have time for your games," Gina snapped. "Take good care of my girls." Opening the door, she pulled it back. Geoff could see the rain coming down in sheets – the streetlights appeared to be out. It was like looking into a black hole.

"Close the fucking door!" he snapped.

"Fuck off, Geoff. I have to go to…"

They both heard it then, and peered out into the rain-soaked night. It was a faint whistle, followed by the sound of someone singing. The heavy rain drowned the words out.

Until the music-maker came closer.

Then closer still, until they could hear the person's

heavy breathing and matching footfalls, and not just the words they sang.

"Who's that tapping at the window? Who's that knocking at the door? I am tapping at the window. I am knocking at the door..." the person sank in a cheery tone.

"Lock the fucking door!" Geoff said.

"Mum, what's going on?!" Rosie asked, stepping into the passageway.

"Get back in there!" Geoff yelled. "Shut the..."

But it was too late — the person's voice was now booming, as they came out of the rain and twisted, nightly shadows.

"Who...the fuck are you?!" Gina's voice warbled.

The strange man who stood before her was over six-feet tall — he wore a Stetson. His hair hung long and his face was painted like that of a skeleton. He sported a large black beard with a smattering of grey.

"Boo!" he said to Gina, bending over and getting close to her face.

She jumped back and straightened. "Look, dickhead, you're a little late for Halloween!"

The wind picked up and blew his long trench coat open and far behind him. Geoff could see that a Welsh flag had been sewn into the lining.

"Davey..." he uttered.

"Howdy, Geoff!" the painted man said, taking his acoustic guitar off his back. He then grabbed it by the neck, swing it over his shoulder like a golf club, and appeared to bring it forward with all the force he could.

The edge of the acoustic connected with Gina's jaw, snapping her mouth shut. The instrument let out a long *boooonnng* sound, and one of its strings came free. Teeth fragments pinged off the walls, floor and ceiling, as she was thrown backward.

"*Ugh!*" Gina groaned, hitting the deck. Blood spurted out of her mouth and nose.

"Nap time!" guitar man said, braying with laughter.

"Oh, fuck!" Geoff said.

"Mum? *Mum*!" Rosie screamed.

"Get back!" Geoff told the youngster. A deafening crash from upstairs, followed by a scream, caused him to snap his head in the direction. "*Susan*!"

"Still touching the kiddies, Geoff boy?!" guitar man said, before violently stamping on Gina's head until it was crushed – her right eyeball popped like a burst water balloon. Blood spurted up his black jeans.

"Mum!" Rosie cried. As she attempted to run to her mother's side, Geoff stopped her.

"No! Get in the living room with your sister. Now!"

She didn't need telling twice.

"I think I'll wait until she's gone cold before I fuck her in the arse!" guitar man said, as he advanced on Geoff. "She's your sister, right? I remember her. I'm surprised she even lets you near her children, Geoff boy. Didn't she know about your reputation?!"

Geoff said nothing, just looked at Davey in surprise. From behind, he heard Susan screaming and crying. "Get off me!"

"*Wooo-hooo*...We're going to have some fun with you, girly!"

"Davey, don't do this!" Geoff pleaded. "I thought you were dead! Had I known, I would never have double-crossed you. You have to believe me!"

"Yeah, we thought you'd be pissing in your pants right about now," Davey said. "Bring her down, lads!"

Geoff looked over his shoulder and saw Needle Sticks and Skull-Fuck. His stomach somersaulted. "Please...Don't."

Davey smiled. "Go on, cry. You know how much that shit makes me hard. We've had a hard time tracking you down, Geoff. You've stayed in the shadows, ain't ya?!"

Geoff nodded.

"Chicken shit knew we were gunning for him!" Needle Sticks said from behind, who hurled Susan down

the remaining stairs. She slid along the floor before slamming into her dead mother. "That one has an innocent smelling cunt!"

Susan screamed.

Geoff looked down at her.

So she was wearing the shorts...he thought. His dick hung lifeless in his pants.

Needle Sticks clapped his hand on Geoff's shoulder and twirled him around. "Hi! Pleased to see your old band buddies?!"

Over Needle Stick's shoulders, Geoff could see Skull-Fuck making his way downstairs. When he averted his eyes, he saw Needle Sticks' drumsticks holstered at his hip. The points were blood encrusted. Like Davey, he too wore a long trench coat. Unlike the vocalist, the drummer had a bald head, but his face was painted the same.

So too was Skull-Fuck's, who donned a patched denim jacket, complete with spiked pads on the shoulders. His hair was cut short – a goatee graced his face.

"Yeah, Geoff. Pleased to see us, old mate?!"

Geoff swallowed, hard. "I'll get you the money..."

"Oh, we're beyond the money, you so-called manager," Davey said. "We're going to fuck your shit right up! Take him in the living room, boys," he ordered Needle Sticks and Skull-Fuck. "Where's the Torturer?!"

"Getting her wires ready for big boy here!" Skull-Fuck said. He slammed his palm against the small of Geoff's back. "Into the living room, fuck-face!"

The front door was thrown shut, as all four men lurched into the other room. Needle Sticks, who had grabbed a hold of Susan by her hair, dragged her behind him.

"Torture!" Geoff said, when he clapped eyes on the fourth band member. Her long, black hair was caveman-wild – she wore spurred boots and leather chaps over blue jeans.

Her hands were covered in thick work gloves. Six-

string wire hung from her left grasp.

"You're looking at me like you want to fuck me, Geoff!" she said, walking up to him. She put her hands around his neck and kneed him in the balls. The air gushed out of him as he buckled and went to ground. "Well, you're going to need a harder piece of wood than that, cowboy!" she told him.

"Their skulls are mine!" Skull-Fuck said, pointing at Rosie and Stephanie.

"Yeah, but their eyeballs belong to me!" Needle Sticks said, withdrawing his tools of the trade and twirling them.

"Have 'em, boys!" The Torturer said, pulling the wire tight between her hands. "This douchebag and his balls belong to me!" she said, looking down at Geoff.

"Please…" he gasped, holding his bollocks. "Let the girls go."

"Not a fucking chance, sunshine!" Davey said, putting his foot on Geoff's chest, pinning him to the floor. "You're going to watch."

The girls screamed as they were pulled apart and held down. They all watched as Needle Sticks raised his drumsticks overhead, with the points facing downwards.

"*Argh*!" Steph screamed, "I thought Doorknob Davey and his gang…"

Her words were cut short, as the drumsticks were shoved through her eyeballs and into her brain.

As her small body bucked, Needle Sticks got off her and straddled Rosie, who lay in a pool of her own piss.

"Alright, the little one is still bucking!" Skull-Fuck said, lowering his zip and removing his cock which he inserted into Stephanie's ruptured eye socket. "Aw, yeah – it's all warm and gooey!" he said, starting to thrust in and out.

The slurping-sucking sounds made Geoff gag. Vomit raced up his throat but he couldn't do anything. He felt dizzy.

"I'm fucking coming!" Skull-Fuck yelled, ramming

himself against Stephanie's skull for the last time. His body trembled as his jism blast out of him. When he was spent, he let go of her small head.

His white, sticky goo could be seen trickling out of her left eye socket.

"Fuck me, that load was just busting to get out of me!" he said, gasping for air. As Skull-Fuck was about to move over to Rosie, the family's cat tried to rush through his legs, but he caught it by the tail, causing the feline to hiss and try to scratch his eyeballs out. "What a viscious fucking thing!" he said, howling with laughter. He then started to swing the cat around in circles above his head, before he brought it down hard onto the hearth. They all witnessed the cat's head explode.

"Wow!" Needle Sticks cried out. "Look at that moggy go!"

Davey had now removed his foot from Geoff's chest and was currently kicking Susan around the room. The Torturer now stood over Geoff. "Offie with the trousers!" she said, unbuttoning them and lowering his zip.

He didn't have the strength to fight her off – his body ached.

As he felt her guitar wires wrap around his manhood, and then he saw Needle Sticks stab out Rosie's eyes with perverted glee. It was the last thing he would ever see, as the Torture pulled the strings tight around his package, severing his cock and nutsack... A scream lodged in his throat. His world turned dark.

FAMILIAR SCENTS
JONATHAN EDWARD ONDRASHEK

Hilga slapped a yellow number 2 card onto the foldout table. "Uno!" she shrieked, her jaw working to keep her fake chompers behind her loose lips.

Johnny sighed as if perturbed, but it was a set-up for a hearty inhalation. Hilga's odor was stronger than usual tonight; it had even permeated the hallway outside her room. He closed his eyes and flared his nostrils, relishing the scent as it clung to his nose hairs. It reminded him of the casts he'd sniffed after they'd been removed from patients. The titillating aroma of sweat and wet, dead, sloughing skin made his dick bulge against his scrub bottoms.

Now, what can I lay down to end this? he wondered. It was getting on past Hilga's bedtime, and Betsy would be waiting for him to come. In more ways than one.

He watched Hilga's bony, wrinkled hands crinkle as she tapped her final card on the table. She licked her lips, her rheumy red eyes fixated on the card she'd discarded.

He debated switching the color, then decided against it. He knew her tell. He plucked a yellow card from the final three in his hand and slammed it onto the pile.

With snowy eyebrows raised, she placed her last one onto the table.

"Dang—ya got me again, Hilga!" Johnny exclaimed, though he tired of all the pleasantries. A nursing home was a death sentence. Joy shouldn't be allowed inside one. *And neither should I…*

She clapped; underarm fat pocked with cellulite and brown spots jiggled. "That's how many now, Johnny? Two, three in a row?"

"At least," he said, a fake grin plastered across his face. "I just can't keep up with you, young lady."

"Oh, Johnny."

Still sucking hungrily at the air through his nostrils, Johnny stood, moved around the table, and placed his hand on her shoulder, his dick rock-hard. "That was fun, wasn't it?"

"Mmmhmm."

He drank in the overwhelming fragrance of old people wafting off her nightgown—moth balls and decades-old, browning newspaper; wood stoves; hard butterscotch candy and excessive VapoRub. His eyes nearly rolled back in their sockets. His fingers wandered to the nape of her neck and raked against the large, hairy warts covering her skin. He leaned forward, face centimeters from her stringy silver hair.

"The fun doesn't have to end," he whispered, moving his hand to the gigantic skin tag on the side of her neck. He fondled it, rubbing the flap as if it were a sexy thigh.

She reached up and placed her hand on his. "Stop, Johnny."

He furrowed his brow. He'd been making advances on her for years, but she'd always rejected them. *Maybe she remembers? Shit… No, don't panic yet,* he told himself. "What? Why? Doesn't it feel good?"

135

"Well, yeah, but it… isn't right. With us being—"

"What, because I'm a nurse and you're a patient?" He chuckled. "Aw, come on, Hilga." His words rushed out in a fine hiss as he whispered in her ear, "Don't you remember what it feels like to have a stiff one in your little pussy, eh?"

Her body quivered. "Oh, I remember everything, Johnny," she said. Her gaze wandered to the clock mounted on the wall opposite her chair. "In fact, if I recall correctly, you should be getting on to Betsy soon, shouldn't you?"

Johnny choked on his own breath and stood to full height. "What?"

"Look, I know. The other day, when we were playing bridge in the commons—I saw the list, Johnny."

Fear coiled within his gut like a serpent poised to strike. *That's where it got to! Shit!* He'd lost his fuck schedule a few weeks ago, but since no one had mentioned it, he'd figured it'd been mistaken for trash and tossed. "I don't know what you're talking about," he lied. "What list?"

"The list of times and room numbers, the ladies' names. It was in your handwriting. I remember it all, and I remember—"

"You stupid bitch. You have Alzheimer's. You can't even remember your own goddamn family!" he said, his mind a whirlwind of red anger and obsidian thoughts. Where was the schedule now? How many people knew about his goings-on at Stoneybrooke Assisted? He'd been careful to keep all the old bitches from tattling on him, but now someone could ruin everything!

Hilga rocked in the chair, stood, and wheeled on him. "How dare you!" she shouted, though her ancient larynx couldn't produce sounds louder than an inside voice.

He glared at her and stepped forward, fists clenched at his side.

Urine trickled down Hilga's legs and pooled beneath the cotton slippers adorning her feet. "Get out," she said,

her voice shaky.

"I'm not going anywhere," he said with a shit-eating grin. "And I don't think you know shit about a list. I think you're just mad I haven't fucked you yet. In fact, I think you're mad because no one's beat up that old vag of yours for decades, ever since your old man left you for that gay hooker. Hell, it probably spits dust!"

She gasped. "Now you've crossed the line. Get out!"

"I'll *show* you crossing lines, you old cunt," he said, shoving her with minimal force. He had to be mindful of leaving bruises, but he knew he could harm her and get away with it. No one ever believed the old bat—her memory was as shitty as a diarrhea-soaked pair of Depends.

She stumbled backward. He shoved her again and again, until she toppled onto her bed. Then he crawled atop her wriggling body, grinding his stiffening cock against her pelvis, nearing climax already.

He clamped his hand over her mouth. Hilga's false teeth mashed against his skin, drenched in saliva. The slimy feel doused his mood in tar; the anger burst from his stomach and plowed into his forearms. He pressed down harder, wishing to smother both his fury and Hilga all at once.

A tiny voice then whispered in the recesses of his mind, reminding him why he'd come to Stoneybrooke Assisted Living in the first place. He'd picked his life up after the restraining order had been lifted and his mother had passed, and he'd gotten his degree just to be at Stoneybrooke. He couldn't throw that away. He had it made here. Offing one of the patients would do more harm than good.

But if it were an accident... He loosened his grip and let the thought teeter on the precipice of sanity. Then he nodded to himself. *Yeah, I need to shut her up anyway. Nosy bitch knows too much. And after her, I can hunt down the schedule.*

He stared at Hilga's bulging eyes, felt the teeth still

137

rubbing against his palm. His raging hard-on threatened to spill seed in his boxer briefs as a new idea formed. He knew exactly how to silence her and make her eat her empty threats.

He slid the fingers still covering her mouth between her lips and yanked her fake set of teeth out. She gasped and sputtered, but before any louder sounds emitted from her throat, he pinched her tongue with his free hand and pulled outward. Then he turned the set of teeth around, pried them open one-handed, and settled the chompers over her tongue. He pressed the dentures together and crammed it all back into her mouth. Her lips stretched around his fingers as if he were fisting her. The image rocked him; come spurted; his body quivered with orgasmic pleasure.

With his fingers still in her mouth holding the dentures clamped tight, he maneuvered off her stomach and knelt on the bed beside her. "Stand up," he ordered. "On the mattress." She didn't immediately move, so he whispered through gritted teeth, "Now!"

She whimpered and tears streamed down her cheeks, but she obeyed nonetheless. As she arose, he stood with her. When her forehead was level with his chest, he wrenched his hand out of her wet mouth, hugged her close, flipped her upside-down as if to pile-drive her, and stepped to the edge of the bed. Her exposed muff was in his face, reeking of tuna and piss.

He let go as another orgasm rocked him.

The top of her head smashed into the ground with a horrendous thud.

As blood pooled beneath her lifeless face, Johnny rubbed at his crotch and then sniffed his fingertips, savoring the bleachy saltwater scent which had soaked through his bottoms.

* * *

Johnny thrust one more time inside Betsy, unleashing a stream of spunk. She bucked and shuddered beneath him, a smile on her face. Since her eyelids were closed in ecstasy, Johnny took the opportunity to sniff her mouth. Decayed teeth and bad breath had always aroused him, and Betsy hadn't practiced good dental hygiene in at least a decade.

He rolled off her and lay on his back, attempting to regain his breath.

"Mmmm, Johnny, dat wuh good," she said in her thick southern accent.

"Goddamn right," he muttered.

Betsy clutched at his bicep and nestled her head against his heaving chest. "An' you smell good as alway', Johnny. Dat Aqua Blue get me e'ry ti'."

Her rancid stenches fell upon him like rabid wolves. "You smell great too, babe." He grinned and moved his hand to the giant goiter at her throat, tracing his fingertips around the protrusion. Raised cherry angiomas jutted from her skin around the abnormality, creating a pleasant, bumpy border.

I wish they'd pop, he thought, like his blisters had when he'd suffered severe sunburn in his childhood, or like the giant ass pimples he'd squeezed the heads off of back in high school. His stomach and sphincter clenched at the thought of oozing pus and weeping sores.

If it hadn't been for you, Mom, I never would've known such pleasures exist, he thought, slipping into daydreams of his past.

His mom had never known what kind of fetishes she'd stirred within her son, and he'd kept it that way until her death ten years ago. Her goiter, compounded belly button lint, Frito-scented toes, and thick, brittle yellow toenail clippings had aroused him long before he'd known what a boner was. The warts, too. He also remembered sniffing toilet seats after she'd used them—even the fetor of shit piqued his interests.

139

Other family members had contributed to his strange desires as well. Holiday settings had been a wet dream back then. He recalled one Thanksgiving in particular, sometime after his cousins and aunt had been in a car wreck. They'd healed up the day of the feast, and he'd sneaked into their bathroom during the meal to sniff and savor the crusty, soiled gauze in the trash can. After that, he'd jerked off onto the shower curtain. His splooge had been rank, yet no one had noticed.

He widened his legs as his cock stiffened anew.

"Whoa, don' lemme fall," Betsy said beside him, yanking him from his reveries.

Yeah, you might break a fucking hip, he thought. *Or your head.* He smiled at that and sniggered.

Ten minutes later, he was dressed and ready for his shift. Betsy hobbled out of the room before him, still in her nightgown, come drizzling down her leg. He waited a few minutes after to ensure the coast was clear, then cracked the door open and peeked out. Geriatrics of all colors and lifestyles mingled in the commons. Cutlery and glassware clinked as breakfast was served to the zombie-like denizens. He slipped through the doorway. Scents wafted toward him: eggs, bacon and sausage; sweet sugary syrup and fresh waffles. Other aromas, too. Familiar scents. Ones which left his balls aching for yet another release.

He smoothed the front of his scrub top and glanced around at the grumpy morning faces when, without warning, all heads turned toward the front entrance. He followed gazes and his heart lodged in his throat.

A nurse wheeled Hilga through the foyer, smiling and waving at the residents who had gotten up from their seats to greet their old friend. Hilga herself grinned wide as a horde of stodgy old folks surrounded her.

Johnny stuck to the shadowy hallway near Betsy's room, sweat bathing his palms. It was the first time in eight weeks that he'd thought of or seen Hilga. He recalled

the blood as she'd lain on the floor, the copious ounces of come he'd splattered on the walls and shower curtain afterward. *Just like the old family holidays.*

He'd heard she ended up with severe brain damage and couldn't speak—half her tongue had been bitten off. She supposedly couldn't write anymore either.

No one had suspected foul play; the investigators had seen much worse from patients with the medical issues Hilga faced. There weren't any cameras, no witnesses, no evidence to contradict a simple (though horrendous) fall from the bed.

Still, he thought, gulping down his fears, *she could remember something. She's said she remembers everything for as long as I can remember her…*

The gaggle of geriatrics whooped and hollered, greeting their healing deathmate. Johnny skirted the commons and rushed into a dark hallway away from the raucous crowd, his mind running amok. He'd finally found the schedule—only one copy—sitting on a table in the commons a few weeks ago. It had faded from memories. But Hilga was back now. What if she remembered something from that night?

What if she remembered…more?

He paused in his flight. The hallway was deserted, and no one saw the sinister grin spread across his cheeks.

Well, let's make sure she doesn't remember a fucking thing then.

Hilga awoke with a start. Her joints creaked as she sat up on the bed. The movements took her breath and energy away.

There had been a noise. That's what had woken her up. But what had caused it?

She groped at the lamp beside her bed. Her trembling, frail fingers finally found the switch and she flicked it. Darkness scampered from the ensuing light. She blinked, clearing crust and drowsiness away. She glanced

about. Nothing moved. Nothing seemed out of place, at least as far as she could recall. Her memory wasn't what it used to be though.

The sensation of a full bladder stabbed at her innards, pleading for release. Perhaps that was what had awakened her? Perhaps it had been a subconscious bodily necessity and not a noise at all?

Sat all the way up, she gingerly moved her legs off the side of the bed, turning her torso. Sharp pangs slammed into her head, neck and ribs. She placed her hands on the bedrails. Something scratchy yet smooth brushed against her skin. She squinted at the items—Velcro restraints. *Were these here before the accident?* She couldn't recall.

Her body throbbed as she stood on wobbly, fawn-like legs. More pains coursed through her, but she felt those pains were familiar. She should've been able to remember them from another time, but she couldn't. Maybe in due time she would. The doctor had told her so—the more she recovered, the more she would remember. He had also stated the memories might hit when she least expected them to. *So standing around waiting for them is pointless,* she thought.

But she also realized she was getting up there in age. She didn't want to wait forever for the memories to return, yet she didn't think she had any other choice in the matter.

She grabbed the walker from beside her bed and shuffled toward the bathroom. Her nightgown flapped against her bare ass, beckoning goose pimples to sprout along her neck. Once inside the bathroom, she flicked the light on. Using her walker as an aide, she hiked her gown up and squatted on the toilet seat. Coldness bit into her thighs as piss tinkled out. She sniffed as she reached for paper to wipe with. The scent of her urine was sour and pungent, almost powerful enough to knock her off the toilet.

That's right, I had pureed asparagus for supper, she thought, holding her breath. *Asparagus always does this to me.* She

almost cooed at her brash certainty of that once-forgotten tidbit.

She pulled herself back up using the walker, turned the light off, and exited the bathroom. She made it to her bed and paused. Several fingers were wet. She had forgotten to wash her hands and flush the toilet.

I forget too easily now...

She stared out the window across the room. Moonlight shone but did not seem to penetrate the glass.

Like the sight of the clouded moon, everything was murky within her mind. Many memories which had once eluded her had returned during her stay at the intensive care unit. Others—things she should've been able to remember with clarity—had run off into the shadows, leaving her paralyzed by her own brain's inability to retain.

She used to be able to eat solid food, she knew. And talk for hours. Like she had with David, her husband, many years ago.

She hadn't been able to remember his name before her accident, but she remembered it now. She could also remember other members of her family, ones she'd forgotten about. David, of course (*the sick fuck—though she couldn't recall why*); her sister, Olga; her sons, Peter and Jack; Mom and Dad and everyone in between. Most of them, anyway. Some, like Olga's son, were still nothing more than whispering, taunting ghosts of her past.

Hilga closed her eyes, drawing on the rich newfound memories. She recalled the holidays now. Some of them. She could almost smell the roasts, breads and melted butter; the stuffing, turkey and ham; the candied yams, chicken breasts and homemade pizzas. She could hear her family's laughter, the pitter-patter of children only waist high, the clinking of wine glasses, silverware and porcelain dishes. She envisioned the fireplaces and Christmas trees, and she felt the warmth of love, a warmth she hadn't felt in far too long.

She sucked in a breath, not willing to shoo the

memories away regardless of how clouded they were. *How long was it before they said they could determine the permanent damage done?* She definitely couldn't recall that. She was grateful for the new mental photographs flashing through her mind, but most recent events refused to peek at her recollections.

Oh, but she remembered the nurse. The kind one. The one who always let her win at Uno and Canasta. The one with the beautiful handwriting. His name, however, remained at the edge of her mind, wrapped in a shroud of mystery.

A sound cut through the room with force, almost like a dog at hunt, sniffing along its prey's trail. Something of that ilk. Hilga peeled her gaze from the starlit sky and glanced around the room again. Nothing stirred. She decided her brain was tired and playing tricks on her. She turned the light off, grabbed onto the side rails, and crawled back into bed. All the random, unknown pains throbbed in protest anew.

On her back, she stared at the ceiling. *What is his name?* she wondered. A familiar scent funneled over her, a manly fragrance, one she should remember well. Then it hit her: *Johnny!* That was his name. The nurse.

A fleeting memory zipped past inside her mind then. Her breath hitched in her throat and a warm smile crossed her wrinkled face. With a fondness she couldn't recall experiencing in years, she conjured the decades-old six-year-old face of her nephew, whose name was also Johnny. *The doctor was right*, she thought. *It's all starting to come back to me.*

Another memory struck, a horrid one which stole her smile away: A man had stalked and tried to rape her many years ago, and she'd gone to the police. She couldn't recall who it'd been, but the overwhelming dread she'd felt back then sent a shiver rippling through her now.

Then she recalled the more recent assault. Disturbing images flooded her mind, and her hammering heartbeat

sounded like footsteps crossing the room.

I'm not going to sit here all fucking night, he thought, moving out from the bathroom with long, angry strides. He'd thought he'd been too loud while moving the shower curtain aside both times. He'd thought he'd woken the dead with his exaggerated sniffing of the toilet seat after Hilga had finished pissing—asparagus urine was one of his favorites. But the old bitch hadn't made a peep about it all.

And she won't anymore when I'm done with her, he thought, stepping up to Hilga's bed. Even without light, he could see well enough. He grabbed the right-side restraint, which he'd installed earlier that day while she'd been enjoying lunch with people she couldn't remember, and undid the Velcro. The noise pierced the silence of the room. Before she could react to it, he snatched her right wrist, placed it against the restraint, and fastened it tight.

The old hag startled, gasping through her toothless lips. As a precaution, he leaned over and cupped her mouth with his gloved left hand. *She can't talk anymore, but I'm not taking chances*, he thought. *Even mutes have ways of speaking.*

He twisted at the waist, stretching until the fingertips on his right hand bashed against the lamp switch. The rekindled light stung his eyes, but he blinked the nuisance away and slipped his free hand into his pants pocket. His fingers wrapped around the syringe contained there, grasping it as if it were his cock.

With her hot breath against his gloved hand, he removed the syringe from concealment and brought the needle-tip to his mouth. He clamped his teeth onto the plastic cap and slid the needlepoint free. Clear liquid sloshed inside the tube.

Johnny noted the many pinpricks dotting the inside of her restrained elbow, a helpful byproduct of her stint in the ICU. A purple-blue vein beckoned from beneath papery, sagging skin. With a true aim and a steady hand, he

145

jabbed the needle into her and forced the plunger down. The clear liquid disappeared into Hilga's circulatory system, carried by her aged blood.

Seconds later, her free arm and entire body stopped flailing as paralysis set in.

Johnny chuckled. "Guess doubling the dose of that sux was a good idea after all," he marveled aloud. Perhaps it hadn't been necessary; she wouldn't have survived even a regular medical dosage of the drug without a ventilator. But he needed to shut her up for good.

He needed to shut her up before she remembered *everything*.

With the syringe tube drained, he pulled the needle out of her vein, carefully slid it back into the cap still clutched between his teeth, and pocketed the instrument. He leaned over Hilga, mashing his chest against her mushy, misshapen tits. Her eyes were wide, unblinking; her chest no longer heaved; warm air no longer flowed against his gloved palm.

He removed his hand, slow and cautious. Her lips had parted in a silent cry. He sighted the sawed-off tongue inside her mouth. Seeing the muscle in its diminished state brought a flutter to his heart.

That tongue will never wag again, he mused.

"Shhh. Shhh," he mocked, noticing a flicker of recognition in her pupils. He placed a finger to her lips to demean her further, knowing the sux had taken hold. It was only a matter of seconds before she would die, choking on lack of air as her lungs and muscles refused to work.

Familiar smells—old folks and nastiness—invaded his nostrils, setting his cock to bulging and throbbing in his pants. He dug his boner into her lifeless arm and stared into her eyes. Though she couldn't speak or move, she still pled for life with those rheumy orbs.

"You've always said you remember everything, Hilga," he said. "And I can't have that. I like this life here. I

146

like these women." He flashed his handsome grin, making sure she remembered his face before she died. "Maybe in due time, the men as well."

He fondly stroked the skin flap on the side of her neck, wishing he could turn back time. "Before you go, I want to thank you for bringing me here to Stoneybrooke Assisted," he said. The wide grin on his face turned downward. "You're the reason I came back home, you know. After your Alzheimer's kicked in and the restraining order expired, the memories—they just wouldn't leave me alone. The smells. The pleasure they bring me.

"I truly am sorry it has to end this way, but I can't have you flapping your gums and spoiling everything I've worked for. This is my new home, and I love the smell of it all. It's familiar. Reminds me of Thanksgiving and Christmastime."

The final flicker of life flashed inside her pupils. He leaned forward and kissed her giant skin tag, relishing its scent of smegma-like sweat cream. He flicked his tongue out, savoring the saltiness and wet little crumbles that found a home on his taste buds.

Then he moved his lips to her ear and whispered, "Goodbye, Aunt Hilga."

ROUND FOUR
WINNER

FAMILIAR SCENTS
JONATHAN EDWARD ONDRASHEK

ROUND FIVE

SIBLING RIVALRY
MATT HICKMAN

VS

ABSOLUTION
MICHELLE GARZA & MELISSA LASON

SIBLING RIVALRY
MATT HICKMAN

The blistering Arizona afternoon heat threatened to melt the entire house as Melissa sat in her office, staring at the horrific images that were displayed on her computer screen. The dull vibrations of the ancient air conditioning unit were the only noises that sounded throughout the home. Despite the air conditioning unit running at full speed, rivulets of warm perspiration beaded on her forehead and trickled down her back.

The horrific images plagued Melissa as she continued to watch the screen, half-enthralled with a morbid curiosity, while also wanting them to stop.

The video, coupled with the intense heat, was threatening to reintroduce Melissa to her light lunch. She swallowed the huge lump in her throat and clicked on the mouse button once again, restarting the video stream. The images slowly pixilated on the computer screen in front of her. Squinting, she took a closer look at the detail. She ran the video back to the same frame again and again, freezing and re-watching the same piece of footage. After the

twelfth time, she shook her head in despair as a single poignant tear ran down her cheek and dropped from her chin, splashing onto the keyboard. It evaporated almost immediately in the heat.

She knew then she was certain.

Michelle Garza sat on the porch in the warm evening breeze, watching as her two little boys played happily in the front garden, the recent heat baking away any traces of grass to parched soil. The joyous sounds of their innocent frivolity filling the air with glee. Michelle groaned; despite it being late evening, the temperature had only cooled down to a mere thirty-eight degrees and the heat and humidity were making it difficult to breathe properly, let alone run around the yard playing.

She shouted out to the boys, "Hey, you two, come on over here for a while, it's still too hot to be running around like that. You'll make yourselves ill."

Both boys stopped running, and turned to face her, dejected, groaning in unison, "Oh, Mom. Do we have to?"

"Yes, for now. Come and have a drink and a rest, at least."

Both boys immediately turned and started heading towards the house, disgruntled expressions plastered across their faces, kicking their feet in the dried-out dirt as they walked.

Michelle smiled inwardly, her heart warming, in addition to the sweltering temperature.

Oh, to be that young again.

She jumped slightly at the sudden touch of a hand placed upon her shoulder.

The soothing sound of her husband's voice came from behind her. "Hey, why so jittery?" Ricky gently rubbed her shoulder blade and ran his hand down the back of her neck, the feel of his strong touch comforting on her taught muscles.

"Your shoulders feel like they're tied up in knots.

What's the matter? Maybe you should lay off writing those horror stories for a while; they're beginning to play with your mind."

He slowly moved his right hand down towards her breast. "Besides, I don't want you going and leaving me…"

She knocked his hand away, playfully. "Pack it in, will you? The boys are right over there."

He laughed. "I'm just trying to cheer you up."

"I'm fine, it's just —"

"Just what?"

"I dunno, maybe I'm just imagining things."

"What things? Come on, how can I help out if you won't tell me what's going on?"

Michelle hesitated for a brief moment, wiping the light beads of perspiration from her brow with the back of her hand. "It's just… well, the last couple of times I've spoken to Melissa, she's seemed a little… off with me."

Ricky immediately burst out into heinous laughter. Michelle turned her head to him, frowning in confusion. "What the fuck?"

Ricky continued to laugh. "Is that it? Jesus, this is you and Melissa we're talking about here. You're closer than anybody I know, or anybody I've ever met. There's no way on earth she's pissed at you."

Michelle smiled. "You think so?"

"I know so. Look, there's no way that the Sisters of Slaughter would ever fall out. God forbid anyone that ever got in your way, but you and Melissa? No fucking way. She worships the ground you walk on."

"As do I, but I swear to you, the past few times that I've spoken to her she's seemed a little off with me."

"You're probably imagining it. It's this damn heat, it's getting to everybody."

Michelle looked at him and raised an eyebrow. "Are you saying I'm insane? You're skating on very thin ice."

"Ice would be welcomed right now. Besides, didn't you say she had invited us over tomorrow for a barbeque?"

"Yes, but she was a little vague about the details."

Ricky leaned forward and kissed her on the top of the head. "Ah, she will be fine, you'll see."

Ricky steered the battered car into the driveway, all of the windows wound fully down. With the air conditioning broken, even during transit, there was barely enough breeze to cool the warm cabin. Pulling the handbrake on, he removed the key from the ignition and turned to the kids.

"You ready to play with your cousins?"

Both boys nodded excitedly. He turned to face Michelle. "You all set?"

Wiping the sweat from her face, she opened the door and stepped out into the afternoon heat. "I guess so. I hope her air con is running."

Ricky smiled, exited the vehicle from his side and joined Michelle on the driveway. He looked up at the house, the eaves appearing to wave from side to side in the hot, shimmering air. It looked unnerving, eerie.

Rick nodded. "Looks kinda quiet, don't you think?"

"Well, it's usually quiet, but yeah, I see what you mean. It's like it's been abandoned."

"What do you think?"

"Stop spooking me out, will you? Let's just go and knock on the door."

The family approached the front porch slowly, a sense of impending dread hanging in the agonising warmth. She glanced at Ricky, who smiled back at her, his look tentative.

"Go on then," he gestured.

Opening the porch door, she balled up her fist, and gently banged on the door, three times.

They waited.

Nothing happened.

She looked at Ricky, a concerned look beginning to spread across his face. He did his best to subdue his

anxiety.

"Try again," he began. "They may be out the back."

Michelle nodded and banged again, this time a little harder.

To everyone's relief, the muffled sound of Melissa's voice floated out from behind the entrance.

"Come on in, guys, the door's open."

Michelle and Ricky breathed a sigh of relief, and she cursed herself for acting so foolishly. Holding open the front door, she gestured to her children. "Come on, boys."

Michelle led the way into the house with Ricky and the boys directly at her heels. Entering the living room, she couldn't help but notice that the room looked untouched - too clean and tidy for a house with a family of four and two young children. There wasn't a single sound in the room, the usual reverberating echo of the air conditioning unit replaced with a deathly silence.

They slowly walked to the kitchen, each footfall echoing across the wooden flooring. Melissa greeted them as they reached the wide doorway, a troubled, forlorn expression upon her usually cheerful face. Her welcoming smile was gone, replaced with deep worry lines around her cheeks and forehead, her usually vibrant eyes sunken into her skull behind two dark bags.

Michelle opened her arms in greeting and offered her a hug, affectionately wrapping her arms around her twin sister, and giving her a kiss on the cheek.

"Hey, sis, how have you been?"

Both women parted from the embrace and Melissa gave Michelle an inquisitive look. Her eyes suggesting a glimmer of suspicion and malice.

"Not too good. They've gone."

"What ... who's gone?" Michelle replied, panicking as she realised that the house was now totally deserted.

"Chris and the kids, they're gone. I'm here alone."

"What? What the hell is... what happened?"

Again, Melissa gave her the suspicious glance, as if

trying to weigh her up. Michelle felt the awkwardness from her sister's gaze, her steady eyes burning a hole straight through her.

Melissa smiled, her usual cheerful facial features replaced with a harsh and punishing expression. A hint of vehemence entered her tone.

"Come into the kitchen, let me fix you guys a drink and I'll tell you all about it. You must be parched."

Michelle cast a concerned peek over at her husband, who interjected into the conversation. "You can say that again, the heat out there is a real killer."

The group followed Melissa into the kitchen. She poured four large tumblers of lemonade from a jug that had been chilling inside the refrigerator. She handed them out to the group with a beaming grin.

"Here you go, guys, utter refreshment. The same recipe as our Mom's."

Michelle and Ricky handed out the glasses, and everyone took a deep swig, the ice-cold contents refreshing and bitter as it slithered down their gullets.

Michelle looked at the glass, and then at her sister approvingly. "My God. That stuff never fails to hit the spot."

She took another large swig, now consuming at least half of the glass.

Michelle wavered, as her vision began to blur. Her world began spinning as she dropped the glass from her hand. It fell to the kitchen floor with a loud smash, shards of glass exploding and skidding along the wooden surface. Michelle fell to her knees, her bare skin landing in spilled liquid and broken glass. The spinning in her head increased and she struggled to stay upright. Sounds began to seem distant and tinny. Somewhere in the distance, she heard someone calling her name. She took a glance to her left just to spot Ricky collapsing at the same time.

She was too far gone to resist it; she fell to her face on the kitchen floor. The side of her cheek slammed the

wooden surface with a wet smack.

Melissa walked over and knelt between the collapsed family, clicking her fingers in their faces, none of them giving a response.

Melissa sneered.

Michelle began to prise open her eyes, the blistering evening heat bearing down on her from above. She coughed, her lips charred and blistered from the soaring temperature, her throat painfully dry. The pain in her head was agonising, seemingly equal to taking a blow across the brow with a sledgehammer. Her long hair clung to the sides of her face and neck with hot sweat.

She felt the bite of the razor sharp steel barbs and yelped. They cut into the soft flesh of her wrists, producing deep cuts as she hung, her arms suspended overhead by a weathered, wooden frame. Warm blood began to sluice down her forearms as she began to writhe.

She whimpered and then screamed out in pain and frustration. Looking down, she saw her underwear and her favorite oversized Iron Maiden t-shirt, but aside from that, she was completely naked. Her feet dangled over the red hot, baked dirt, barely low enough to be able to support her weight; she could barely stand upon her tiptoes. Her slim ankles were bound with the same barbed wire.

She frantically looked around her, and immediately recognised her surroundings—Melissa's back yard. The familiar silhouette of the red brick, low-rise buildings stood in the distance to her left, scorched from years of exposure to the Arizona sun. She reminisced on the countless times that both of their families had shared many poignant and happy memories.

She called out. "*Hello? Melissa? Ricky? Kids, are you there? What the fuck is going on?*"

From behind her, came the familiar voice of her husband. "Michelle? *What the hell?* What's going on?"

Michelle attempted to take a glance over her shoulder,

but failed to see anything. She sensed the closeness of her husband's body. Frantically, she tried peering over her other shoulder to no avail. The barbs continued to produce fresh blood as she attempted to squirm. "I don't know. Tell me what you can see. I'm tied up."

Ricky winced. "I am too. Barbed wire around my wrists and ankles. What the fuck is this all about. Where are the kids?"

Michelle swallowed the lump in her throat. "I... I don't know. The last thing I remember is having the lemonade in Melissa's kitchen. What the hell is going on with her?"

"I'm not sure, but you can ask her yourself."

In the distance, Ricky's eyes squinted against the glare of the sun, he spotted the familiar outline of his sister-in-law walking slowly from the back entrance of her house. She appeared to be dragging something behind her.

Ricky called out as the woman approached and came into clear view. "Melissa. What the fuck is going on here? Get us *down* from here, now."

Melissa continued to approach. Ricky noticed she had changed her clothes, and she was now wearing a simple pair of black shorts complete with a black vest top and open-topped sandals. Her brown hair disappeared behind her head, pulled back in a tight ponytail, and her eyes now hid behind with a pair of dark sunglasses. Despite her cool appearance, her whole body glistened with a perspiring hue. In her right hand, she carried a large bottle of water; and in her left she appeared to be dragging a large, filthy woven sack. Letting the sack fall to the ground, it gave out a dull metallic clunk.

She stopped and took a long, deep, swig from the water. She replaced the cap and looked up towards Ricky. Gesturing with the bottle, she mocked, "Would you like some?"

Ricky looked at the bottle longingly as beads of water spilled down her hand and dripped to the scorching dirt at

159

her feet. "Yes ... please, Melissa. What the *fuck* is going on?

Melissa walked up to him and loosened the cap before placing the rim of the bottle to his parched lips. He did his best to pucker up before she pulled the bottle away and slowly began to pour the full contents of the bottle into the dried earth. A slow, guttural, demonic laugh escaped her lips.

Ricky frowned. "What the fuck, Melissa? What are you doing, you mad bitch? Have you gone fucking insane? We're cooking out here."

Melissa threw the bottle over her left shoulder, the glass shattering as it smashed off a rock in the distance. Without a word, she approached Ricky and grabbed his chin between her forefinger and thumb, forcefully.

"Listen to me, you patronising little bastard. I meant what I said earlier. My whole family is missing, and I intend to find them. You two are going to tell me everything you know."

Ricky's eyes widened, an incredulous look appearing on his face. "Missing? What do we know? What are you talking about?"

Melissa frowned. She let go of his chin and stepped back, shaking her head. Springing forward, she threw a left hook that connected with Ricky's cheek. His head snapped violently backwards, smashing into the head of his wife behind him.

"Don't come out with that shit. I know full well that you're involved." She took a step towards him, thrusting her face into his own, close enough that he could see his own reflection in the lenses of her sunglasses, "And trust me. You're going to spill the beans."

Michelle called out to her sister, her head held high. "Melissa. Melissa, please, whatever you think is going on, this is the first that we've heard about this. Please, you have to *believe* me."

Melissa walked around so that she was face to face

with her twin sister. Pulling her sunglasses down to the bridge of her nose, she stared at her, her gaze dripping with menace.

"Don't give me that shit, sis. We both know you're involved. Trust me, before long, you'll be singing like a canary."

"Please, Meliss—"

Her statement was interrupted as Melissa unleashed a wicked, backhanded slap across her right cheek, directly below her eye. The blow was hard enough to make the bright evening sun turn a deep shade of brown.

Michelle slumped, her legs going limp at the knees, the steel barbs cutting further into the flesh of her wrists. Drooping her head, a thick line of spittle mixed with dark crimson hung from her mouth.

Michelle sobbed, still peering downwards. "Please, Melissa, where … where are my kids?"

Melissa laughed. "*Your* kids? I was about to ask you the same question."

"Please, Melissa," she pleaded. "We don't know anything."

She stopped to look at her sister for a brief moment before shaking her head. "Okay, if you want to do this the hard way."

Michelle watched as she sauntered off into the distance and disappeared into the brick outhouse. A few moments later, she reappeared along with two children, their hands bound behind their backs, their frail torsos stripped to the waist. Melissa motioned them forwards towards where their mother hung like a slab of putrid, rotting meat.

Michelle called out to them. "Boys. Are you okay? Melissa, if you've done any —"

"Oh, *shut the fuck up* will you, you blithering cow."

Melissa stood with both hands resting on the shoulders of her nephews. "Now, sister, dear. I'm going to repeat myself once again, and you know I don't like

repeating myself. Tell me where my family is.

Michelle screamed at her. "*I keep telling you, I don't know anything about it.*"

Melissa didn't reply, she quickly placed both palms, gripping onto both sides of the eldest boy's skull, and twisted his head around violently. His slim neck immediately snapped under the imposed burden. The sickening sound of cracking vertebra filled the thick, desert air. His young, thin carcass dropping to the heated ground with a thump, chest first, his face protruding at an unnatural angle.

The thump was followed by Michelle's tormented scream.

Then, a scream from the victim's younger brother.

Melissa mocked them both, producing a scream of her own that echoed into the afternoon heat. .

Michelle screamed hysterically. "*You fucking sick bitch, how the fuck could you do that to a child* ... to your own nephew, *your own flesh and blood?*"

Ricky called out over his shoulder, his tone filled with concern and panic. "What. *What the fuck has she done?*"

Michelle sobbed, tears streaming down her face. "She killed him. She *fucking* killed Junior."

Ricky bellowed, "*You fucking bitch.* I'll get out of here and I'll *fucking murder you.*"

Melissa didn't respond, she placed both hands on the sides of the other boy's skull and shrugged her shoulders, gesturing towards Michelle.

"No, please, don't," she pleaded. "Please, don't *hurt him.*"

"Tell that dickhead of a husband to wind his neck in then, before I wind his up."

Michelle screamed out to her husband. "Ricky, *shut up!*"

"But ..."

"But *nothing*, for God's sake. Just be quiet."

Ricky immediately obeyed his wife's instruction.

Grabbing the boy by a handful of his blond hair, Melissa dragged him off to the side away from his parents. They both looked around, giving them a clear view.

Melissa positioned the boy in place and instructed him not to move. Ambling over, she grabbed the filthy sack from where she had discarded it earlier. Dragging it through the sand, she returned to the boy, who dared a quick glance whilst swallowing the huge lump in his throat.

Reaching into the bag, she produced a large axe. She held it aloft, both hands gripping the wooden handle, the sunlight reflecting from the steel head and casting rays of light across the boy's face.

Melissa looked at Michelle and Ricky. "So, let's try this again, and see if we get any more sense out of you. Now, bear in mind that I know that you're involved in this. If I suspect that you're lying, or you refuse to cooperate," she held up the axe, "Well, I'm sure you can guess where this is going."

Michelle cried. "Please, Melissa, you've got to believe me. I don't know what you think you know, but..."

Melissa casually shoved the boy in the small of his back from behind, before swinging the axe in a massive arc overhead. The nauseating sound of steel slamming through flesh and colliding with the vertabrae of his spine spat a hollow echo through the air.

Both parents screamed.

The boy hit the deck and Melissa placed the sole of her foot on his shoulder, struggling to work the blade loose from his back. An eruption of blood decorated the surroundings as she worked the blade free. Without hesitation, she swung the axe again, embedding the blade into the back of the boy's skull with a heavy clunk.

Both parents continued to scream and wail.

Letting go of the axe, Melissa stepped away. She grabbed the sack and began storming towards Ricky, dragging it behind her. She slumped it down in front of him with a clatter.

He looked at her through tears and blood shot eyes. He attempted to spit at her but in his dehydrated state, the miniscule strand of saliva only dribbled down his own chin.

"You sick slut," he spat.

Melissa approached and laughed. "Slut? *I'm* a slut? Who was the one that tried to come on to this *slut* on the very same night that his wife was in hospital after giving birth to his first child?"

"You lying bitch."

"What the fuck did you just say?" Michelle shouted over her shoulder.

"That's right, sis, the night that you were in hospital, giving birth to your now dead son, lover boy here was attempting to get me into bed." She turned to face Ricky. "And let's face it. It hasn't been the only time now, has it?"

Ricky drew his eyes narrow. "You sly cow. What exactly are you trying to pull here?"

Melissa's right knee shot forwards, connecting with the man's groin. He exhaled deeply and groaned as the wind immediately left his sails. If it hadn't been for the sparse contents of his stomach, they would have reappeared.

Melissa leaned in towards his face. "Oh, I'm sorry, did that hurt? Now, I'm not sure of your involvement in all of this, Ricky boy. I know for certain that your wife, and my so-called twin sister is, and for that, she has directly caused the death of your children. So, what's it going to be, are you going to tell me what you know? I mean, what can I possibly have that you need, Ricky? I have no money; my family is all I have."

Ricky took a second to compose himself; he looked over to the fallen body of his youngest son. His eyes connected with Melissa and a solitary tear ran down his cheek, the bitter salt stinging his lips.

"My family was all I had, too. You murdered them in cold blood, you sick bitch."

Melissa examined him for a moment, her eyes turning into slits, cautious.

"I do believe you're actually telling the truth. Well, how about that, Michelle? Crafty. Not even telling your own husband about your antics. I guess you knew he could be broken."

Melissa reached down to the sack and produced a large hunting knife. Instinctively, Ricky started to thrash about, opening the wounds further on his wrists as Melissa held the blade up towards his face.

"So, Michelle. What's it to be? Your husband here claims that he doesn't know where my family is. I, for one, believe him. So the real test is whether you're prepared to sacrifice his life for the sake of your insane scheme."

Ricky screamed. "You'd better fucking kill me, because if I get out of here, you're a dead woman."

Melissa beckoned over his shoulder towards her sister, "So, what's it to be then, Michelle? You have three seconds."

"Please, Melissa, I kno—"

"One."

"Pleaaasse. I don't know where—"

"Two."

Michelle screamed as loudly as her lungs would allow. "*I don't know* —"

"Three."

The sound of Michelle's screaming was immediately drowned out by Ricky's pained shriek as Melissa drove the tip of the knife into his exposed sternum, right to the hilt of the blade. Warm blood spurted from the wound and coated the back of her hand and arm as she continued to cut upwards through flesh and viscera, a determined, maniacal look across her face.

Ricky continued to scream and buckle as Melissa sawed the steel, determined, backwards and forwards through flesh, a deep pool of claret now sluiced from the open cavity in his stomach and spilled down his legs,

pooling on the floor at his feet.

Michelle continued to scream out. *"Ricky? Ricky?"*

Within a few seconds, his body went into shock and he fell still, hanging limp from his wrists like a spoiling carcass. Melissa wiped away the sweat from her brow with the back of her arm. The perspiration mingling with Ricky's fresh, spilled blood.

Melissa left him dangling, the body continuing to bleed out. She faced Michelle, her sister, her twin. "I never thought, you of all people would ever do anything like this to me."

Michelle continued crying. "Melissa, I don't know what you're talking about, *please.*"

The shrill sound of a phone ringing shattered the tension, the noise emanating from the pocket of Melissa's shorts.

She ignored it.

Melissa lifted the blade and ran the tip across the front of Michelle's t-shirt menacingly. The woman flinched. "You see, you made one simple, stupid fucking mistake when you sent me the video of my abducted husband and children."

"Mistake?"

Melissa nodded.

"Video?"

Again, the woman nodded.

"I… I don't know what you mean."

The phone in Melissa's pocket rang again but she ignored it.

"Many people wouldn't have noticed the finer details, but I freeze framed that fucking video a thousand times until I was sure it was you."

"Until what was sure? Melissa, I don't understand," she pleaded, tears streaming down her burning cheeks.

Annoyed by her continuing lack of compliance, Melissa grabbed Michelle's arm. Twisting the surface of the skin around towards her, her hand forced back the sleeve

of Michelle's t-shirt, the large tattoo on her upper left arm exposed. Taking a moment to check the design, she ran the edge of the knife along the surface of the detail, opening a deep laceration across the woman's bicep. Michelle screamed as Melissa's mobile rang again.

Infuriated, she ripped the phone from her pocket, checking the screen.

Unknown number calling.

She placed the phone to her ear. "Yes?"

Michelle observed, the pain in her arm nearly causing her to black out. A short silence ensued, the colour appearing to drain from Melissa's face. She looked at Michelle before speaking into the handset.

"What did you say? Where are they?"

Melissa terminated the call and looked at her sister, the feeling of dread consuming her.

Michelle spoke. "What's going on? Melissa... what the fuck?"

Melissa didn't answer; she just turned and ran towards the house. Bursting into the kitchen, her feet slid on the wooden floor, hastily attempting to take her towards the front door.

A loud banging noise stopped her in her tracks, the door threatening to shake itself loose from the frame. Without hesitation, she opened the front door; she failed to react as the stranger raised the butt of the shotgun. The blow was effective and instantaneous, colliding with the side of Melissa's jaw. She was out cold before she hit the deck.

Melissa began to rouse, groggy. The pain was immediate and explosive inside her cranium. The sour taste of copper filled her mouth. Running her dry tongue against her gums, she felt the wobble of loose teeth.

Fully opening her eyes, she glanced around the room. She found herself bound to one of her kitchen chairs by her wrists and shoulders, the abrasive edge of the thick

duct tape scraping her skin. Directly across the room, a few feet away, her twin sister sat in the same quandary. She appeared to be semi-conscious, babbling away incoherently, covered in sweat, blood and dirt.

A voice came from her right; an accent that she didn't recognise.

"Oh good, you're awake."

"Who's there?" she asked.

The silhouette of a large man, tall with broad shoulders, stepped from the shadows, a shotgun resting over his right shoulder. Melissa's large knife protruded from his left hand, the blade still encrusted with dried blood.

She looked at the man. "Who the hell are you?"

"You don't recognise me, Melissa? I'm a little disappointed."

Melissa looked again, the slightest hint of recognition creeping into her eyes. "Wait a minute are you... Matt?"

The man laughed and winked. "None other."

"What the fuck is going on?" she spat. "You disappeared."

"That's correct. Ever since you and your Sister of Slaughter here beat me at the hands of the judges in that anthology."

"Wait. What? *Versus*? Is all of this about that *fucking* competition?"

Matt laughed. "A competition, yes. A competition that I lost. Ours was the deciding battle, after that, everyone else blamed me. I was fucking ruined."

Melissa screamed. "You fucking crazy son-of-a-bitch. I'll fucking... wait, wait a minute. I saw the video. The evidence was clear. I knew it was her, it had to be her."

Matt laughed and rolled up the left sleeve of his shirt, displaying a tattoo, an image identical to the one that adorned the arm of her twin sister.

"You like it?" he asked. "I got it done especially. Even had to shave my arm."

Michelle suddenly spoke, and continued with her bleary vocabulary.

"What ... what the fuck is going on here?"

Matt turned to her. "I got here just in time," he shouted in her general direction. "Your own sister went insane and slaughtered your whole family."

The man leaned forwards, cutting at the tape that bound her to the chair; it fell to the ground, releasing her. He held out the knife, towards her. In her cowed, intoxicated state, she attempted to grab it by the blade.

"No, other way round, sweetheart. Do what you need to do, I'm sworn to secrecy."

Michelle stood up straight, unsteady on her feet, confused. She looked at her sister.

"You killed my family, bitch."

Michelle stepped forwards, the knife held aloft.

Melissa screamed.

Matt smiled.

ABSOLUTION
MICHELLE GARZA & MELISSA LASON

"I give easement to thee. Go down and rest. Come not to walk these woods and valleys. For your peace, I pawn my own. For your sins, I claim…"

A heavy thud rattled the wooden door. The old woman halted in her speech as it immediately shook a second time, and perturbed, she looked over to the homeowner. "Open it," she instructed.

The wiry haired gentlemen across from her hesitated before hobbling from his seat to stand before the door. The granny woman knew that his apprehension would stay his hand, though she couldn't blame him for being anxious. She reminded him, "Dead the dead shall remain this night, open the door, for it is the living that disturb us."

"Who's there?" he hollered over the storm winds that raged beyond the threshold. There was no answer, only the howling mountain gales. He shrugged his thin shoulders then hurried to reclaim his seat beside the oblong table as a flash of lightning lit the interior of the small shack with

white-blue brilliance. Thunder rolled through the old woman's chest as the door came flying in, two shadows stood black against the flashing storm; filling the doorway. The men stepped inside, battered with rain, sopping wet as they entered unwelcomed. The door was slammed shut behind the intruders leaving only the wide-eyed homeowner and the old woman as witnesses to their faces.

"What have we here?" the taller of the two asked. "Got supper just waitin' for us." He spoke again turning to his partner who nodded eagerly then agreed. "So nice of you to invite us in!"

"Light a fire, old man. It's rude not to be hospitable," the obvious leader said as he shed his coat. They were stout of build, wearing dark clothing and the scars of men that were no strangers to physical violence.

"I have nothing for you to eat and nowhere for you to sleep."

"What do you call that there?" the drifter asked, pointing a grubby finger to the rectangular table where a small loaf of bread sat beside a jar of homemade liquor.

"That is for the granny woman…" he began to reply, only to be silenced by the ancient-looking crone seated at the opposite side of the low table.

"If you claim responsibility for it, then you may eat it, but remember there are some lines you can't uncross." She grinned.

"That a threat, hag? You gonna sick the law on us?" He came to sit upon a splintered chair, folding his arms over his chest. "I ain't scared. I take responsibility for everything I eat, everything I fuck…everything I kill."

"Maybe she's gonna sick the lord on us, Willy?" his partner laughed, shaking the rain from his greasy blond hair while dragging up a seat from beside the door.

"Ain't scared of him either, Jeremiah. You know that's for damn sure!"

"Then have your supper if you accept it," the granny woman spoke.

171

"Don't mind if I do." Willy snatched up the stale bread, it was dwarfed in his calloused hand. He winked over at the skinny older man whose eyes never ceased to be filled with terror before shoving half the loaf into his mouth. He picked up the jar, slurping its strong contents in to moisten his meal. Jeremiah looked on in disappointment as his partner commenced to finish off the bread then emptied the jar down his throat before throwing it against the stone fireplace. Willy belched then rubbed his stomach.

"Very kind of you folks to take us in out of the storm." He turned to Jeremiah who scratched the stubble on his face in agitation. "Next house you can eat, partner."

"What's yer name, old man?" Jeremiah asked.

"Thomas."

"Well, Thomas, where's that fire we asked for?" He kicked his muddy boots up to rest on the long low table, dirtying the quilted blanket used as covering.

Granny woman nodded to Thomas who rose from his seat to build up a fire.

"We're criminals, you know. Blood as cold as a cottonmouth." Willy spoke directly to the old woman who sat stone-faced.

"I've met many like you."

"No. Not like me," Willy corrected. "You wouldn't be alive if you had."

Willy felt his stomach lurch, a pain blossomed within his gut. Though he tried to keep up the appearance of being the devil himself, he soon found that sweat was beginning to dampen his already soaked shirt. He gripped his abdomen as it grew to an agonizing degree. The granny woman raised one white eyebrow. "Probably better that you do eat somewhere else, Jeremiah," she cackled.

"What did you do to me?" Willy demanded as vomit rose in his throat. "Poison me?"

"In a way." Her smile was black with tooth decay; he could smell it across the odd table as he bumped his knees

against it to run into the storm. He emptied his stomach in the mud just beyond the entrance, liquid fire that tasted of soured stomach and bush whiskey.

Willy returned, trembling at the knees to find that Jeremiah had the hag by the throat.

"What did you do?" He was hollering while he shook her. When he saw the look in Willy's eyes he knew better than to interfere with what happened next. Jeremiah's hands had never extinguished a life, yet he had witnessed his partner's rage turn to murder on a few occasions, and only once was he foolish enough to question it.

Willy yanked her from his companion's grip, held her out by her neck. Though she knew that she was going to die, he could feel her pulse was still steady and slow. It enraged him to think that she was not afraid of the end he had planned for her. With his opposite hand, he pummeled her face, blow after blow that decimated the frail bones of her wrinkled visage. Her blood ran freely as he lifted her above his head before bringing her down face-first into the table. When he picked her up once more, her head lulled limp upon her crooked neck. When he was satisfied with the amount of abuse he afflicted upon her lifeless body, he turned to see Thomas cowering like a malnourished rat in a trap, the old man couldn't get by to the only door, and his cowardice held him from intervening in the granny woman's murder. Willy brandished a knife from his belt, held it out to the firelight. Thomas shrank into the darkened corner of the one-room shack, waiting to die. The criminal crossed the floor in three long strides to grab Thomas by his frail shoulder. Willy plunged the blade into the withered man's gut in numerous quick thrusts. He watched as Thomas's eyes continued to stare until they no longer seemed to see into the living world, before dropping him to bleed out upon the wooden floor of the shack.

The two stayed on for a spell, lying beside the fire while Willy nursed his aching stomach. Jeremiah had

drifted off to restless sleep, snoring so loudly it nearly drowned out the storm that still gripped the mountainside.

A whispering caught Willy's ear, a faint yet distinctly feminine voice. He sat forward knowing that it was not possible, for what rambled through his ear like a song to be originating from out there in the wind and rain. He could not make out a word, yet it was there.

"Do you hear that?" Willy asked only to be answered by his partner's snorting inhalations. It grew louder as he concentrated on it until he could decipher a single line...a question within a song.

"Did you keep my teeth in your front pocket?"

Willy shot to his feet, looking about the dark corners of the cabin. His eyes fell upon the corpse of the granny woman as the voice filled his ears once again.

"Did you make a ring from a lock of my hair?"

"Get up, goddammit!" He kicked Jeremiah in the side, jarring his partner awake.

"What, what, what is it?"

"Do you hear it? The girl's voice?" Willy asked.

"I don't hear shit!"

"Listen!!"

Jeremiah got to his feet, then cocked his head, focusing his attention on his surroundings. Willy stomped over to where the woman lay on her face. "What did you say?" he asked. Her face was an unrecognizable mess, her mouth hung open and her head swung loose on her broken neck as he picked her up...she was quite dead and silent like any corpse should be. He shook her then threw her head first into that odd shaped table only to have her skid across the top of it, the quilted tablecloth wrapped around her like a cocoon as she slid out of sight. Jeremiah jumped when he realized that it was no table at all but a long box...a coffin sitting on short wooden blocks.

The voice filled Willy's ears again, his gut knotted as it seemed to grow in intensity.

"Did you pry my breastbone open to see what was

hidden there?"

He spun to search Jeremiah's face, his partner had not heard the morbid question posed in a sing-song voice. "You don't hear it?" he asked, though he knew the answer.

"That's a damn coffin!" Jeremiah said, ignoring the question that had already been answered by Willy's nervous pacing. The drifter turned to face the truth that Jeremiah had brought to his attention, his breath caught in his lungs. "You don't think the voice is coming from there, do you?" Jeremiah asked.

Willy searched beside the hearth until he located a long iron poker used in the fireplace, only he intended to pry the lid from that casket and silence whatever laid inside.

"Wait! Don't you think if they were going to bury her, they had a good reason?" Jeremiah asked, stepping into his companion's path.

"Get out of my way," Willy said through gritted teeth, maddening rage burned in his eyes.

Jeremiah had never seen him in such a state, he was usually unnervingly calm even while committing the vilest of crimes. He stepped aside to allow Willy to have at the poorly constructed burial container. He beat the thin wood, sending splinters flying with each powerful stroke of the iron rod. Willy managed to knock a hole into the coffin lid so he jammed the end of the poker inside to pry free the large slats of wood. It was impossible to see inside so he grabbed a candle from the mantle, thrust it into the fire below to light its wick then turned back to illuminate the black void beyond the broken coffin lid. He gasped then fell backwards, dropping the burning candle to the floor.

"What is it? Is she in there?" Jeremiah asked.

"It's not a woman, but a man," Willy answered, tears gathered in his eyes. "She won't stop singing! Let's get out of here!" he screamed, gripping the sides of his head then took off out the door of the shack into the storm.

Jeremiah scooped up the candle before it was snuffed out upon the wooden floor by the winds that came sweeping into the shack. He crept close to the stinking box, he could see the opening that Willy had made. His arm shook as he stretched the light out over the dark hole. He had never seen such an abused corpse in all of his brutal life. The man had the hair at the crown of his head torn out, not a tooth could be seen in his gaping violet mouth. The candle's glow revealed that the chest of the poor bastard had been wrenched apart. Jeremiah could hear Willy screaming as he ran for the forest; he too had seen enough and fled the house of death.

Willy had a head start on Jeremiah who tracked his companion by his cries alone, until he found him writhing on a moonlit river bank in the mud left behind from the passing storm.

"Willy!" he hollered. "Get yourself together!"

"I can't, she's here, she won't stop singing... her voice hurts so bad!"

A line of pale yellow orbs shone through the tree line on the far shore of the river causing Jeremiah to fall upon Willy. He clamped his partner's jaws shut as an approaching procession of people drew near. He dragged Willy over to take cover in the thick reeds on the bed of the river to wait until the group had passed over a small bridge not far from them. Jeremiah could feel the brawny man's body quivering as he wept, snot poured from Willy's nostrils down onto the hand that held him silent. The lanterns revealed a group of men, solemn faced and intent on whatever journey they were making. As they slipped into the forest that Jeremiah had just exited, they began to sing, a low hymn deep in sorrow. He released Willy, leaving him weeping in the cattails, to observe the train that had just passed...a funeral procession. His intuition told him to follow the group for he knew their destination, it could not be a coincidence that the shack held a corpse in a casket, and that these earnest men set out through the

storm adorned in funeral garb. Jeremiah ran through the wood in their trail, hoping to find a clue as to what plagued his partner with phantom voices. Their lantern light eluded him a few times, yet he meant to cut across the country anyway, to beat them to the door of that hovel. Jeremiah took off as the crow flies through the wood, and although it was not the country of his birth, he had spent months there with Willy playing highwaymen, robbing and pillaging as they saw fit to survive. He, at last, came to the tiny house surrounded by pine and oak trees, and there beside it, he found a thick patch of bushes to conceal him. He was panting when the procession came down a rutted dirt road; he held his breath in an effort to calm himself. They halted before the door, and a man that had been leading them spoke.

"The sin eater has been paid to be certain that his spirit will not roam. I know that was a concern after all that he did to that poor girl, Rose. Rest assured that this nightmare is now over."

"What of Thomas? How do we know that he ain't just like his brother?" a grey-bearded man questioned.

"Thomas is a good Christian man. He didn't harm anyone. Do not take out the sins of his blood upon him," the leader answered, as Jeremiah watched from his thorny hiding spot. He could see that the man wore the collar of a preacher. He cringed as the men pushed the door open; the sight of the murders became evident as the pallbearers stepped inside.

"Preacher! The sin eater is dead!"

"She couldn't withstand the burden?" the pastor questioned.

"No, sir. It appears she's been murdered along with Thomas. There was a struggle for sure, and we recovered two men's coats."

Jeremiah crawled from the bushes, around the house into the dark woods, only to hear a scream cut through the cool night air. He came to stop as he recognized it

instantly as being from his longtime partner, Willy. He peered around the edge of a hickory tree to see the tormented man come running down the dirt road, tripping over his own feet, rolling in the muddy puddles left behind from the storm.

"She won't stop singing to me. She's here!"

Willy began rending handfuls of hair from his own scalp, leaving bald bleeding patches behind. A few of the gravediggers met him, brandishing their shovels as weapons. He scooped up a jagged rock from the road then began bashing himself in the mouth, he spat a handful of blood and teeth into his palm.

"Will you keep my teeth in your front pocket, make a ring from a lock of my hair?" Willy sung in a soft voice that mimicked a young woman's.

"I believe we have found who is responsible for the granny woman's death," the preacher said.

"How are you certain?" the man with a grey beard asked.

"He exhibits the same mannerisms as Thomas's brother did before he killed himself."

"The preacher tells the truth. I just witnessed the fiend's corpse," a pallbearer spoke. "This fool must've eaten the corpse bread. He swallowed the sins and is not strong enough to hold them at bay."

"Not with the tainted soul of a man with hands eager to murder," the preacher agreed. "His fate is a dreaded one indeed."

"He did not act alone," the pallbearer said.

"We shall wait the other out," the preacher answered softly.

Willy brought the sharp stone into his own chest, its impact was a moist thud. He screamed in torment, though his actions were no longer his own, they were those of Rose.

"Did you pry my breastbone open to see what was hidden there?" Willy sung.

He repeated the same vicious abuse to himself until he had gouged a deep pit into his flesh. Jeremiah watched him bleed, could hear the rock as he bashed it into his sternum full well knowing that the bone could not withstand such cruelty. Willy lodged it within the hole, twisting it, rending the meat away. The entire time he cried out, heaving as he wept. He yanked the bloodied stone from his flesh, readied himself to jab it in farther. Jeremiah could see Willy's eyes pleading while the group only watched his self-torture. With sickening determination, his partner drove the gory stone into his chest, this time a snapping echoed through the eaves of the trees. Many in the procession now turned their backs, refusing to witness his madness any further. Jeremiah ran from his hiding spot to fall upon his knees before the preacher.

"Please. Make it stop. We are not good men, but you cannot allow him to open his own rib cage up!"

The holy man looked down at Jeremiah shaking his head. "Two coats. Two men. Two murderers? I knew that you wouldn't stay in the shadows while he cut out his own heart."

The crowd of men dressed in black came to claim Jeremiah who fought in vain to break free.

"I didn't kill anyone. Willy did, but don't let him suffer. I beg you," Jeremiah said. His ears were filled with the sounds of Willy's misery, for he had dropped the stone to tear chunks of his flesh away with his bare hands; his screams were now nauseating... inhuman.

"You seek absolution for your sins and mercy for him?" the preacher asked.

"Yes, sir," Jeremiah answered.

"He's a liar and a murderer too!" the grey bearded man accused.

"No, he isn't. If he was a killer, then he would have left his companion to die and never looked back. He would never have sought mercy for this other one here," the preacher spoke, motioning to Willy who clawed at the

179

cavity in his chest, revealing a portion of his broken rib cage.

"Mercy granted," he said, drawing a pistol from his coat, the preacher fixed his sights on Willy who feverishly worked his bloodied fingers between pieces of shattered rib bones with only inches to go before he could pull his own heart from his chest. He squeezed the trigger removing half of the criminal's head. His free hand moved through the gun smoke in the sign of the cross.

"Absolution is something you will have to earn."

Jeremiah was made to dig four graves, two of which were filled anew once the old woman and the man dubbed the fiend were laid down in them. Thomas, along with Willy, were stretched out upon the dark soil beside their designated holes to wait. The sky burned red with dawn's awakening when at last, the shovel was pried from his blistered palms.

"Sit down." The preacher pointed to the damp earth beside Thomas's white, bloodless corpse.

"Now you will get to see why that old woman was so vital to our community," he spoke, placing a small loaf of bread upon the dead man's chest before marking it with the initials T.T.

"Read this aloud, young man. Prepare to show me that you deserve absolution... the forgiveness you seek."

Jeremiah unfolded a stained scrap of yellowed paper, looking at it in embarrassment. "I can't read, sir."

"Very well, then. I shall whisper it into your ear while you say it in a loud, clear voice. These words shall never leave you until your task has been fulfilled."

Jeremiah nodded weakly, eyeing the men circled about him with their pistols drawn. He knew that if he did not do as he was bidden, he would soon be digging a fifth hole... his own.

The reverend came close beside him, bringing his lips to the dirtied lobe of Jeremiah's ear. As the preacher spoke, so did the criminal, sealing himself to a wretched

fate.

"Thomas Trudeaux, I give easement to thee. Go down and rest. Come not to walk these woods and valleys. For your peace, I pawn my own. For your sins, I claim responsibility."

"Now, eat the bread," the preacher instructed. "Slowly, though, you are no stranger to sin it can be quite painful," he cautioned.

Jeremiah tore a small portion from the stale loaf then brought it to his lips, it rested on his tongue tasting like mold. As he swallowed it, his throat tightened as if it could force the tainted repast back out onto the ground.

"Accept it," the preacher said. "Or accept your grave beside your partner."

He forced the bread down, it felt heavy in his stomach, though it was hardly a mouthful.

"Take another bite."

Jeremiah repeated his actions, each time he swallowed a bit of bread it felt as if something had dug down into the lining of his stomach, writhing and burning until at last, the entire loaf was consumed. It filled him up inside to the point that it gripped his lungs in a tight fist. He fell back onto the grass, moaning in agony.

"I knew what he did… to that girl, Rose. That poor young thing only wanted to go to the city to sing for folks. I followed him down to the creek bed. He was yanking out her teeth. My god he pulled out her hair…he tore her open! All he kept saying was that he wanted her heart, that he NEEDED HER HEART! I've always been yellow-bellied, nothing more than a coward! He never saw me watching him while he ate it. He ate her heart raw!"

Jeremiah writhed while the fire inside of him was fanned by memories of only echoes, things he had never heard… they were Thomas's recollections. The sound of river rocks being pounded into flesh, lungs expelling the last of their air though the body, was long dead. Somehow, Jeremiah knew these things first hand, even though his

181

Michelle Garza & Melissa Lason

eyes had never beheld them. The old man's regret liked to devour the young man from the inside out. A voice broke through the beating, a winded, haunting voice... the fiend had sung her a song while he dismantled her. It was the very same tune that Rose had repeated and drove Willy to insanity.

"I'm gonna keep your teeth in my front pocket, make a ring from a lock of your hair. Gonna pry your breastbone open to see what is hidden there."

Jeremiah cried out as the fires, like those of the depths of hell, ravaged him. A sudden wave of cold swept over him, it ran down his throat strangling his shrieks. He sat forward, coughing, to see the preacher holding an empty bucket; evening was now upon them.

"Ready for supper?"

Jeremiah knew the reverend did not refer to any ordinary afternoon meal, but the dining upon the sins of his comrade, Willy.

He swallowed bits of bread from Willy's cratered chest well into the night, felt the trespasses of his former friend growing within him like some insidious parasite. Jeremiah lost control of his own extremities as they clawed at the earth, then at his very own skin. The visions of past deeds committed by the cold-hearted drifter stained Jeremiah's psyche and marred his soul with wounds that would never heal. He opened his eyes to utter darkness, a canopy above him blocked out all the starlight. He hadn't the strength to rise, yet he was aware that he was no longer lying beside the fresh dug graves. There was a trickling of water nearby, a terrible thirst prompted him to crawl on his belly until he reached the stagnant trickles gathering between the rocks of the river's edge. He lapped at the green pools that crawled with larvae before falling out again, exhaustion began to darken the edge of his vision as a pair of boots came into view followed by a familiar voice.

"You lived. Seems absolution is in your future," the preacher said.

182

A baying of hounds echoed down the creek side. "He's over here, boys. Take him to his new home," the reverend called, then squatted down to whisper in Jeremiah's face. "There's just a few more souls that need tending before it's granted."

ROUND FIVE
WINNER

SIBLING RIVALRY
MATT HICKMAN

ROUND SIX

THE MIDDLE OF NOWHERE
KEVIN KENNEDY

VS

PRANK
PETER OLIVER WONDER

THE MIDDLE OF NOWHERE
KEVIN KENNEDY

Ryan was ten years old when his little sister went missing; she was nine. The family had gone on their regular yearly camping trip to the Scottish Highlands that year. Ryan spent ages researching Scotland online and couldn't wait to get out into the hills and visit the old castles and ruins. He had shown Denise lots of pictures of the old buildings surrounded by forests, and spoke about how they would search and explore while they discussed games they could play. Ryan had always loved his sister. He didn't understand why the other boys and girls at school always seemed to moan about their brothers and sisters; he always had the most fun when he was with Denise.

They had driven out into the hills as far as they could before parking up and gathering their equipment and supplies before heading even further out. Each year, the family ventured further away from civilization, and the kids seemed to love it. There was something feral about children if you took them away from all the wonders of the modern world, and their parents enjoyed seeing them

without a computer or phone in their hands as they had grown.

Linda and Ian started making dinner on the first night of the trip and had only taken their eyes off the children for a few minutes when Ryan came screaming out of the woods, "They've taken her!" Ian hadn't stopped to ask who, as he flew past his son into the woods. As he ran, he saw the scratches on his son's face and picked up his pace, knowing something was very wrong.

After searching frantically for close to two hours, Ian returned and tried to find out from his son what had happened. After ten minutes of getting nothing from the boy other than "They took her," Ian returned to the woods to continue his search after sending his wife with Ryan to the closest town to inform the police. Ian found nothing that day, and neither had the police or search parties who searched those woods for close to two weeks.

Life after Denise disappeared was different for everyone in the household. Ian and Linda didn't speak anymore, and neither of them spoke to Ryan other than to ask him if he had eaten on the days that one of them remembered to do so. Ryan's father blamed himself for the loss of their daughter and dealt with it by shutting everyone out. There was a constant blackness hanging over the house, one that was suffocating for everyone inside. Ryan's father continued to work and pay the bills, but he forgot about the people he still had. As time passed by, Ryan's mother left; she never said goodbye to either of them. She just couldn't take the life anymore. Ryan was only twelve when she left, but in a way, he understood. He wanted to leave himself.

Over the next few years, Ryan had started experimenting with drugs. It was pretty easy to get weed and when he had a smoke, it seemed to take away all the troubles of the world. There wasn't a day that passed where Ryan didn't think of his little sister. He knew if she was still alive, she would look very different, but as he

grew, the picture of his sister in his mind didn't. She was still the same little girl she was when he last saw her. After a few months of smoking weed, it didn't seem to have the same effect on him, so he started borrowing the odd pill from his father's medicine cupboard. After experimenting with a few different ones and realizing that they didn't all make him feel good, he settled for the Valium. Valium made him feel even more relaxed than the weed, but again, he didn't feel much of an effect as time went on.

By the time Ryan was fifteen, he felt angry all day, every day. He still took more drugs than most, but due to his tolerance levels, he functioned like most normal people while he was high. It was when he wasn't taking something that problems arose. Ryan started getting into a lot of fights; he needed a release for his anger, and it seemed the best way to let it all out. He never fought someone that he didn't think could beat him as the challenge was one of the most important things about it. In a way, he wanted to get hurt, but he never seemed to lose. Maybe he was just angrier than most. His mind always raced a thousand miles a minute, but the drugs should have slowed it.

After beating down a particularly large kid who had tried to bully him for his weed, he decided that selling drugs was probably the best path to take. People always wanted drugs, so he knew he could make some quick cash, and the fact that he was regularly getting the best of lads at eighteen and nineteen years old meant he doubted he would face many challenges or lose money. Ryan knew there was no way he would pull the money together to buy anything to sell, so he started working his way round anyone he knew that sold drugs at school, and then started moving out into the surrounding neighbourhoods. The dealers he targeted were all under eighteen, and he knew that a comeback was doubtful. He also knew they might go running to the guys they got the drugs from, but he couldn't see anyone who made a lot of money bothering about someone like him.

By the time Ryan turned seventeen he was the only dealer in town, of anything. Everyone knew who he was and no one got in his way. The steroids intended for horses he had been taking for the last year did wonders at transforming his physique. Ryan spent a massive amount of time alone and used a lot of that time to either train, take drugs or drink. Many a day, he could be found in his home gym doing all three at once. The people closest to him feared him more than most, as they knew of his capabilities and also his mood swings. Ryan had planned to be dead before he hit his mid-twenties but had decided he was going to cause a lot of pain and carnage along the way. His father, who had been a zombie since Ryan lost his sister, had tried to intervene once when Ryan had just turned seventeen, but a savage beating that had surprised the old man was enough for him to kick Ryan out of the house and cut all contact. It didn't matter. Ryan already had more money than he knew what to do with.

On Ryan's eighteenth birthday, he stood on a chair, an almost empty bottle of vodka and an empty strip of Valium on the floor, and a rope around his neck. He had made it eight years now without allowing one single person to get close to him. He had a few dealers he trusted, or at least knew they were too scared of him to let him down, but not one friend, not one person who knew him or his pain. Just as he was about to step off the chair he caught a glimpse of the only picture he had of his sister out of the side of his eye. Although he had more money than he could ever spend, and anything he owned was top of the line, he had rarely bought anything he didn't need. He was a minimalist without even trying to be one. He had just realised early that nothing really made him happy. Well, not since his sister. She had been his best friend, his only friend. He knew that's when everything had gone wrong for him and his family. His mind was fuzzy at best. He had been questioned so many times about what happened, and he could never find the words to describe what exactly

happened, but he remembered them, the ones that took his sister. He had often wondered if she was still alive but had long ago made peace with the fact that it was almost impossible. As the alcohol and Valium kicked in, he could feel his legs becoming like jelly. The rope bit into his neck. As his eyes started to close, he slipped the noose from around his neck and collapsed to the floor. "I'm coming for you, cunts!" was the last thing he muttered before he passed into oblivion.

Most people would have died after consuming so many Valium and coupling them with straight vodka, but Ryan had a much higher than average tolerance to both. His hulking body meant he could almost always outdrink anyone, but he was never completely sober at any one time. It had been a long time since he went a day without taking a handful of Valium when he wanted to relax. A few lines of coke in the morning, onto the gym for a hard training session, deal with any business that needed taken care of, then home to get fucked up. Ryan had never planned on the drink or drugs killing him; they had just been for a buzz before he kicked the chair out from under himself. He went into an almost comatose sleep, but woke up the next morning with his mouth stuck together and a throbbing in his temples. Sleeping on the floor hadn't helped either. Knowing the best cure for himself, he sat up, lifted the open bottle of vodka, and finished off the one drink that was left. He was drowsy from the Valium but knew he had to get himself together today. He had plans. The last eight years had been wasted on a happiness he was never going to find. Through a drug-addled haze, he had powered on, making sure he'd done nothing of benefit to anyone, but today, that was going to change. Today, he was going to start preparing for his trip back to that very forest in the Highlands where his sister was taken. He would either find her, find the fuckers that took her, or die trying. It was a win-win situation. He had nothing to leave behind that he cared about anyway.

It had taken Ryan a few hours to get himself together enough to be able to drive. He knew he was many times over the limit but didn't really give a fuck. In the space of a few hours he had been to the top outdoor store in the area, left them with a list of everything he needed before heading on to pick up the two guns he had organised from home earlier in the day. No mean feat in the UK, but connections were everything. He swung by his lockup that was in his ex-girlfriend's name and picked up some weed, Valium and coke. Ryan knew that no matter how much he planned to find his sister or her kidnappers, he couldn't do it straight. His body was dependent on the drugs he took. He grabbed a few bottles of his testosterone and a bag of needles, too. He had no plans to come back from his journey, so wouldn't be selling any of the stuff left behind and had no need of money where he was going, but he didn't know how long he would need to search. He even planned to double his dosage of the steroid, deciding that losing his temper would not be a hindrance where he was going, and a little boost in his already freakish strength would only help. Ryan knew there would be a lot of them but a child's mind could play tricks on them, and Ryan had, on more than one occasion, fought groups of four or five full size men and come off the best. He didn't care if he died, but he knew he would kill others first.

Ryan pulled into the very same parking lot he had left behind eight years earlier without his sister. He had sworn as a young boy never to return here, but as he parked the car, it felt like he never left. It looked the same, but even more than that, he felt like he had always been here. This is where he had left the only part of him that mattered. Stepping out of his Audi, he looked on at the forest in the distance. He went to the back of the car, opened the boot and removed his backpack. It was stuffed with food, his drug stash, water, vodka, the guns, a few spare clothes and his collection of knives. He had only picked his favourites to bring along. None of them were legal in the UK, but

they had been a treasured collection of Ryan's. Now he savoured the thought of testing how they sliced through flesh. With his backpack on, he started his walk. Money was no issue, the list Ryan had left at the outdoors store meant he was more than prepared to go out into the wild and survive with the minimum he needed, though they were the absolute best. Although Ryan had abused his body from a young age, he had never gotten ill and always felt in great shape. His problems were all mental, and his body had never failed him. Camping was something he had given up at the age of ten but he didn't plan to camp. He would move at pace and sleep as little as possible, The drugs and drink were to keep him ticking over, but he had no plan to get fucked up.

The sun set as Ryan started his march towards the woods. He had no issues with night time. Truly scary things happened in the day, as well as the night. Ryan wasn't afraid of ghosts and the things that took his sister took her in the middle of the day. The sooner he met them, the better.

As Ryan reached about thirty feet from the treeline, he stopped and took his pack off. He removed both guns and slipped them into the back of his army trousers, before sliding knives into the two straps with sheaths crossing his chest. He had been taking sips of the Vodka on the drive up but still felt fresh as a daisy. He hadn't touched any of the drugs and felt surprised that he wasn't craving them; this was the first time his life had any purpose as far back as he could remember. He had no idea how long he would have to search the forest, but he had no plan on leaving alive unless he found his sister. Would he even recognise her, he wondered. He took another drink of the Vodka, slipped it into his pack, pulled out one of his needles and the little vial of testosterone and jabbed it into his bum. He upped the dose a little from his usual, and once he was packed up, he slipped his cleaver from his pack. He had actually cut another dealer's ear off with it

when he was sixteen and it had been used to threaten many others. Feeling like he was prepared for anything, and with his adrenaline pumping, he resumed his walk towards the treeline.

Entering the forest brought a hundred memories flooding back, the smell of the trees and the plants, the sounds of the birds, his sister's laugh and those things approaching and snatching her. He remembered it as if it were seconds ago. Stood frozen to the spot, Ryan wondered if he could go through with this before he looked down at his body and remembered he was no longer a scared, helpless little boy. He pulled a joint from his bag and lit it thinking it would do no harm to take the edge off. With the joint hanging from his lips and the cleaver at his side, he started his journey deeper into the forest. He had no idea which way to go as they had been attacked a few steps inside the tree line, so he decided he would just keep walking in as straight a line as possible. He knew the search party all those years ago must have covered every inch of ground on their search, so he had to go further.

After six days of hiking, sleeping as little as possible and daydreaming about the carnage he would cause if he actually found the fuckers, he realised that everything had gone quiet. The sound of the birds and other animals had died away. He felt the hairs on the back of his neck stand up. He lifted the cleaver with his right hand and drew the dagger from the strap on his chest with his left. Nothing moved. He tried to steady his breathing as much as possible. Nothing. After an agonizingly long minute he started moving forward at a much slower pace. The silence was beyond eerie. As he continued forward he started to hear voices, but couldn't recognise what they were saying. A smile crept across his face. Who else would he be likely to find in the middle of a forest in the middle of nowhere?

As Ryan crept closer to the voices, he decided it was

time to ditch his backpack. Taking it off and setting it down quietly was a challenge with the floor of the forest covered in twigs. He managed to rest it against the base of a tree and started removing what he thought he might need. Most of what he brought was food and a mat and bag to sleep in, but he was going nowhere without his knife collection. A few of the knives had sheaths he could attach to his person and a few others folded up so he could slip them in his pockets. After watching mainly gangster and crooked cop movies his whole life, he knew if he was going to go out, it would be in style. Fuck taking precautions and planning. These motherfuckers were in trouble. He finished checking himself to make sure he hadn't forgotten anything that he could cause pain with before picking up his bottle of Vodka. He took a huge double swig and dropped it open on the ground. He wouldn't need it again. Ryan had walked into many dodgy situations over the years and caused plenty more himself, but this was different. Here he was a hulking monster who would be described as unstable on a good day, walking into his childhood nightmare, kitted up like a one man army. Ryan normally liked to sniff a few lines before taking part in any planned violence, but today he didn't need them.

He could tell the trees were thinning out as he got closer. He didn't give a fuck if they knew he was coming now, so he picked up his pace. He could feel the straps across his chest pulling tight as he flexed his muscles. He felt stronger than he ever had. He didn't know if it was the lack of Valium and weed, or if it was the fact that he was going to finally get revenge for his sister, but he felt like he had just won the heavyweight title of the world, and he hadn't even started his fight yet. As he crossed the tree line he stopped dead. What he saw in front of him would have shocked anyone. There was an entire tree village like the fucking Ewok village from *Star Wars*, although maybe not quite so grand. It shouldn't be possible, but it was.

There were a few of the things on the ground. They were almost exactly as he remembered but not quite as big. They were humanoid in form but misshapen. There was no way they could have ever been fully human, but they looked like some kind of missing link. They were around six-feet tall but their heads and shoulders were massive. Their arms and legs were extremely skinny, as were their torsos. It almost looked like they had children's sized footballs in most of their joints. Their skin was stretched tight over every inch of their bodies, and as far as Ryan could tell, they had no genitalia. The creature's faces were the most horrifying. Their eyes were similar to his, but much darker and with much larger pupils. They had no noses though, just two holes where their noses should have been, and their mouths were much larger. Even though they were still at a distance, Ryan had seen them closer and he could remember their mouths were ragged rather than a straight line and that it had looked like the skin from the lips had grown over the teeth.

There were five of the things on the ground, but there were many more watching from the tree village above. Ryan started walking again. He didn't make a line for the creatures. He was heading to where he could see a ladder leading up into the village. Let them come to him. As he started walking, he heard them start to move quickly towards him. All five carried clubs that looked badly carved from wood. Ryan smiled. He continued to watch them from the side of the eye as he got closer to the ladder. He was about halfway when the first three ran out in front of him and two came from behind. Ryan stopped where he was, holding his cleaver and one of his hunting knives at either side.

"Where's my fucking sister?"

The things looked at each other, but as they did, Ryan had already taken three quick steps forward, buried the cleaver in the middle of the first one's face, and slammed his dagger upwards through the other's chin,

197

piercing it right through the top of its skull. Before their bodies had even hit the ground he had slipped his other dagger from the chest strap and buried it in the third one's ear. He turned to face the two behind him, only to see them flee further into the forest. Ryan hadn't realized he had been grinning from ear to ear since the creatures appeared. Years of anger and pain had all been leading to this moment and he just hadn't known it. Today would not be a day of understanding or change; today would be a day of carnage that he had spent most of his life unknowingly preparing for. The adrenaline rushing through his system felt good; it was the closest feeling he ever got to happiness. Ryan started his ascent of the ladder, wondering if there was any chance at all of finding his sister alive. He expected to face a barrage of creatures as he climbed onto the wooden platform, but there were none. He wondered just how tough or intelligent the creatures were. Were they setting a trap or hiding from him? When they took his sister, he had only been a child and he had run instead of fought. His sister was small and weak and would have been easy to carry off. What had they wanted her for?

Ryan climbed up onto the next platform and was on a walkway that led past several small huts. He decided to start at the beginning and enter the first hut. As soon as he walked through the door, he could see a figure crouching in the corner. Although he could see no weapon on the creature, he felt no sympathy. He had never had a chance to use his new butterfly knife so he slipped it from his pocket and flicked it open as he had practised many times. He walked over to the creature that was shaking and pressed his fingers lightly against its head. The fact that the creature let him push its head back so easily made no difference. With one lightning quick slash the abomination's throat was opened and Ryan was heading back out the door. The second hut held two of the creatures who again put up no fight. Nonetheless, Ryan executed them quickly. By the time he had made it to the

end of the walk way he had been in ten huts and mercilessly slaughtered sixteen of the beings.

The platform running out from the end seemed to lead to one central platform where five more of the things stood. Ryan wiped the blood off of the two knives he held against his trouser leg before walking towards them. He had expended very little energy and had no doubt that he could clear out the whole village quickly if things stayed as they were. His body was now covered in the blood that had sprayed from his enemies. He stopped just before entering the main platform and removed the straps across his chest, followed by his t-shirt. He stood topless, muscles tensed, face red from blood spray, several knives attached to his person, one in each hand, and the guns still tucked down the back of his army trousers. He had no intention of using the guns unless it was absolutely necessary. He didn't know how many of the creatures there were, but so far, he had no substantial challenge.

As Ryan stepped onto the main platform, four of the creatures slowly made their way towards him with their hands up and out to the sides, while one stayed centre platform. The one in the middle was at least a foot taller than the others and had a bigger frame. Ryan's hands hung at his sides as he studied them, there was no fear, and yet they held no weapons.

"Do you know me?" he asked, directing his question at the taller creature. A nod was his response. "Where's my fucking sister?" The creature in front of him gently waved him to come forward as the four in front split to make way.

He marched, confidently, burying a knife in each of the two closest creatures stomachs as he passed. The other two looked at him but made no move to run. He took the final few steps and stopped an arm's length in front of what he guessed to be their leader.

"Where's my sister?" Ryan asked, the veins in his temples standing out as the blood pumped through him.

The creature very slowly raised both hands. It moved forward at a snail's pace and without taking its eyes from Ryan's, it slowly placed both hands on Ryan's head. A million images rushed through his mind, a jumble of imagery, but it all seemed so clear. Ryan understood everything. They weren't monsters, their whole civilization was sustained on one child every two years. The whole village could live healthily and happily on that one child. They could have taken an adult and that would sustain them for much longer, but it was too dangerous for them to try. They were weak and had no fighting ability. Human meat and blood was literally the only food source for these creatures, they hadn't chosen this life. It was given to them. The creature hadn't managed to convince Ryan of these things. He just knew they were true. It was no different to humans eating meat. Some people may choose not to eat meat and be able to survive, but these creatures had no other dietary options. They didn't eat for pleasure, only for survival. The creature took its hands from Ryan's head and took one step back. He had no idea how it had been able to show him so much by only touching him. He wondered for a second if they could all do it, or if it was a special ability given to the leader. Ryan thought about all the things he had done throughout his life and wondered how much control he really had over the decisions he had made.

Ryan realized everything was still silent. He looked around at the faces that peeped out from windows on the edges of the main platform. They were all scared. A part of him felt sorry for them. He knew his sister hadn't suffered and he knew they had no choice. He also knew that the pain and suffering he had caused himself was tenfold what this entire race of people had caused between them. He wondered if he believed folks had no control of their decisions, or life in general, just before he pulled his guns from the waistband of his jeans and shot the leader in both of his bulbous kneecaps. As the leader went down, he

made no noise.

"You know I had no fucking choice in doing that," Ryan said, smiling. He shot the leader several times in the stomach before turning to shoot the other two on the platform. He made sure there were no head shots or chest shots. They could die slowly. Cunts! His sister wasn't coming back and neither were they. It took Ryan over three hours to slaughter everyone in the village. As the time passed by, he had found more creative and brutal ways of slaughtering his prey. When he was sure he had murdered every last one of them apart from the two that had run away, he sat down against one of the little huts. He was drenched in blood that was at varying stages of drying. His knuckles were a mess as he had started beating some of the creatures to death. He looked out into the distance at the forest and realized he had never felt quite as happy in his entire life.

"I'll find the last two, sis. I promise."

PRANK
PETER OLIVER WONDER

From around the corner, Hank watched. It was his favorite part—watching just before his little plan came to fruition. The unsuspecting mark blindly walks into a situation they have no control over. Just another mundane task to go about and then, BAM!

Hank's roommate, Phil, placed the hot dog into the bun and opened up the refrigerator. He pulled out the mustard and mayonnaise and set them on the counter top. It was all Hank could do to remain silent as he watched Phil squeeze out a line of mustard and then a line from the mayo bottle. The condiment containers were placed back into the refrigerator door before he finally took a bite of the hot dog.

"What the fuck?" Phil shouted into the empty room as he spat out the hunk of meat and bread into the sink.

Hank burst forth from around the corner, doubled over with laughter.

"Goddamn it, dude. What the hell is this? Soap? You really need to knock this shit off."

"It's Sarah's shampoo. I couldn't resist."

"Did you buy hot dogs just so this would happen?" Phil asked.

"You're the only weirdo I know that puts that nasty crap on a hot dog."

"And you're the only nutcase I know that still thinks it's fun to play these silly games when you're pushing thirty years old. Honestly, Sarah is getting sick of it, too. She's not going to be happy when she finds out you wasted her shampoo to play some stupid trick on me."

"Oh, who cares? It's just shampoo. She can get some more."

"That's not the point, Hank. These pranks need to stop. Or at least slow down. Dealing with your crap every day was fine when we were younger and I didn't have a girlfriend that lived with us. But, she and I have been talking and we would really like it if this crap could just stop."

Hank dropped his head slightly and glared at Phil. Phil took a step back from the evil expression. "You have fun when I do these things. We have fun. If she has a problem with it, she can go fuck herself. What happened to bros before hoes?"

"She's not a hoe, dude." Phil reached into his pants pocket and looked around. Sarah was nowhere in sight, so he pulled out the black box and opened it for Hank to see what was inside. A diamond ring shined under the kitchen light. "I'm going to ask her to marry me."

Hank's stomach churned at the thought of such a thing. "You're going to marry that stuck-up bitch?"

Phil snapped the box shut and stuck it back into his pocket. "You're such a child, dude. There's no talking to you." Phil turned his back and headed back to the bedroom.

There is nothing childish about a prank between friends. That bitch has his mind all twisted around. I'll fix him. I'll fix both of them.

Hank looked around the room. This whole goddamn place was about to become a prank. He was determined to scare her off. If Phil decided to go with her, so be it. Hank wasn't going to change who he was just for some bitch.

The pair emerged from the bedroom and into the hallway, arm in arm. "Since the food here seems to be tainted," Phil said, "we've decided to go out for dinner. I'm feeling like something kind of fancy anyway."

Hank gave a nod and watched the two of them as they left through the front door. Sarah, with a sour expression on her face, bumped him with her shoulder as she walked past.

Best friends since the second grade and now this? Pranking one another has been a way of life for as long as I can remember. He's going to throw that all away for some cunt he only met six months ago? Not after tonight. Things will be different after tonight no matter what happens.

He walked down the hallway and opened the door to Phil and Sarah's room. The room was spotless. The bed was made and had two stuffed bears resting at the top— one on each pillow. He lifted the one on the left, the one that had a pretty pink bow on the side of its head, and examined it in his hands. He didn't know if it was old or new or if it held any significance to it at all. But to him, it was the perfect representation of Sarah.

Out of anger, he squeezed the bear as hard as he could with both hands. His left gripped the head while his right clung to the body. He gave a slight twist, pulling the head off, and threw the two pieces across the room.

It's time to get busy.

Hank walked down the hall and into his own room. He had some items in store that would be fun when utilized at the appropriate time. Putting so many of them together would drive Sarah apeshit. The usual tape on the bathroom faucet to direct the water at the victim, move all of her stuff around, glue items together, and all of the other standard things were going to happen, but Hank needed

something even bigger. It was time to pull out all the stops.

The couple stumbled through the door. They were wrapped around one another and laughing hysterically. Hank was sat comfortably on the couch with a book to read.

"My, my," he said, watching the two. They had clearly been drinking.

Through her laughter, Sarah slurred, "Hey there, Hank!" She dropped her handbag onto a nearby table.

"Hanky Panky," Phil said before the two nearly collapsed from a new burst of laughter.

"Ah, charming. It looks like you two had a good time. Strange that something as simple as shampoo on a hot dog can have such a pleasant outcome. Don't you think?"

"Oh my god," said Sarah as Phil continued to laugh while holding onto his abdomen. "You're still hung up on that? Jesus Christ, no wonder no girls ever come around this place besides me. You're a fucking weird, creepy dork, you know that?"

"Oh, yes," said Hank. "I'm very fucking weird. No matter, though. I'm quite certain the two of you will be seeing the last of me very soon. What with the extra-special engagement dinner that just transpired. I'm sure you'll be heading out of here in favor of a bigger place in which to raise a family, am I right?"

"Well, yes. Eventually, I imagine the two of us will be needing a bigger place, but that doesn't have to happen tomorrow. Sarah has essentially been living here for the past four or five months anyway. This will just give us a chance to save up for a place and we can work on the two of you getting along a little bit better. After all, just because I'm getting married doesn't mean my life is going to stop having room for you in it. I'll always need my best buddy around." Phil sat down beside Hank and placed a hand on his knee. "You know I love you, brother. Sarah is well aware of that fact as well. She's going to try to be nicer to

you—despite the most recent slur of insults—and maybe you could try to lay off the pranks a little bit in return."

Sarah let out annoyed sigh. "I'm sorry for calling you a weird dork, or whatever. I totally didn't mean it. I actually think you're a pretty cool dude and some of your pranks have been really funny." Her fit of drunken giggles overcame her once more.

Hank smiled at her, unconvinced that this wasn't just an act. In all likelihood, she was just trying to play the part of the angel in front of her man. Hank wasn't naïve enough to trust a woman that he didn't depend on for sex. A tiger doesn't change its stripes. That goes for Sarah being a selfish bitch as well as for Hank being the prank master.

Tonight would be the night of pranks that would end all others. It was going to start off small at first, but it would work its way to a grand crescendo that would leave everyone in stitches.

Sarah began to walk down the hall, giving Phil a seductive look as she did so. The very inebriated Phil began his own laughter, released Hank's knee and made his way toward Sarah. "I'm glad we had this talk, buddy," he said over his shoulder. "Things will start to get much better now, alright?"

"Mmhhmm," was Hank's unenthusiastic reply. Even though Phil probably really believed this would be the case, he was also blinded by love. More likely the case was that he was blinded by the lust at that body which was to die for. Hank turned back to reading Stephen King's *It* to finish his page before getting back to work.

Inside the bedroom, Phil and Sarah were getting pretty hot and heavy. "I think I need to wash my hands before we continue," said Sarah. "I spilled some of that last drink on my hands and now they're all sticky. They keep getting stuck in your hair."

Phil continued to kiss at her neck as she stood up until she was completely out of range. He sat back on the bed

after slapping her tight ass as she made her way to the connected bathroom. She let out a playful moan a little louder than she knew Phil would have liked.

"You did that just so Hank would hear it, didn't you?"

A devious smile found him in the form of a reflection. "Whatever do you mean, darling?" she asked with false innocence. She twisted the knob for hot water and was frightened and confused by the alarming amount of water that shot out and covered her clothing. "Oh, that fucking twat-waffle," she growled just loud enough to be audible to Phil, who had seen the whole thing and was now doing his best not to laugh. He didn't want to destroy all chances of fucking his brand new fiancée tonight.

"Would it be considered rude to go out there and rip that fucking head of his off? Psycho boy is reading that damn Pennywise book. He's doing that just to mess with me. He knows I hate clowns. That movie fucked me up so bad when my dad made me watch it as a kid. And now this? Baby, I'm afraid there is a lot more to expect from him tonight. That quietly reading on the couch thing is just an act. Would it be too much to ask you to go out there and talk to him?" she asked sweetly, batting her eyes at him. She walked over and grabbed his partially stiff cock through his pants to drive her point home.

He bit at his lip as she gently massaged his meat through his jeans. After letting out a groan, he said, "I'd better go do it before a certain situation arises, and it would be awkward for me to go and talk to him." Sarah released his slightly harder dick and allowed for him to stand up.

"I really have to do this right now?" he asked.

"While you're off doing that, it'll give me an opportunity to get out of these wet clothes. If you hurry, you might get back before I've found a suitable replacement for these." As she bit at her red lips and twirled her blonde hair around her index finger, the strap to her dress mysteriously began to slip down her shoulder.

Phil let out a sigh as she shut the bathroom door to shut out his gaze. "Goddamn Hank," he uttered to himself. He adjusted his trouser snake before turning to the bedroom door and walking toward it.

This will be over quick. I just need to find out if there's any other bullshit he's got planned for us, and then I can get back to business.

After a quick twist of the knob, he pulled the door open—a big, fake smile plastered across his face. Though he was quite pissed off at the distraction from much, much better things, this was to be a friendly conversation. This was to be a discussion between two friends to try to create some sort of bond between his two favorite people in the world.

When he made it to the end of the hallway, he found that Hank was no longer sitting on the couch with his book. As he looked around the area, he heard water rushing through the pipes as the shower started up. *I guess Hank decided to take a shower.* Phil gave a shrug and walked back to his room. There was no sense in shouting at him through the door. Best to have a quick plow and then talk to him after.

As he made his way back toward his room, he stopped halfway down the hall. He looked to the bottom of the closed door on his left. There was no light coming from underneath, but Phil knocked anyway. There was no response from the bathroom, so he opened the door. "Hank?" he called out into the darkness. The shower was off and there was no one inside. Clearly, Sarah had thought the conversation would last a little longer than she'd liked and decided to take a shower as she waited.

Phil shut the door and turned around to face the door on the right side of the hall. The light was off, but he knocked anyway. "Hank?" he called out through the door.

Again, he was met with silence. He took a step back and looked at the bottom of the door. No light was coming from inside the room. Perhaps Hank either fell asleep or decided to go out for a smoke. If Sarah was

taking a shower, it was going to take quite some time. Realizing all stiffness had left his dick, he walked to the front door to see if Hank was out there enjoying a cigarette.

Though there was a streetlight off in the distance, most of the light outside came from the moon and stars on this very clear night. The smell of cigarette smoke wafted to Phil's nose as the cool breeze swept through the street. He made his way to the end of the walkway and found Hank standing in the driveway and gazing up at the stars.

"It's a beautiful night, don't you think?" Hank asked without even looking over at Phil. With his cigarette in between his middle and index fingers, he pointed up at the sky. "That right there is Orion. He's always been the easiest to find for me, due to the stars that make up his belt. One of the stars that make up the constellation is called Betelgeuse. What a lot of people don't know is that it's from Arabic Bait al-Jauza which translates to Armpit of Orion. It's my favorite star because when I was growing up, I always thought it was named after Beetlejuice."

"I didn't know you were so into space," Phil said.

"I'm into a lot of things you don't know about. I'm not all pranks and laughs."

"I know that, man. That's actually why I came out here. Are there any more pranks you have set up for tonight that I should know about? Sarah got hosed by the sink and we don't want any more of that funny business tonight."

Hank's face lit up with an evil grin as he dropped the butt and crushed it beneath his shoe. "I assume the answer to that will be apparent once we go back inside."

Phil's face contorted in confusion. Before he could ask what the hell he meant by that, there was a scream coming from inside the house. "Son of a bitch!" he said before running back up the walkway. Hank was immobilized by the laughter brought on by knowing what his friend would find.

Bursting through the bedroom door and closing it

behind him, Phil was shocked by what he saw. Sarah was standing naked, staring at herself in the bathroom mirror. Clumps of loose hair filled both of her hands. "Holy shit! What the fuck happened?" Phil asked with his mouth agape. There was a chemical smell in the air that stung his nose.

"My shampoo... He must have done something to my shampoo..." She reached up to her head and grabbed another handful of hair which fell free from her scalp. "I'm going to kill him," she said calmly.

"It's okay, baby. We'll get this taken care of. This is the last straw. We are done with Hank and we're not going to see him anymore after tonight. He has gone too goddamn far and I'm not going to stand for it."

Phil left the bathroom; Sarah slammed it shut behind him. He made his way to the bedroom door and it swung inward. The fright he felt was immediate and intense. The shock of the cold blade penetrating his stomach was entirely unexpected and only caused further confusion. The Pennywise mask that glared at him was something he had never seen before, but the clothes matched what Hank had been wearing earlier.

"Why?" he asked as blood trickled from the corner of his mouth.

"Every word. I heard every word you said to her. You're right about never seeing me again after tonight. While I am indeed into a lot more than just pranks, I tend to find the humor in just about everything." He began to laugh gently through the mask as he continued to work the blade. The laugh got louder as the last life dimmed in Phil's eyes. The sound he now made was something evil. It was the laugh of a distant nightmare that had somehow become reality.

Sarah couldn't take it anymore. Her anger had reached an all-time high as she listened to the stupid laughter outside the bathroom door. Filled with hair, her hands clenched

into tight fists and she grit her teeth as she turned to open the door. The clump of hair fell from her right hand as she grasped the door knob and violently pulled it open. "You're not going to be laughing much longer, you fucking piece of shit!" As she pulled an oversized shirt over her head, the laughter got louder and farther away. Then it stopped suddenly.

Sarah rushed out of the bathroom in a fury but was stopped dead in her tracks at the sight in the bedroom doorway. How it was even possible to have lost so much blood in the amount of time from when Phil left the bathroom until now seemed impossible, yet there was a substantial pool of it in which he was currently lying. He had been split from his navel up to his solar plexus. His throat had been slit and his tongue pulled through the wound. The frame of the door was smeared with blood, and hand prints were all over the wall that led down to Hank's room.

Once her mind had processed this gruesome scene and moved on from the anger she felt in regards to her hair, the feeling inside melted away into a puddle of fear. An ear-piercing scream broke free from her throat. Were the hand prints on the wall intended to draw her to his room? The sick, sadistic fucker was dumber than she had initially thought if he assumed something that morbid would draw any sane person down the path.

Once her scream came to an end, she decided to take the quiet approach. Doing her very best to not make a single sound, she made her way back to the bathroom, silently shut and locked the door, and took a seat on the lid of the toilet. Tears raced down her face as she tried to fully comprehend the implications of such a situation and just how fucked she was. Her phone was in her purse, which she had left on the table by the front door when she first came in. She was unable to call for help unless she was able to get to Phil's phone, and there was no way in the name of all that was holy that was going to happen any

time soon.

No windows meant no escape. In order to get to a situation that was even a fraction better than this, she would have to run. Hank likely knew that, which put her at a great disadvantage. Running would probably lead to a fight, and she was still a little drunk and not nearly as strong as Hank. She would need a weapon. She stood from the toilet, tears still sliding down her cheeks. There was no time to grieve for the loss of her fiancé; it was time to get busy saving her own life.

She looked at the counter that was covered in all manner of beauty products. Makeup was less than useless in a situation such as this. She had brushes and combs, but they would be about as helpful as a toothbrush against a murderer. The hair dryer wouldn't do any good either, but . . . Of course! The curling iron would be able to do some damage. It wasn't as effective as a knife, but she had burnt herself on that thing more than a few times and it hurt like a son of a bitch every time. Though Phil had gotten upset at her a number of times for leaving it plugged in all day long, she still hadn't learned her lesson and, for once, it was finally about to pay off.

She put her hand over it and felt the heat radiating off the barrel. When it was this hot, it was sure to do plenty of damage. Especially if it were applied to a face or, better yet, an eyeball. She unplugged it from the wall and wrapped the cord around her hand. She had a firm grip on the weapon and was physically ready to fight.

The alcohol that still coursed through her system lowered her inhibitions, but to fight and possibly kill or die was something she was not mentally prepared for just yet. The tears were now soaking into her shirt as she did her best to keep her loud sobs at bay. She looked down at the ring she had gotten just over an hour ago and knew that the future she had just been planning had all been dashed away for no reason. That once more fueled her anger and she clutched tightly to the iron. Her lips curled and she

resolved that she would not be the one to die tonight. After what Hank had done, she still didn't want to be responsible for taking another human's life, but she would do whatever was necessary to keep herself from being the next victim.

Motherfucker. Not tonight. Not fucking tonight, you sick piece of shit!

With her free hand, she grasped the doorknob and slowly twisted it open. She rushed from the bathroom like she was storming Normandy beach. She didn't get three steps out the door before being blasted by the artillery that was the sight of the evil clown sitting on the floor on the other side of her bed. His left forearm rested against the bed while his right elbow rested beside it vertically to support his chin. "Beep, beep, Sarah," he said through the false set of razor sharp teeth.

"NO!" she screamed before stumbling backward and falling onto the bathroom floor.

"What's the matter, Sarah?" Hank asked, still impersonating Pennywise. "Would you like a balloon? They float. And when you're down here, you'll float, too!" He went back into his evil laugh and began to stand.

As he was resting on the bed, Sarah hadn't noticed, nor was she in the frame of mind to think of the weapon he picked up off of the bedspread. The blade, the handle, and his hands were covered in blood. As Hank calmly walked toward her, he drug the tip of the blade across the top of the bed.

"Please, there's no need to be *so* afraid. I'm not really Pennywise the Dancing Clown that haunts your nightmares and plagued your childhood. I'm just a man. A man you've known for a long time and have lived with. I'm just a man. A man who grew up without much of a family and without many friends. A man whose one friend that became family to him has been taken away from him by a pathetic piece of pussy. A dumb, scared little bitch that's going to pay for tearing apart the only family I've ever

213

known."

Sarah didn't hear a word he said. She was busy studying his movements so she could plan her move at exactly the right time. When she fell back, her arms went behind her, concealing the iron from Hank's view. He took slow, methodical steps as he spoke, wanting for each word to sink in. He was savoring this moment. There was no telling how long he had been waiting for an opportunity like this to come along—how long he had been planning this.

His head was cocked to the side and he was carrying the knife down by his hip, at first. When he had closed half the distance, he straightened out his head to gain a new perspective on the situation. In his head, this sick fantasy was playing out like a movie in which he could change his own camera angles. As he proceeded, his knife hand rose into the air, ready to drop down on her and puncture her in one of many places that would lead to either instant or delayed death. Obviously, a delayed death was preferred. Why end something as glorious as this? Phil's death was too quick as it was. It wasn't as though he could toy with the both of them and have no concern of losing control of the situation.

In his head, there was no sorrow over what had just transpired. He had lost his friend before killing and mutilating him. Once that happened, Phil had already been a stranger thanks to the woman that was on the ground before him now. This shallow whore who couldn't take a joke was the root of all of his problems, and now it was her turn to pay. Behind the mask, he was smiling as wide as a child on Christmas morning and his cackle was growing ever louder.

"You're going to die, you little bitch! You fucking homewrecker! You think you can tear friends apart and not have to pay the consequences?"

He dove down on top of her but as he did so, Sarah lifted up the curling iron like a sword. The tip went straight into his eyeball as the blade of the knife sunk into her

temple. The bathroom was filled with silence and the smell of burning flesh.

ROUND SIX
WINNER

PRANK
PETER OLIVER WONDER

ROUND SEVEN

SQUIRM
DUNCAN RALSTON

VS

MISERY ARTIST
RICH HAWKINS

SQUIRM
DUNCAN RALSTON

The sun wakes me, the sound of sparrows outside the open window. A summer breeze blows in, cooling the sweat on my bare skin where I've kicked off the sheet during the night.

I find it difficult to sleep in the summer. The heat makes me uncomfortable in my own skin. Erratic breeze from the fan startles me awake as it blows past, fluttering my hair in my face. Noises outside rouse me too easily with the window open: raccoons rattling garbage cans, distant sirens, drunken partiers. I've always been a light sleeper, but so much more so since the children came. Bill could sleep through the Apocalypse...

I lie there for half an hour, just listening to him breathe and watching the birds outside our window. I've always envied his ability to turn off his brain and recharge for eight hours a night. The boys don't wake him, creaking their way down the hall to pee or get a drink of water. When they were babies, it was always me who would wake first to shake Bill awake for his turn to change them or

shush them back to sleep. Even now, I'd be lucky to get a few hours uninterrupted before my brain started circling around things that didn't bear thinking about so late at night.

I roll over to watch Bill sleep. In the dead of night, I may begrudge him, but watching him like this in the morning makes me smile. I think of how lucky I am to have such a perfect family, a perfect *life*, and the thought makes my heart swell with joy, bringing me close to tears. Few better ways to start the day.

The alarm clock on his side of the bed tells me it's still too early to wake him. I consider creeping out of bed and heading downstairs to read a little of my book, but a tiny twitch in Bill's cheek concerns me—something like a facial tic. I've never seen him do that before. He usually sleeps so peacefully, never shifting, eyelids barely fluttering, just lying there on his back like a man in his grave. The tic is something different. I don't do well with different.

He rouses a moment later to find me watching him. His lips upturn in a smile as he takes in a deep breath of morning air through his nose. "Mmm... Morning, honeybear."

"Morning," I say. He kisses my closed lips briefly, before I pull back, not wanting to give him a face full of morning breath.

Bill leans in again and kisses me deeper. Watching me. *Wanting* me. I let my lips part, despite my breath issues. I watch him as his eyes close, getting into it. I imagine him getting hard in his boxers, and the thought turns me on.

It's been weeks since we've had alone time (it's hard for me not to think of it as "Mommy-Daddy time," despite how fully it kills the mood), with the kids in bed, at their grandparents, or sleeping over at one of their friend's houses. I feel a deep urge to be with him, to have him inside me, his hands roaming over my skin. Then my mind starts circling. Stupid things. It's so hard for me to just be

in the moment sometimes.

Should shower first. Brush my teeth. But then the kids will wake…

Bill's eyes open. A hand slips over my clavicle, down to my breast. All thoughts dissolve. His eyes follow the progress of his fingers, widening in hunger as the rough pad of his thumb circles my areola, bringing blood to the surface.

He blinks then, but his eyes don't close. He's too engrossed in his stroking, fingers tracing my freckles, the mole above my nipple. He blinks, but a translucent film closes over his eyes instead, shuttering over them from side to side, like an animal's, keeping them moist but wide open.

This is not my husband.

I tear my lips away from him, certain I must have imagined it. Pulling back in horror, I try to blink the image away, to look at him from a distance. To *study* him.

"What?" he whispers. "The kids won't be up for another half hour…"

Even if I knew what to say, I can't speak. It's impossible. My lips won't form words.

Bill pouts like a little boy, his typical reaction when he feels scorned. No evidence of anything different in his eyes now. Of anything *other*. But I can't forget I'd seen it. The facial tic while he slept… had that been part of it? I'd been stressing myself out lately, looking for full-time work now that the boys were older, still doing my regular duties as a wife and mother. Trying to be the Supermom society expects of me. Compounded with the lack of good, solid sleep… is it possible I'd imagined it?

As I lie there considering how to reply, the boys come bursting into the room in their pajamas, all smiles, giving me the opportunity to separate from Bill without making it something to fight over.

"*Mommydaddymommydaddymommydaddy!*"

They leap onto the bed and climb in between us. Bill

play-wrestles Dylan over his shoulder, making a monstrous growl. Dylan giggles uproariously, his laughter high-pitched, almost a squeal. Ryan climbs over Bill's legs and snuggles up between mine. Any other time I might have found the scene cute, but the image of Bill's eyes closing without closing has filled me with such confusion and dread I can't enjoy our morning routine like I normally would, his playful growl—the Mattress Monster, the kids call him—now vaguely sinister. Ryan crawls up my legs and cuddles into my lap, wrapping his little arms around my waist. He looks up at me with a wide smile.

"G'morning, Mommy," he says.

He sticks out his lower lip to blow shaggy brown hair out of his eyes, and translucent shutters close over them, just like his father's.

Ice cold fingers run up the nerves in my spine, despite the summer heat. I so desperately want to jump out of bed, to run screaming headlong down the hall and into the street, but then they'll know that I've seen them, that I know what they are—or what they *aren't*. So I force myself to sit perfectly still, and it takes a concentrated effort of every muscle in my face to return the smile.

"Morning, honeybear," I say to the creature that used to be my youngest son.

Nictitating—that's what they call it. Translucent membranes below the eyelids that protect the eyes and keep them moist. Birds have it, snakes have it. Some mammals. I spent most of the morning on the internet after dropping the kids off at school, looking it up, hoping it was possible for humans to have it. Some sort of vestigial thing. A holdover from our ancient ancestors.

After kissing Bill perfunctorily on the lips—with my eyes open to watch *his*—and whisking him out the door, I'd packed the boys' lunches into their backpacks and their backpacks over their shoulders, and hustled them off to the car. Driving behind the school bus with them sitting in

the back seat, I found myself sneaking peeks in the rearview, worried they'd blink their membranes while I wasn't looking—or *worse*. I'd made sure they were buckled in tight, knowing I would hear the *click* if one or both of them decided to climb over the seat for a concerted attack while I had my hands on the wheel and couldn't defend myself without crashing the car.

I assured myself I was being crazy, a mantra I repeated in my head, one I hoped they couldn't somehow overhear. Thinking this, that they could possibly hear my thoughts, I peered at them in the mirror again. Their brown eyes met mine instantly, as if they'd only been waiting for me to look. Their pale, gentle faces wore broad, innocent smiles. *Loving* smiles.

But when I looked away, I caught them turning their smiles on each other in my peripheral vision. And the smiles twisted into something menacing. *Knowing*. Their nictitating membranes flicked closed, and I swear I could almost hear a dry click, like a camera shutter.

It took all of my strength not to jerk the car into oncoming traffic.

I spent a lot of the day looking up postpartum psychosis, using terms like "delayed onset" and "late life" to narrow the search. Hoping desperately that what I'd seen was just a hallucination, something I could possibly suppress with pills or alcohol. I read that most sufferers experienced symptoms within the first six months after childbirth. Since Ryan, my youngest, was now five, postpartum didn't fit as a diagnosis.

Clearly I was hallucinating, though. You don't just wake up one morning to find your husband and kids have been replaced by humanoid reptiles. Things like that don't happen. This isn't Kafka. This is reality. There are rules.

Humans don't have nictitating eyes. That's something I *know*.

I look at the clock on the computer, and realize I've spent the whole morning sitting here fretting. My coffee

cold, a skim of clotted cream on the surface. I erase the browsing history, and close the laptop. It's time to pick up Ryan from school.

He kisses me on the cheek, and I buckle him in. No evidence of the creature I saw this morning, he's the perfect little angel he's always been. We drive in silence, while he holds a toy car up to the window, pretending to be driving alongside us. Shame twists my insides, making me queasy. How could I have ever believed he wasn't my son?

Ryan flops down and watches cartoons for an hour before I tell him to go out back and play. I can't think with the sound of the TV, and I need to think, to hold on to the notion that everything I'd seen wasn't real. My gaze falls upon an opened bottle of red on the counter while prepping for dinner.

Wine before dinner? Why not?

When Dylan arrives home, he looks at me sitting at the table in front of an empty bottle of wine and a stained wineglass, and scowls in confusion. I realize I haven't greeted him like usual, and smile. It's much easier to force a smile after two glasses of wine. "Hi, honeybear. How was school?"

He cocks his head, unsure of me. Then he shrugs. "School was school. Where's Ryan?"

"Out back."

He sets his bag down on the floor, and heads past me to the backyard. I watch the boys through billowing curtains. They stand very close together near the shed, speaking to each other. Then, as if they'd been talking about me, they turn to the window.

I wave cheerily. It's easier to cover my increasing sense of panic now that I'm slightly drunk.

The boys turn to each other, confused. As if *I'm* the one acting strangely, and they've been perfectly normal. Perfectly *themselves*. Then they separate and throw the ball back and forth.

* * *

Bill watches me floss through the bathroom mirror. I can tell he's been wanting to ask me about the wine all night, and I've been preparing myself for it.

"Are you all right?" he asks finally.

"Uh-huh," I say, running the dental pick between my incisors, putting too much force against the gums.

"It's just..." He hesitates, trying to think of the most delicate way to put it to avoid an argument. "You don't seem yourself today."

You don't seem yourself today either, honeybear.

"I'm fine. Maybe a little stressed. Job hunting and all that."

Bill nods, seemingly understanding. He watches me a few seconds longer, then picks up his Robert Ludlum from the bedside table and opens it, settling into the pillows.

I spit a mouthful of blood into the sink. Looking at myself in the mirror, I stare until my eyes blur from dryness, until I can't hold them open any longer and involuntarily blink.

I look at the dental pick in my hand.

Eyeing Bill, I gently close then lock the door.

I return to the mirror, hold my left eye open with thumb and forefinger, and bring the sharp end of the pick toward it. I've never been able to touch my eyes. Can't even put in drops without blinking furiously like I've been splashed in the face with acid. Just watching someone else deal with their contact lenses makes me cringe.

The pick end blurs it's so close to my eyeball.

Ohgodohgodohgod—

The mint green plastic barely grazes the spongey lens of my eye and I blink it away hard. Feels like I've scratched the cornea, even though I know it wasn't enough pressure to injure me. Tears already streaming down my cheeks, I bend over the sink and splash warm water on my face. Blink blink blink away the pain.

226

All I wanted was to see the membrane. To see if I'm one of them.

Now I'm sure I'll never know.

Morning. I've been awake all night. I look a mess. I feel like a train wreck. I laid there beside Bill watching him sleep while the sirens wailed and the raccoons rummaged. He didn't move all night, but his skin did. The tic I'd noticed the previous morning had spread, his whole face suddenly doing the jitterbug. That's what I'd thought for the first hour or so as I lay there in the semi-dark, our bedroom illuminated by the fingernail moon. Over time, I realized it wasn't his skin moving at all, nor was it nerves. It was something *under the skin*. The flesh moved in ripples and waves, as if parasites were living inside him. Or an alien presence had dressed itself in his skin.

It *squirmed* under his face, flesh rippling.

Tentatively, my own heart beating so hard I could hardly breathe, I laid my head on his chest and I couldn't hear his heart. There was no heart to hear. I couldn't feel it, pulsing below his ribs. But I felt the creature under his flesh move, like snakes in a burlap sack. A living thing in a dead body.

I wondered what might happen if Bill's skin could no longer contain the thing beneath. If it suddenly split open and peeled back while I laid there, revealing its true form, blood and extraterrestrial goo soaking into the good sheets.

After a while, I realized I could smell him. Not his usual scent; not the sharp tang of man-sweat under a light breezy cologne, and the flat smell of clean hair. He reeked of cloves, like how I imagine a mummy might smell, and the salty smell of mucous as he breathed in and out deeply through his nose, so cloying it made me gag and I had to turn away.

I laid there beside that awful thing all night, knowing I'd have to kiss it in the morning. Knowing the creatures

227

wearing my boys' skin would scurry in once the sun was up, and expect me to hug them and tell them good morning. Bizarre, once-impossible thoughts circled my mind like sharks, terrifyingly plausible now.

I slipped out of bed as the sun rose so I wouldn't have to reenact our morning routine. After the night I had, I knew I couldn't have possibly dealt with it.

I drank a vodka and cranberry juice before they came shuffling downstairs wearing my family's pajamas over my family's skin, appearing bewildered and even a little upset, hair a mess. The vodka took the edge off, but I'm still jittery. Jumping at any sudden movement.

Somehow I manage to get breakfast made. Pancakes. Still their favorite, though I'm certain the things they've become are only eating to appear normal. To avoid detection, conflict. I'm watching the two smaller creatures eat, cutting up the food I've made into bite-sized chunks with their forks and spooning it into their toothy orifices. I'm frozen with the milk jug extended in my hand, and when the thing wearing Bill's skin asks me to pass the syrup, I snap out of it, but I still can't seem to make my hand pour the milk.

My limp hand quivers, milk splashing against the inside of the jug.

"Honeybear?" it says.

The two smaller creatures look up at me, forks poised before their opened mouth-holes. Their eyes nictitate, unblinking. The creature wearing my husband's skin cocks its head to the side and watches me, as if I'm the one who's abnormal.

I can't take any more of this. This can't be my life. Only yesterday I was reflecting on how perfect it was...

Now. Have to act fast.

Instead of the syrup, I calmly pick up the knife. I don't even excuse myself as I stand with it clenched in a fist and leave the table. The things wearing Bill and the kids stare up at me with their mouths open, not sure how

to react. It's not until I've bypassed the counter and left the kitchen that the Bill-creature's concern becomes evident. I hear his chair squawk as he gets up quickly to follow me, but by then I'm already running down the hall.

I'm in the en-suite bathroom with the door locked when the creature raps gently on the door.

"Hon, what are you doing?"

I need to know.

"Honeybear, why did you bring that knife into the bathroom?"

I wonder, if I was one of them, would I even know it? Would I act any differently? Would I feel the same?

If my skin was a jacket, how could I be certain? If my insides squirmed, would I see it? *Feel* it?

He pounds on the door with his fist, but I know he's too cautious to break it down. I have time.

I need to know.

"I know what you are!" I shout at the door, moving in close to the mirror to study my reflection.

"*What?* Libby, what's *wrong* with you? What the hell are you *talking* about?

His fist on the door rattles the toothbrushes in their cup.

"Open the door!"

"Mom?" Dylan cries. "Mom, open the door!"

Ryan is weeping. I can picture the two of them, holding hands just outside the door. They sound so much like my family, but I know it's a trick. They're trying to lull me into a false sense of security, and when I open the door they'll spring their attack. They'll drag me back to their mothership or their underground lair to begin the change, to become one of them.

If I'm not already.

I grab my hair and pull it back, exposing my face to the naked white light of the vanity bulbs. I haven't looked at myself this closely in months, ever since I noticed the frown lines expanding between my eyebrows, and saw how

229

large my pores looked in the makeup mirror. Aging is the least of my worries now.

I wonder if they age, the creatures. Do they mate? Procreate? Or do they just steal our bodies, using us like cuckoos use the nests of other birds?

I raise the knife to my face. Just below the scalp. This is where surgeons would cut me to erase the signs of having lived. Peel down the skin and sew it back together, tighter. The knife quivers in my hand, the edge of the blade resting against my forehead.

"Libby, open this goddamn door!"

It clatters against the jam. I've never heard Bill raise his voice like that before, and it startles me. I need to move fast. I need to finish this.

Cutting yourself deliberately takes much more force than you'd think. The first cut I make merely brings blood to the surface, leaving a raised pink welt that burns like a stinging swarm of bees. The second cut is deeper. The flesh blossoms open and blood trickles down my forehead, pain bursting in white stars before my eyes. The vodka I drank before preparing breakfast barely dulls it, but instead of making me stop, it's galvanizing. I cut deeper, dragging the blade, tracing an upside-down smile below my hairline, opening my flesh to the bone. I cry out in pain and frustration, finally allowing myself to grieve the loss of my family, blood spilling in rivers down my furrowed brow and into my wide, wet eyes. The creatures just outside the bathroom, faking tears, using Bill's fists to pound on the door.

"*Lib!*"

"*Leave me alone, you freaks!*" I scream at him, my face painted red like a woman warrior. The blood-drenched knife clatters into the sink, and I reach up with both hands to grasp the ragged edge of flesh I've carved. It feels like warm, raw chicken, but the mental image makes it no easier to pull apart flesh from bone. I watch my fingers peel my skin, the pain so far beyond anything I've

experienced that I'm now mentally detached from it, as if I'm watching it being done to someone else's body, through someone else's eyes. This flesh is no longer mine. This body is merely a vessel. A husk.

The door frame splinters.

I watch Bill's shoulder smash against the door through the wide, angled crack. Behind him, I catch glimpses of the little ones, the boys who were once mine. Then the flap of skin falls over my eyes with a wet slap like a damp hood.

For a moment, I see nothing, blinded by flesh. Fingers peel away the darkness to bright white. The lids pull away from my eyes with a terrible sucking sound.

I can see.

In the mirror I see a woman, thirty-five years old, blonde hair. The beginnings of laugh lines and crow's feet obscured by a jagged, curved flap of glistening, angry red flesh draped over her nose. The eyes now perpetually widened in horror or fascination. The mouth open, smiling, whitened teeth stained pink as she laughs.

Glimpsing bone amid the raw meat of her forehead, she's unable to blink away the sight of her insides squirming as the door smashes inward and her husband stumbles in, his own eyes widening in revulsion, terror, stupefaction. The boys behind him, *her* boys, now screaming and huddling against each other.

Bill staggers back, a hand over his mouth. "Oh, dear God... *Libby!*"

A gauzy film draws over her eyes like curtains, moistening them. Nictitating.

I see the woman leave the mirror. She moves toward the creatures in the hall. No longer fearing them. She drops to one knee, and Bill and the children fall into her arms, weeping, afraid, relieved.

Creatures, like her, dressed in hand-me-down flesh.

"*We are family,*" I say, and the body I wear hugs them tightly.

MISERY ARTIST
RICH HAWKINS

Prentiss climbed the stairs to the room at the top of the house. He shut the door behind him and flicked the light switch to reveal depictions of monsters upon the walls. The fumes from oil paint and turpentine thickened the air, mixing with the dank smell of the loft conversion. It enlivened him, and his pulse quickened with the riot of his heart as he closed his eyes for a moment to savour it all.

He crossed the room and opened the window, and the maddening fumes dispersed in the winter cold. Gusts of wind spat rain into the room. He regarded the gunmetal sky above the city. Within minutes his teeth were chattering, so he closed the window, moved to the worktable alongside the wall, and tied an apron around his waist. He arranged a fresh canvas upon the stand and stood back with his hands to his chest, recalling the images he'd seen in the previous vision. They were still vivid in his mind, as they always were immediately after sleep, and he would capture their essence and power or collapse to his knees in failure.

He muttered a folk song from his youth as he gathered his materials and instruments. Ancient songs for old gods forgotten by the fickle minds of men.

He started work.

Lurid, aching colours. Vivid crimson and scarlet, awash with speckled black and streaks of jaundice. Prentiss wiped sweat from his bow and hunched over with his pallid face close to the canvas, like a medicine man attending to the wounds of a blighted creature. His breath came in harsh rasps through the pained sneer of his mouth.

The serpentine shape took form. A row of black spikes pushed through the skin of the back from the spine underneath. The curved, segmented body. The bone jaws yawned as if to emerge from the canvas and devour him. A fever-vision. Grimacing, dripping sweat, his head aching with euphoria, he put the finishing touches to the awful mouth of serrated teeth. He painted the sightless eyes of something that dwelled in darkness, and augmented its flanks with scraps of skin he'd taken from the homeless man he'd killed in the underpass last night.

The skin, mottled and bloodless as it was, added depth to the painting, and once he was finished and the creation was complete he stood back from the glistening canvas and admired his work while whispering the name of the terrible god.

He sat with a microwave dinner on his lap and watched a black-and-white film on some obscure cable channel. The greying slop in the plastic tray tasted as bad as it looked, and the smell of it was like a neglected wound, but he ate without complaint or hesitation and never took his eyes from the TV.

He followed the turgid food with several pulls from the whiskey bottle at his side. After that, he smoked a cigarette during the end credits of the film and struggled to remember what it had been about. He remembered a man

and a woman in love, and in the end they had to leave each other. Their names were lost to him.

He extinguished the cigarette in the leftover juice of the food and took a small plastic bag from the pocket of his jeans. Inside the bag were the dismantled pieces of several black toadstools. He opened the bag and inhaled the contents. The smell reminded him of peaty forest floors and childhood days with his mother.

Pinching a black stem between two fingers, he placed it on his tongue.

He swallowed the stem and followed it with another gulp of whiskey. Then he sat back on the tattered sofa and closed his eyes. Soon there were bursts of white light behind his eyelids and a vague ringing in his ears. He thought he heard faint voices. The muscles twitched in his face. His blood thickened with a riot of chemicals. The hairs on his arms stiffened and his hands tingled. His eyelids fluttered. Thunder inside his head.

When he opened his eyes, the room was awash in white strobe-light and the walls were swarming with shadows.

He screamed to announce himself to the oil-slick, apelike creature hanging from the ceiling.

When he woke and his head cleared of the chemical fog, he looked around to see he was alone in the room. There were no writhing shapes on the walls. Cold sweat dripped into his eyes. He stumbled to the kitchen sink and splashed tap water over his face. He remembered the wet rasping of the creature he'd seen; the thing that had visited him in the dark.

For a long while Prentiss hunched over the sink, the hiss of the running water muffling the panic of each gasping breath. And once he had calmed down and the quivering of his heart had relented, he retreated from the kitchen into the cramped hallway and dressed himself in his long coat and boots.

There was work to be done, out in the night.

Prentiss walked several streets away from his house before something drew him to the graveyard surrounding the abandoned church. He stepped lightly amongst the derelict graves and the sleeping dead, listening to the wind in the trees. He stopped under the skeletal bough of a tired-looking oak and crouched behind a lichen-covered headstone.

Candlelight flickered in the remnants of the stained glass windows. Drunken voices echoed within the ruined walls.

A short while later, a bedraggled man emerged from behind the broken doors of the church and stumbled into the cold drizzle. He was mumbling to himself, coughing and gasping into his hands.

When the man began pissing on a gravestone, Prentiss came up behind him and smashed the back of his head with a lump hammer. Prentiss felt the man's skull crumble upon contact. The man sank to his knees, murmuring wetly, and put one hand to the place where his head sagged inwards. Then he fell forward onto his face and fell silent. Prentiss hit him again to make sure, then put the hammer in his bag and took out a hypodermic needle, a pair of scissors and a scalpel. And in the rain and dark Prentiss went to work on the body to take the things he needed.

On the way home, passing between the faltering street lights, he thought he saw a tall man standing in the shopfront shadows of a closed Chinese takeaway. A fleshy grin formed on the man's face. His eyes lacked definition; they could have been crude holes in a pallid mask.

Prentiss kept walking, holding the bag to his chest and quickening his pace.

* * *

He spent the rest of the night working on the new painting, absorbed in the act of creation, muttering as his hands worked to depict the apelike thing skulking upon a plinth of small bones. Gulping the whiskey to numb the pain in his head, he enriched the painting with scraps of skin robbed from the vagrant man's stomach. He used strands of the vagrant's hair to depict the mangy hide of the beast. The man's blood was used for the ape's bleeding eyes. These materials enlivened the creation, consolidating the vision and the brushstrokes from his trembling hands.

Perception of time fell away. Prentiss began laughing when he recalled the appalling mouth, its blackened gums drawn back to display carnivore teeth. And he realised it could have been laughing with him.

Later, he fell asleep on the floor in front of the wet canvas, the exhausted acolyte of a simian god.

He woke in the morning and noticed he'd added a human face past the shoulder of the carnivorous ape. He realised it was the grinning visage of the tall man he'd seen whilst walking back from the church.

He quickly turned away to go downstairs. He couldn't remember painting the man's face.

Prentiss ate breakfast at the kitchen table and listened to the local news on the radio. A dog walker had found the vagrant's body earlier that morning. But he wasn't concerned, because even if the police discovered him it would be too late; the God of Gods and its kin would arrive soon, and that would be that.

Prentiss lit the last cigarette in the packet and thought about the approaching Dark Age of monsters and exquisite agonies.

* * *

The day was all grey light and heavy rain. The roads were black under the streams of muddy water. Prentiss was one of the few to venture out into the wet streets, pulled and pushed by the cold wind, hands forced deep in the pockets of his waterproof coat. His boots splashed in shivering puddles.

He had to stop when a scraping pain bloomed in the centre of his skull. Hunched over and rubbing his head, he leaned against a garden wall and ground his teeth. A ringing sound grew louder in his ears until it seemed that red bells clattered inside his skull. His eyelids fluttered.

When he raised his face from his hands, he heard the screeching wail of something lurking behind the houses on the other side of the street. He squinted through the rain and opened his mouth, made a noise like a pained whimper.

The creature was taller than the houses and made of flesh so black it could have been shadow. An insect-like thing composed of pincers, crooked limbs, claws, and a glistening carapace larger than a double decker bus. When it paused between two of the houses, and turned its blazing red eyes towards Prentiss, he thought his heart would stop.

Then he smiled.

The thing let out a high-pitched shriek that made him lower to a squat and cover his ears. And the call was answered by a similar cry from directly above him. He looked up into the falling rain and watched a titanic shadow ripple across the cloud ceiling. The sight reduced him to tears of joy and awe.

Later that night he ate a few pieces of the black toadstools and fell into a vision of mountain ranges and derelict pagan temples. And in one of those temples, where ghosts still walked and muttered, he found a crippled god in a rotting nest.

* * *

It was just after midnight when he left the house. Wary of police patrols on the streets, he kept to the shadows, but he was confident of remaining undetected. Due to the Brexit and new austerity measures, the police, like all emergency and public services, were stretched past breaking point. Also, his victims were only vagrants and transients, and were of little interest to the police. It was a society awash with apathy and ignorance. No one cared. Ideal conditions for his work.

The rain pressed upon his shoulders like insistent fingers. He blinked water from his eyes, wiped his face, spat on the pavement. Looked around the street at the fronts of darkened shops and fast food restaurants. Scraps of litter rustled against the kerb. The black road glistened with reflected street lights.

He walked deserted streets, past tower blocks and council estates, listening to far away thunder brooding in the east. His lonely footsteps on tarmac. Concrete shadows.

When he saw a girl slip from the shadows ahead and cross the road and disappear into the next street, he quickened his steps but kept his distance, careful not to lose her in the incessant downpour.

Prentiss followed her until she stopped and sheltered in a shop doorway. Shielded by wind-blown flecks of rain by the hood of her coat, she unshouldered her rucksack then sat in the doorway with her knees drawn to her chest.

Concealed in the shadows beneath a huddle of trees across the road, he watched her. He figured she was a runaway. And he wondered if she had loved ones missing her. Would anyone care about her death? She'd be another lost face in the countless ranks of the murdered and abandoned.

Prentiss was not without sympathy for her.

He reached into his pockets, melding with the dark, waiting in the rain.

Once he'd checked for cars and other people, he emerged from the shadows. The rain hid the sound of his footfalls as he walked towards the doorway at a wide angle to hide his approach. His shoes splashed in puddles.

He attacked the girl with the lump hammer held high in one hand. And she opened her eyes and revealed her hands and one of them held a knife; a little blade that swung outwards in her thin arm and scored a line of intense heat and pain across his right thigh.

Prentiss cried out and doubled over against the edge of the doorway. As the girl scurried past him, ducking underneath his flailing arm, she slashed at his exposed flank. He swung the hammer back towards her, but she was already running away with her rucksack slung over her shoulder.

He slumped in the doorway, and by the time he turned again to face the street she had already disappeared into the rain.

The front door slammed shut behind him. He gasped and whimpered, his hands held at his wounds, soaking wet and half-drowned. He stumbled upstairs and grabbed the medical kit from the bathroom then sat on the toilet and tended his injuries. His clothes stank of rain and blood. He wrapped a bandage tight around his thigh then pressed a gauze pad against the slash on his left side. The bleeding had stopped from both wounds, which were fairly superficial.

After dry-swallowing some painkillers, he sat back against the cistern, closed his eyes and dreamed about the girl, craving the chance to use her blood upon a pristine canvas.

* * *

239

Prentiss woke on the bathroom floor with his hands clutched to his chest. Grey daylight filled the window's frosted glass. He rose to his feet, wincing at the pain in his thigh and side. His head thumped. The inside of his skull felt swollen and full of sour juices he could taste on his tongue. Waves of nausea shivered at the back of his mouth. He had to rest his forehead against the wall before he moved. And he went downstairs, gripping the bannister with both hands to keep his balance.

When he stepped into the kitchen, he found the girl sitting at the dining table, slumped back with her face raised towards the ceiling. Her throat had been cut.

He stood in the doorway and looked at her, unsure if he was still asleep and dreaming. He moved towards the girl. There was no blood on the floor or the table – she'd been killed somewhere else and brought here.

Who had done this?

He dismissed the possibility that he had killed her and forgotten about it. He shook his head, and then he saw the piece of paper left on the table. He looked closer. It was a note.

A GIFT FOR YOU, MISERY ARTIST. THE TIME IS NEAR. WE LOVE YOU. YOU WILL BE GLORIFIED.

He picked up the note and held it before his face. Red ink. Neat handwriting from a delicate hand. He sniffed the paper; it smelled of ashes. He placed it back on the table and stood beside the dead girl. He closed her eyes then examined the killing wound in her throat and deduced it'd been made by a blade of impressive sharpness. Much more efficient than his clumsy wielding of the hammer.

He looked at the note. "Who are you?"

Prentiss peered through the windows and watched the street outside, but there was no sign of the visitor who'd entered the house last night while he slept. He checked the doors were locked and the windows were shut. And once that was done, he grabbed his scalpel and

took what he needed from the girl then returned upstairs to the painting room.

Hours had passed in the act of creation, and he was still working when midday arrived. He hadn't eaten or drunk anything, and his injuries ached, but he was so immersed in his work that he barely noticed.

The smell of the girl's flesh and blood was delightful.

Upon the canvas, he depicted an image of something so hideous that when he looked at it, he felt the edges of his sanity crumbling like sand. He opened his mouth and laughed. His eyes dampened with tears as he offered a prayer.

It was the God of Gods, created in obscene angles and red brush strokes, surrounded by a maelstrom of tortured faces. Prentiss drooled as he worked, wiping his mouth with his wrist, his hands trembling with palsy and excitement. And then he stood back and surveyed the painting and put his hands to his face. The painting – this offering – would open the way for the God of Gods and its kin to emerge into this world.

He sighed, spat by his feet. He was perplexed. His voice was a whisper when he spoke. "It's missing something."

The light began to fade from the day. Prentiss lit a candle then sat on the floor in one corner of the painting room. He chain-smoked cigarettes and downed vodka, searching his thoughts for what the painting needed. And all the while the painting dwelled in the middle of the room, half-doused in shadow. When he absently looked up at it, he averted his eyes and whispered a prayer to be spared the approaching insanity that would consume the Earth.

He dozed restlessly, dreaming of black canyons and ocean trenches in alien seas. When he woke back into the doomed world, he listened to the hard rain upon the roof and examined the memories of his dreams to discover the

painting's missing ingredient. But his search was fruitless, and all that returned to him were flashbulb images of terrible creatures and organisms drifting in the void of space.

Downstairs, the front doorbell rang.

Prentiss sat up, wiped his eyes. Listened.

The doorbell rang again.

"Fuck off," he murmured.

As he was gulping more vodka, the doorbell rang yet again. But this time it was a continuous ringing, as though a finger was constantly pressing the button.

The sound grated inside Prentiss's head. He put down the vodka and climbed shakily to his feet. He pictured a gaggle of police officers outside the front door. But they would just smash down the door, surely?

The ringing didn't stop.

"Bastard," Prentiss said, as he crept downstairs. He took a kitchen knife and held it behind his back as he went to the door. The ringing stopped, as if the visitor knew Prentiss was about to answer.

He opened the door. Rain fell against him, swept by the wind.

A tall, hooded man in a long coat stood just beyond the doorway. When Prentiss had first opened the door, the man's head was bowed, but now he raised his face to Prentiss and grinned, and there was something wrong with the shape of his mouth. It was bloodless and fleshy. He had a lean look to him, like he hadn't been eating well for a while.

Prentiss thought he recognised the man. Then the realisation hit him. The man had been watching him from outside the Chinese takeaway a few nights ago, after he'd killed the tramp.

"You..." Prentiss's voice trailed off.

The man's grin never left his face. He spoke in a clipped accent. "Greetings."

Prentiss tightened his hand around the hidden knife.

242

"Who are you?"

"An admirer," the man said.

Prentiss swallowed. "You've been watching me."

"Of course. I had to keep appraised of your progress."

"My progress?"

"You're very talented, Mr Prentiss. You are a true misery artist. I'm here to help you."

"What?"

"We're on the same side, you and I. Did you think that the dead girl walked here to sit at your dining table? I procured her, after she eluded you."

"I don't understand," Prentiss said.

"My *employers* are great supporters of your work and your vision for the world. I'm here to help you find the missing ingredient for your final painting."

"My final painting. How did you—?"

"And *what* a painting. A true work of art. The God of Gods."

Prentiss realised he was nodding. "The God of Gods."

The man's grin lengthened so that the corners of his mouth drew level with his eyes. His teeth were very white. "Exactly. That's exactly right."

Prentiss blinked, frowned, shifted on his feet. "What's the missing ingredient?"

The man put his hands together. "It's you, misery artist. It's always been you."

Prentiss awoke rope-tied to a wooden chair in the painting room, blinking in the light of a lone candle placed on the floor. Rain falling upon the roof. He'd been positioned before the painting of the God of Gods. He struggled against the rope, but his bonds were secure and tight, knotted about his wrists and arms. Eventually he relented and slumped in the chair.

The man appeared from behind him and placed one

hand on Prentiss's shoulder and squeezed lightly. Prentiss cringed, expecting a slap or punch to the face, but the man simply stood to one side and looked down at him. He was still grinning.

"You're awake." His voice was jovial and damp. He licked his lips then wiped his mouth with his hand. "I'm sorry about the needle, but it was the only way to make you compliant."

Prentiss suddenly remembered the man had pulled a syringe from a hidden pocket and stabbed him at the base of the neck. The man had moved too fast for Prentiss to react, and by the time he realised what had happened he'd already collapsed into the man's waiting arms. And the last thing he'd seen before he passed out was that grinning face staring down at him.

"What are you doing?" Prentiss asked, squirming on the chair.

The man leaned over him with his own scalpel, and in one movement slashed Prentiss's face, scoring a deep line from chin to forehead. Prentiss screamed and thrashed as blood ran onto his face and into his mouth and dripped from his chin. It was a hot, stinging pain. His screams dulled to weak murmurs and muffled grunts.

The man used his hands to collect some of Prentiss's blood and then smeared it upon the painting of the God of Gods.

"Your blood is very special," the man said. "And like I said: you are the missing ingredient."

Prentiss understood.

"We've been watching you for some time," the man said. "All the killing you've done, and the art you've created from it, using the flesh and blood of your victims to bring the gods into this world. And now your flesh and blood will be used to finish this final painting. You should be proud. It is a great honour."

Prentiss screamed again as the man resumed working with the scalpel. By the time the man was finished, most of

Prentiss's face had been cut and peeled away, and a pint of his blood covered the painting of the God of Gods.

Prentiss cried until his throat was raw. He almost passed out. The man injected him with adrenaline to keep him conscious. He slumped, head bowed, dripping blood onto the floor.

The man patted him on the head and ruffled his hair. He offered comforting words and sweet promises. Shivering with agony and the sopping rawness of his grievous wounds, Prentiss raised his flayed face to look at the man. He tried to open his mouth to speak, but the man shushed him, cooed soothingly and muttered an apology.

The rain stopped pattering against the window. Everything faded to silence. The air stirred with static. The floor creaked and the walls seemed to shift and warp.

The man's eyes gleamed with excitement. "Can you feel them? They're close. Oh, they're so close."

Prentiss only whimpered and trembled, staring at the painting. The God of Gods, stained in his blood. The dripping canvas.

The man muttered a prayer.

The candle went out and darkness filled the room and the world beyond. The sound of gods and monsters all around, past the walls, under the floors, high in the sky towards the stars.

Within the cacophony, and the chaos of emergence, Prentiss heard the canvas ripping wetly, as though torn apart by something sharp. And he closed his eyes and bowed his head to accept the embrace of slick, squirming tendrils upon him.

ROUND SEVEN
WINNER

SQUIRM
DUNCAN RALSTON

ROUND EIGHT

THE FALLEN
SALOME JONES

VS

YOU REAP WHAT YOU SOW
KITTY KANE

THE FALLEN
SALOME JONES

Sam woke from deep sleep, shards of dream lingering in her fogged brain. She lay still, listening, blankets pulled up over her head. The traffic outside hissed past on the rain-soaked street. The metal heater pinged several times. A moment of silence had allowed her to almost slip back to sleep when a series of thumps and a splintering crash from the other side of the ceiling set her heart throbbing painfully in her chest.

"It's Saturday," she muttered. She pulled the blanket down and gazed up at the ceiling. There was another set of sliding thumps — something, someone thrashing around. "Shut up!" She growled the words, her fists clenched at her sides. The noises from above continued undiminished.

Every day this week. What the hell is going on up there?

The quiet isolation of the flat had been one of the things that had made her sign the six-month lease. Only a month in, and she was beginning to feel duped.

She dragged herself up and out of bed, stepped over to the window, and slid back the curtains. The day came in

to meet her, along with the other thing that had sold her on the fourteenth floor apartment – the view of north London laid out beneath the cold grey morning sky like a perfect miniature. Victorian buildings stood proudly next to newer, squarer ones. The spires of churches silhouetted against the horizon, row houses, trees... so many trees, though at this time of year they were nothing more than leafless, black skeletons. In the distance, the rain was visible as a mist over Hampstead Heath.

She glanced up again. "At least some things don't change overnight."

In response, there was a sliding noise and a thump from the ceiling. She gave it the finger and started getting dressed.

It was cold in London in February. Only a pair of electric baseboard heaters battled the chill that came through the big windows, so it tended to be nearly as cold inside as it was out. She put on one of the sweaters she'd brought from home – reminding herself they were called 'jumpers' here – and a thick pair of jeans. It made a nice change from the suits she wore during the week. She was sure she'd look American in Maida Vale, but she wouldn't be the only one.

She left the bedroom, picked up the door phone and called down to the front desk to ask if there was anything they could do about the noise. It rang five or six times but no one answered. She shrugged. After hanging up, she rounded the corner into the apartment's tiny kitchen. She was badly in need of caffeine, exhausted after the working week. This was supposed to be her day to sleep in. As she glared at the stack of dirty dishes and the bag of trash needing to be taken out, her motivation to make coffee deserted her.

The noises started up overhead again, now in the kitchen. That was new – usually they were confined to the bedroom. She was not really awake enough to be rational, but wasn't this excessive?

"That's it. I've had it."

She slipped her shoes on and picked up her keys from the coffee table. As she was leaving the flat, she heard a creak and, from the corner of her eye, saw the door across the hall open an inch. She pretended not to notice and it closed again. Sam had seen a middle aged woman go in and out of that apartment a couple of times. She could see a shadow under the door, could feel her watching through the peephole.

Nosy neighbors.

Down the hall, one of the elevators had an 'Out of Order' sign in front again, so she took the other one. She stood stiffly inside it, aware of the security camera. On the ground floor, the porters' desk was unattended, but she could hear voices inside the small office where they stored their coats and kept their lunches. She went to wait at the counter, listening to the agitated commentary coming from the slightly open office door.

"I can't believe you took my hamburger."

"It didn't have a label on it."

"You knew it wasn't yours. You owe me a hamburger."

She recognized the speakers. The manager and apparent hamburger thief, Martin, had a distinctive adenoidal sound to his voice. The other voice was Tony's. Of the three porters, he was the least pleasant.

They continued to argue, Tony getting louder and more shrill.

Bad timing. Maybe I'll just handle this myself. She pressed the elevator call button. The door opened right away and she got in, only relaxing slightly when the door closed and the lift began its climb. She took it up to the fifteenth floor and got off, walking around as if she were going to her own apartment. She had never been up here before. She might have thought she was on her own floor, except that the carpet in that section of hallway was brown instead of blue.

As she approached the door to the flat above her own, her lungs tightened. A heavy silence lay over the entire floor. It made her feel like she was violating some unspoken rule.

Maybe this is not such a good idea. But then she thought about how good it would be to sleep in on Sunday.

She stood outside the apartment for what seemed like five minutes before getting up the courage to knock, timidly. She felt an immediate desire to flee, but before she could put her hand down, the door swung open as if it hadn't even been latched.

She could see into the living room. It was empty, nothing but the carpet. She swallowed and cleared her throat.

"Hello?"

When there was no response, she put out her hand to push the door open a bit further. She felt all her muscles tense as if preparing to fling her backward at the slightest unexpected sound.

The kitchen was just as empty as the living room. How was this possible? Someone had definitely been up here.

She glanced down the corridor she was standing in, and seeing no one there, she stepped inside the entryway. "Hello? I'm from downstairs. I wanted to ask you if you could possibly keep it down in the mornings."

She walked cautiously across the room, leaning forward to see into the bedroom. No, this was probably over the line. She turned and took two steps toward the door she'd come in through. She's was still more than arm's length from it when it swung shut. The slam seemed to echo through the room. She flinched, and froze where she was, listening intently.

A soft rustling floated from the direction of the bathroom.

"Hello?" she called again.

Silence. She felt an overwhelming desire to get out of

there. She reached for the door handle and turned, both ways. It barely moved. She yanked on the handle, but it wouldn't open.

"Shit." She picked up the door phone and called down to the desk.

A crackly voice answered.

"Who is this?" she asked.

The reply was broken by static.

"Listen, this is Samira Evans. This is embarrassing but I'm up in 15L. I can't seem to get out. Can you come up and get me?"

There was more static.

"Did you hear me? I'm in 15L."

The line clicked off. She hung up and dialed the desk again. It rang and rang, but no one picked up. She replaced the handset and stood next to it, heart racing.

The rustling sounds came again and some other noise she couldn't place. Taking a deep breath, she crept across the living room to stand at the edge of the short hallway between the bedroom and bathroom. That was when she noticed the toe of a black shoe sticking out from behind the bathroom door facing.

"I know you're there!" She half shouted the words.

There was a burst of sound and movement. She screamed. A pigeon flapped off from the ledge of the open window.

"Christ." She put a hand to her chest. Surely no pigeon would be in a room if someone were standing there. She moved forward until she could see into the bathroom. A single shoe lay on white linoleum floor, unattached to a person – a woman's shiny leather shoe, mid-heel, stylish. A gust of air blew from somewhere, upsetting a small cloud of dust and tiny feathers. She felt a sudden dread, like something was about to happen. She made it back to the door in three long steps. It opened just as she reached it, with a sound of jangling keys.

She let out a shriek and the person outside did the

same.

"Sam! How did you get in here?" said the large man in the crumpled suit.

"Oh, god, Tony. You nearly scared the life out of me."

"You shouldn't be up here." He stepped out of the way so she could get out.

"I know. I'm sorry. It's just that every morning there's a lot of noise up here. I tried to get you on the phone but no one answered, so... I came up here. The door was open." She stepped out in the hallway. "Close the door, please. It's creepy in there."

"As you can see, there's no one here."

"Why is it empty? I thought these flats were in demand. I've had three letters this month addressed to the owner of mine, asking if it's for sale."

"Tied up in a legal case. It can't be sold until that's settled."

"What legal case?"

He looked down the hall in both directions before he whispered, "England is a very strange place. There's something here that keeps spirits close to earth. Many ghosts." He closed the door and locked it.

"Are you saying there's a ghost here?" They started walking toward the elevator.

He shrugged. "I'm not saying there is, but I'm not saying there isn't."

"If there were a ghost, whose ghost would it be?"

"There was a woman who lived in that apartment. An actress. Very beautiful."

"What happened to her?"

He was quiet for a few steps. Finally, he said, "She fell."

Sam considered the possible meaning of his words. "She fell... from the building?"

He nodded.

"Oh my god. When was this?"

"Fifteen years ago."

"Did you work here then?"

"No, I started after all that. It was just Martin and James back then."

They reached the elevators. Tony pressed the down button and they waited.

Sam folded her arms across her chest, rubbing her hands together for warmth. "How did she fall?"

"Very mysterious. Big kerfuffle." He stopped and paced around, looking up and down the various hallways. When he returned, he leaned in and in a quiet voice said, "Martin found the body on the street. He doesn't like to talk about it."

"I can see why. How horrible."

The elevator chimed its arrival.

They got on and stood in awkward silence as they descended a floor. The door opened. Sam got off and waved to Tony. The door closed. As she walked back to her flat, it occurred to her that they hadn't solved the problem of the noises from upstairs.

"Pigeons," she muttered. "Just pigeons."

The remainder of the weekend passed uneventfully. Sam slept in on Sunday morning and started the work week feeling rested. Her job at the accounting firm wore her out, but it gave her the opportunity to work in London, so she was happy to do it. The first part of the week went per usual: work, rain, quick meals on the run, sleep, repeat. Thursday evening she decided to treat herself to Indian takeaway. She'd been dying to try *jalfrezi*, the legendary British Indian curry she'd heard so much about, so she picked one up on her way home.

Sam came into the building through the big front gates. She waved to James who was sitting at the counter. He lifted a hand and gave her a smile. She rode up in the lift, thinking that he was actually the only one of the staff she'd seen doing anything besides sitting there. He walked

the corridors, making sure they were clean. He checked the trash rooms on every floor and took away anything people might have left there, despite the large, multilingual signs telling them not to. She had taken to trying to help him, by picking up anything she found on the floor there herself and carrying large boxes down to the recycle bins when she had time.

She got off the lift on her floor and turned the corner toward her corridor. Someone had opened one of the elevator lobby windows again. She suspected the cleaning crew, who she heard vacuuming every weekday morning.

She let out an exasperated huff and stopped to shut and latch it. Having it open made the door and windows of her flat — and she assumed other people's flats — clatter. Plus, it was bloody cold.

As she reached the door to her own flat, she noticed that it was rattling violently and a howl was coming from inside, like someone blowing into a bottle, but much louder. Her heart jumped, and a weird feeling settled in her stomach. She stood there for a moment, trying to reassure herself that there was some natural explanation. She'd closed the lobby window. Maybe it was air coming in through the kitchen vent. Yes, that had to be it. Her heart continued tapping far too quickly in her throat. She'd managed to put the events upstairs out of her mind until that moment, but now she found herself remembering the eerie feeling she had in the fifteenth floor apartment.

She took a deep breath and unlocked the door, turned the handle and pushed. The door opened about an inch and then slammed itself shut. She swallowed. *Weird.* She took another try, and had to put her shoulder against it to get it open. When she stepped inside, the door hurled itself shut. A gale howled through the flat. She dropped her bags in the kitchen. The kitchen vent was barely affected by whatever was going on, the window tightly closed. She moved on to the living room. The big glass wall and the two windows and the door onto the balcony were all

257

closed and locked.

She moved to the bedroom doorway, and saw the curtains blowing in the wind. One of the windows was fully open. It must have blown open. That seemed unlikely, admittedly. The windows were new and had serious latches on them, and she'd never had a reason to open any of them. It had been far too cold since she'd moved in. But still, it had to have opened somehow. The wind was the only explanation.

She closed it, turned the handle ninety degrees and tugged on it to make sure it was really latched. All the windows had key locks. As an extra precaution, she locked it and put the key in her nightstand drawer.

She got a plate and fork and served herself some of the *jalfrezi*. It was full of tiny chili peppers, and came with a side of lime pickle.

She clicked the television on and sat watching it while she ate. When the news started, she turned the volume down. Lime pickle was amazing, she decided. Spicy and tart, and tasting nothing like the original lime. The next time she glanced at the television, it held an image of Stuart Tower, the building she lived in. She put down her fork and turned up the volume.

"…judge will decide today whether there are grounds to pursue murder charges in the death of Suad Hosni, who fell from the tower in 2001. Officials suspect foul play, but the lack of clear evidence has hampered the case."

They flashed to a man with a thick accent. The titling on the page listed him as a dentist.

"Suad was very happy about the work we'd done. She was looking forward to going home and returning to work…"

Tony had said that she was an actress.

The TV flashed to another man. She missed the caption.

"In the absence of a note, there was little about the woman's death to suggest suicide, leading... Officials found

one of Hosni's shoes in the bathroom and the other with her body."

She was listening so intently to the commentary that she didn't immediately hear the screams. At first it was just a metallic buzzing in her ears, but something in the tone bothered her. She muted the TV, and heard it clearly.

Someone was screaming repeatedly from upstairs. She picked up her cell phone and turned on the audio recorder. At least this time she would have some proof. The door phone started ringing then. She got up and trotted across to it.

"Hello?"

"Sam, it's James from downstairs. Are you all right? Someone has reported they hear screams coming from your flat."

"It's not me. It's upstairs."

"Ah, okay. Apologies."

"Listen, I have an idea what's causing it. This is going to sound crazy, but—" She was interrupted by a huge crash of shattering glass. "Um. James, it sounds like a window just exploded in my bedroom." She could hear the wind howling again. The door to the bedroom slammed shut.

"Can you go see what happened and let me know?"

She took a breath. "I don't really want to go in there right now."

The bedroom door, which had been rattling savagely, fell quiet. A rush of wind whistled through the room, scattering the napkins on the coffee table. The temperature plummeted. Fear flooded through Sam's body, stiffening her joints, turning her arms and legs to rubber.

"James, I might need help," she whispered.

"What's wrong? What's happened?" His voice was faint and she realized she had dropped the handset. "Sam? Sam!"

She stopped listening. Something floated toward her out of the bedroom. Barely visible, she might have missed

it if it had not brought with it a blast of unnaturally icy air and a deep sense of dread. It was making an inhuman, metallic screeching.

"What do you want?" Sam tried to shout the words but they stuck in her throat. *What are ghosts afraid of? The cross?* No, that was vampires, and anyway this ghost had probably not been Christian.

"Are you Suad Hosni?" she whispered.

The figure stopped where it was.

Dredging up all her courage, she repeated it, louder this time. "Are you Suad Hosni?"

The screeching began again. It almost sounded like words, but she couldn't make them out.

The wind howled around her, blowing her hair across her face. The coffee table flew across the room, crashing into the book shelf. Books tumbled off the shelf and swirled around as if caught in a whirlwind.

Sam took the opportunity to move for the door. Her body felt stiff, barely her own. She tasted the iron flavor of her own blood, heard it pounding in her ears. She felt her feet lift off the ground.

"Oh, god. No, no!" She started screaming as she was pulled toward the balcony. The glass door slid open. She kicked and flailed, trying to pull away from the force that held her. The screeching continued.

There was a pounding on the door into the hallway.

"Sam! Sam!" It was James's voice. She recognized his soft Filipino accent.

"James! Help me!"

She heard keys banging against the door, and then it opened.

"Sam!" James ran into the flat.

Sam reached out her hand, and he grabbed it.

"Let go of her!" he yelled. Then he made a roaring noise.

Everything stilled. She dropped onto the carpet.

James bent down to help her up. "Come on. You

should sleep downstairs for tonight."

Sam took his hand and let herself be guided to her feet. He gently pushed her toward the door and followed her, closing it behind them.

They moved toward the elevators.

"She was saying something," Sam said.

"Yes, yes. Let's worry about that later."

She didn't remember the trip down the elevator. The next moment they were in the lobby and she was sitting on one of the sofas. She was wrapped in a wool coat she didn't recognize.

James was pushing a paper cup into her hands. "Tea."

"Thank you."

The warmth felt good. She was shivering so hard her teeth were clicking together. She clutched the cup, afraid she'd spill it if she tried to drink.

"Rest here. We'll get your flat cleaned up when it gets light."

She nodded, finally daring to take a sip of tea. It was weak and unsweetened, but she didn't care. When she finished drinking it, she felt warmer. She put the cup down on the small table next to the sofa and leaned back into the cushions. She dozed uneasily for a while, waking every time the door opened or a car engine revved outside, reassured by James's presence. Then she was alone, and panic washed through her. He came out of the office a moment later.

"All right?" he said, and smiled.

"All right." She willed her breathing to return to normal, but it took quite a while before it did.

After that, she couldn't fall asleep again. Dawn came incrementally, changing the building's front garden from deep black to winter grey to pale grey-blue. Cars began to appear on the road out front. A big, red bus came to a hissing stop out front and drove away again, an advertisement for *Les Miserables* splashed across its side.

When Tony arrived for the day shift, James went with

her to her flat. She stood in the hallway, not wanting to go in.

"Don't worry," James said. "I've brought some protection for you." He reached into his pocket and pulled out a tiny green soldier.

She squinted at him and shook her head. He smiled and for some reason, she felt reassured.

The apartment was a disaster. For the first time, she was thankful she didn't have a lot of belongings. Nearly everything she owned was scattered around the place. She began cleaning up the glass in the bedroom first, while James wandered through the other rooms. The window looked as if it really had exploded, tiny shards glistening across the carpet, the nightstand and the bed.

From time to time she would call out to James to make sure he was still there. She wasn't sure how she was ever going to stay in the flat by herself again.

After she finished picking up broken glass, she moved into the living room to tidy there. Her cell phone was still lying on the coffee table. The screen was black and it didn't respond when she touched it. She remembered then that she'd set it to record. She took it into the bedroom and plugged it in to charge.

James helped her move the sofa back into its place along the wall, and then he took her around the flat and showed her the little soldiers he'd placed on the sill of every window and next to the doors, the silver coins in every corner.

"Don't move these," he instructed. "They will protect you."

She knew it was only superstition, but she right now she was willing to take comfort where she could. She nodded.

"You should go home." She said it half-heartedly, hoping he would say no. He looked exhausted though, and she felt guilty keeping him.

He must have read it in her voice. He looked at his

watch. "I'll call down and get Martin to come up. He should be here by now."

"Thanks, James. I'm going to have to be alone here eventually."

He shrugged. "Okay."

She looked around. The apartment looked almost normal. "Thanks for all your help."

"We'll get someone to replace the window. Maybe not until Monday, so I'll send Martin up with some cardboard and tape to put over it for now. Will you be okay for a little while?"

She nodded.

After James left, Sam found herself jumping at every sound. The heater came on and popped several times, and she almost fled downstairs. She went to check on her phone. The green light showed it was fully charged. She brought it back to the living room and sat down on the sofa.

As she debated about whether she wanted to listen to it, there was a knock on the door. She let out a little shriek, and then she heard Martin's voice in the corridor.

"Sam? Are you all right?"

She got up and ran to the door to let him in, the phone still in her hand. "Sorry. Just a bit jumpy."

"I heard you had a visitor." He came in. He had a large sheet of cardboard in his hand "Where's the broken window?"

"It's in the bedroom. I'll show you." She led him into the bedroom and gestured toward the broken pane.

"So, tell me what happened," he said. He took a craft knife and a roll of heavy duty tape out of his pocket and set them on the night stand.

"She burst through the window and came at me gibbering."

"Hold on. What do you mean by she?"

She felt her face flush. She'd assumed everyone

already knew whose ghost it was. "I... I think it's Suad Hosni."

"Oh, right," he said. He nodded slowly.

"James said it was you who found her. I'm sorry. He said you didn't like to talk about it."

"No, no. It's okay. So she came at you, you said?"

"Well, at first she was just screeching. I felt like she was trying to tell me something, but I couldn't understand anything. Then without any warning, she grabbed me and started dragging me toward the balcony. If James hadn't come in when he did, I don't like to think what would have happened."

"How terrifying!" He'd cut the cardboard to the size of the window and started taping it in place. "But you say you didn't understand anything?"

"No, though it occurs to me that she might not have been speaking English. You knew her, right?"

"I did, yeah. Did you know she was a famous actress in Egypt?"

"Oh, really? Tony told me she was an actress, but he didn't mention where."

"Yes, very famous. She was known as the Egyptian Cinderella."

"If only I'd realized, I might have understood some of what she was saying."

"Oh? You speak Arabic?" He turned to face her.

"I wouldn't say I speak it, but I grew up with it, so I understand a bit."

"Too bad you didn't know."

She nodded. "Yes, but I recorded it."

"You recorded her...?"

"Yes. I didn't mean to. I just turned on the recorder when someone started screaming upstairs. I was starting to feel like I was just imagining the noises from up there."

"Well, where is it? Have you listened to it?"

"No, not yet. I'm not sure I want to. Maybe I'll just email it somewhere to be analyzed."

"Too bad. I'm curious now."

Sam took a breath. "Okay. Let's go into the lounge and get something to drink. I need alcohol if I'm going to go through this."

"Booze? Count me in."

"I've only got rum," she said.

He nodded. "I'll have a taste."

She poured out two small glasses and sat down on one end of the sofa. He sat on the other end. She downed most of her glass.

"Get ready. As I said, it starts with screams." She clicked the forward arrow and strange screams came from the tiny speakers. She pressed stop. "See? It's really unsettling."

"Just skip forward. Let's see if we can understand anything."

Sam nodded. "Yeah, okay. Thanks for sitting with me through this. I'm not sure I can even stay here now."

She scrolled forward a bit and pressed play again. The gibbering shrieks poured out of the phone. Sam focused on the central sounds, which were the most like words. It sounded different in the recording, like an extra layer had been recorded over it.

"Oh, wait. Maybe I heard a word there. Let me go back." She dragged the bar back slightly, let it go for a few seconds, and then pressed stop. "Yes, I think… it sounded like, 'He stole…' Hm. Then a word I don't know, but basically, 'he stole something of mine.'" She pressed play again and listened. "And then she's saying the same thing over and over. He *did something* to me."

"Are you sure?"

"No, not at all, but I'm sure she's saying things in Arabic. I'd want someone else to listen to it. I think I should give it to the police."

She pressed play again. "I think she's saying he *killed* me. Now, '*Wa kana*' is 'it was'…'" She desperately tried to keep the realization off her face. *'It was Martin.'*

265

Before she could move, he slid down the leather sofa and grabbed her. He clamped a hand over her nose and mouth and began dragging her toward the balcony, overturning the coffee table, nearly falling over it. She scrabbled, trying to get some purchase, failing, lungs already aching for air. He braced her against his shoulder, bruisingly hard, and unlocked the sliding glass door. She clawed at his arm, looking around wildly for anything she could use. Her eyes lighted on the tiny solder James had left near the door jamb. *Hey!* She lashed out at it with her foot, and saw it fly off the balcony.

As he began to pull her outside, she clutched desperately at the door facing. Black spots danced in front of her eyes.

There was a rush of freezing wind. Her hair whipped in front of her eyes, and she felt Martin let go. She pushed away, gasping air, running for the front door. Angry screeching made her turn, for a moment, to look back. Martin was struggling against an invisible force holding him against the balcony railing. Slowly, he was bowing backwards. She dashed out into the hallway and banged on the neighbor's door.

A startled looking woman in her sixties answered. "Yes?" She gasped. "You're bleeding." She pointed to her nose.

Sam put a hand up to her face. It came away red. "Please! Call downstairs. Get help. Martin killed Suad Hosni. She's trying to throw him over the balcony!"

A loud scream of anguish cut her off, fading into the distance. Behind her, the gale faded away.

YOU REAP WHAT YOU SOW
KITTY KANE

Chester Postlethwaite had relatively few problems in his life. He was a corporate lawyer with an ex-wife (naggy), a current wife (saggy), and a beautiful eighteen-year-old bit on the side (shaggy!). Yes, he had relatively few things of which to bemoan, except one rather large, blatant and recent issue that had arisen. Chester Postlethwaite was dead.

Dead as a door nail, dead as a dodo, deader than the morning fish catch on Grimsby docks. Simply dead, deceased, an ex-Chester, gone, ceasing to exist.

Now, thought Chester, *I wouldn't mind this dead malarkey quite so terribly much if I had died a noble and heroic death.* But Chester didn't die a noble and heroic death. Oh, no. No bravely fought terrible illness, no laying down his life to save another, nope. Chester Postlethwaite died from auto-erotic asphyxiation.

The last thing Chester recalled was going into the

stationary cupboard at the law offices where he was employed. Goode and Partners. This name had always made him chuckle, because if you could find a single corporate lawyer that was anywhere close to good, he would show you a man in the wrong job. But I digress.

Chester had checked the coast was clear before picking up his kit. This kit he lovingly referred to as his "wank bank kit," a large duffel bag containing silk scarves and several pairs of panties that Chester had procured from the washing line of the penthouse apartment opposite his own. He had gained panties from both the mother and the school girl that lived there, and they were among his most prized possessions.

Also contained in this duffel bag, a small tablet computer, laden with porn. Most of it illegal, all of it immoral. *But then*, thought Chester often, *show me a corporate lawyer that wasn't immoral.* It simply went with the territory.

In the bottom of the bag lay an item which Chester had struggled heavily to procure a nondescript silver coloured ring, approximately the diameter of a side plate, nothing special to look upon, but a clever little item indeed. This was a magician's ring, a trick ring with a stealthily hidden, but strongly sprung trap door, which fooled onlookers into believing that the magician would be passing solid hoop through solid hoop. Entertaining trickery however, was not the reason Chester had this ring. Chester had this ring to hang himself to the point of passing out.

Using a silken scarf passed through the hoop, and also the metal bar running along the low ceiling of the supply closet was perfect to utilise this hoop and scarf combination. Wrapping the cool silken scarf around his fat neck, taking his feet out from under him, not too far. Just far enough to experience that extra rush at the point of climax. Only this time, the rush had ended his life. Well, life as Chester knew it.

ultimate high, coming whilst almost blacking out. His silken sock-clad feet slid right out from under him, his magician's ring trapdoor sprang, throwing the ring off the rail sideways, but catching upon a hook. Chester, cock in hand, experienced his last orgasm as his neck snapped, his tongue lolled out, and his vile little life drained away.

The next thing Chester saw were two pin pricks of light, one up, one down, floating in the void. Chester felt confident that he would be heading upwards, but then his stomach churned as he plummeted downwards. Down, down, down, towards the red light. Chester screamed, incredulous that he, Chester Postlethwaite, would be treated so appallingly as to be sent to this nasty red light, when he so preferred the gentle pale blue light he had briefly glimpsed above him. Then, Chester was dumped unceremoniously on to his ample and still naked rear, onto a huge and seemingly endless highway.

Looking around, Chester spotted a signpost with at least sixteen different arrows pointing to places called names such as Purgatory Point, Blasphemer's Way, Lucifer's Rest, and so on. "I'm not loving this crap!" Chester muttered, and set off down the seemingly endless highway.

Out of the corner of his eye, he spotted movement. He turned his head and saw rats scurrying towards him. These rats were not ordinary rats - they were mutants. Some of them had eight legs and scuttled like spiders, others looked more rat-like but had a scorpion tail curled above their heads, and still others had multiple heads with teeth that pointed down like vampire fangs.

Chester was not exactly what you would call an animal lover. In fact, Chester didn't like animals at all, and these mutated abominations were even worse than any other animal he had ever seen. As he looked on in horror, his mind flashed back to primary school, when he and his school pal Corin Ledbetter had played a nasty, sick prank

on the rest of the class.

The class, as a collective, had a pet fancy rat named Burt, and each member of the class got a chance to take Burt home and care for him for a weekend. The members of the class adored the little rat, but Chester and Corin had an idea, a very sick idea. When it became time for Corin and his twin sister Corina to have a turn at looking after Burt for the weekend, the two boys had come up with a plan with which to amuse themselves.

As expected, the moment the three children walked out of the school gates, the little girl pursed her rosebud lips and proclaimed that she would be looking after Burt. Corin would be allowed to look at him, maybe stroke him. However she glared at Chester and told him he was to come nowhere near Burt, or herself for that matter.

Chester remembered all the way back then, thinking to himself how much he would like to ram his penis between her rosebud lips that she pursed so self-importantly. Chester thought he shouldn't push his luck too far, she was his mate's twin sister, so he just had to grin and bear her precociousness. The weekend passed, and by Sunday, as suspected, Corina had lost interest in Burt, and then the boys got chance to execute their plans.

Taking the tame rat out of its cage, they climbed up into Corin's tree house where they would not be disturbed. In a box with air holes, the two boys had collected a multitude of spiders of all different sizes, millipedes, centipedes, slugs and ear wigs. The inside of this box was an undulating mass of legs and slime. Chester grinned at Corin, who reached for the claw hammer the boys had purloined from next door.

Swiftly and efficiently, Corin, using his father's fishing knife, dispatched Burt's life and split the poor creature's stomach open. Scooping out what they found inside the body cavity, the boys put the steaming and bloody mass outside for closer inspection later.

Taking handfuls each of the wriggling, crawling mass,

the boys stuffed poor Burt's carcass with the insects, and using his father's fishing twine, Corin sewed up the cavity. Taking care to arrange the cage just so, Chester placed the insect filled rat corpse carefully into the sleeping end of the cage. The moving, trapped insects gave the illusion of Burt breathing, making it seem he was simply asleep.

Corina, having lost interest in the pet over the weekend, simply shoved some food into the cage on Monday morning, then picked up her book bag and the cage. Almost bumping into her brother on the landing, she thrust the cage towards him and announced that he must carry it to school. Corin simply grinned and accepted the cage.

The twins left the house and met Chester at the gate. He winked at Corin and performed an exaggerated bow to Corina, knowing it would piss the prissy little madam off. As soon as Corina was out of ear shot, Chester asked Corin if everything was still going according to plan. "Yup," Corin said, "Gettin' a bit stinky, but rats stink anyways, innit?" Chester could barely contain his excitement. He also was finding it increasingly difficult not to get aroused at the thought of the faces of some of the pretty girls in class, ones who would never look at Corin or himself, when the show began.

As the school bell rang, Corina snatched the cage from Corin and marched up to the teacher's desk. In her shrill, sing song, baby doll voice she proclaimed that she had looked after Burt really well. Just her though, not her brother, he had done nothing, not even touched the rat all weekend. No, all the work had been done by herself.

The teacher Mr. Cullum smiled and said, "You sure have done a great job, Corina. As it happens, I need Burt to accompany us to the assembly hall today, so if you wouldn't mind bringing him along, please? Not the cage, just Burt; there will be nowhere for the cage to go."

Corina pursed her lips together, and with a self-important shake of her curled hair, reached into the cage.

As she took hold of the unfortunate pet and pulled him from the cage, she gave a shriek. Burt didn't feel warm and fuzzy anymore, he was cold and stiff. She dropped the rat in disgust, and as the poor thing hit the floor with a squelch, its hastily sewn belly ripped open. Out into the classroom poured all the spiders, millipedes, centipedes, slugs and worms that the boys had shoved onto the body cavity.

The smell was nauseating, and Corina and the girls in the front row of the class started to scream. Chester and Corin looked at one another, Corin had turned green. Chester glared at him, issuing an unspoken command that he was to remain silent. Mr. Cullum was visibly shaken and he grabbed hold of Corina's wrist and tugged her to him. He looked her straight in the eyes and said, "What have you done, Corina?" He even shook her a little. She simply opened her mouth, but no sound came out. She, her pretty little curly head shaking from side to side, imploring the teacher to understand that this vile act was not of her making. But she had dug her own grave, in proclaiming everything regarding the rat's care had been done by her, there was no other to blame.

The rest of the class scrambled out of the door, away from the critters scuttling across the floor. When they finally returned to the classroom, of the cage, rat corpse, insects, Corina, or Corin for that matter, there was no sign. Chester called round that night only to be told that no visitors were allowed there ever again.

Much later that night, he managed to call Corin. Corin said his sister had been taken away, as she must have lost her mind. She had started screaming that morning and didn't stop until they had placed her in a straightjacket and taken her to the asylum. Two days later, Corin's family had moved out, and Chester never saw his friend again.

Jerking back to the present, Chester saw that more and more mutated animals were scuttling, crawling, squelching and scurrying towards him. Disgusted, he tried

273

to run, but a large frog-type creature with huge barbed horns caught him around his thighs, and to Chester's horror, the creature let loose from its teeth-filled maw a huge tongue, which also contained a mouth of its own, and this mouth also had teeth.

Chester screamed and futilely batted his hands at the monstrous pincers holding his legs. Looking up, Chester screamed again, because coiling itself from a burnt and scarred tree, was a huge snakelike being. Unlike any creature Chester had seen before, not even in nightmares. It had the body of a snake, the head of a vulture, and the dorsal fins of a great white shark. With lightning speed, it struck, wrapping itself around Chester's torso, clamping his arms to his sides.

The vulture-like head swung around, and stopped in front of Chester's face. His eyes widened as he saw the tongue inside the mouth. All along its tongue were razor blades.

Jolted once more into his murky past, a game flashed through Chester's mind. A sick little game with which he had amused himself for a while after his friend, Corin, was stolen from him—just because his frigid stuck-up bitch of a twin went crazy and was sent to the loony bin. Being bored, Chester had decided that, to amuse himself, he would attempt to liven up the activity in and around the dull and boring places around town that were meant for folks' enjoyment.

Taking razor blades from his father's drawer, and from the bits and bobs drawer on the kitchen some thumb tacks and spare Stanley knife blades, he put these treasures into his pockets and set off to the park. Stopping on the way at the paper shop on the corner, Chester, pretending to look at the latest football sticker collectables, surreptitiously shoved packet after packet of chewing gum into his shorts pockets.

The shopkeeper was well aware he was doing this, but last time he had challenged Chester, his beloved pet duck

had been poisoned. Having replaced him with a fluffy new duckling, he decided that discretion was the better part of valour where this vile little asshole was concerned. The door dinged as Chester left, and the shopkeeper breathed a sigh of relief; there was something not quite right with that child.

Arriving at the play park, Chester had been glad to see he was pretty much alone. Only the small bespectacled form of Pussy Pete could be seen in the whole park. Chester wasn't bothered by him; the guy couldn't see much without his glasses, and that was easily arranged. Walking faster, almost breaking a slow jog, Chester clotheslined Pete off of the swing, his glasses flew into the air, and landed in front of Chester, who promptly stamped on them. Pete probably never even saw his assailant attack. Brushing off his hands, Chester turned his mind back to his plans.

All the way to the park from the shop, Chester had been chewing an obscenely large wad of stolen chewing gum. Now he reached into his mouth and took it out. Breaking it down into six parts, Chester walked towards the large climbing frame which also incorporated a hut with slides coming down to the ground. One was straight and open, and one was enclosed and spiralled. It was the spiral to which Chester headed. Placing his backpack on the floor at the bottom of the slide, Chester removed the purloined Stanley knife blades from the pocket. Carefully cooping down and walking into the spiral slide from the bottom, at roughly spaced intervals up its length, Chester placed the still pliable pieces of gum and pushed them hard onto the slide. And now the coup de grace - into each bit of gum Chester embedded a Stanley knife blade, sharp side up. Hurrying out of the hut end, Chester grabbed his backpack and set off again, thinking of the carnage this could potentially cause.

Wanting to witness his handiwork at its best, Chester settled himself on a bench outside the cricket pavilion and

waited. The first people to enter the park were a mum and toddler, but they simply went to the swings and stayed there. Just as boredom was setting in, a woman with two kids entered. One, an eighteen-month-old little girl headed for the baby swings, but with glee, Chester saw the boy of about three head straight for the climbing hut. He held his breath as the lad climbed the steps, and then was annoyed to see him come whizzing down the straight slide. At the bottom, face full of joy, the lad turned and ran for the steps again, and this time Chester was rewarded by an agonised howl. Before the unfortunate child exited the spiral slide, a trickle of blood ran out of the exit, followed by the screaming boy, who appeared to be bleeding from both palms, both buttocks and both calves. His mother screamed and ran towards him, her eyes beseeching Chester to help her. Shaking his head, Chester backed away trying to look horrified, but inside, he was laughing.

Having seen the success of his sick plan, Chester decided to up the ante, and off he went to the local swimming baths. Once again, chewing an enormous gob of gum, Chester mumbled "one child swim" to the pretty lady behind the counter, who gave him a blue wrist band. These were supposed to signify when your time in the pool was up, but Chester never took any notice of the announcements telling folk with particular colour bands to leave the water. Why should he? Stupid rules.

Chester changed swiftly into his boardies and sloshed through the ice cold foot disinfector pool and entered the main pool. Secreted in his inner pocket of his swimmers was a pack of razor blades, and a few thumb tacks. The latter he had needed to leave the majority of in his locker, stupid things kept poking him, and that simply wouldn't do. As he entered the pool the tannoy announced it time for folk with yellow bands to leave the pool, and Chester smirked as they all got out and did as they were told, but this also enabled him to get into the pool unobserved. Swimming over to the stairs that went up to the two

waterslides, Chester ran up the slide for the rainbow river. The other slide, Thunder Road, was way too fast for him to be able to stick his vicious little surprises to the flume's bottom. Using his feet to slow his descent, Chester repeated the chewing gum sticking down the length of the flume. This time he embedded razor blades in some bits of gum, and thumb tacks in others. Completing his task, he retreated to the main pool unnoticed, and waited.

In time, he spotted a man carrying a very young girl up the steps of the slide, Chester's cold heart began to race as he watched the man position the girl between his legs and push off down the flume. After a couple of seconds there came two unholy shrieks of pain, one childish and high pitched, the other the agonised grunting shout of a man. The water gushing from the exit of the flume began to turn red, as it poured out into the splash-down area. Two blobs came twisting and plopping out, scarlet arterial blood was shooting up in a crimson geyser, and the young girl flew from her father's grip, landing face down in the mixed blood of herself and her father, swirling around with the chlorinated pool water. Panicked people were running everywhere; a woman had grabbed the child and had her bleeding young body laid out on the side of the pool, her breathing shallow. The lifeguards grabbed the man to safety, his legs and back were cut to ribbons, and the blood poured. The girl was also cut, but not as severely. Chester, trying to hide the maniacal grin threatening to spread across his face, got out of the pool unnoticed in all the commotion. Later that night, on the six o'clock news, Chester had been a little startled by the announcement that the man had died from his injuries; it seems he was something called a "haemophiliac," apparently, he simply didn't stop bleeding, he had expired right there on the pool side. Chester was gutted he hadn't stuck around to witness a real death! Nobody ever traced the two separate blade antics to Chester, and this made Chester very smug indeed. He always cherished the

memories of that river of scarlet running from the flume.

Coming back to himself once more, Chester looked into the razor-filled mouth of the vulture's head, noting that also lining the inner cheeks of the creature's mouth were gleaming thumb tacks. He tried to pull backwards, but the hell creature's vicelike grip simply tightened. There came a sound very much like a wheezing laugh from deep inside the vulture head which made the small amount of natural hair Chester actually had on his head stand up.

While he attempted to remove his face from harm's way, an icy cold feeling flooded his bowels, for dragging itself towards him over the hellish, roiling landscape, was what first appeared to be a bundle of filthy rags. As the bundle approached, Chester shook his head in disbelief. A matted, blood-soaked, but unmistakably curly haired head became apparent. Swaying and jerking from side to side in such a violent fashion, it reminded Chester of condemned prisoners taking their final seat in an electric chair, jerking and stiffening as the current passed through them, frying their internal organs, until they were declared dead by the state executioner.

However this was no condemned prisoner jerking its way towards him, and as it stopped three feet from where he was being held by the Hell fauna. The blood soaked head jerked back exposing a hellish visage that Chester recognised at once. Slashes and cuts and bruises covered the once-pretty face, and maggots were wriggling around in the empty socket of one eye. The eye itself hung upon the slashed cheek, and was ragged around its edges where the maggots had been feasting. Upon the ear lobes hung dung beetles, pincers so tightly gripping the flesh that they had pushed all the way through the lobes.

The bundle, with effort, arms and legs unnaturally bent back into the gymnastic position known as the crab, showed itself in all its bloody glory to Chester. He knew of course who this was, had been. Corina was semi-crouched in front of him, centipedes and spiders flowed in a

continuous stream from the place under the tattered dress where her legs met. In her broken hands, fingernails long ripped out from their foundations, she held the corpse of a rat. A rat that seemed familiar to Chester, a rat with no insides left, in place of the rodents innards, writhed a mass of oozing putrid slugs, green phlegm like gunk dripping to the ground.

Chester tried to speak, to attempt to tell the Corina creature that he was sorry, to beg forgiveness, but only the true thoughts came out in gasps from his parched lips. "Serves you right, you little prissy bitch." Chester's mouth was operating entirely under its own volition. Panicked at the lack of control over his own vocal cords, he spat, "Always did fancy ramming my cock into that frigid rosebud mouth of yours." Alarmed, Chester made to cover his uncontrollable mouth with his hands but the Hell creature still held him tight. Looking once more to the horizon Chester felt his bowels finally let loose all down the backs of his legs, the stench nauseating. The mutated rat-type beings scurried forwards and began to lick the foul, liquid-like excrement with much gusto.

Approaching the nightmare gathering now were two more figures, a relatively normal (normal for here) looking man, and a semi-naked girl wearing just the tattered remains of a school skirt. One thing she didn't seem to be wearing though was a head. As the pair got closer Chester could see her head was actually present after all, but was hanging on by just a small strip of flesh, and the spinal cord, oesophagus and muscular structure was visible upon the neck stump. Chester vomited. Chunks flew across the creatures and the walking dead with cataclysmic force. The mutant rats squeaked their pleasure at this new culinary offering.

"What do you want from me?" screamed Chester, his sanity beginning to fray. "Anything, I'll give you anything, just let me go!!" But being let go was not to be Chester Postlethwaite's fate that day, no way. The man lumbered

towards him, maintaining eye contact. The smell emanating from him was sweet but rotting, a little like a trash collection truck. As he stood in front of the still captive Chester, he turned around, revealing several deep slashes down his back and legs. His kidneys and spine, along with his curled intestines and liver could be seen through the slashes, the organs all had a coating of vile smelling mould growing upon them, and of course, Chester realised who this was: the unfortunate haemophiliac from the swimming pool. His bowels let loose again.

The almost headless girl shuffled clumsily forward; it was hard to see where she was walking with her head hanging off. "We are the products of your warped and twisted pleasures, Chester Postlethwaite." she said from behind herself. "We are your demons. Now, you must face us."

"Indeed," said the slashed and moulding man. "We hear your thoughts screaming to let them out. You would give or do anything to make it so right now—wouldn't you, Chester Postlethwaite?"

Nodding furiously and trying to agree, Chester started to cry rivulets of salty tears, tears he had never once in his life cried for anyone other than himself. "What...what do I need to do?" he gasped. The child-sized bundle of rags that once was Corina, pretty, pesky Corina, slittered forward once more in her crab-like stance.

"Indeed, we are your demons, Chester," the sing song voice still had the lisp of which Chester and Corin had ridiculed the little girl so often. "You CAN escape us Chester. You can be free of here.

"HOW?" he screamed. "Tell me how, you little bitch!"

The Corina demon scuttled aside to allow the mouldering man, and beheaded and violated girl, to step in once more. "It's simple, Chester Postlethwaite," said the slashed haemophiliac, "You can win the right of rebirth, it

is the only way out of Hell."

The man stepped back allowing the school skirt-sporting headless (almost) corpse to approach. From behind the decapitated torso came the girl's voice, "To win rebirth, Chester, you must conquer and endure. If you cannot do these things, you will not win reincarnation, and myself and my friends here will use you as our play toy for all eternity. You enjoyed so much to be amused by the suffering of others, we, as your personalised demons, also feed from that feeling, but for us, it is your suffering that we crave. If you successfully endure, and conquer us, your demons, you shall be reborn, if you fail, nothing will help you, nobody will hear your screams. Do you accept?"

Nodding furiously Chester agreed, past even being able to think clearly about what might happen to him, he just wanted to save himself. Thirty seconds later, he began to find out exactly what would happen to him, a cowardly bully all his life. He began to reap just what he had sown.

The pincers of the frog-like return tightened, cracking the bones in Chester's legs like matchsticks, and something, almost a tickle, was moving over his still naked bottom. Suddenly it bit down hard, rammed itself between the stained cheeks of Chester's ass, and entered his rectum. Up into his colon, the thing continued until it met resistance, then Chester felt the extra mouth within the elongated tongue bite. It chewed its way through any obstacles it encountered on its journey through Chester's insides, and Chester felt each and every bite. The slowly wavering vulture type head upon the finned snake body froze. Chester saw the gleam in the beast's eye and knew what was coming. Opening its razor and tack filled mouth, it began to lick every part of Chester that it could reach. The razors split his skin wide open, the cuts and slashes were legion, and every cut that opened immediately attracted the mutated rats, who were jumping and suckling the blood from these lesions as voraciously as newborn piglets feed from the sow.

Chester didn't need to wonder what was going to happen next, so many times had thoughts of ramming his dick into Corina's mouth crossed his mind in the past, he knew for sure what was coming. Hooking out his flaccid member, the demon child placed it in her unholy mouth and began to suck. Against his will Chester felt the beginnings of an erection stirring, regardless of the horror of the situation. Then, what Chester knew was coming came. The child from hell bit down so hard on his semi-hard cock that he heard and felt the thing snap like bone. Chester tried to shriek, but as he opened his mouth, the razor- and tack-filled vulture mouth landed over his. The tacks acted much like carpet gripper; he was going nowhere.

The Corina demon, apparently pleased with her prize, scuttled off once more in her crab-like pose. The near headless school girl approached, staring at the gaping and bloodied hole between Chester's legs, her muffled voice came once more. "That is very much how a certain part of me looked just before that Russian bastard cut off my head. What was the reason this was done? To amuse sick, sick assholes like you, Chester!" As she shouted, her foot connected so hard with Chester's now openly exposed scrotum, his testicles flew from their wrinkly sack and hit Chester's chest with a double splat. The delighted mutant rats fought among themselves to be the first to chew away the stringy bits of flesh holding Chester's really not impressively sized bollocks on, and four delighted victorious rats chowed down immediately on their bloody, semen-filled prizes.

Chester wanted to pass out, boy, did he, but the blessed blackness was not forthcoming here in Hell. His final tormentor stepped forward and whispered something in tongues to the snake creature. The head came around, looking him up and down. From between his legs, the horrendous mouth of the frog mutant appeared once more. Rat insect mutants positioned on either side of him,

drooling bubbling black saliva upon Hell's barren earth. The spider-like rats shot from their misshapen mouths a strong putrid smelling silk, which wrapped around Chester's arms and legs. Yet more appeared around his fat neck. The slashed man walked stiffly towards Chester, flecks of mould dropping off in his wake.

"You lived your life, Chester Postlethwaite, in a way that caused untold suffering to others. You used this for your own entertainment. Today, Chester, you are our entertainment here in Hell. For your pleasure, pain we had to endure, now, for our pleasure, you will reap what you have sown!" As he said his final words, the creature surrounding Chester pulled, bit, and rent at his body. The pain was excruciating. He tried to scream, but blood filled his mouth. His flabby unkempt body was torn into a thousand pieces. Finally, there was a huge flash of lighting, and for Chester, all went black.

The next thing he became aware of, was opening his eyes, but they weren't his eyes, they were in the wrong place, on the side of his head. Confused, he looked around him and saw that he was in a cage with some straw, and what looked like a bowl of muesli. A bottle containing what looked like water was poking through the bars of the cage. 'Rebirth!' he thought to himself. 'I must have won the right to be reborn because I was able to endure and conquer!' Feeling pretty smug, he thought he would rather have not come back as a furry animal, but anything was better than the torture the hellions had been using upon him.

Hearing a noise, he looked up through the bars of the cage and saw two school boys approaching. They looked at each other and grinned as they reached for the cage. Lifting it up level with their own eyes, the boys stared in at Chester the rat, eyes sparkling with thoughts of their plans. Oh yes, they had plans for this little caged rat. Sick plans, horrid plans, not unlike the plans of two other school boys a few years ago. Two boys named Chester Postlethwaite

and Corin Ledbetter. Chester the rat heard these plans running through the sick minds of the two boys. Chester the rat tried to scream, but defenceless animals can't scream, can they? No, they can't scream or cry for help at all, and with the words of the slashed and mouldering man ringing in his ears, Chester Postlethwaite went to his eternal cycle of damnation, rebirth and suffering - hearing over and over:

You reap what you sow.
You reap what you sow...

ROUND EIGHT
WINNER

YOU REAP WHAT
YOU SOW
KITTY KANE

ROUND NINE

HAVE A NICE DAY
MICHAEL NOE

VS

RIDING THE WAVES OF LUMINESCENT TRANSDIMENSIONAL SEA TURTLES
DANI BROWN

HAVE A NICE DAY
MICHAEL NOE

Ever have one of those days where nothing goes right? It seems as if the moment you wake up, everything begins to fall apart. You can lie and say no, but I know you're lying. It's okay because everyone lies. It's all a part of what makes us human. Lying makes us feel good about ourselves. Why be like everyone else? Lying is good for the soul. We all do it. When the clerk hands you your change and tells you to have a nice day, you may say something nice, but on the inside you're saying; "Fuck you, and gimme my change, asshole." Let's be honest and say that they don't care if you have a nice day. They're taught to say that. They say it to everyone, and you can be sure that over the course of any given day, they've told a thousand people the same damn thing.

You're just another face that blends in with countless others. They don't care about you, or your dog. They couldn't give two shits about your grandmother or her heart attack. They're programmed to *act* like you matter. In the grand scheme of things, you're about as important as a

fart. It sounds pretty cruel, doesn't it? You go into countless establishments over the course of your day and you're *supposed* feel as if you matter. You really don't. Odds are, if you go to a restaurant and don't tip, you're remembered as that cheap bastard at table five or wherever they put you. Odds are, someone has just spit in your food or stirred your drink with their dick. Remember, people remember when you don't tip or happen to be rude.

I'm a waitress. I know these things. I haven't done them myself, but I know people who have. Customers are all the same. I personally don't care if you tip or are rude to me. Karma's a bitch and I'm sure at some point, you'll get yours. Life has a funny way of working out. You may call me an idiot, and then as you're fucking your wife or girlfriend, you might have a heart attack, and it'll be your own fault. The motto is simple. Don't be a dick. People have feelings. Hard to imagine isn't it? It's an insane concept that people just don't or won't grasp. Our society is fucked and thanks to the Internet, it's only going to get worse.

I want you to understand that I may just be a waitress, I know what my job is, but would it kill you treat me like a human being? I'm not just a serving wench. I only waitress while I'm at college. I only took the job because it fit into my schedule and allowed me to pay my bills. There are days that I hate my job. Fucking hate it! Each Monday to Thursday I show up and plaster on a fake smile and pretend to give a shit, even though I don't. I put up with screaming babies and assholes that think I'm too stupid to put in a drink order.

I could be a stripper. I've thought about it, but the thing is I have too much self-respect to show strange men my titties. The money would be better, but I would also lose a great deal of dignity. I know how men feel about strippers and how easy they assume they are. They think that if a woman takes off her clothes for money, she must

be an easy lay. What kind of bullshit is that? I get how attractive the female body is. I've seen myself naked, but do men really think that women choose to strip because it has good health and dental? The idea could be that I show these guys my pooter in hopes that they'll want to marry me. A lap dance shouldn't be high on the list of things men look for in a wife.

I bust my ass waiting tables. I hear what you're saying. If I hate it, then why am I doing it? Surely the job can't be that bad or you wouldn't still be doing it. How bad could the people be? It's not a difficult job and yes, anyone can do it. Well, almost anyone. If you have a crappy attitude, you won't last long. I can promise you that. People like me, despite the fact that I hate most of them. The needy few outweigh the genuinely nice people. America is full of selfish, needy bastards who assume that their needs come before everyone else's.

Here's the thing: if you didn't know, you would just assume that I was a nice girl with a kind word to say to everyone. I make a lot in tips because I *force* myself to pretend that you are the most important people I have seen all day. The reality is that you're just a blur. You're holding me back from my fifteen-minute break, and when I smile, I'm secretly calling you a dipshit. You have no idea how much it pains me to smile for eight hours a day. They pay me to be nice to you. You aren't special. You're just another asshole sitting in my section. I smile and chat as if we've known each other for years, but if I had to pick you out of a police lineup, I'd fail miserably.

I would like to tell you that I had no idea why I did what I did. I could blame it on stress, or any number of things, but that's a lie. It was coming for a really long time. Imagine a tea kettle for a moment. What happens when it heats up? It screams, and lets you know that the water is boiling. I reached my boiling point. It was just a bunch of isolated incidents that led to the boiling point. Rude customers were just a small part of it. The reason that I'm

even telling you this is so you have some sort of reason behind my actions. Does it make it excusable? It doesn't. Nothing is going to change it anyway. There's no way to say I'm sorry. Odds are you won't believe me, and why should you? Everyone lies. It's human nature.

I started my shift at the restaurant at my usual time. I worked seven in the morning until three in the afternoon. Looking back, the only thing that happened was that I had been running late and I was just in a horrible mood. There was nothing I could do to shake myself out of it. No amount of coffee made my mood lighten. As I watched people streaming in for the breakfast rush, I felt my skin crawl. It was as if I were stuck in some kind of time loop. No matter how much time progressed outside, it was as if time stopped once I stepped through those doors.

It seemed as if I were staring at the same exact people, and the days themselves never ended. It would just pick up right where I left off. I was disoriented for a moment and had to close my eyes to keep myself from passing out. By closing my eyes, I hoped to make the feelings go away. When I open them, I know that everything will be back to normal. My mood will lighten and most importantly, I won't feel as if I'm stuck in some strange time loop. All I had to do was close my eyes and everything would be okay. When I was a young girl it always got rid of the boogey man that hid in the closet, so it would work here.

As I opened my eyes I held my breath, afraid that it wouldn't work. Everything would be the same. I would be stuck in this weird moment where nothing changes. I would be trapped here forever. The same people eating the same food over and over again. The crying babies were my new music. The clack and clatter of silverware would be unending. My lungs constricted as the urge to breathe became a dull throb that vibrated my chest. Dots pulsed and waved in front of my rapidly blinking eyes. Maybe I died and this was my own personal hell. All I needed were

flames and the smell of sulfur.

Everything was normal. I breathed a sigh of relief and went about my normal routine. It's true what people say. Routine defines us. No matter how singular we think we are, we all have routines. It's who we are. We can pretend to be different and sure, we can even pretend that we're better than everyone else, but our routines give us away. We're easy to spot that way. You ever wonder how stalkers have such an easy time pinning us down? Our routines make it too easy. If everyone altered their routines, then it would make it harder for them to do their stalking thing. If just once you skipped the bagel and headed out the door ten minutes earlier you wouldn't be so damn easy to spot.

Is this making any sense? I've had a bit of time to think about that day, and while it seems so clear in my head it just seems to come out jumbled. I can tell you the smells from that morning. They come to me late at night in the dark when I'm trying to sleep. Black coffee and bacon. It's a smell that seems to trigger the memories. In the dark, I can hear the whimpers and the crying, but it's the smell of bacon and black coffee that make me smile. Smells and memories are all we have, aren't they? They can bring back things long forgotten, or they can remind you of a time, when for just a moment, everything made sense. Isn't that what we all want? We want things to make sense.

No matter how much they seem to make sense to you, they never make sense to everyone else. I also think that decisions good or bad define us. Think about it. While you're staring at your significant other you're there by choice. No one held a gun to your head and said you have to be there. Good or bad, it's these decisions that give our lives meaning. We all need our lives to have some kind of *direction*. Without some sort of direction, what do we have? We have nothing. We begin to have regrets, and those regrets all pile up until the moment we die, and we wish that we had done something with our lives. Made people remember us. No matter who you are or what you believe,

there's nothing scarier than not being remembered.

When I woke up that morning I had no idea that a decision awaited me. It was a chain of events that led to it. It was like a stack of dominoes. You knock just one over and then they all come crashing down. The domino effect affects all our lives. Look at your own life and you'll begin to see it. I'm not saying it's all bad, but it could be. When you set one domino into action, it starts the chain moving and once it's put into motion, there's no stopping it. All you can do is watch as it all falls apart. Life isn't really as complex as people make it out to be. Everyone tries to compartmentalize it and make it mysterious, but when you really think about it, it's all about simplicity and choices. You're the domino knocking into everything else. Everyone around you is the next piece destined to fall over. It begins a chain reaction that affects others around you.

I bet you never thought about that, did you? Whether you realize it or not, you're a part of someone's history. A first date, or the ending of a tumultuous relationship. You could be a part of someone else's domino effect and not even know it. The world isn't as small as you make it out to be. There's history happening all around you and in some small way you're a part of it. You aren't as special as you appear to be. We are all linked together and no matter how much we try and rationalize everything, there's no escaping the fact that we're all connected.

That morning the panic I felt threw me off a little. I had heard about feeling *trapped* before, but I never felt it. What was so different? Aside from the fact that I was running late I can't think of one damn thing. When I step back and observe everything and my emotions at the time I think maybe there was something different. Why did I feel so trapped? I could have quit my job at any time. Just walked away and this story wouldn't even exist. The fact is that I didn't. I had no idea that anything was going to happen. I was thinking about what I was going to do after

work. Simple mundane stuff that everyone thinks about. Not once did I harbor any malice or ill will toward anyone. I wasn't wired that way. It wasn't who I was.

I am a woman who avoids conflict. When things go wrong, I don't voice any complaints at all. I just accept it and move on. Maybe I was storing it all and squashing it down until there was simply no more room. I was surrounded by rude people that lashed out at other people who they felt were beneath them. Having a bad day? Take it out on the people at the laundromat or that poor clerk who had maybe fifteen minutes left on her shift. We forget that these are people with real lives and real problems. They aren't there because they want to be. It's a job. It may not be the best job, but that doesn't make them worse than you. They aren't there for your abuse or amusement.

We all need to feel superior to everyone else. It makes us feel better to treat others like shit. Entitlement is a bullshit concept. We aren't owed anything and no matter what you think, you aren't any better than anyone else. You just think you are. I wonder sometimes if the hippies had the right idea. The whole peace and love thing seems like a weird concept, but is it? Human decency shouldn't be a foreign concept. First world problems are a bullshit concept, aren't they? The problem is they exist, and because of that, there's this idea that we're more important than everyone else.

When you look at the ideas that the hippies had, there was no self at all. It was all about loving everyone, and treating everyone as if they were your brother. We only think about the sex aspect of it and never imagine that there's more to it than that. These were dirty, delusional hippies after all. They had these archaic ideals that made no sense. Why should we love everyone? That's fucking crazy! It had to be the pot, right? It affected their thinking and gave them these crazy ideas that would never work in a free society that's force fed violence and hate. There's no room for compassion at all. How can we love others when

we can't even love ourselves? We demand respect, but can't respect anyone else.

I had just reached my breaking point. That moment of panic *affected* me. I was able to go through my normal routine, but there was something different. I felt as if I was falling apart; the ledge that I was standing on was slowly crumbling. I could feel it, but there was nothing I could do to save myself from falling. It was just a matter of time before the ground gave way underneath my feet. Everything I had squashed down came bubbling to the surface. I wasn't as strong or as confident as I appeared to be. I was no different than anyone else. There was nothing unique or special about me. None of us are.

My mom used to tell me that I was a special snowflake. Different than everyone else. She would sit me down and say: "Jill, you may think you're just like everyone else, but you're just like a snowflake. You're unique and special." When she told me this, I wasn't sure what she meant. Weren't we all supposed to conform and be like everyone else? I know what she meant, but the concept was foreign to me. No one wants to think that they're unique. When you fall into that mindset you begin to feel like a freak. We all want to be accepted and loved. That's what we all want from life. When people stand out, they're ridiculed. I didn't want to be like a snowflake. It was too damn hard to be different.

I emerged from the kitchen as If I were awaking from a bad dream. My thoughts were going in so many different directions that it was hard to focus. Faces and orders all blurred together. It was as if it all became a language of its own. I forced myself to smile and pretend that I was listening, but in reality, I was miles away. My eyes scanned the crowded dining room and the sound of the silverware clattering on the ceramic plates seemed louder than usual. They morphed into strange creatures with gaping maws and wild boisterous laughter. Instead of humans, I was looking at oinking pigs. They would all laugh and slurp up

Michael Noe

their coffee as they stuffed more food into their pudgy little faces.

I needed a break. In the open air I felt a bit better. I lit a cigarette with shaking hands. I thought about just leaving. If I had left, things would have turned out quite differently. Looking back, I know what I should have done, but I didn't. The cigarette calmed me. I went back into the kitchen I felt normal again. I no longer felt trapped. I couldn't understand why I had felt the way I had. It had to have been the stress that I was under. School, and the job. I was worried that my grades weren't good enough even though I knew they were. I had nothing to worry about. I was one of the lucky ones, wasn't I? There were so many that had it worse than I did, and they were doing just fine. Wasn't it all mental?

Everyone handles stress differently. You never know when someone's about to go postal. There's never a warning or anything. Just that one moment of clarity and then it all fades to black. I was just having a bad day. I was *entitled* to it. I could plaster on a fake smile and plow through my day, and when it was all over, I would go home and have a good cry and focus on tomorrow. One step at a time. One day at a time. That was how you got through life and all of its hazards. In with the good air, out with the bad.

"Pardon me, Missy, but could I trouble you for just one tiny second?" I turned toward the voice and tried to smile, but that voice was like listening to Freddy Krueger drag his steel claws on a chalkboard. The woman was maybe forty or so with dark circles under her eyes and brown lipstick that made her mouth look less like a mouth and more like an asshole. I suppressed the urge to laugh as I walked over to where she and a group of her friends were all seated in a corner booth by the front window.

"Of course." I refilled all of their coffees and cursed myself for even coming. This wasn't even my section. Whatever issues these women were having wasn't a

concern of mine. *Out with the bad air in with the good. You are a tree waving in a forest of peace and calm.*

"Don't smile at me. You see these eggs? These are runny. Not at all what I asked for. What kind of idiots does this place hire? You're not as stupid as the twit that took my order, are you? Are you even listening to me? Jesus, I swear you people are all fucking idiots."

I felt my peace and serenity drain away as I watched this woman drone on and on about how stupid we all are. Anyone could waitress. It wasn't rocket science. You simply took orders. How hard was it? I guess it was too difficult for her server because she was a complete and total fuck up. "I'm sorry. Let me take this and I'll bring you new eggs," I reached for the plate and heard her breathe as if I had I just offended her.

"Don't bother. My breakfast is ruined. If that cunt had done her job correctly, we wouldn't be having this conversation at all. Obviously you don't understand the problem. It's beyond the eggs and down to stupidity. You, my dear, don't strike me as intelligent either."

I felt the smile slide from my face as the anger took hold. I reached out and grabbed the fork from the cunt's plate. I jabbed it into her hand as hard as I could, enjoying the squeal of pain that erupted from her mouth. I could see blood pouring from the wound as if it weren't even a hand at all, but a fat tick that was feasting. No one at the table spoke. They were too stunned to do anything but stare. I smiled and smashed the half full coffee pot into her temple. Bright red splotches exploded onto her skin. Bits of glass stuck into her head like porcupine quills. Now, people began to notice. The sound of the breaking glass and the smell of coffee was overwhelming.

"You are one rude bitch! Why don't you go fuck yourself!" I screamed. Out of the corner of my eye I saw someone coming toward me. I knew that someone was probably filming this and soon the cops would be there. I needed to make this count. I grabbed a plate full of

sausage gravy and biscuits and just swung. The food splashed against the stunned face of my manager and the plate broke against his forehead turning the running food into a clumpy crimson that reeked of pennies.

I made a beeline to another table and spotted a knife that I could use to ward off anyone that came near me. The thing was that no one did. The room was eerily silent as I made my way through the dining room. Blood had splattered into my eyes momentarily obscuring my vision. I stood behind a customer and howled as I stabbed him in the neck, relishing the feel of his arterial flow against my shaking hands. The paralysis broke, as people screamed and ran toward the doors in a mad panic. One of the customers tried to tackle me but I was able to jam my knife into his fat stomach. It was like sticking my hand into a warm bowl of pudding.

"You feel brave now, asshole?" I spat in his face as I kept jamming the knife into his fat quivering stomach. His mouth moved, yet no sounds came out. I laughed as I kept stabbing not even caring that he was already dead. It wasn't important anyway. I was teaching this bastard a lesson and all of those around me should have been paying close attention.

The anger washed over me, but I can't really remember killing anyone. It all happened so fast, it felt as if I had just stepped out of my body and was allowing someone else in. It was as if I were possessed by the anger. It was controlling all of my thoughts and actions. I lay next to the dead man and rested. I watched as people streamed by, and occasionally I would reach out and hit a calf or two. Their screams were music to my ears. They were all invited to witness my breakdown. It was a beautiful thing that no one would soon forget. As I lay there, I remembered reading stories about people who had just snapped and there was never a reason. They ended up dying at the hands of the police, or they realize what they've done and end up killing themselves. Not a noble

way to go, is it?

The cops did arrive and off I went covered in blood and laughing as if I had just heard the funniest joke in the world. The smell of blood, piss and coffee reminded me that no matter what I did from this moment on I would always be remembered for this. This was my moment where all the dominoes clickety-clacked together and my history was forever altered. There were of course other ways to handle things, but I was just acting on instinct. I didn't plan to kill anyone. I sometimes wish that it *had* been premeditated.

If I had planned this ahead of time, then I would have taken out so many more people. All of those rude instinctive people would have paid dearly for thinking that they were better than me. That's the real reason people kill. They grow tired of feeling as if they don't matter. There is always someone that has to make someone else feel like shit. No one takes the feelings of others into consideration anymore. There was a time when respect and common courtesy mattered. We weren't entitled to anything and if we were, we didn't make others feel inferior. Now? There just isn't any respect for anyone.

Does it justify what I did? Of course not, but there are those that see me as a kind of hero. They use me as an example of a variety of issues. At my trial I had to lie and say that I had a great deal of remorse. The truth was I had none. There wasn't a moment to think about anything or even stop myself from harming anyone. They were dead. That bitch got what she had coming to her. I feel nothing at all for what I did to her. If I could go back in time I would probably do it again. That look on her face was motivation enough. I wanted to make her pay for what she said, and how she made me feel. I wanted to show her that I mattered. All of those bitches at that table would never forget what I had done.

I hope it haunts them in their sleep. I want them to close their eyes and see me killing that bitch. She had

deserved to die. That fat guy wanted to be a hero, and what happened to him? He ended up dead too. I felt a bit of remorse for that one because he did nothing wrong. He was just in the wrong place at the wrong time. They never asked me, though. They just assumed that I did. It all goes back to choices, doesn't it? We all have to make them, and as I write this, I know that there's nothing I can do. I do have a nice clean bed sheet though, and if I do this right I can escape from this predicament that I'm in. I just need to be patient and bide my time.

Writing this has been therapeutic. People have wanted me to tell my story, but I just never felt as if was important. A year is a long time. I've had a lot of time to think and figure out what I wanted to say. Why would people care anyway? Apparently a lot of people do. I leave this as my suicide note, and now, I have a sheet waiting to take me out of my prison and into sweet oblivion.

RIDING THE WAVES OF LUMINESCENT TRANSDIMENSIONAL SEA TURTLES
DANI BROWN

Balancing on top of their shifting plastic island riding the waves of the Pacific, the cruise ship passengers realised no food had washed up with them. Licking crusty crustaceans off the plastic was thirsty work; not enough bottles of water had washed onto the floating island, and those that had weren't full and were at least two years old. Water all around them and they couldn't drink it.

The indignity of clinging to floating plastic, the sun scorching blisters onto their skin, hair extensions and false eyelashes long gone, was too much for some. They dropped away as the sun set.

Land was a distant memory. The cruise was meant to

be the height of luxury—stops at every major port in the world. Money was meaningless to these people. All they gave up was their time. As the super-rich, they hired people to wipe their arses. Surviving without servants was a fun bragging right as long as that time didn't stretch beyond twelve hours. It had been six since cartoonish pirates with birds on their shoulders and missing limbs forced them to walk the plank. They would have preferred actual pirates, despite their chances of survival being even lower. Actual pirates had almost as little humanity in them as the cruise ship survivors, but they could be bought.

The few people left fought over the bottles of water—each drop precious—as more of them fell away from the floating plastic island. The cruise ship in the distance looked like it might have been on fire, but that could have been the setting sun. It was easy to stab each other with jagged pieces of plastic on top of the floating island, and it wasn't necessarily the man or woman with the fattest wallet or biggest offshore account who won these duels.

The blood attracted sharks. The plastic in the ocean had broken the bottom of the food chain, and these effects were finally being felt at the top; these remaining sharks were really hungry and pissed off. Cannibalising each other had lost its appeal. Every shark for a two-hundred-mile radius was circling, eating its competitors.

Once the sun fully set, the only light to be seen were the stars in the sky. They didn't illuminate much. The sharks had an extra sense. They knew where a leg dangled into the water. They knew where the plastic was thin and weak.

The water beneath them became lighter. At first the survivors thought it was a trick of their minds. It was easy to go insane out here with no chance of rescue. Some were beginning to wonder if they had been set up. The pirates were too childish, exactly the sorts of things that those who opposed tax rises for the poor and tax cuts for the

rich would send out. The cruise had seemed too good to be true. It was the task of the accountants to cover costs but never before had such a cruise been attempted.

Orbs of light danced beneath the surface of the ocean. Promises of far off lands, rescue, food, water and servants called to the survivors. The sharks needed to be defeated first. The super-rich weren't good at anything much really, except pushing people into a rut and keeping them there. The very richest among them even had servants for that task.

There was no one around to suggest to the survivors that it perhaps wasn't such a good idea to go diving for the light orbs. A lifetime spent with servants wiping their arses meant they didn't have the sense to think it wasn't a good idea.

One-by-one, the people clinging to the floating island of plastic dropped away. The sharks had no class preference for what would serve as their late night snack. Rich, poor, man, woman, transgender—it didn't matter. They all tasted the same. Sure, rich people could eat better but they often made the decision to eat deep-fried, heavily processed endangered species, which really was no better than the highly processed poor man's diet. The sharks noticed no taste differences.

Not every person diving after the orbs was eaten by a shark. Some sharks were too full after gorging on others of their species and too bloated to swim away. One man managed to catch an orb. They weren't as deep as first thought.

He forgot he couldn't breathe underwater, or more likely, there wasn't a servant there to tell him he couldn't. It didn't matter. He grabbed onto the orb by a tail. Orbs shouldn't have tails. But he didn't know that. He didn't know much of anything except that if paper money was still in use, he would have a fat wallet. His fat wallet sat on the lost cruise ship with lots of pieces of plastic in it. There wasn't any orb to guide it to safety up the man's arsehole.

Where he was going, he wouldn't need a wallet.

The gills appeared just in time to save him. It was another thing he did not know. He felt them pushing up against his neck skin as he clung to the tail of the orb. The orb didn't explain what they were. It wasn't needed—he didn't even notice himself breathing.

He only noticed the speed at which he was moving through the water when he let go. There was no slowing down; on the contrary he was speeding up. Faster and faster. Where he'd stop, he couldn't say. But then he couldn't say much.

The orb began to take shape. A giant turtle came out of the glow. If he'd tried to speak, he would have been greeted by a mouthful of giant, glowing turtle shit. There was a lot of glowing turtle shit in the ocean. Other than sharks and the occasional whale, it was about the only species the oceans could support these days.

All that plastic hadn't been so good for the oceans. Deep below in the vents, a new species was being born of the molten plastic, but it hadn't yet worked out evolution. That would come in time, when plastic ruled the Earth. It wasn't of any concern to the man, former owner of a fat wallet and an even fatter off-shore account. He might have been a root cause; he might not have been.

He was caught in the tide of the luminescent sea turtles. They only came around once every ten thousand years to bring the seas of change. The turtles of ten thousand years ago were documented as some sort of god, passed down through oral traditions. The man had never come across them. Not many people had.

He was spinning. And then he stopped. It was sudden. His bones should have shattered. Instead, he found drugs had been shoved up his arse.

Turtles surrounded him, their colours so bright. He was their mule. He didn't volunteer to have them shoved up his arse. When he left the floating plastic island, he hadn't given consent to anything else.

The gills retreated back into his neck. He was standing on dry land, naked with blood dripping down his thighs.

The turtles stared at him. A moon glowed in the sky. She was beautiful, but that was impossible - there was no moon on the night he found himself stranded on the floating plastic island. Full and bloated, she had a friend walking across her with eight legs. She was eclipsed by a spider in the sky.

He wondered if the package shoved up his arse was breaking apart and its contents leaking into his blood stream. He didn't have time to wonder for much longer. It was ripped from his insides with a pop and little ceremony. The turtles followed it with their eyes. It wasn't for them. They were only the smugglers. Luminescent sea turtles never touched the stuff.

Instructions were to leave it on the beach and they could have their children back. Now there was a man shaking, naked and cold standing before them, complete with a vacant stare. He didn't know who he was or what he was, let alone where he was. They couldn't leave him stranded there, but they couldn't bring him back to his own world either. That door was closed. Even if it wasn't, it wasn't such a nice place, what with the plastic spawning new life. The people there were too greedy.

A thunderclap in the sky echoed off the rocks on the beach. It was time to go. They nudged the man along. On land, they lost their glow and speed and became slow, sluggish creatures. The thunderclap growled a threat, "Move along, move along." The addicts wanted their drugs from that other world.

The man walked with the turtles. He couldn't think of anything else to do, being too used to having people tell him what he should or should not do. The wind howled behind them, moving them along. The turtles were used to it. The man wasn't. He didn't know what was happening. The people he ruined would have loved to have seen him

walking naked, drooling and escorted by turtles. Without his power suit and team of yes men, he was reduced to nothing.

The sea was getting angry. The turtles nipped at his ankles to try to move him along. They didn't want to be anywhere near the beach when the drugs were picked up. Red foam forced the tide in. The customers were here. The man shat himself—a half-remembered nursery rhyme about the red tide. He always thought the red tide referred to a woman's monthly cycle. His yes men agreed because that is what they did. (He'd found a way out of paying them; slave labour at its finest.)

The turtles found their voices and squeaked. There were words in the squeals but the man couldn't understand them—too high pitched to make any sense. The red tide was the customer. Sea turtles stood before it and the drugs.

Withdrawal was unpleasant, even for microscopic specs of red from a different dimension. Symptoms included diarrhoea, projectile vomiting, and tearing a hole in reality.

The man's mind was already blown and shattered into over a million pieces, left to rot on the beach. Nothing more could be done to him. The red tide viewed this as a challenge and accepted.

The turtles were brushed aside; they wouldn't glow again lying on their backs, not for anyone. The red tide surrounded the man to suck him back into the water. He didn't put up a fight. He didn't know how, not without someone shielding him from reality and scooping his brain back into his head.

There was no plastic in this patch of ocean. All life was dead and floating to the surface, murdered by the red tide on their drug run. This didn't bother the man. Death was part of life; a part he wasn't often exposed to, yet seeing it up close and personal had no impact on him.

His gills returned the moment he was dragged into the water. Deeper he was dragged. Down below, he

discovered all was not dead. It may not have ever been alive. That didn't matter to him. The glow was different to that belonging to the sea turtles.

Eels swimming below, thousands of feet long, belonged with the red tide – the sea turtles were just the drug mules. Gravity in this strange ocean was different, stronger.

He never felt like he was drowning. He could breathe even with the pressure on his chest. The sun was blotted out by something dead floating above him. He looked down.

The sea floor was alive with coral that belonged with the red tide, shooting a creamy white substance into the water above. The red specs that caught it turned pink and bloated in instant pregnancy.

The man remembered a snippet of childhood; his mother, a governess, saying "It was all just a dream." He didn't think this was a dream. He didn't have much of a brain left to think with. It was left behind on the beach. He would never experience thought again.

Creamy white bubbles found their way into his eyes. They drifted into his gills but caused no blockage. An eel wrapped itself around him. Spikes entered his skin. He cried out and received a mouthful of creamy white cum bubbles, red tide and sea water for his efforts.

Up above, something glowed. The turtles were coming to rescue him, diving around dead animals and fish floating to the top. He was their mule. They demanded him back. The red tide was too strong to swim against. Even grouped together as one powerful creature, swimming to the sea floor was impossible. It was easier to tear a hole through reality and come out beneath the coral.

Creamy white bubbles weren't the only things these coral could spew. A sack beneath the cum sack produced an array of things designed to cause pain. Old coral had a selection of fishing hooks from various oceans lapped up and collected through time. Animal skeletons from ancient

beasts could be broken into spears.

The turtles felt the force of these spears puncturing their glow sacks. Luminescent cum was released into the ocean. The man became covered in that too. The ocean did nothing to wash it away.

The turtles did manage to break a hole into the coral. The sea floor wasn't beneath them but a window into the man's own world. He saw his cruise ship on fire and his cruise mates being torn to pieces by sharks. Except that one guy. He seemed a bit odd. Watching him with an erection trying to violate a shark's eye confirmed it. Trouble was, the shark seemed to enjoy it. Shards of plastic floated down into the water. There weren't any small fish left to eat it. Time sped up and everything became sludge. Watching his world crumble, the only thing he missed was his wallet and the power that came with it.

There was no desire for change on his part, unless it was removing the spikes of the eel. He looked up only to see more eels circling above him, some watching him, some watching the window. There weren't any people left in that world for them to hurt. He had hurt many himself, with a little help from his friends (who he would throw under a bus if given a chance).

An eel bit off his toe. What it tasted must have been good because it swallowed it whole. It didn't go back in for a second bite right away. The other eels needed a chance to taste the man. Fairness and all of that. One head-butted him in the shoulder, drawing blood but not attracting any more creatures. They probably didn't notice the blood in the red tide.

With the fracturing of the coral, stones on the sea floor were revealed. An enterprising eel thought these would make a good plug for the man's gills. And they did. It was like the gravel on the bottom of a fish tank clogging a filter. He found he was drowning after all. Not before another eel took off with another of his toes and the few remaining corals spewed more creamy white substance

into the red tide.

It was birth-giving time. Pregnancy didn't last long with the red tide. Slowly at first, then gaining momentum. Red specs burst in an explosion of red pus, leaking tinier red specs into the ocean. The pus and casings of the original pregnant red tide found its way into the man's eyes.

Another toe for another eel. He didn't know what he'd done to deserve this. He'd kept his head down, moving people around like chess pieces just like his peers.

"It's just a dream."

No it fucking wasn't. With a dream, he would have woken up by now in his four poster bed, on an orthopaedic mattress, next to a cheap hooker with blood leaking down her nose.

His few remaining brain cells, the ones that stayed in his head instead of being left to rot on the beach, wanted to shield him from the eels and the drowning and the red tide. There weren't enough of them left to do much good. He didn't treat them very well. They were stuck spending eternity with him. If they could commit suicide before he died, they would be free to join their brothers and sisters on the beach. Collective brain cell suicide would not leave him brain dead. They left behind pain receptors and broken neuro-highways. They'd take away the thoughts and memories of this being just a fucking dream. If it was, he would awaken in a puddle of his own piss next to his cheap hooker. There was no awaking.

The eels had taken away all his toes. They were starting on his feet. They left just enough space free in his gills so he wouldn't drown, only experience the pain of drowning.

Due to the eels not letting him rub his eyes, he had to die without seeing the light that followed. Fire consumed him. If only he could open his eyes, he would have seen an orb of light and an urging to follow.

The eels started on his fingers. They were the fire, but

they weren't. The fire came for the parts of him in their stomachs. More and more of him was lost in various eels but he was still alive.

For a brief moment, he saw the light. He couldn't move towards it though. His eyes were the last to be eaten but the eels had to lap away red tide casings first. First the right eye, then the left eye was swallowed into the stomach of an eel.

The fire found him a few seconds later. He was whole again in the pits below all dimensions. Devils found his brain cells and forced them back into his head via his nose.

Other cruise ship survivors on the island of plastic were afforded a better circle of Hell. All except the shark eye fucker. There was a special place for people like him. But not as special as the Hell in which the man found himself residing.

The devils told him he was special and therefore he must suffer. As centre of the universe, he needed to be chained down and kept so things could return to the way they were.

Fire washed over him every night and was his cereal every waking period. Sometimes his devils looked like turtles, other times they resembled sharks. Eels weren't uncommon either.

Servants would never be able to save him, even if they had the will do so. Video footage of them dancing on a memorial meant to represent his grave were beamed to him on Saturday night movie screenings. No chance of redemption down here. It was small and cramped with offenders of the worst sort on 'all-of-eternity' sentences.

Memories of time spent in cold climates flooded him. He'd hated it then, now he longed to be frozen. It could be arranged, his devils informed him. He declined. Each day, new experimental ways to torture were tested on him.

He still remained himself. There was no escaping that. That was the worst punishment of all.

ROUND NINE
WINNER

HAVE A NICE DAY
MICHAEL NOE

ROUND TEN

CERNUNNOS
DANIEL MARC CHANT

VS

ONE NIGHT OF SLEEP
ESSEL PRATT

CERNUNNOS
DANIEL MARC CHANT

The call that cut short Detective Inspector Lydia Brooks' vacation came in at 0832 hours. There'd been a suspicious death in Saighir Village and they needed her there as soon as possible.

In a way, she was glad. After only a few days, London had already lost its allure. Next time she wanted to go somewhere noisy and expensive, she told herself, she'd go to Beirut. At least there she'd get a tan.

Displaying what she considered a healthy disregard for traffic laws, she arrived at Saighir Village in record time. The sight of its thatched cottages and quaint shops improved her mood to no end. She wasn't even put out at having to stop to allow a mother duck and her brood to cross the road.

Lydia drove on past the Norman church and the village green where a game of cricket was underway and came at last to the scene of the putative crime. Although Cowan Cottage was no bigger than most cottages in the village, its grounds were large enough to incorporate an ornamental

pond and an apple orchard. Five cars were parked in the driveway. Lydia recognized four of them, which presumably meant the fifth belonged to the victim. It was an SUV – the sort of vehicle Lydia despised.

As she pulled into the driveway, a cloud of steam floated up from beneath the hood of her car, causing her heart to sink. She hoped nobody would notice. The last thing she needed was some patronizing flatfoot telling her, 'It's your manifold, love.' So she quickly killed the engine and headed for the front door. It opened just as she reached it.

'Morning, ma'am,' said Sergeant Steele, touching the peak of an imaginary cap. Holding the door open, he stepped aside to allow Lydia in. 'You're going to like this one.'

Lydia couldn't help but give a slight shake of her head. It was the way she reacted nearly every time Steele opened his mouth. Despite knocking on 30, he was inclined to act like a teenager and to make asinine remarks. As usual, his slightly too small uniform was in dire need of being ironed. 'I should be on holiday,' she retorted, her tone making it very clear she wasn't about to like anything. 'Where's the body?'

'This way, ma'am.'

'Stop calling me *ma'am*. I'm a detective inspector—not a bloody school teacher.'

'Yes, ma'am.'

Resisting an urge to kick him where it would hurt most, Lydia followed Steele into the surprisingly spacious living room. It was crawling with policemen in a way that made her think of maggots inhabiting a corpse. 'Anyone who doesn't need to be here—out now. Go on. Scram.'

Making no attempt to hide their resentment, the cops shuffled out, leaving the room to Lydia, Steele and Roger Fleetwood, the police medical examiner.

Fleetwood had made himself at home in an armchair and was busy doing the Times crossword. He waved

315

Daniel Marc Chant

briefly to acknowledge Lydia's presence then carried on as if he were at home.

Lydia cast a quick eye around the room. It was expensively furnished, mostly with antiques. A large television and a stereo system seemed to be the only concessions to modernity.

The first thing that caught her interest was a skull—clearly not human—sitting on the oak desk next to a small forest of empty beer bottles. She was about to make a comment about it when she noticed the pile of ashes on the chair in front of the skull. A crate of beer on the floor beside the chair obscured her view of something she could just about see the edge of. Closing in, she found herself looking at a slipper full of ashes.

Sergeant Steele wore a smug expression. Lydia knew he was dying to say *I told you you were going to like this one*, so she quickly treated him to a look that said, *Don't you dare*.

Steele took the hint and said, 'Meet the late Donald Haig. Male, Caucasian. Mid-50s. Weight: approximately 140 pounds. Height: just under 6 foot. Hair: grey.'

Despite herself, Lydia was almost impressed. 'You can tell all that from a pile of ashes?'

'From CCTV footage. There are cameras on the roof. They show Mr Haig entering the cottage and nobody coming out. Ergo: this must be Mr Haig.'

'What happened to him?'

Roger Fleetwood looked up from his crossword, scratched the side of his nose with his biro and said, 'Spontaneous human combustion.'

On the last day of his life, Donald Haig went for a walk in the woods. His therapist had promised it would do him a world of good, both physically and mentally, but he wasn't in it for his health. He'd moved to Saighir Village with the intention of becoming a country squire and had a notion that going for long walks was part of that particular lifestyle. So every day, he'd spend an hour or two traipsing

around the countryside in his tweed jacket and matching cap.

As he came to a small stream, he had a feeling of being watched. It brought about a momentary attack of paranoia that caused him to duck and almost run for cover. But the feeling quickly passed and he laughed inwardly at himself. What was he thinking? That he was about to be torn apart by a lion? Here in the English countryside where the most vicious thing he was likely to encounter was a mosquito?

The snapping of a twig caused him to turn his head. Brown eyes regarded him through the foliage. They were inquisitive, intelligent, and seemed to be asking him what he was doing in the wood. Although they showed no hint of belligerence, he would not have called them gentle. Rather they seemed to be the eyes of something that wanted no trouble but knew how to deal with it should it have to.

The stag stepped out of the undergrowth. Impressed with its majesty and strength, Haig turned slowly, careful to show he presented no threat. This was as close as he'd been to a wild creature in a long time and he was as thrilled as he was wary.

He couldn't help himself. The predatory instincts that had made him a successful stockbroker caused him to point an imaginary rifle at the stag. Closing one eye, he aimed for the creature's forehead and squeezed his trigger. 'Kapow!'

The stag blinked. A look of disdain seemed to settle on the creature's face as it moved on, leaving the path and disappearing back into the undergrowth.

Haig felt cheated. If he'd had a real gun, he would now be the proud owner of a genuine – albeit illegal – hunting trophy.

For a brief moment, he contemplated buying a shotgun and going after the stag, but a better idea occurred to him. He would buy a stag's head and hang it on his wall. And if anyone asked if he'd killed the beast himself, he

317

would look them in the eye and say *yes*.

'Spontaneous human combustion?' Lydia snorted her contempt.

'It's where a person bursts into flames with no apparent reason,' said Roger Fleetwood, putting aside his newspaper and lifting himself out of his chair.

'I know what it is, thank you very much. I also know there's no such bloody thing.'

'And yet here it is.' Fleetwood walked up to Lydia and put on a pair of half-rim glasses. He squinted at the chair. 'To reduce a human body to ashes like this takes a temperature close to 3,000 degrees centigrade. And yet the chair our incinerated pal was sitting in has one or two minor scorch marks and that's it. From which we can conclude that whatever caused Mr Haig to turn into a human bonfire came from within rather than without.'

'Assuming this *is* Mr Haig. How can we be certain these ashes are even human?'

'Right now, we can't. We'll know for sure once we've run some tests.'

Lydia turned to Sergeant Steele. 'I want this cottage searched thoroughly.'

'Already been done.'

'Then do it again. And this time look out for secret passages, priest holes or anywhere else Donald bloody Haig might be hiding. If he's making a fool of us, he's going to regret it big time.'

With a shrug, Steele left the room and began shouting orders to have the cottage gone over with the proverbial fine-tooth comb.

Lydia turned her attention to the skull. 'What's this?'

'A skull,' said Fleetwood.

'I can see that. But the skull of what?'

'A stag, if I'm not very much mistaken. Minus the antlers, of course.'

'So what's it doing sitting on this desk?'

'You're the detective. You tell me.'

The shop was small and dingy. It smelt of damp, dust and other things Donald Haig didn't much care for. Since moving to Saighir Village, he'd passed it just about every day without giving it much thought. According to the sign over the doorway, it was an antiques emporium, but Haig had it marked down as an overpriced junk shop and would never have set foot in it but for his encounter with the stag.

A quick glance around the gloomy interior was almost enough to make him walk right out again. The place was filled with old furniture that had seen better days and curios that no one in their right mind would wish to purchase.

A picture on the wall caught his attention. It was an oil painting of folk in peasant garb performing what was clearly a pagan rite of some sort. They were gathered in a woodland clearing, dancing around a fire in front of which stood an effigy that appeared to be made of twigs and bones held together with tar.

What fascinated Haig about the picture was what the effigy was wearing on its head: a skull replete with antlers.

'May I help you?'

The voice startled Haig. He hadn't seen its owner – an old man wearing a velvet smoking jacket – come in.

The old man stood behind the counter looking every bit as much an antique as anything in the shop. 'Are you interested in purchasing that painting? I can do you a very good deal.'

'Actually,' said Haig, 'I'm looking for a stag skull.'

'You are?' The old man seemed surprised. 'I'm afraid I can't help you on that one.'

'Oh, well. It was a long shot.' Haig decided to leave before the old man tried foisting on him something he didn't want. As he headed for the door, he came upon a glass cabinet. Its contents stopped him in his tracks.

'What's that?'

'That?' said the old man, without even looking. 'That's just junk. I've been meaning to throw it out.'

'Looks like a stag skull to me.'

'Perhaps it is, but without the antlers it's worthless.'

'I'll take it.'

'I'm afraid it's not for sale.'

'A hundred quid.'

'I beg your pardon?'

'You heard. A ton.'

'As I say: it's not for sale. Not at any price.'

'I'm offering you a lot of money for something you just said is worthless.'

The old man shrugged his boney shoulders and went up in Haig's estimation. No stranger to haggling, he knew when he was being played and right now he was being played as well as he'd ever been. Common sense dictated that he leave the shop immediately and track down what he wanted elsewhere, but he was in no mood for rationality. If he wanted something badly enough, he was always prepared to pay over the odds, and right now he wanted the skull in the glass case as badly as an addict needs cocaine.

He held up his arm and pulled back the sleeve of his jacket. 'You see this watch?'

'Not from here.'

Haig marched up to the counter. 'See it now?'

The old man bent forward. 'Vintage Rolex. Do you mind if I...?' He placed his ear to the watch. 'Oh, yes. That's the real thing all right.'

'Of course it's the real thing.' Haig deftly removed the watch and dangled it in front of the shopkeeper's face. 'Yours for that skull.'

Haig was pleased with himself. The fact that he'd paid way too much for the skull didn't bother him in the least. He'd got what he wanted and there were plenty more Rolexes in

the world.

There was, in his book, only one thing to do after closing a deal like this, and that was to celebrate. In the past, that would have involved cocaine and other illegal substances, but not anymore. Having seen many of his colleagues destroyed by drugs, it was a source of constant amazement to him that he'd made it to the end of his career without suffering the same fate.

I am one lucky bugger, he told himself as he placed the skull on the table in his living room. *Seems like I can get away with anything.*

With narcotics being off the menu, he went to the kitchen and brought back a crate of Old Growler Premium Bitter, a local beer he'd started drinking as part of his drive to fit in.

The two pubs in the village served Old Growler and whenever he went into one of them he made sure the locals saw him drinking it. He didn't want them to see him as some ponce from the City flouncing around with his fancy City ways. The sooner they accepted him as one as their own, the better.

So he drank Old Growler despite the fact he didn't really like the stuff. It had far too much flavour for his taste, but he was determined to get used to it.

Sitting down at the table, he aimed a remote control at his state of the art stereo system and hit the on button. His flat screen television came to life and offered him a menu of over a thousand acts starting at Aerosmith and ending with ZZ Top. Now what was it to be? He fancied something retro, something that had stood the test of time and was unarguably classic. The Beatles? No. Too obvious. Chuck Berry? Getting closer.

'David Bowie,' he decided and almost instantly changed his mind. Instead he selected the Rolling Stones and what he considered their greatest album—*Beggar's Banquet*. As the opening strains of "Sympathy for the Devil" issued from telephone box-sized speakers standing like sentinels

either side of the ornamental fire place, a sense of almost transcendental calm descended on Haig.

He took a gold plated bottle opener from his pocket, grabbed a bottle of Old Growler and opened it. *Life*, he told himself, *doesn't get any better than this.*

Sergeant Steele ambled back into the living room. 'There's some old geezer outside. Says that there skull belongs to him and he'd quite like it back.'

'Oh, does he?' Lydia felt her hackles rise. 'Tell him to fill out a claim form at the nick. Right now, that skull's not going anywhere.'

'He also says there's a curse attached to the skull.'

'That's all I bloody need.' Lydia pictured the headline in tomorrow's Saighir Chronicle: *Village Resident Struck Down by Ancient Curse.* Somewhere in the story, her name would almost certainly crop up, leaving everyone to assume she believed in the curse. Something similar had happened when she'd investigated a so-called Satanic blood sacrifice which turned out to be a pigeon killed by a fox; she wasn't about to let it happen again. 'An old man, you say?'

'He didn't give his name. Says he owns the antiques shop down Southside Road.'

'I suppose I'd better go talk to him then.'

By the time Haig had finished his second bottle of Old Growler, he'd decided it was the perfect accompaniment to the Rolling Stones. After all, what could possibly be more English than the Rolling Stones and beer the colour of ditch water served at room temperature?

With a satisfied belch, he cracked open a fresh bottle and poured it into his glass. As he did so, it occurred to him that the deer skull was a better, more fitting drinking receptacle. Isn't that what big game hunters did? Drink a celebratory drink from their victim's skulls?

As much as the idea appealed to him, he decided to forego the pleasure for now. Before his lips went anywhere

near the skull, he was going to have it thoroughly disinfected. Then he was going to invite friends around and have them drink from the skull as a way of acknowledging kinship.

Friends? He chuckled at the thought. What friends? Before he became a stockbroker, he'd had quite a few friends, mostly old school chums he'd known for half his life. But as their lives diverged and they all settled down to mediocrity while he made a name for himself in the City, he'd cast them adrift one by one almost without noticing, and replaced them with a different kind of friend.

By the time he started thinking about getting out of the rat race, he had friends galore. Friends at the office. Friends in business. Friends in the City. Friends eager to spend his money and abuse his hospitality and stab him in the back for the sake of a quick buck.

When he announced his retirement, they threw him a lavish party, shook his hand, thanked him for this and that, and told him not to be a stranger. They reacted with enthusiasm when he invited them to visit him in Saighir Village any time they liked. 'We'll be down as soon as we can,' they lied. 'We'd hate to lose touch.'

And that was it.

No phone calls. No emails. Not so much as a card on his birthday.

'Bunch of bastards.' He took a healthy swig of Old Growler. Smacking his lips, he wondered why he hadn't gotten into real ale before now. So much better than that gassy piss-water called lager.

He decided to get drunk.

'The skull,' said the shopkeeper, 'is older than you think. It belonged to the Druids who lived here in the days before the Romans came. That was a time when the people lived peacefully and in accordance with Nature.'

'I don't give a flying monkey's how old it is,' Lydia responded. Now she was outside with fresh air in her

lungs, she realised how unpleasant the air inside the cottage had been, carrying with it as it did the faintest hint of compost and stagnant water. 'The skull is part of an on-going police investigation. When we're done with it, we'll see it's returned to its rightful owner.'

'I advise you, dear lady, to hand it over before it harms anyone else.'

'And I advise you to get lost before I stick some handcuffs on you.'

'Please. I implore you. You don't know what you're dealing with here.'

Lydia's stomach grumbled, reminding her that she'd skipped breakfast. 'You have ten seconds to get off this property before I arrest you.'

'Very well,' said the shopkeeper. 'I've tried to warn you. What follows is on your own head. May the gods have mercy on you.'

When *Beggar's Banquet* finished playing, Haig decided on a bit of Bowie after all. Although he considered *The Rise and Fall of Ziggy Stardust and the Spiders from Mars* to be a seminal work of art, he much preferred *Aladdin Sane*, the album that came after it. Critics and fans alike seemed to regard *Aladdin Sane* as being slightly inferior to *Ziggy Stardust*, but so what? When they had a music system like his, then they could voice an opinion. Until then they could kiss his rich, successful butt.

As the intro to "Watch that Man" kicked in, he allowed himself to fantasise that Bowie was singing about him and for him. Donald Haig might be retired, but he wasn't about to go away. If the people of Saighir Village didn't want to embrace him, that was their lookout.

For a while, he'd thought about abandoning his plan to buy the whole village and turn it into a holiday resort for the rich and selfish. But the way he'd been treated since arriving had strengthened his resolve. Buying Cowan Cottage had proven easier—and cheaper—than he'd

expected, and he could see no reason why he couldn't acquire the rest of the village within year.

Of course, the villagers would fight him tooth and nail, but he knew how to deal with people who got in his way.

'Bloody yokels. They'll be better off in tower blocks. This place ought to belong to people who appreciate the finer things in life.'

The room swayed gently. Haig gripped the edge of the table and grinned. The beer was going to his head and he liked the sensation. In the past he'd tried all sorts of chemical aids to help him relax and feel happy, but nothing compared to a bottle or two of Old Growler.

He pushed at the stag skull with his finger, causing it to spin a couple of times before coming to a wobbly stop. Tomorrow he would hire a craftsmen to mount it on a suitable base and attach it to the wall.

For want of anything better to do while he got drunk listening to David Bowie, he tipped some beer from his glass into the skull. There was a slight hiss as the froth settled to expose the bronze liquid beneath. The winking lights of his stereo system were reflected on the surface of the beer, allowing him to fancy he was looking into a pool full of nymphs or whatever it was that lived in water and glowed.

The level of the beer dropped noticeably. Haig put his hand on the table, expecting it to land in a puddle of ale.

The table was dry.

He leaned forward and tried to work out where the beer was going. There was no sign of it reaching the table and the outside of the skull looked and felt dry.

Soon there was no beer in the skull. He ran his fingertips over the inside of the cranium and noted with wry amusement that it was *as dry as a bone.*

'Well, blow me down.' The skull must have absorbed the beer, leaving behind not a single trace. He couldn't see how such a thing was possible, but then he'd never claimed to be a scientist.

The skull went out of focus. He blinked and it came back into focus surrounded by a haze of light.

Being no stranger to intoxication, the sight neither alarmed nor perturbed him. After so much beer, it was to be expected and a sure sign he was having a good time. Feeling suddenly playful, he turned the skull right side up and leaned forward to whisper in the hole that had once been its ear. 'You and me, buddy: we're going to take over the world.'

He leaned back and stared at the eye sockets. They seemed to stare back with unexpected malevolence. Beyond them lay shadow which seemed to pulsate as if crawling with thousands of tiny organisms. And though he thought it unlikely, he was certain he could make out his reflection in the darkness.

Some perverse inner compulsion made him want to dip his fingers into the shadow, but he was forestalled by a sudden dread. As his hand hovered over the skull, the shadow shifted and begin to ooze out of the sockets and drip down onto the table.

It was at that point that he decided he'd had quite enough to drink. Maybe if he'd thought to eat before going on his binge, he'd be all right. Now it would be all he could do to make it to the sofa to sleep off the Old Growler.

'Enough!' he cried, slamming his bottle onto the table. He tried to stand but his legs failed him. 'Bugger.'

The darkness kept pouring from the eye sockets. It seeped beneath the skull, pushing it ever upwards, forming a black column about two feet wide. Haig recalled a film he'd seen in a biology class many years ago. It was a time lapse recording of slime mould, which (if memory served) was a mass of single celled organisms that would from time to time come together to form a multicellular structure.

Was that what he was seeing now? Billions of microbes acting as one? It was as close as he could get to a rational explanation and he determined to hang on to it for

as long as he could.

When the column had risen high enough for the skull to be almost touching the ceiling, it stopped its upwards progress and grew outwards to twice its width. For a while, it quivered like a jelly, causing Haig to fear that the ungainly edifice was about to collapse on top of him. But it held firm and became still.

As Haig studied it, he was forced to discard his slime mould hypothesis, for the black mass was filled with what looked like random junk. As well as twigs, leafs, moss and tree bark, he could make out bones, teeth, ears, lips, veins and a host of other animal organs.

With a plop that made Haig picture a champagne bottle being de-corked, the column sprouted appendages near its apex. They protruded horizontally like branches on a tree. Five small columns germinated from the end of the appendages. As he formed the thought that the smaller appendages looked like fingers, the ones that might be branches bent upwards at right angles then flopped down to dangle at the sides of the column.

With another plop, the column's lower half split and moulded itself into two legs.

Haig's mind flipped back to the picture in the antiques shop and the effigy in front of the fire. It seemed the damn thing had found its way into his cosy cottage and was standing on his table. All that was missing were—

'Damn!' Haig was more annoyed than surprised to see a pair of antlers suddenly blossom from the skull. All he wanted was a few hours listening to music and abusing his liver, and what did he get? A bloody tar monster! Angrily, he jumped to his feet and gave the monster a mighty push which had no effect whatsoever.

As he sat back down, a voice spoke to him. 'Mortal, why doest thou disturb my rest?'

Haig looked up at the skull. His heart seemed to come to a juddering halt; for a long moment, he was unable to breathe. Things were getting out of hand, and for a control

freak that was close to intolerable. *It's an hallucination*, he told himself. *Your brain conjured it up; your brain can make it go away.*

His heart leapt back into action and he was able to breathe again. As he exhaled, he pointed a trembling finger at the apparition and said, 'Get lost, you abomination!'

The tar monster shimmered. Haig sensed anger and contempt radiating towards him, and he immediately regretted opening his mouth.

'Freak?' Putting his hands on his hips and bending down like an adult confronting a naughty child, the tar monster spoke in measured tones. 'Hold thy tongue, mortal, lest I rip it from your mouth.'

Haig swallowed hard. He wanted to tell his unwanted guest to go to Hell, but the very thought of what might follow caused his stomach to contract. As much as he believed he was being threatened by a figment of his own imagination, there was a part of him that wasn't so sure.

Straightening up, the tar monster looked around the room. 'This be Joseph Wyatt's abode.'

'No.' The single syllable escaped Haig's lips as a coarse whisper. 'Mine.'

'Aye. That it might be, Joseph Wyatt being dead one hundred winters or more. Thee then must be the current master of Cowan Cottage.' The tar monster paused in expectation of a response which, due to his mouth being dry, Haig was unable to supply. Losing patience, the apparition roared, 'Speak, mortal!'

'Yes,' Haig squeaked. He took a quick swig of Old Growler and found his voice and his courage once more. 'I am Donald Haig. Who the hell are you?'

'I am that which I was and will always be. Throughout the centuries, I have had many names. When your ancestors lived in caves, I was known as the Monarch of the Hunt. When they learnt to farm the land, they called me the Spirit of the Harvest. These days, I am most commonly addressed as Cernunnos.'

'So what are you? A god?'

'To those who wouldst have me as a god, a god I am.'

'You think a lot of yourself, don't you?'

'In the presence of one such as thyself, why wouldn't I? Thy life is but a blink of an eye to me. I roamed this land in the days before Man and I here I shalt be when thee and thy kind are but a memory.'

'Is that meant to impress me? Because I have to tell you, it ain't working, pal.' Feeling a surge of machismo, Haig opened a fresh bottle of Old Growler with his teeth and spat the top at Cernunnos. It disappeared into the creature's leg. 'I've had enough of this. I'm going to bed.' Haig got to his feet and felt the floor shift beneath him. With one hand resting on the back of the chair, he stood still until he was sure of his balance. When he was half certain he could at least make it to the door without falling over, he began the short but hazardous journey, laboriously placing each step with the greatest of care.

'Thou shalt stay,' said Cernunnos. Though his tone was soft, it conveyed all manner of threats. 'We are not done yet.'

'Wanna bet?' Hands at the ready to catch himself should he fall, Haig took another step and was preparing for yet another when he was arrested by a sound that reminded him of the rustling of autumn leaves. Something dark flowed from beneath the skirting board on all sides of the room. It crept towards him, a sphincter of menace constricting around his feet.

Instinctively he kicked out at whatever it was. It momentarily retreated before coming back at him amidst a fluttering of wings.

Aghast, he realised he was surrounded by cockroaches.

Bile rose in his throat. There was nothing on God's earth he hated more than cockroaches and the germs they carried.

Well, they weren't going to stop him going to bed. In fact, he relished the thought of walking across them,

crushing their vile bodies beneath his feet.

Determinedly, he started for the door again. As he raised his foot, a legion of cockroaches rose up before him, but could not shake his resolve. He swatted at the creatures and took a step forward.

The cockroaches attacked. They were suddenly all over him, crawling up his arms and over his face. He spat some from his lips, snorted a few from his nostrils. He felt them creeping into his ears and down the front of his trousers.

Brushing frantically at his face, he was unable to stop them covering his eyes. He grabbed a fistful and squeezed the life out of a dozen of them.

He staggered back. His leg brushed against the chair and the next thing he knew he was sitting down and the cockroaches were retreating, dropping from his body and scurrying back to the skirting boards. Haig had no doubt they'd be back should he attempt to leave the room again.

'Ah, yes,' said Cernunnos. 'Thy ancestors had another name for me: Lord of the Cockroaches.'

Haig shivered as a fever came upon him and recognised that he was in shock and might very well faint. 'What do you want from me?'

'That which is mine to take.'

'The cockroaches? They're all yours. You can have them and all the other creepy-crawlies in this dump. First chance I get, I'm having this place fumigated.'

'Like many of thy kind, thou knowest not of that which matters. Greed is thy master. In its name, thou wouldst destroy that which is good, that which is right and in accordance with nature.

'I see what lies in thy mind. It is filled with dark thoughts and hatred. Thou wouldst take this village from its rightful owners. You wouldst destroy that which generations have built and fought for.

'I am Cernunnos, Monarch of the Hunt, Spirit of the Harvest, Lord of the Cockroaches, Defender of Saighir. And you, Donald Haig, are no more!'

Haig's fever intensified. Heat radiated from his abdomen and raced through his veins. He could smell burning meat but wouldn't—couldn't—admit it had anything to do with him. A whiff of smoke spiraled from his nostrils.

Searing pain ripped through him, forcing a scream from his lips. With the scream came fire. It gushed from his mouth, ensuring that the last thing he saw in this world was the means of his destruction. A moment later, his eyeballs exploded.

Flames erupted from all his pores and orifices. Despite his torment, he did not move. His muscles were turning first to liquid and then to smoke. For a moment that seemed eternal, Donald Haig was deaf, blind and in the grip of an all-consuming agony.

Cernunnos was merciful. With a gesture of his hand, he granted Haig the gift of death. Then he let go of his earthly countenance and flowed back into the skull where he would sleep until he was called upon once more.

Lydia decided she'd seen enough. 'Bag everything up and let's get out of here before the peasants surround the place and try to burn it down.'

'Ma'am?' Sergeant Steele looked at her blankly.

'I think,' said Roger Fleetwood, popping a mint into his mouth, 'Detective Inspector Brooks is inferring that the people of Saighir Village are an ignorant bunch of superstitious yokels.'

'But I'm from Saighir Village. And my folks before me. And my folks before them.'

'Which rather eloquently puts paid to the Inspector's hypothesis. Doesn't it, Inspector?'

'Sure,' said Lydia, thinking that if ever there was a prime example of the sort of hick she had in mind, he was standing right in front of her with three stripes on his arm.

A constable walked in carrying a small, cordless vacuum cleaner. He proffered it to Fleetwood.

'And what,' asked the medical examiner, 'do you expect me to do with that?'

'Dunno, sir. I was told to fetch a vacuum cleaner for you.'

'Do you know how to use it?'

'Of course.'

'Good.' Fleetwood nodded in the direction of the ashes that had once been Donald Haig. 'Try not to leave anything behind.'

Lydia enjoyed watching the constable's face as he got to grips with what was being asked of him. A hint of a grin suggested he thought he was having a joke played on him, but the grin quickly vanished to be replaced by a look of near-panic. He turned to Lydia in the hope that she would spare him.

'When you've done that,' she said, putting on her best poker face, 'my car could do with a clean.'

As the constable set about his unpleasant task, Lydia found her gaze being drawn to the skull—specifically to its empty eye sockets. It made her think how she would look—with luck many years hence—when Death had claimed her and her flesh had gone the way of all things. She hoped her end would be more dignified that the late Mr Haig's.

As happens when someone stares at something too long, Lydia's eyes lost their focus. The skull now appeared as two dark patches floating in a mist. Everything else around her vanished.

She watched as the patches seemed to melt and trickle onto the table where they coalesced and formed a pool of absolute darkness. Amused by the tricks her eyes were playing on her, she fought an urge to blink and spoil the illusion.

Somebody screamed.

Lydia snapped out of her reverie as the constable drop the vacuum cleaner and leapt away from the table.

Roger Fleetwood and Sergeant Steele both had a hand

over their mouths and were staring at the skull. Or rather they were staring at the tar-like substance that had filled the skull and was now pouring onto the table.

'knew he's be back. knew he's knew he'd be back.'

ONE NIGHT OF SLEEP
ESSEL PRATT

The full moon's glow glared through a part in the bedroom curtains, sending a sliver of iridescence across Marc's closed eyes. A slight irritation to his soporific slumber, he rolled over to face the center of the bed while draping an arm across his partner. The pair shuffled under the sheets as their bodies warmed in peaceful slumber. Their minds settled in dreamy relaxation, the two became one in a tender embrace as the night's decree ushered serene respite. The cool night and plush bedspreads cradled them in comfort, ensuring nothing would disturb them until morning's light welcomed them to a new day.

As the clock's faint glow showed 10:37, much earlier than a normal night's sleep, the day's hectic chores of yard work and the construction of an outdoor dog pen for their Chihuahua, Scottie, exhausted them to an early slumber. The promise of a quiet night in each other's arms, holding their bodies close, was worth it all.

"Arr, arr, arroooo!" Scottie's high pitch howl cut through the silence like fingernails on a chalkboard.

In unison, the couple shifted their bodies and wedged their heads underneath the luxury down pillows.

"Aroooooooooooooo..." Scottie howled nonstop, barely pausing to take a breath.

"Holy hell, Daniel, you have to do something about that damn dog."

"Christ," said Daniel. "I'm sorry, Marc, I really thought keeping him outside would at least buffer his howls so we could get some sleep."

Marc sat up in bed, glaring at Daniel in the darkness before turning on the light.

"You need to do something," said Marc. "I cannot keep doing this. Every damn night that little disgrace for a dog howls from moonrise to sunrise, non-stop. I can't keep staying up all night long. I'm going to lose my mind."

Daniel rolled over to his back, looking up at Marc. He could see the weariness in the dark circles beneath his baby blues. Propping himself up onto his elbows, Daniel closed his eyes and let his head fall back into the wall, knowing that neither of them had a full night's sleep since adopting Scottie a month prior. They tried everything they could think of to keep him quiet: draping a blanket over his crate, constricting him with a muzzle overnight, surrounding the dog cage with pillows, and finally keeping him in a pen outside overnight. Nothing could muffle the incessant howls that returned each and every night.

"I don't know what to do," said Daniel. "We've tried everything. I want it to stop as much as you do, I really do."

"Then do something, tonight," said Marc. "I don't care what you do, just make that dog shut up."

"Honey," said Daniel. "I will sell that dog's soul to the devil for one night of restful sleep; I'll do it right now. I don't have a clue what else to do."

There was a brief silence in between the howls as Scottie caught his breathe, before continuing again. "Arr, arr, aroooooooo!"

"Go dump him in the woods while I sleep," said Marc. "Maybe a night outside in the wild will do him some good. If he doesn't get eaten by a wolf or coyote, maybe he'll find his way home and learn to respect our sleep patterns."

Daniel glared over at Marc with his head cocked to the side. "You want me to take him out in the woods and just drop him off?"

"Honestly," said Marc. "I really don't care anymore; throw the little fucker off a cliff for all I care."

"You know what?" asked Daniel. "Fuck it, I'll do it. We've taken him out there plenty of times during the day, I'm sure he'll find his way home in the morning."

Daniel twisted his legs off the side of the bed and grabbed his shorts from the armchair to his right, slipping them on over his loose boxers before putting on his tennis shoes. Before he could stand, Marc already turned off the light and clutched the pillow tightly over his head, ready for the howling to stop.

Daniel crept out of the bedroom door and down the stairs. The high-pitch howl of Scottie's voice ripped through his eardrums, dulling any doubt that he was doing the right thing. He hurried his pace, nearly tripping over the last step as he turned toward the kitchen, following the memorized path around the table and stepping over the paisley rug that always bunched up in front of the back door.

Fumbling with the lock in the dark, Daniel reached his left hand over and grabbed his car keys from the hook on the wall. The knob had a habit of sticking and it took some fidgeting to open it in the dark. He was determined to quiet the little mutt outside; allowing his frustration to use a little extra force to coerce it open. It only took a few seconds, but seemed much longer.

He stepped out onto the patio, the cool air sending a chill down the back of his neck, and hastened his pace over to Scottie's brand new kennel. The high pitch howling

didn't stop until Daniel descended the stairs and turned the corner, his eyes meeting Scottie's under the full moon's glow.

"Damn dog," Daniel grunted as Scottie looked up at him with his big brown eyes. "All we asked for is one night of sleep. One fucking night. Instead, you have to be a little bitch."

Scottie remained seated, his tail wagging from side to side and his mouth agape as though he was smiling at Daniel's arrival.

Daniel unlatched the kennel gate and reached down with both hands to pick Scottie up. He slipped in the wet grass, catching himself before falling as a sharp pain surged through his back. "Fucking dog, I hope you rot in hell for all the damn trouble you've caused. The devil can have your soul and fuck you over for eternity."

In the car, Scottie sat impatiently in the passenger seat as Daniel backed out of the driveway. He enjoyed car rides to the woods and loved to run about in the underbrush while chasing butterflies and bees. Going out at night was a new experience, but the full moon made it seem like a dark dawn. Daniel looked over at him, anger fed by sleeplessness surged through him, ready to dispose of the damned pup and get back home to sleep.

The unpaved dirt road was bumpy, tossing Scottie in his seat, nearly knocking him to the floor on multiple occasions. Despite the wooded area being only half a mile up the road, it seemed to take an eternity to arrive at the regular location. Daniel could have sworn it took longer to drive there than it did to walk.

When he arrived, Daniel wasted no time to exit the car as he grabbed Scottie and carried him about ten feet into the woods. In the face of the full moon, the area was quite dark, concealing fallen branches and holes dug by various critters. Daniel was careful not to fall and hurt himself, his back was still sore from nearly slipping in the

back yard. The last thing he wanted was to fall in the woods, in the middle of the night, with no one to come to his rescue until morning. Rather than go in too deep, he decided to ditch Scottie where an old oak had fallen and the stump still stood in remembrance of its once regal majesty.

The spot seemed better than any other around and he really didn't want to waste time pondering locations for fear he would change his mind. As quickly as he arrived, he plopped Scottie onto the soft soil and whisked him onward to play. He waited a moment to ensure the little dog was preoccupied, before leaving, hoping it wouldn't follow.

He was quick to return to the car, turn the ignition, and perform a U-turn to make his way home. The moon's glow seemed brighter than on the way out, almost blinding in the darkness. It was quite mesmerizing and he took his attention off the road for a second or two, just enough time for him not to notice the large deer at the side of the road until it jumped in front of his car, causing him to swerve to the right and smash right into a large tree.

The impact set off the airbag, hitting his face hard enough to cause a broken nose and send a horrific pain down his back where he twisted it just prior to making the journey. Pain rushed through his body. The pain was so great, he was afraid to move at first, unsure if he needed immediate medical attention or mot. On instinct, he reached to his left pocket for his phone, realizing he left it on the nightstand at home.

With no way to contact Marc at home, he had no choice but to try and walk the rest of the way. His head was fuzzy from the impact and pain surged through his muscles, but with caution, he managed to emerge from the wreckage without dropping to the ground in despair. Other than his back, he didn't seem to be harmed much at all.

Hunched, he held on to the car and surveyed the

damage. The car was totaled. Anxiety filled his head as pressure filled his chest; wondering how Marc was going to react. They just purchased the car a month prior, right about the time Scottie came to live with them. He tried not to focus on the insurance claims and Marc's reaction, though. He looked up the road toward home. The ditch on either side of the road would make it difficult to hold on to the trees as he hobbled homeward, and creeping down the middle of the road was not an option. He figured he might as well begin the journey, hoping the trek wouldn't take too long.

Maneuvering down the ditch in front of his car was difficult as the wet grass left little grip for his shoes to remain firm on the ground. Making his way up the other side with the back pain fighting his every movement was even more difficult, but he managed to make it and rest against a young mulberry tree. He tried to catch his breath, its ghostly expulsion dancing in the cool air, reminding him of youth and summers camping with his father. He longed for the comfort of his father at his side, wishing he was there at that moment.

Just as he was ready to begin his journey onward, a creature on the other side of the road exploded with a deep growl, its hum rustling the leaves low to the ground. Daniel glanced in the sound's direction, hopeful his mind was playing tricks on him, only to see two beady red eyes glowing under the moon's embrace. The creature's breath erupted from within the low vegetation, the eyes moving forward an inch or two as a deeper, more hungered growl warned of its impending attack.

Without much thought, Daniel immediately ran into the woods, questioning why he didn't just get back into the car for safety. His hunched back and gimpy gait made the escape difficult as he traversed fallen trees and soft soil under his feet. He didn't look back though, and focused instead on escaping whatever beast approached, hoping, whether wolf of coyote, it would have mercy on his injured

soul.

Cracking twigs and rustling leaves let him know that the creature was approaching with haste. Daniel continued onward, the pain slowing him down with each step, hopeful that something smaller might grab the creature's attention and veer it toward a more familiar snack. Nothing else made a noise in the darkness, under the thick canopy, so Daniel traversed onward, finding his way into a moonlit clearing.

Daniel dropped to his knees, propping himself up with his arms until they began to violently shake and his body collapsed onto the ground. He was helpless; his only hope was for the creature to lose interest and leave him be until morning when Marc came looking for him.

Daniel looked into the trees, hoping to identify the creature. Its eyes glared back at him, staring him down, refusing to show itself. To his left, another deep growl signaled its presence, to the right, another did the same. Behind him, a much deeper howl yelled into the night, sending shivers down his back as he struggled to stand, only to fall to his back, helpless to defend himself.

The four creatures emerged from the trees, revealing their identity as massive wolves with fur as dark as the night sky. Each approached one step at a time, deep growls conducting the night's eerie symphony. Daniel wanted to scream for help, yell at the beasts to get away, but nothing came from his throat. He was helpless to defend himself in any way.

The wolves were at his side in no time, each standing above him, their drool spilling onto his exposed flesh. The warmth was foreboding as its gooey damnation stuck to his skin like honey. As they stood, waiting for the unknown, another creature snapped a twig in the brush line. Each of the wolves glanced in its direction, as if awaiting orders. The air was silent, all but Daniel's labored breath, until two consecutive scratches within the ground's brittle leaves cut through the air. In an instant, two of the

wolves bit down into his ankles while the other two clasped onto his wrists, securing him into place with no room to move. Their quick action caused his spine to lurch and he thought he heard it snap as the pain from waist down ceased to irritate him, while the waist up felt as though it was on fire.

He fought the urge to pass out from the pain, anxious to see what beast could summon the will of the wolves and coerce them to hold him in place while he writhed in agony under the strain of their clutches. His head turned toward the noise, and he strained his eyes to catch a glimpse of the beast.

The creature wasted no time revealing itself. Scottie the Chihuahua emerged from the bushes and sulked toward Daniel. His eyes glowed hellish red as he traipsed upon his four stick legs, his mouth agape with the farce of a smile. His little body approaching with haste.

Daniel tried to apologize to Scottie, hoping to stop the torture, almost hoping it was a dream.

"Scottie, here boy," he said. "I was only playing hide and seek, I didn't mean any harm. Let's go home and snuggle in bed."

As he spoke, Scottie jumped up onto Daniel's chest. His breath was as warm as the flames of hell, his drool burnt like acid upon the bare flesh.

"Please," begged Daniel. "This is all Marc's fault, don't hurt me. I'll take you home and you can let him know you are angry. I'll even let you sleep in the bed."

Scottie cocked his head to the side, as though he could comprehend what was said, contemplating his decision. Then, without warning, Scottie opened his mouth nearly three times as wide as it should, and bit down upon Daniel's neck, ripping his throat out in a bloody explosion, as his jugular severed and let loose a red sea of death.

In unison, the wolves released their grasp and howled to the heavens, cheering for the demise of Daniel and the inaugural kill of their new master. Their praise echoed

through the woods, waking the fauna that slept peacefully under the night's cover, and sending those that scavenged for food to seek shelter away from the hellish sacrifice.

Up in the bedroom, Marc slept peacefully in the silence of the night. Sprawled out in the bed, he was having the best sleep he had in a long time. His body numb in relaxation, he allowed the memory foam mattress to accept his body into its warm hug. Not quite asleep, his awareness of the peace and quiet was comforting.

As he felt sleep coming on, he decided to thank Daniel with extra snuggles when he returned. Rolling to his side, from his back, facing the window, he allowed his eyes to glance up at the moon one final time before surrendering to sleep. The brightness seemed to dim a bit, creating a sense of calm within the room, until the victory howls of the hunting wolves pierced the quiet and echoed within the room.

"Fuck!" yelled Marc as he rolled to his side, covering his head with the pillow, drowning out the noise as he drifted off to dreamland.

ROUND TEN
WINNER

CERNUNNOS
DANIEL MARC CHANT

ROUND ELEVEN

GONE
THOMAS S. FLOWERS

VS

BROKEN THINGS
KYLE M. SCOTT

GONE
THOMAS S. FLOWERS

Danny Jarvis loved looking up at the stars. Especially late at night when everyone else had gone to bed, the best place to be was on the roof just outside his bedroom window. Head craned upwards toward the heavenly host of breathless constellations and shooting stars and cosmic dust seemingly floating along the stratosphere, glittering greenish yellow as hydrogen gives birth to carbon, eventually forming into oxygen-rich iron. He loved coming up here, more so on nights when his Pa was laying heavy on the booze. Drinking himself into a comatose stupor. On nights when his mother would refuse to leave her room, praying until she fell asleep to whatever *god* she believed cared two rat shits for the Jarvis family. He loved coming out here most of all because he was alone. Alone to take comfort in knowing his kid sister was safe and fast asleep, tucked under an oversized comforter with Mr. Buttons, her teddy bear, cradled in her arms, without much knowledge of what was *really* going on. He took comfort

knowing despite everything, despite his drunk of a father, despite potentially losing the farm to the bank, despite watching his mother becoming another frantic pew-warmer do-nothing, or worse, having to move far away from the fields and streams and woods he'd known since he was much younger then he was today, he would still be twelve years old tomorrow. *Tomorrow was another day with troubles all its own*, or however that saying goes, the one from Ma's church, some piece of cheap grace he'd heard once in bible class. He loved coming out on the roof to look at the stars because late at night, when he was alone, the world seemed to slow down. Everything was calmer up here. The clock didn't tick as fast as it normally did during the day. Up here on the roof, outside his bedroom window, with his *Transformers*-pajama-ed knees tucked into his chest, head craned upward toward the infinite glowing white and yellow orbs, he could imagine a place far away from all the woe and hardship.

If he let himself, Danny Jarvis could disappear.

Pa was on another bender. A bad one. Eight months and still no work. His interview from today didn't seem to have gone very well. He'd come home in a rush, burning gravel and dust down the long stretch of dirt road, over the elms and hills that smelled heavily of spruce this time of year, when every flower was in bloom. The exhaust on his rusted brown baby blue 1973 Chevrolet pickup belching grey smoke. Transmission rattling.

"How'd it go?" Ma had asked. Still wearing her strawberry rose apron, putting the finishing touches on the chicken in the oven.

"What's for supper?" was all Pa had said on the subject.

Ma simply nodded her head. *She knew.* "Chicken and greens." And then she went about her business in the kitchen. She knew her husband well enough to leave it alone, at least for now while his temper was still hot. She knew when and where to press. After twelve years of

347

marriage, Margarete Jarvis approached her husband as she did most things in life. She diluted with prayer and dutiful negligence.

Tonight, high above, the moon looked large and dingy, as if dulled somehow with yellow dye. The pit marks in the face of the man on the moon seemed darker, more menacing then Danny had ever seen before. The night breeze was comforting, despite the strangeness of his mood. The wind cooler compared to the midday's summer heat. The cows out in the field slept standing up, box jaws still grinding cud, but otherwise motionless. The tall grass that stretched out over the Jarvis Farm swayed slightly. Glowing emerald eyes sparkling every now and then between the brownish blades as the tomcats hunted for mice. Blue Bonnets were in season, as were yellow daises, and sunrise-red Indian blankets. The odor of manure wasn't altogether unpleasant. Souped with the flowers and the mild summer night wind and chicken coup out back and the hay and rolls of grass, everything came together into a smell of natural familiarity. This was home. And everything was wonderful here. Or at least, it could be. The folds of hill country. The countless, endless stars open to the naked eye. No light pollution. No world pollution.

Well, Danny guessed that last one was a lie. Even in what the old timers called "God's Country," the world and all its troubles seeped and polluted the waters.

The boy stretched out his knees. Laying back against the roof, he rested his head on his hands like a pillow, never taking his gaze from the stars tinkling above him. Despite the beauty of God's Country, Danny couldn't shake his woes. *Was Pa ever going to find work? Will Ma ever get off her high horse about church? Will we have to move? Where would we go?*

He didn't know.

He didn't know.

As he gazed, wondering with worry much too mature for his age, a low rumble echoed in the distance.

One of those 747s passing, he thought, looking around for the blinking lights. But there was none to be found. Only the stars and a growing orange illumination as if some artificial sunrise had come earlier.

What is that? Danny wondered, sitting up now. Head turning every which way.

Meteor shower?

—*No meteor showers glow like this.*

What then?

Danny scooted back toward his bedroom window. Eyes darting across the sky, searching for the cause of the sudden glow and the low rumbling that began to quiver up the spine of the Jarvis house. The cows in the field woke, complaining and stumbling with low grunted moos.

Earthquake?

—*In Texas? Okay… but what about those lights? Those sounds?*

Scooting farther, Danny fell backwards into his room. Toys and books knocked from his desk and shelves. He thumped on the floor. The sound of metallic screams howled far above. The house vibrated and shook. The wood creaking.

Danny jumped to his feet and ran to the window. Peering out he watched with held breath as the world seemed to ignite in flame. Dazed, he blinked and watched, rubbing tears from his eyes, as something came falling from the sky high above, rocketing past the house. Dark grey clouds billowed out in front of the object, a disk-shaped ship like a Frisbee, though impossibly large, blinking frantically in a kaleidoscope array of colored orbs fixed along the mass. Metal moaned and thundered like some monstrous Lovecraftian beast, unable to thwart its destiny with Earth. The object came down in hour-like seconds, impacting on the far side of the hills with a sickening thud that gave one final horrible tremor, sending the cows fleeing for the chicken coop on the opposite side of the farm.

And then the world was silent once more.

"No way," Danny whispered, unable to take his gaze away from the kindling-orange glow, turning the hills into dark-shadowed humps. He could no longer see the ship, or whatever it was, only the smoke that now started to rise, billowing into the once pleasant manure-rich summer night wind.

Is anyone awake?

Did they hear?

Danny bolted from his room. Without knocking, he ran to his mother's bedside.

"Ma! Ma! Come quick, you'll never believe what—"

"Danny? What are you doing out of bed?" Ma sat up, rubbing the sleep from her eyes.

"Something fell out of the sky, Ma. Come see—"

"If your father sees you out of bed, he's gonna tan your behind."

"But, Ma, something—"

"Back to bed, Danny." Ma laid back down.

"MA!"

Nothing. His mother was fast asleep. Danny huffed, as all young children did when adults never listened. He looked at her nightstand, frowning not at the open Bible, but at the nearly empty beige-colored bottle of some kind of prescription meds. Morosely, he left her room, closing the door gently so she could sleep, uttering under his breath, "No-good pew warmer."

The hallway was much darker than he remembered. Downstairs he could hear some after-hours infomercial selling some kind of stain-be-gone product and the heavy snores of his father, still passed out.

Am I the only one who saw?

Danny reached for his door knob.

"Danny?"

Danny froze. The voice calling his name was no louder than a squeak. He turned, suddenly chilled. The floorboards creaked. Sour air. Heart hammering against his

frail, thin chest. Had they come for him? From the wreckage of the crashed ship? Slithering wet tentacles and enormous insectoid teeth? Hungry for a snack? Or worse…?

He breathed a sigh of relief.

Hellen May, his baby sister, stood in the darkened hallway clutching Mr. Buttons. Her pearl white nightgown tickling the floorboards.

"*Hellen May*, what are you doing out of bed? If Pa sees you!" God help him, he sounded like his mother.

"I… I had a bad dream, Danny." Hellen squeezed her teddy bear. Eyes large, strangely white and innocent in the gloom of the hallway.

"What dream?"

"A fire."

"Fire?" Danny kneeled next to her. "Outside?"

His sister nodded.

Danny took her by the shoulders. "Hellen, that wasn't a dream. The fire's real."

Hellen squeezed Mr. Button even harder. "Don't be mean, Danny."

"I'm not! It happened. Seriously. Come and see." Danny led Hellen into his room. The glow outside his window far over behind the hills still kindled in that dark angry orange bonfires get after burning past the gasoline and working on into the plywood and cardboard and rubber and all the other random junk you could see smoldering over on Johnson's Farm. Duke Johnson and his brothers hosted barn dances on Saturday nights and the fires could get rather high. Or even farther up Highway 59 toward Sinclair's place, but no one ever went there to see those bonfires, not if they didn't want to get peppered by a nearly always half-naked senile Joseph Sinclair holding a twelve-gauge.

The smoke on the other side of the hills billowed upwards, but not nearly as thick as before. Danny watched his sister as she inched toward the window sill. Mr. Button

clutched tightly to her chest.

"What is it?" Hellen finally asked.

Danny stood beside her. Both looking out toward the glow in the otherwise pitch black night. "Something came crashing out of the sky."

"What?" Hellen asked, but just barely. Danny imagined she didn't really want to know, but like most people was inclined to ask by sheer curiosity if nothing else.

Danny looked back over toward the glow. "Aliens," he said matter-of-factly.

Hellen jumped. "*Aliens!*"

"Hush. You want to wake Pa?" Danny pressed his finger to his lips.

Hellen looked away. "Maybe," she whispered.

"What was that?"

"Nothing."

"Better be."

They were both silent for a while. Each gazing out the window in Danny's room. Tracing the soft orange glow on the horizon. The wisps of smoke.

Strange, Danny thought. *You'd think someone from the government would be swooping in or something. Like in that movie with Jimmy Hunt whose Pa got his brain zapped. Or at least the sheriff, someone, anyone. Surly I'm not the only one to have seen this ship crash?*

Danny put his head out the window, much to Hellen's nudging discomfort. The night sky was as it had been. Quiet and calm, all but for the smoldering remains of whatever had landed behind the hill.

"I wanna go take a look." Danny came back in from the window, suppressing a laugh from looking at his sister's deadpan stare.

"No, Danny. Don't," she moaned.

"Why not?"

"It might be dangerous."

"I'll be careful."

"What if something... survived?"

Danny thought about it. That same movie, *Invaders from Mars*, came to mind. But Jimmy Hunt had been okay. The aliens never got him, no matter how hard they tried. Jimmy was smart, and so was Danny. And Jimmy had saved his town, if not the entire world, from those invaders. What if something similar was going on here? How could Danny not go? And besides, the bad guys never got the boy in those stories. The boy always became the hero and was rewarded somehow by the president or governor.

Rewarded?

Danny looked again out the window. Licking his chapped lips as if he'd gotten a taste of something too sweet not to eat. Images of the Jarvis farm and the bankers came to mind. Of the Travis County Sheriff and mayor shaking his hand. Of his Pa hugging Ma. Everyone with smiles and praise. Without further hesitation, he sat on his bed and tied on his sneakers.

"Danny, please. Don't go." Hellen followed her brother, pulled on his *Transformers* PJ sleeve.

"Come with me," Danny said without looking at her.

Hellen stared. Mouth hung wide, as if she'd just been told the most ridiculous, impossible thing she'd ever heard.

"Come on," Danny pressed. "Don't be a chicken. It'll be fun. Aren't you at least curious what's over there?"

Hellen hugged Mr. Buttons. "What if Pa wakes up?" she whispered.

Danny huffed. Standing, he looked out the window and then back at his sister. "What if... what if," he mocked. Slowly, he took Hellen by the shoulders. "If that spaceship crashing didn't wake him up, what makes you think he will now?"

Hellen shrugged, looking away.

Danny smiled. "Come on, Hellen May. How often does something like this happen? Never, that's what. How cool would it be if we were the first humans to make

contact with an alien? We'd be famous! That's what. News reporters would want to talk to us. The government might even give us a reward! Someone'll write a book about us, Hellen. Think about that. We could be rich… we could save the farm. Ma and Pa wouldn't have worry so much. Do you want to move?"

Hellen shook her head.

"Good. Neither do I."

Hellen shuffled her feet. "But—"

"But nothing, Hellen. This is our golden ticket."

Hellen brightened. "Golden ticket? Like in *Charlie and the Chocolate Factory*?"

Danny nodded. "Exactly."

Hellen chewed on her lip and said, "Okay."

Danny and his little sister, Hellen May, snuck past their slumbering, passed out father, still snoozing on his recliner, empty bottle of Jack Daniels resting beside his unmoved hand. The screen door had popped shut behind them, causing them both to jump ten miles in the air. But when they heard their father sawing logs, they both exhaled with a sigh of relief.

The grass on the hill was slick with early pre-dawn dew. A set of emerald eyes watched them carefully from the safety of a nearby sycamore. The cows refused to venture on this side of the farm, choosing instead to roost with the hens. Nothing else stirred, not even the coyotes that loved to come prowling about this time of night for an easy meal.

While Hellen seemed to tease, moan, and wheeze with each step closer to the glowing orange embers, Danny looked enthralled with wide eyed curiosity. Taking wider steps. Banking toward the cusp of the hill.

The orange glow softened as they climbed. A smell of sulfuric smoke, billowing slowly still, muddying the night sky with dark grey clouds.

His eyes teased the top.

Just a few more steps, he thought, licking his lips, again imagining news reporters and the governor handing him some sort of reward, a huge check written out to him. And his parents, smiling and laughing and hugging both Hellen and himself. *Just a few more steps!*

"Danny?"

Danny halted. Turned. Hellen stood several yards back. Her face frighteningly pale in the soft amber glow. "What's wrong," he asked, even though he knew exactly what was wrong. She was scared. And plenty reason why. They were out in the farm at night and alone, climbing the hill, toward the dying flame of some wreckage belonging to an unidentified flying object. Their parents didn't know where they were. And something could have survived. Something… alien.

"Let's go back, Danny," Hellen pleaded. Mr. Buttons looked strangled in her arms.

"Go back?" Danny laughed. "It's just over the hill. Right in front of us. We can't go back now," he protested.

Hellen took a step backwards. "I don't want to."

Danny glared. Angry. Frustrated. He understood why she didn't want to go any farther. Hell, he was scared too. But with everything going on, the bankers threatening the farm. Pa drinking all the time. Ma locked behind her bible. How could he just turn tail and run? He couldn't. He wouldn't.

"Go then, if you're scared. *Go*," Danny shouted. Not waiting for any response, he turned and stormed up the rest of the hill. At the top, he stopped and turned, giving one final look at his sister before venturing down the other side of the hill.

Hellen didn't move, but shouted, "Stop, Danny. Please, come back!"

Danny ignored her. He waved and then disappeared down the other side of the hill.

* * *

"*Danny*?" Hellen May had been shouting. Her throat hurt. Her body ached. She was cold and hungry and unsure how long she'd been standing there, shouting her brother's name. Minutes? Hours? Forever, maybe? And with each shout, nothing could be heard from the other side. Only the strange orange glow from the crashed spaceship or whatever it was, and the frustrated moos and clucks coming from the cows and hens near the chicken coup.

"Danny?"

Still nothing.

"Danny, *please*!"

Hellen took a step forward and froze. Cupping her ears from a horrible sound coming from the other side of the hill, some sort of trumpet blast, echoing across the predawn sky. Rumbling along the ground. Shaking the earth. Blinding and unforgiving.

Hellen fell to her knees. Mr. Buttons pushed against one ear, and with the other, a cold trembling hand. *Lord have mercy*, the sound was like something from Ma's bedtime stories, stories from Revelations about angels and horsemen, of death and pestilence and famine and war, a sound taught to give solace to pew warmers and parishioners of cheap Sunday comforts. It was thunder, yet not; more. The scream had color, bright dazzling color. This was the Days of Elijah. The End Times. The trumpet was unmercifully *forever*.

At the top of the hill, tall shadows grew from the blinding orange light. Impossible forms taking shape. Dark, almost grey. Elongated limbs and starved swollen bellies, reminding Hellen of those African children in the *National Geographic* magazines Pa kept in the potty. Narrow heads and unreadable faces with massive black eyes. First one, then two, and three, and now dozens more came into view, forming in the orange amber fog that rolled down the hill. Hellen watched. Frozen. Somehow, they were communicating with one another, the shapes spoke, unaffected by the unmerciful trumpet blast.

One of the slender shapes pointed at Hellen.

Another nodded in whatever agreement they'd made.

Hellen did not wait.

Unglued, she ran. Danny now far removed from her mind. She ran. Her short legs pumping faster than she'd ever moved before. The emerald eyes in the trees vanished. The moos and clucks stopped. There was nothing but the sound of the trumpet and her own heartbeat thundering, pulsing in her ears.

Pa tipped over in his recliner and pounded the floor. Dazed and frighten, but unsure why, he rose just in time to see the blinding orange light disappear and the rolling echo of something that sounded eerily like trumpets. He winced as something thumped the floor above him, Margarete must have slipped out of bed. Woken by the same noise that tipped him out of his slumber. He walked to the front door and opened the screen. In the distance a spotted a tiny shape bolting toward him.

"Hellen May?" Pa whispered, squinting against the night's gloom. He wasn't angry. What he felt was fear, more than anything else. Fear, the same bubbling poison he felt when he was first laid off from the mill. Fear of not knowing what he was going to do, how he was going to provide for his family, how they were going to keep their home, their farm. Now, his fear came from watching this small child sprinting down the hill toward the house, but more so the look on her face.

Hellen came bounding up the porch. Breathless and cold, Pa caught her in his chest, like a linebacker catching a long pass. She kept trying to run through him, but he held her fast.

"Hellen? Baby girl, what's going on?" Pa spoke in her ear, hugging his daughter tight. He could feel her heart, pistons pumping on high octane.

"Hush, now. It's okay. Whatever it is, it's okay. You're safe. You're safe," Pa sang softly, remembering the way he

spoke to her when she was an infant. Rocking her gently with her head rested on his chest. Singing her country songs. Singing about the day's events. Anything. But he didn't know what to sing now. There was no comfort he knew to give except holding her tight and refusing to let go.

"Hush. Hush."

And after a moment or two, Hellen stopped fighting and stood terrifyingly still.

"Hellen?" Pa took her shoulder to get a good look at her. Her skin was horribly pale and ghostly. Her teeth chattered. Her body quaked. But her eyes, her eyes were the worst. Large and moonlike, unblinking and empty.

"Sweet pie, please. Tell me what happened. Why were you outside?" Pa asked again.

Hellen muttered something unintelligible.

Pa leaned closer. "Say what, baby?"

"*Danny*," Hellen breathed, softer than a whisper.

"Danny? What about Danny?" Pa pressed.

"What's going on?" Ma was standing by the staircase. Bedhead and still half asleep.

Pa glanced at her. "I don't know. Hellen May came running from outside. Something about Danny."

Ma turned and ran upstairs. Pa could hear her feet pounding the floor above. Her shouts. He knew. She came back looking jarred and frightened.

Pa turned back to Hellen. "Sweet pie, where's your brother? Where's *Danny*?"

Nothing. Hellen was catatonic. Pale as death; as famine; as pestilence; as war.

"*Hellen May*, you answer your father. Now, where's Danny? Where's your brother?" Ma came beside Pa. The fear in her voice was unmistakable.

Still nothing. Hellen stared somewhere far away. Lost.

"Hellen?" Ma shouted, slapping her daughter across the face. Her hand drew back, her face said everything, how terrified she was for what she'd just done, and the

growing painful realization something more horrible had befallen her baby boy.

"*Where's Danny?*" she shouted one last time.

Hellen said nothing. The mark her mother's hand had made was red across her white, delicate skin. With one outstretched arm, she pointed toward the crest of the hill, the place where the strange orange light had glowed, the place where the trumpet blasted and she'd seen the tall elongated shapes of the silent whisperers.

There's a saying that time heals all wounds. It's a miserable promise. Wounds never heal, we just forget to lick them from time to time. And when we do remember, the sorrow returns just as raw and painful, if not worse, than the moment the wound was first carved into our flesh. Some wounds are easy enough to prolong remembrance. Others, such as the loss of a child, those kinds of wounds are never forgotten for long periods of time. The wound seeps and oozes constantly. So much so that it eventually becomes a natural part of you. You are no longer who you were before the *unexplained* disappearance. Now you're this whole *new* person. A miserable wreck people tiptoe around, refusing eye contact. *Shunned*, almost. Suspected. The person tabloids and Lifetime made-for-TV movies love making accusations about. *Sex pervert. Murderer. Scandal. Sinner. What are they really hiding?* Etc. etc.

Pa sat on the roof of the porch just outside his son's bedroom window. He sat watching the stars twinkle above, hoping, or as much of hope's sting he could endure. His face was slick. He'd been crying again. Eyes red and irritated and full of guilt. *Guilt* for his selfish behavior. For his drinking. All his relentless failures as a father. And whatever else he could blame himself for. Ma was asleep inside, in Danny's bed. Hellen tucked beside her. Safe in the embrace of her mother's arms. Her bible collecting dust in her bedroom.

The Huntsville sheriff's department was still looking

for Danny. Though to be honest, after four months, there wasn't much hope anymore. Experts say child abductees are typically slain within the first forty-eight hours. *Still*, Danny's photo was plastered everywhere in town.

Over the hill, the place Hellen had said Danny had gone, was the focal point of the investigation. Just over the hill, deep grooves had been dug into the soil, as if maybe something massive had crashed there, or been driven into. The latter was the determining factor. Crime scene investigators took soil samples, molds of tracks, photos, lots of photos. And statements, to which Hellen was unable to give a full testimony, only that Danny and she had gone out to the hill and there had been an orange glow. And shapes. And sounds. Both Pa and Ma confirmed the odd glow and the sounds. Whatever it really was, whatever had sent Hellen into a catatonic shock, it was gone. And so was her brother.

The *official* statement made by authorities was that the grooves found at the scene were no doubt made by pranksters and that Danny had more than likely been abducted by a person or persons unknown. *Unofficially*, the Jarvis family were not without suspicion. But who could say, really? Sometimes people just walk away. Sometimes children just disappear.

BROKEN THINGS
KYLE M. SCOTT

Josh let the small, severed arm roll from his fingertips, let gravity claim it as its own. It dropped to the floor where it landed on the small pile of mutilated bodies.

With growing horror, he surveyed the devastation wrought on the soft purple carpet of his bedroom.

The tears came, bitter and stinging, as he began to recognise small parts of his loved ones. A leg here, a head there, a torso—limbless—laid on its chest, discarded like it was nothing more than trash.

I won't cry. I won't cry.

I won't.

That was bullshit, though. He'd cry. He knew it. It was as sure as the sun hanging in the sky on a summer's morning.

He *always* cried.

It was a power that Gerry had held over him all his years, and it wasn't going anywhere soon.

The tears were flowing already. That was a given. It was the childish wailing that fuelled Gerry like it was the

air he breathed. It was watching Josh crumble and break into a million little pieces right before his eyes that got him off.

I hate him. I hate the monster, and I wish he was dead!

It was wrong to think such thoughts about his older brother. He knew that he should *never* think such thoughts, even if they were about a person who really, *really* deserved it.

And Gerry... he deserved it.

Gerry.

The golden boy.

Mum and Dad's prodigal son, blessed with movie star looks, a sharp, keen mind and a charm way beyond his years.

Gerry.

What Mum and Dad didn't know could fill a book.

They saw their first born son through a shining, glacial prism, filled with light and hope and pride so potent it made Josh want to choke. What they didn't understand, in any way, shape or form, was Gerry's inherent cruelty.

He had a mean-streak that ran deep and dark. So dark that often, in times like these, when Josh was sat on his floor rummaging among the debris of his dead friends, he truly believed his older brother to be evil.

Yeah, that was the word... evil.

Gerry was an evil, twisted guy.

But he hid it well...

Their parents didn't know. His aunties and uncles didn't know. His friends didn't know, either.

In all their eyes, Gerry was Jesus with a better haircut. A saint. A prince. A poster boy for all that was good and right in the world.

And Brandi, his utterly gorgeous girlfriend of three months and counting, she'd seen glimpses of it, but even *she* didn't know what he truly was.

What he was, was a *monster*.

What kind of brother, with six whole year's seniority,

would do such a thing as what Josh was bearing witness to on his bedroom floor?

I'm only twelve. He's practically a grown man, and he does this…!

Josh picked up one of the severed heads, reeling with disgust.

He studied it in his hands, willing the tears to stop their flow. Willing the heartbreak to be stemmed. Willing those shameful, child-like whimpers to stay tucked away, deep down in his gut where they couldn't prove his brother right about him…

That he was a wimp.

A little girl.

A sissy.

A 'little fucking pussy.'

He looked into the dead eyes staring back at him from the head, and felt the anguish swell.

"What did he do to you, Han?" he asked the tiny plastic head.

The small likeness of Han Solo's head stared back at him with jet black, lifeless eyes made of paint, yet judging him all the same.

He dropped the small head back on the pile of the ruined and the broken toys.

He didn't want to look. Didn't want to study the horror before him, but he couldn't look away.

There was Optimus Prime, his shining metal body pulled in half.

And Gizmo—the Mogwai—with both its arms ripped off its small, plush body. White cotton oozed like candy floss blood from the wound.

And Lion-O, leader of the mighty *Thundercats*, his muscular legs bent and stretched completely out of shape.

There were more, too.

Many more.

The violence that Gerry had committed in his room was nothing short of a massacre.

Here it comes.

Josh's vision blurred, making the pile of broken action figures melt into one awful whole.

I won't cry.

I won't cry.

I won't cry.

From his doorway, came that all-too-familiar voice. How he hated it.

The mirth… the *glee*… was unmissable.

"What do you think of *that* shit, pussy?" Gerry asked. "Did I hurt your widdle toysies?"

Rage, hate and misery warred within Josh, as his brother burst into wild roars of laughter.

I won't cry.

It started low, deep in the back of his throat, before rising in pitch to a keen whining, and then…

Gerry had won.

He always won.

Josh couldn't help it.

He wept openly, unable to stem the flow of his emotions.

He cried and he wailed, and the snot ran and his chest heaved, and he was no young man.

He was no young man at all.

He was a little boy… a wimp… a *pussy*.

Just as Gerry always said he was.

Josh sat alone in his room, sorting through the pile of broken toys. Some of them could be saved, maybe, but most of them were destroyed forever. The tears had stopped flowing half an hour ago, replaced by a tired numbness that washed over him like a cold wave.

Why was it always the same with Gerry? Why did he have to do these things? Why were older brothers always such *assholes?*

It's not all of them. Mike's brother is a great guy. And Tommy's two brothers are really cool, too.

He'd always felt a certain jealousy when visiting at his friends' houses. Their older siblings were their heroes. They looked out for them, protected them, *loved* them.

Josh had just been unlucky.

Born the second in line to the future 'King of Shits.'

Often, he'd fantasise about taking a stroll down to the local gym, working out till he was every bit as big and strong as John Rambo, and then...

Then he'd show Gerry who was boss.

He pictured himself stood over Gerry, triumphant, while his brother wept and grovelled at his feet, cowed before his better. Josh would lay a foot on his chest, staking his claim as a mountaineer would do, having climbed the highest peak of the highest mountain.

It was a lovely fantasy, but Josh knew it was all bullshit. He was the runt. The weakling. He'd be laughed out of any gym he entered, and would run from the building to a chorus of ridicule from boys stronger and better than him.

But fantasy was all Josh had.

And now, the conduits of his fantasies—his precious toys—had been further decimated by the cruel tyrant who lived just down the hall, in the bigger bedroom, with the bigger television and the latest, flashiest Super Nintendo console.

It wasn't right.

It was all kinds of wrong.

He pictured himself stood over his brother once more, this time, his boot was on Gerry's face.

And he was crushing him.

Someone needs to teach him a lesson.

Someone needs to show him he's not the biggest and the strongest.

He's just a mean bully who likes to terrorise the little brother he should love.

Again, the thought came, whispering in the back of his mind, insidious in its seduction.

I hate him.

I wish he was dead.

He was drawn from his reverence by the familiar sound of muffled laughter coming from the adjacent room.

Gerry's room.

The deep rumble of his brother's laughter was accompanied by the soft, lilting giggling of his girlfriend, Brandi.

Josh shuddered as he sat there, staring at his broken things, while they laughed and joked and enjoyed their positions as the lord and lady of the whole damn town. Prom king and queen. Beautiful yet destitute. Shit wrapped in the finest silk.

I bet they're laughing at me.

They think it's so funny, don't they?

So funny...

He got to his feet, his muscles aching as he said his final farewell to his beloved action figures, and ended his sorrowful vigil.

The walls were thin in their house and he didn't want them to hear him. Slowly, Josh tiptoed to the wall he shared with his brother. He placed an ear against the cold wall and listened.

"You should have seen the little shit's face. Fucking snot and tears *pissing* out of him. It was awesome."

Josh's face burned with shame as he heard Brandi giggle. "You're so mean to him!"

"Don't act like you don't find it funny. We both know you get off on it."

"On what?" she protested, in a mocking, playful tone.

"You love the bad boys. Don't deny it."

Josh gritted his teeth, seething with rage and humiliation as Brandi confirmed what he'd already suspected. She was every bit as poisonous as Gerry.

"You should have made a video of it with your dad's camcorder! We could have shown it to the guys at school."

Gerry groaned. "Fuck... I never thought of that."

"And *that's* why you love me."

There was a pause, then Gerry said, "There's always tomorrow. If I can be bothered."

"So bad... breaking a little boy's toys..." she purred.

"Well," Gerry drawled. "Maybe the little shit will thank me for it one day when he grows up, and gets himself a *real* toy to play with."

Her girlish giggling again, flirtatious and alluring.

Josh felt sick.

"Is that what I am?" she asked Gerry. "A toy?"

There was the sound of movement. The squeaking of a mattress. "You know you are... you're my sexy little fuck toy. And guess what?"

"What?" she asked, coyly.

"My old folks won't be back for at least another four hours."

"Is that right? And what about the pipsqueak next door?"

"Let him listen. It's the closest the pathetic little bitch will ever get to a real pussy. I think he enjoys it."

"You're so mean."

"Take your skirt off."

"Yes, sir."

"Now spread your legs wide."

"As you wish."

"Play with yourself."

"Yes, master."

"Now suck on it. Keep doing what you're doing. Suck on it while you're doing it."

Brandi's next words were muffled. Josh felt an excitement stir deep in his loins that only deepened his shame.

"Good girl. Now... bend over and show me that ass. Pull your cheeks apart. That's it. Nice and wide. I wanna see both holes."

"I'm all yours, master. Put it where you like."

"Say you're my fucking sex toy."

Brandi panted, "I'm your fucking sex toy."

She let out a prolonged whimper.

"You feel that?" Gerry's voice was hoarse. "You feel it deep?"

"I do. Push it all the way in."

"Say 'please.'"

"Please."

"Say 'please master, fuck your little sex toy.'"

She was panting now. Lost in carnal rapture. "Please master, fuck your little sex toy. Fuck you're sex toy in the ass."

With that, the talking stopped.

Josh was glad of it.

He moved away from the wall, repelled by it, just as he was repelled by his own excitement.

He was every bit the pathetic wimp they took him for—a dumb kid with no balls, who's only chance to be near a girl was to listen up against a wall while things were done to her by another.

It was hard to determine who disgusted him more.

His brother.

Or himself.

And there it was again, playing over and over in his head like a mantra.

I hate him.

I hate him.

He deserves to die.

All he does is ruin my life.

All he does is cause me pain.

Hatred welled inside Josh, shaking his small frame where he stood. Years and years of torment, humiliation, helplessness and pain, coursing through his veins like liquid fire. In the theatre of his mind's eye, a hundred awful memories lit up the darkness like a horror movie made just for him.

A cavalcade of degradation.

368

His brother, sitting on his face, expelling wind.

His brother, laughing as he wet himself in the school playground, only a boy of eight, while the whole school—boys and girls—all joined in.

His brother, ripping up a drawing he'd lovingly etched, depicting the recently deceased family cat. A cat Josh had loved and adored above all else. The last and most precious thing he had, with which to remember his pet.

On and on the memories played.

And always at their centre… his brother tormenting him.

The poisonous cyclone in a whirlwind of cruelty.

Making Josh's life a misery.

A living hell.

Well, Josh thought. *No more.*

He strode to his bedroom door, opened it, and made for downstairs. Ignoring the moans as he passed Gerry's room, he took the stairs two at a time. Then he passed through the living room and into the kitchen, where the afternoon sun pierced through the windows and kissed his pale skin.

He walked past the breakfast table, past the sink and past the fridge and when he reached the walk-in cupboard, he took a deep breath.

Then he stepped inside.

He'd find what he needed in there.

After all, it was where Dad kept his all his tools.

Josh opened Gerry's bedroom door, ever so slowly, quietly as he could. Despite the animalistic sounds coming from within, fear gripped him.

If Gerry caught him entering his room…

Especially while he was doing what he was doing to Brandi.

That would be it.

Game over.

His older brother would beat the living shit out of him, then force him to explain to their parents that he'd been attacked by a gang of local thugs. Or fell over. Or took a tumble off of his BMX…

It was always something.

And they *always* believed their golden child.

The door was silent as he pushed it open, just a fraction.

He peered inside, feeling immediately repulsed.

The first thing he saw was his brother's naked ass, rising and falling rhythmically as he thrust in and out of the girl beneath him. Her legs were splayed to either side of Gerry's, feet pressed against the bed, hips high, urging her lover forward, deeper.

Brandi's face was buried beneath Gerry's chest as he grunted like a wild beast, his sweat-soaked flesh meshing with her own as she moaned and writhed and bucked.

Josh opened the door a little wider. Just enough so that he could enter the room.

He approached the bed, treading as softly as he could, his eyes never leaving the two rutting bodies. He stepped over the bed sheets, discarded on the carpet; his heart thundered in his chest as though aching to smash free.

Gerry was biting into her neck as Josh moved behind him. His brother thrust harder, angrily, into Brandi. Josh imagined he could hear his brother's heartbeat meet and match his own. The stench of sweat and something else, musky and sweet, hung in the air around the rutting couple.

If his brother turned round now…

There was no going back, even if he wanted to.

No going back at all.

Josh raised the hammer above his head, freezing only for the tiniest fraction of a second.

Then he brought it down on the back of Gerry's skull.

The dull thud as steel connected with bone sounded

more satisfying than all the Saturday morning cartoon theme tunes in the world.

Combined.

Gerry was coming round.

That was good.

For a while there, while he was positioning his brother in the chair, Josh was worried he'd hit the bastard too hard. Maybe killed him.

That would have been disastrous.

His brother had to *see* what was about to transpire. He had to see it with his own two eyes. Take it all in.

He watched with muted interest as Gerry began blinking the blood from his eyes. Squinting as though looking into the sun, his eyes met Josh's.

Josh smiled.

"Whuhthefuhsis?" Gerry mumbled.

Maybe I did hit him too hard.

You didn't. He's alive, isn't he?

Yes, he was alive, but it looked like the hammer blow had knocked out of his skull everything that made Gerry, well… Gerry.

Having him brain dead was no different to having him dead-dead.

Shit.

Again, his anxieties were alleviated, when his older brother licked the drying blood from his lips, focused his baleful gaze on Josh, and said, "What… the… fuck… faggot? I'll murder you, you… little cunt."

Yeah… Gerry was still in there.

And it appeared he hadn't yet grasped the severity of his predicament.

Josh's mood brightened. He flashed Gerry a huge, beaming grin.

"There you are, big brother. There you are…"

"What… you… doing… you… little… shit…?"

"I'm snapping, Gerry. That's all. I'm snapping."

Gerry's eyes were clearing now, the dark fog of oblivion dispersing like black clouds as consciousness dawned.

He looked around himself, finally taking in his situation. Slowly beginning to understand his plight.

The first thing Gerry's eyes fell on were the ropes that bound him to the sturdy wooden breakfast chair. His legs were bound roughly together at the ankles. His wrists secured to the arms of the chair.

Instinctually, Gerry immediately struggled against the binds, but soon realised it was no use. Josh had made sure there would be no way for him to release himself. He understood that, should Gerry get free, he'd be beaten to within an inch of his life; perhaps even a few inches more than that.

His brother soon figured out he was trapped.

Then, in an amazing feat of selflessness for such a cold-hearted, cruel and petty bastard, he slowly took in the environment around him, mumbling her name: Brandi.

On the bed, Brandi writhed, screaming a muffled plea for help. Her eyes bugged out of her head as she fought to form words around the filthy gym-sock Josh had stuffed into her mouth.

Her arms were splayed above her head, bound to the headboard of Gerry's bed with small plastic tie-wraps.

Her legs remained free. She twisted and flailed like a docked fish, howling muffled obscenities at Josh as he knelt down to meet his brother's face, up close.

Gerry's rage was quickly being eclipsed by terror. His eyes burned with dread as he saw what Josh was holding in his right hand.

Josh savoured the fear.

The misery.

The horror.

In the wide, black, startled pupils of his lifelong tormentor, he saw himself reflected back, and for the first time in his lonely, unimportant life, he liked what he saw.

Confidence.

Determination.

Purpose.

"You beginning to get it yet?" he asked Gerry.

"Get what, you little bitch?!" Gerry was trying so hard to sound tough. Nonplussed. In control. The tremor in his voice betrayed him. "I'm gonna fucking *slaughter* you when I get out this chair."

"When you get out the chair? What makes you think you're getting out the chair, Gerry?"

The golden boy was cracking. Josh watched intently as his sibling's lips quivered as his own had so many times before. Gerry wasn't a man now. He wasn't a tormentor stood in Josh's doorway with a malicious grin, delighted at his own cruelty...

He was a boy. A weak, scared little boy, teetering over the precipice of pure terror.

He was helpless, and he *knew* it.

"Let me go!" he demanded, his voice cracking from low to high. It reminded Josh of his own voice a little... the way it changed in pitch.

With Josh, though, it was puberty.

With Gerry, it was the tremulous dawning of his new reality.

"Let me fucking *go*!" he barked; his muscles tensing in his arms, his biceps rippling as he fought once more against his restraints.

"Give it up, Ger," Josh said, flatly.

On the bed, Brandi continued her ridiculous flailing, cursing as she battled against her binds.

"What the fuck are you *doing*?!" Gerry screamed as tears flowed over the lids of his eyes.

Josh had never seen his brother cry before. Never in all his years. All the tears that had been shed in their happy home, had been shed by Josh himself.

Years of them.

Rivers of them.

Josh reached forward, ran his forefinger along his brother's cheek. He savoured the tear's wetness, just for a moment, before he slipped his finger into his mouth. It tasted salty. No different to the taste of his own tears, really.

"Are you deaf, Gerry. I told you what I was doing," he finally answered his captive. "I'm snapping..."

Gerry sputtered blood down his chin as he huffed. "You're already all the way snapped, you fucking nut!"

Josh raised the hammer, swivelled it in his palm like he'd seen so many of his heroes do with their swords and guns and knives. He felt something right then he'd never felt before in all his life...

He felt... *cool*.

"You're not getting it, Ger, are you?"

Gerry growled something indecipherable.

Josh gripped the hammer tight.

"That's not the kind of 'snapping' I'm talking about..."

With a grunt, Josh swung the hammer down onto Brandi's ankle, snapping the bones like brittle twigs.

Brandi wailed, urine pooling out from between her legs as she instinctively pulled them closer to her body, minimising the target as best she could. Her foot flopped around beneath her already blackening ankle as Josh swung wildly. He caught her on the toes of the dangling foot with the second blow, grinning as he heard the bones crack. His heart thundered as the toes cracked under the hammer's vicious force. Blood immediately filled the twisted digits, turning them a sickly black-blue. Brandi's toenail—the large one—must have been clipped by the hammer's edge. It hung by a few tiny fleshy strands, dangling like a grisly decoration from her seeping, ruined toe.

Behind the sock-gag, she howled like a beaten down dog.

Josh grew hard.

Ignored it.

Focused on the matter at hand.

His brother was screaming something. It all sounded a little distant, as though he was hearing the foul-mouthed protestations through thick glass.

He turned to face Gerry, lowering the hammer, letting it swing. He gave his sibling his full attention.

Brandi would wait.

"What's that, Ger?" he asked.

"Why are you doing this!?" Gerry wailed, crying openly now. A savage pride welled in Josh's heart, seeing the golden child in so fragile a state.

"Why… WHY?!" he shouted, spittle peppering Gerry's face as he leaned in close. He lowered his tone. "This is about my toys, Gerry. It's about your toy, too."

"I don't…"

"I *know* you 'don't'… you're too fucking stupid to grasp it, so I'll make it simple for you, big brother. It's not rocket science, but try to keep up."

Gerry nodded, complaint. His gaze darted between the bawling, writhing Brandi, and the blood-flecked hammer held in Josh's hand.

"You've bullied me for my whole life, Gerry. Mum and Dad don't see it. They don't see what you are. They never will. You're a small, cruel, vicious parasite and you don't deserve all you have.

"And you have it all, Gerry… you have the world in your hands. Girls, the car, the friends… it's all yours and it always has been. You took it for granted, Ger. All of it. Like it was your fucking birthright to be adored.

"You know what I had, Ger, while you had your great fucking life…? I had my toys."

Gerry's frown was almost comical.

Josh went on. "That was all I had. Nothing else. You took any chance at happiness from me like it was nothing. Made me miserable my whole life just because you could.

And I put up with it. I had to. And the only way I could put up with it, was by having my action figures to comfort me.

"They were my *friends*, Ger. I loved them. They were all I had, and you *knew* it."

Gerry was shaking his head—a surreal gesture of denial. Josh wondered momentarily what it was that his brother was attempting to deny to himself.

His cruelty?

His malice?

His own well-earned predicament?

It didn't matter, Josh surmised.

"I'm… sorry…" Gerry whimpered. "Don't hurt her anymore."

There it is.

He does *care for her.*

Good.

Josh grinned. "You're not sorry *yet*, but you will be. You cracked and snapped my action figures like they were trash. You took my precious things, and you turned them into useless, lifeless, broken things.

"You broke *my* toys, Ger. And now I'm going to break *yours*… I'm going to break *your* 'toy' till it's as useless as you made mine"

"No… no…"

Josh rose to his feet.

He felt like Thor, the mighty god of thunder, as he held aloft the hammer. He brought it down on Brandi's kneecap. The bone pulverised beneath the blow. Blood welled. Muffled screams filled the room.

It didn't sound right.

Josh reached forward and removed the filthy sock from her mouth. She gasped for air, coughing.

Josh raised the hammer.

Her left hand this time. The heavy hammer caught her on the knuckles, crunching bone and flesh. He struck again. This time, hearing the bones succumb, relishing the

way her misshapen fingers pointed in wild directions, brutalised and mangled. Brandi screamed her heart out; begged for mercy, for God, and for her big, brave Gerry to save her.

Gerry wasn't saving *shit*.

Josh swung again, this time, driving the hammer's solid steel head into the small of her hip with a savage crunch.

The sounds coming from her now were barely human.

"How does it feel to have your things broken, Gerry?"

Gerry was crying for their mother.

"Don't cry for Mummy yet, Gerry," Josh mocked, licking sweat from his lips. "We haven't got to the best part yet."

A dark, wet stain flowered from Gerry's crotch.

Lots of people wetting themselves, this morning, Josh mused.

"Come on, Ger. You know what the most *fun* part is, don't you? It's not maiming someone else's things that brings the most pleasure…"

In his mind, dark wraiths floated.

Dead things made of dead materials.

He-Man. Skeletor. Luke Skywalker. Batman.

A funhouse of plastic treasures, all broken.

All ruined.

Josh took a deep breath. "The most fun part, Gerry… is *obliterating* someone else's things…"

Josh gripped the hammer in both hands. He rose, stood over Brandi as her moon-sized baby blues shone with stark terror.

He brought the hammer down hard on her face.

Her nose exploded like a ripe tomato, as the bludgeoning hammer connected. Blood and snot sprayed from her flattened nostrils. Bone, splintered and spiked, pierced the skin from within, jutting out from the flattened mess where her pretty nose had been. Beneath her eyes,

deep, dark bruises formed. She spat blood from her mouth, trying her best not to choke on it.

Taking a pained, sputtering breath, she opened her mouth to scream, or plead, or beg.

Josh swung the hammer down on her open mouth, hard as he could.

The teeth shattered as the steel smashed through them. Tiny broken shards of her molars clung to her bleeding, caved-in gums. To Josh, they looked like little white boats, clinging to the surface of a red, churning sea. Brandi gurgled thick blood in her throat, swallowing her own teeth like bitter pills as she fought to breathe.

His brother cursed and roared and wept.

He raised the hammer high as he could.

Brought it down with all his might.

He'd meant to hit her on the jaw this time.

He'd wanted to see it crumple.

He missed his target.

Instead, the flat, solid head of the hammer came down on her right eye-socket. The bone around her eyeball caved inward. The eyeball itself turned up into her head.

Fun!

He struck again. Same place. Harder this time.

The eyeball erupted in a splash of jellied mulch and blood.

Her one good eye stared at Josh, questioning.

She was still in there.

Even *more* fun.

He swung at her forehead.

Watched it dent inwards.

Swung again.

Marvelled at the way her skull opened up, and how the brain seemed to push out of the wound, as though seeking escape. It was a different colour than he'd imagined.

He swung again.

The blow hit the brain itself this time. Josh giggled as

red, shiny chunks of matter spurted from the sides of the brutalised skull.

Another swing.

Then again.

Then again.

By the time Josh had worn himself out, her head was little more than a viscous soup of brain matter, splintered skull and blood.

It looked like someone had spilled half-cooked bolognaise all over Gerry's pillow. Steam rose from the raw, mangled flesh as Josh finally dropped the hammer, breathless. It fell to the bedroom carpet with a dull thud as he leaned in close to the pulverised meat above Brandi's neck, studying his brother's most precious thing.

"D'you like how it feels, Ger… losing what's yours?"

"I'll… kill… you…"

Josh ignored the idle threats. He allowed himself a moment to regain his composure. Bludgeoning his brother's girlfriend to muck had been hard work, and he was no athlete.

He expelled a weary sigh.

"Can you guess what happens next, Gerry?"

The older brother's eyes darted to the discarded hammer. Josh followed them to the weapon, then back to look at Gerry.

He laughed. "You're not getting off that lightly, brother…"

He wouldn't have thought it possible for a person to look more terrorised than Gerry had this whole time, but the dark promise in his words really did the trick.

Without another word, Josh made for the bedroom door, opened it, and reached for something just outside the room.

With a grunt, he lifted the heavy object and moved back inside.

Seeing what Josh had in store for him, Gerry bucked like a wild horse, driven near insane with terror.

Josh unscrewed the seal.

"The worst thing wasn't you breaking my toys." Josh said calmly, as though Gerry had asked. "It wasn't you ripping their arms off, either. It wasn't even you ripping their *heads* off. It was something that happened a long time ago. *That* was the worst thing.

"Do you remember my sixth birthday? I do. I remember it like it was yesterday. I remember it because it was the year that Gran bought me an eight inch Superman figure. I loved that thing with all my heart, for the two or three hours I had it, I was in heaven. Superman was my idol, and you *knew* that. That's why you did what you did. I remember how much I cried when you ruined that perfect day. I bet you do too, Gerry…"

Josh allowed the memory to wash over him…

The tantalising unwrapping of his gran's gift, so much more special because it came from her… his favourite person in the world.

The beat of his heart as he unwrapped then held the huge Superman figurine high, like a treasure; immeasurable in worth.

His gran's sweet, kind face as she bathed in her grandchild's unbridled delight.

Running upstairs to his room, hungry to concoct myriad adventures for his hero in the imagined metropolis of his small bedroom.

And then Gerry, stood in the doorway.

Josh was unsurprised to find his own tears flowing, as the black memory of what came next washed away all the joy.

All the light.

There was only Gerry. His cruelty. His malice. His sick need to hurt and to break.

Josh sighed. He raised the canister above Gerry's head as Gerry begged.

His brother's screams went up a few octaves as the petrol poured over his scalp, over his face, down his chest

and over his groin.

"The worst thing you ever did, was setting my Superman on fire."

Josh reached into his pocket. Brought out the matchbox.

He removed a match. "He was so handsome. So clean-cut and perfect."

With a quick flick of his wrist, Josh scraped the match along the rough surface of the box's sandpaper side.

"He was my hero, and you melted him down to nothing."

The flame flickered before Josh's eyes. He watched the light dance; marveled at its terrible hunger to devour.

"*That* was the worst part. You made a *monster* of him! You…" Josh paused.

Gerry mewled like a kitten.

"I think you get the idea…"

Josh tossed the match into his brother's lap and watched the flames burn bright.

The sirens were getting closer.

Josh had always had a hard time distinguishing the different tones used by each of the emergency services.

But not today.

The fire engines would be pulling up outside his home at any moment now. He briefly wondered who'd called them. After all, there wasn't much smoke. He'd already put out the flames.

He'd let Gerry cook just long enough that he was no longer recognisable as 'The Golden Child.'

In fact, he was no longer recognisable at all. The blistering, blackened thing that twitched in the still-smouldering chair barely resembled a human being. The eyes were melted away, scorched to nothing by the searing flames. The lips were entirely gone, affording Gerry a devilish, skeletal grin. His hair was burned away too, and in some places, even Gerry's skull showed through, starkly

contrasted against the black, crispy flesh.

From top to bottom, Mum and Dad's favourite son was little more than a seeping, melted heap of cooked meat.

But he was *alive*.

Josh had made sure of that.

Hadn't he promised Gerry that his fate would be worse than Brandi's?

He'd keep good on the promise.

He briefly pondered what lay in store for the charred, blackened freak in the chair.

Endless pain.

Isolation.

A future trapped within a hated shell, sightless and speechless, unable to escape from a darkness that could never be alleviated.

Endless and bottomless despair.

Josh smiled.

His own fate, he was sure, would be far less severe.

A decade or so in a mental asylum, then rehabilitation, then back out into the world.

He was twelve years old. He'd be out by the time he was twenty five, easily.

He could live with that.

Nothing out here, anyway, he mused. *It's not like I have any friends, and like Gerry said, I was never going to find a girlfriend. No pussy for me, out here or in there...*

He'd be going away a long time. God only knew when he'd even set *eyes* on a girl again...

Then it came to him.

Josh smiled as the idea took hold.

He looked at the broken, naked body on the bed. It was bent out of shape, sure... badly bruised too. Not to mention that the hardening soup of pummelled bone and brain, where Brandi's head had been, was a little off-putting...

But...

Beggars couldn't be choosers.

And it'd be kind of fun to play with someone else's toy.

Especially Gerry's.

Pulling down his pants, Josh climbed onto the bed.

It was eight long minutes before the firemen arrived. Enough time for Josh to play twice.

ROUND ELEVEN
WINNER

BROKEN THINGS
KYLE M. SCOTT

ROUND TWELVE

BLOCK
JAMES WARD KIRK

VS

ZOMBIE DAD
KIT POWER

BLOCK
JAMES WARD KIRK

1.

Block is a giant. However, he slumps, because his soul shines diminished. His heart hurts. He sleeps on the floor of his home, next to the bed his wife laid in. His dark suit is tailored to fit, but doesn't, like the rest of him.

The murder scene is larger and bitterer than even Block. Blood will never completely dissipate from this kitchen. Some small part of this human sacrifice shall live here forever, even when the house is lost to time, some soft cell of her melting into the earth below, a specter eternal that haunts Block until he offers his own mortality to the universe.

The esoteric of this woman, the parts that comprise the human body, lay displayed for review. Each organ is exposed and beside each is a small, yellow sign marked with a number, embossed in black; all quite in contrast to

the red—but not all blood is red. Liver blood is as black as ink, perhaps God's comment upon the human condition. The numbers run high as nothing much remains inside Mary's habitus.

The refrigerator kicks on.

Her eyes, also removed, stare at Block from atop the refrigerator. Her face, deftly removed, lay perfectly wrapped around her eyes. She seems more curious than angry. Her heart is in the sink, with fresh apples. Her intestines hang from the ceiling like sticky flytraps and are already at work. The buzzing is loud. The woman's brain is on the counter next to the microwave, split in half, and smells like fresh mushrooms.

Block's feet are too large for crime scene covers. He reaches into his jacket pocket and removes a roll of green-black thirty-gallon plastic trash bags. He uses a shoestring to tighten one around each calf. He steps into the lake of blood, sending ripples like lunar tidal waves splashing against the floorboards. Block cannot avoid all the hanging entrails, and flies, angry for being distracted, form an anti-halo around his head. Congealed blood mixes with his hair, clings to his face and shoulder and, as he turns away, I imagine a tear forming in his eye.

Block imprints her pain upon his soul, incapable of *not*, of not knowing, not absorbing, like hovering near a loved one, a cancer patient, and listening to the final murmurs of life.

"This is the twelfth of the first," he said. His voice is as big as his body, and in the other room, a paramedic began weeping.

Block bends at the knees as if in prayer. He removes a tongue suppressor and gently pushes at the stomach; he

sniffs gently at the cut esophagus and says, "Peppermint schnapps." *The girl was just having a little fun, perhaps a first date.*

The Coroner tells Block he shouldn't have done that and Block tells her to go fuck herself. Block will read the woman's report, words surgical and clean as if she is above human sentiment. He has absorbed the facts he needs from this theatre of the absurd.

Block walks to the edge of the kitchen and removes the bags from his feet. He steps into the hallway. People move away from him like sheep and he their shepherd. "What is Mary's last name?" He knows her name is Mary. All twelve of these poor souls are.

"Benevolentia," the Coroner says, still new and unaware of the anger residing within Block.

"Mary Benevolentia," says Block.

The Coroner starts, "It means—"

"I know what it means," Block says. "It's Latin for 'good will.'"

The Coroner enjoys the last word. "The subject's liver is in the refrigerator. The time of death is compromised."

No, though Block. *The time of life is compromised.* Like his wife's, Luna, strangled purple-black with a scarf. Block places his right hand upon his chest. His heart hurts.

2.

Alexander Ashmedai is shopping for a silk scarf.

"For your wife?" asks the sales girl. She is perhaps twenty-six. Her red hair is the death of her.

"No, it's for you. Which scarf do you most enjoy?" Ashmedai is tan, thin, and handsome. He is charismatic,

like sunsets.

"That's easy," she answers, apparently fine with allowing a stranger to buy her a scarf she could never afford, choosing a green scarf the color of spring grass, the Eiffel Tower patterned into the silk scarf.

Ashmedai asks the girl for her name.

"Abby," she says. She has a card: Abby Gramsci.

How many Gramscis are there in the phone book? he wonders. Not many, he thinks, and later he will find her on Facebook too.

Ashmedai gives the girl some cash and concludes his transaction. He neatly folds the receipt in half and places it in his wallet. Ashmedai has seventeen similar receipts at home pinned to his bedroom ceiling.

Ashmedai moves artfully toward his Vienne French four-poster bed. He is nude, semi-erect, and carries the scarf with him. He sighs as he lies down upon five thousand dollars of silk bedding. He ties the scarf tender and tight around his neck, a knot perfect for choking oneself. He takes his fully erect member in his right hand and begins strangling himself with the scarf with his left.

Ashmedai is not abused as a child, or molested, or suffers pain of any kind. He does not go hungry or want for things other children less fortunate than him envy. He is a bright and meticulous student and earns the praise of his teachers. Peers admire and like him, and seek his company and companionship. Girls want to kiss him.

He does not kill small animals. He loves Mother and Father.

He does not murder until one night under a harvest

moon, in the company of a young woman from a neighboring university—a spontaneous event while trolling the streets for pleasure.

Ashmedai is quite bored with life. He absorbs the information his professors offer effortlessly, and in a short time understands their areas of expertise perhaps even better than they understand. He is comfortable materially. Money is no problem for him. Mother and Father take good care of him, when they visit and when away. Ashmedai wants for nothing, but his lust is overwhelming and finds it sovereign. He does not work.

Ashmedai and Amanda are sitting in a white convertible, the top down, fondling one another. Ashmedai is unable to achieve an erection. An idle thought excites him: he might enjoy taking her life. He begins the process, uncertain at first, fumbling around until he discovers that he truly enjoys the erotica of his hands upon the girl's delicate neck. His erectile dysfunction problem resolves as the natural life of the young woman flees him.

His orgasm is a life-changing event.

Sated, he looks about and finds no person has witnessed his murder. As he returns his attention to his date, he discovers the rub—moonlight reveals his fingerprints upon his lover's throat.

Ashmedai drags the young woman's corpse to a copse of fir trees and hides it there. He fumbles around in the dirt, comes upon a sharp rock, and obliterates her throat and his fingerprints. Returning to his car, he finds the woman's purse on the floorboard, and her red scarf. He uses the scarf to lift the purse, and his member stirs at the sensation of silk rubbing leather. He leaves the scarf and the purse beside the corpse.

The memory of the scarf elevates his spirits for several months. Then reminiscence is not enough.

Ashmedai researches serial killers. He does not delude himself. He understands his undertaking. The first to turn up on Google is the Green River Killer. He turns away in disgust. He will kill regular women. How nice to begin with a policeman's wife? He trolls the local newspaper online and reads about a giant.

Ashmedai sits up on the bed, frustrated. He cannot climax. He has a man in mind. The man's name is Alexander Mort. Mort is stealing his limelight.

Ashmedai and Mort kill in harmony one night, a year ago, albeit on opposite sides of town and each unaware of the other, and Mort gets the headlines. Television is atwitter about the man named Mort. Mort is brutal. Ashmedai likes to think of himself as humane. To discover his art regulated to the second page of the paper, a mere afterthought of reporters because of Mort, infuriates Ashmedai. He is chagrined that he and Mort share the same given name.

The police are bereft of information regarding Alexander Mort. Ashmedai is not. He has seen Mort. He has witnessed the work of Mort and explored the aftermath. Mort is a brutal, ugly, and stupid man. Ashmedai has decided that if the police cannot locate Mort then he shall assist them. He has all of the necessary information.

Ashmedai decides he will visit the public library, access a public computer, and send the giant all of the information he needs to apprehend Mort—all contained in a tidy email from a temporary account.

Ashmedai freshens up. He's decided one more night of surveillance is required before he greets his new lover, Abby.

3.

Mort is comfortable in his lair. He lies upon an abandoned mattress.

He lives in an abandoned stand-alone wood frame building once owned by a Russian who sold tobacco out the front door and heroin out the back door. He lives here alone having frightened away other would-be squatters with a simple meeting of the eyes. One man did not look away from Mort's eyes and died.

Mort is not retarded, as Ashmedai suspects, but he is brain damaged because of poor nutrition as an infant and repeated punches and kicks to the head as a toddler. He is self-aware.

Mort is good with his hands partly because of growing up on a farm in California, and working construction as a teen. He has secured his home from would be intruders. Police are content to leave it alone, as the building's outward appearance resembles any other well-kept building closed because of the poor economy. The windows are covered with thick plywood. The doors are secured with premium locks. Drug dealers and prostitutes do not frequent the corner—and this *is* a surprise to local police. As one patrolman said of the surrounding neighborhood, "You can't throw a rock in this area without hitting a whore or a drug dealer." Mort does not tolerate people near the building, transient or not.

Mort often sleeps in the chicken coop as a child,

especially when Mary has masculine visitors. Sometimes they stay awhile but eventually they all leave. He does not mind sleeping with the chickens. The mild cooing of the sleeping chickens calms him. The stench is preferable to that encountered in the house.

At age five, Mort's mother takes him between her legs. Mort's penis is huge, but it is not his member visiting her dark place. He is awkward at first, and struggles for breath, but Mother That Becomes Mary is an excellent if cruel tutor.

At age eight, and beyond Mort's understanding, his member becomes tumescent when servicing Mary. Mary is outraged: "How dare you!" She lights a cigarette and burns his penis. Mort never experienced another erection after that, not even upon awakening or if needing urgently to urinate, but the burning of his penis continues. A ritual develops.

As a man, Mort's penis is scarred from base to tip. When he touches its leather-like surface to urinate, he becomes furious. A rage builds. The rage becomes frenzy. He uses a phone book to find Mary, and his wrath is released with Mary's death.

For a while, anyway, as alas, the rage builds like the need for inhalation. Mort will find Mary again and she will die like an exhalation—spent. In death, Mary is Momma again.

Mort moves to a sitting position. He is troubled regarding the last Mary.

She says, as the knife descends, as its point penetrates, "I forgive you."

Several minutes pass before her words come to life in his thoughts, like a ghost ascending from its grave. He is sitting, a kidney

in each hand, and he hears her words echo in his mind like the "who?" of an owl.

No one has said these words to Mort.

Standing behind Mary's house, hiding in the shadows of the alley, Mort says, "I forgive you."

He looks back at the house and sees a man entering. Mort returns to the house and peers through a window. He sees a man standing there, holding a silk scarf. Mort gets to know this man named Ashmedai.

Mort stands and leaves the mattress. He urinates into a coffee can. He returns to his mattress and lies down again—and at that moment, another voice cracks through his consciousness.

The voice says, "I am God. I forgive you."

Mort brings his hands to his head and says aloud. "Thank you, God." Mort has heard of God. He is a kind man who lives in Heaven. Heaven is a nice place.

God says, "I demand recompense."

"What does 'recompense' mean, God?"

"You must give Ashmedai to the giant."

"Okay, God." Mort knows the giant. He always goes to Mary. Mort thinks the giant wants to put the Mary back together again, and this is fine because the Mary is cleansed.

Mort rises, and begins the work God has given him. Crucifixion comes to mind.

4.

Ashmedai sits in his car outside Abby's apartment building. Abby's apartment is at ground level. Ashmedai is happy about this as it will make his entrance and exit less

dangerous. There is a copse of maple trees behind the apartment complex and a small lake. As Ashmedai contemplates the subtleties of variance between suffocation by silk and drowning, he sees Mort leave the apartment, carrying Abby.

Ashmedai understands this is no coincidence. Mort must have some plan. Ashmedai is not concerned. Mort is a brute, and it follows that his plans are brutish. He watches without agitation as Mort disappears into the woods behind the apartments. He wonders if Mort can get home without interference from the police. He imagines Mort making the trek home with success, as Mort enjoys at least the cunning of a coyote carrying its prey. He knows where Mort lives, and even has a master key for the locks there. Ashmedai is comfortable. He has planned the eventual congress of the two.

Ashmedai starts his car and leaves for Mort's den. He will wait in the rafters, like a bat.

5.

Block awakes from his slumber. The moon is bright for a moment, but then clouds move over like a sheet over a corpse. The floorboards beneath him creak as he rises to his feet, as do his bones.

Block has not slept upon his bed since Luna died.

He's hungry, goes to the kitchen, and finishes the remains of a pizza. He washes it down with tepid tap water.

Block checks the voicemail from his phone. *If you want to find Luna's killer, come to this address.* Block writes down the address, but memorizes it, and forsakes the

paper beside his phone as he leaves his home.

Block looks to the moon. A soft breeze scuttles leaves across the driveway. They sound like the scraping of bones.

Block looks at the Crown Vic assigned him by IPD, and his Ford pickup truck parked on the other side. He looks at the sky and with all of his agony wishes to see the moon shine. Rewarded, he shines too, but for the moon quickly cowers again behind silver clouds.

Block knows that if he chooses the truck he will die.

Block has lived too much, suffered the touch of madmen, tasted the ugly redolence of death, and outlived the only human being that ever loved him. Even for a giant, death cultivates life too dear; death draws final breaths, as frosted flowers do in the season of fall. Death allures even giants.

Block arrives at Mort's warren in his truck. He has a police-issued Glock in his right hand.

The door is open and Block enters. Block takes in the scene before him. He sighs deeply, one of but a few exhalations left him.

Block sees Mort nailed to a cross, a crucifixion in all ways realized. A spear protrudes from his side. A nude young woman lies at his feet, dead. She wears a silk scarf around her lessened neck.

There is candlelight.

Block is not surprised when the man on the cross moves, but it is not Block addressed.

Block hears the man say, "God, have I recompensed?" Block watches the man on the cross die, consumed within a shudder.

Ashmedai emerges from the shadows. He holds two

sticks, one in each hand. "Old Mort was a fool."

Block sees Ashmedai as one sees the world as it slips away forever. Block sees in the shadows surrounding Ashmedai appendages, or tumors, a beautiful cow, a dragon and a ram.

Ashmedai says, "I bring hell with me. You shall see."

Block's places a bullet between the eyes of Ashmedai anyway. He asks, *Why not?*

Block's heart spasms and he bends to his knees; and again Block's heart spasms. He drops face-first upon the floor and before the cross. He pulls arms under him, puts his hands to his chest, as if cupping his essence. Block's heart stops and the giant dies.

Ashmedai bellows. No one hears his cry.

6.

The giant sees radiance in the distance. He is in a line of people leading toward the light.

Block says, "The line to Heaven is a long one."

The man just in front of him tugs at the giant's arm.

Mort says, "At least we're in it."

"You got that right," Abby adds.

ZOMBIE DAD
KIT POWER

My dad's got a pretty good left jab, especially for a guy who's been dead for two years. He catches me in the gut as soon as I walk in the door, and it takes the breath out of me. I stagger back, pushing the door shut with my body, my hands already moving to cover my abdomen.

The next blow catches me on the cheek, bounces my head off the wood, bam bam bursts of pain, front and back. Tears squirt.

"Jesus, Dad, what the fuck?"

"Where's my beer, you little bastard?"

I hold up the blue carrier bag, the tins clinking together inside. He grabs it out of my hand. The skin on his fingers is grey, dry, flaky. As he snatches the bag, his smell rolls over me, and I have to choke down the urge to gag.

I straighten up fully, expecting another blow, but he's already turned away, muttering under his breath. He goes into the living room and slams the door. I wait until the sound of his chair creaking tells me he's sat down, then I

open the front door again, quietly, and pick up the second bag—the one containing another round of tinnies and my microwave lasagna.

It's experience, that's all. Give him all the beer upfront, I know I'll face a screaming fit around 10:30 and end up hoofing back down to the shop for another round. Also means I'm liable to be up until 3am listening to him yelling at the TV. This way, when he runs out, he'll shout at me for an hour or two, but when he goes up the stairs he'll find the second bag. It's enough to get him through the evening, and means I get some sleep.

I stash the second bag in the fridge for now, nuke dinner, then take it upstairs to eat. I try and listen to the radio in my room, but the TV is too loud. The football game commentary bleeds through the floorboards, making it sound like two people talking at once, having different conversations. I turn it off after a few minutes and just eat.

Afterwards, I sneak downstairs and wash up, remembering to grab the bag out of the fridge and put it at the bottom of the stairs on my way back up.

I take a shower, pull on my dressing gown, and crawl into bed. The TV booms on downstairs. I close my eyes and try to sleep.

Dad got laid off when I was thirteen. I came home from school one day and instead of an empty house, there he was, sitting on the sofa, drinking beer and watching TV.

He stayed there for the next ten years.

Mum stuck it out for a while after my brother Jack and I grew up and left, but eventually she decided that she deserved a shot at having a life. She walked. Jack wanted nothing to do with him, but I felt a responsibility. Jack was younger, couldn't remember as clearly what Dad had been like before. He'd been an okay father. I missed him.

So I visited, a couple of evenings a week, brought takeaway, talked football. He'd been going downhill anyway, but with Mum gone, things got worse in a hurry.

He stopped eating regularly, and I got the impression that sometimes he didn't leave the sofa in between visits, except to piss. I noticed the post building up, the red letters, and I twigged that the situation wasn't sustainable. The evening I got there to find him sitting in the stink of his own urine was the clincher.

He moved in with me at the end of the month.

"Hey, George!"

I look up from my coffee, startled clean out of memory lane by the friendly voice.

"Jenny, hi. Thought you were on the 10:45 break?"

"Call ran over. I swear, nobody understands these new overdraft rates. Might as well have put that bloody letter out in Swahili."

I chuckle, and the sound of my own laughter startles me a little. She smiles back, and it warms me.

"Anyway, mind if I join you?"

"Nah, yeah, great." I point at the chair next to me.

"Cheers." She goes over to the kettle, starts making her drink—teabag, two sugars, milk.

"Jesus, how is it only fucking Tuesday?"

I laugh again. There's something about the way Jenny swears that really lights me up.

"Dunno, mate. I know what you mean about that letter though. Been a pain in the ass all month."

She's nodding as the kettle boils, and she turns away to pour the drink. I let myself look at her as she does it, taking in her blonde hair up in a bun, the back of her neck above the collar of her shirt.

"Morons. I tell you what..."

She trails off as she turns around. She's looking at me, and I'm so stupid it takes me a second to realise why. By then she's already saying, "Shit, George, what happened to your face?"

"Nah, nothing, it..."

"Someone hit you? You been in a fight?"

I can feel the flush rising, shame burning in my cheeks. I hate it. Can't stop it.

"Nah, just walked into a door on my way out the loo. I was shitfaced."

She looks at me, eyes sad, and I feel my jaw clench. In that moment I hate her, for her friendship and her awful sympathy.

"Must have been. Looks like the door lamped you a good one."

"Yeah, innit?"

"You know, George..." She trails off. There's a lot going on behind her eyes. She's frowning. She still looks sad. Lovely, though. I wish I could help her, talk to her. I wish... but then I get a flash of Dad, hitting me in the face.

I can't.

She comes over, sits next to me. Normally this'd be the highlight of my day, but her face is still so sad, and I just know she's going to say something, something real, and I don't want her to.

But then she surprises me. She takes my hand. I flinch but don't pull back. The touch is warm. I feel light-headed. She turns my hand over in hers, stares at it; opens her mouth to talk, then stops. The frown goes deeper. She opens her mouth again, and I follow her eyes down as she says, "Looks like you got the door a good one back."

I take in my bruised knuckles and I don't say anything. I remember punching my pillow in frustration, missing and hitting the bed-frame. But what's the point of telling her? Sounds like a lie.

Feels like a lie, even though I was there.

I take my hand away and look at her face. Her eyes meet mine. She holds my gaze calmly, with no front. I suddenly feel on the edge of tears.

"How's your dad, George?"

I manage not to jump, not to look away, but it's an effort.

"Not good. Can't remember anything now, most of

the time. Has a lot of nightmares."

Cover story—dementia. Close enough. Explains why I can't go out of the house, don't have any kind of social life. I don't like lying to her, but given the options...

She shakes her head, and I realise she's on the edge of tears, too. "God, George, I'm so sorry, really..."

"Hey, it's okay..."

"No, it isn't, it's..."

She's up suddenly, and a single tear falls from her eye. It hurts me to see it.

"I'm sorry, George..."

And she's gone. I don't get up to follow her, I just let her go. I stare into space, not thinking of much. Before I go back to my desk, I tip her tea down the sink and wash her cup for her, putting it next to mine in the cupboard.

I don't see her for the rest of the day.

It took me a while to realise he'd died. I'd come in from work, dropped the beer by his chair, noticed he was sleeping. I let him be, went up and showered, heated up dinner. I'd walked in with his dinner on a tray and noticed he was still asleep. Put the tray on the sofa. Shook him to wake him. He just pitched forward, fluid flowing from his mouth. The smell was vomit and fermented hops. It was like he'd drowned in it.

I phoned an ambulance. His dinner was still cooling on the tray when they declared him dead at the scene and zipped him into a bag.

Chronic liver failure. No surprises. Well, one. At some point, he'd taken out one of those 'pay-for-your-funeral' insurance schemes, and kept up the payments—or at least forgot to cancel them. Either way, I didn't pay a penny for any of it, and he got a good suit, a nice casket and a decent burial.

I was the only family there.

We buried him on a Thursday. I took the Friday off. It seemed like the thing to do. Was going to clean out his

room, but he'd hardly been in there since he moved in, so there wasn't much to do. The living room was worse. I tidied, dusted, hoovered, but I didn't move his chair. Couldn't. It stank of him, that was the thing—sweat and rotting beer. I knew I needed to be shot of it, but it was all I had left of him. It was real, like he'd been real. I wanted it to stay.

So I tidied and cleaned and scrubbed and at the end, the room gleamed. And in the middle of the room sat his chair, untouched, the blue carrier bag on the right hand side.

Tinnies in reach.

I remember feeling something then—a pain bigger than tears, something shifting in my chest, in my head. I staggered over to the chair, and sat in it.

It felt comfortable. Worn in. I could feel the shape of him pressed into the old fabric. I inhaled deep through my nose. Took him into my lungs. Dad. The remote was there on the arm. I flicked the telly on to Sky Sports and reached down for a tinny. I was aware that I'd started crying as I cracked the can and brought the beer to my lips, but I was okay with that. *I love you, Dad. I miss you, Dad.*

Things went grey for a while. I sat and drank and watched and cried and drank some more. At some point, I drifted off, and I was having a nightmare, and in the nightmare someone was letting themselves into the house. I could hear someone move the plant pot with the spare key under it, hear the lock turn, hear footsteps coming into the house, the front door slamming shut, loud, and still I couldn't wake up... The lounge door banging open now, someone stomping over to me, a familiar smell hitting my nose... and that let me open my eyes.

He was wearing the suit I had buried him in. His eyes were open and sunken back into his skull. His skin was pink, but this close, I could see the make-up smearing already, the yellowing flesh beneath poking through on his cheeks, his hands. He grinned, and his teeth were the

same, rotting and yellow, and as he leaned forward and placed his hands on my shoulders, his breath rolled over me. I felt myself gag.

He stared at me for a split second, eye to eye, leant back, and slammed his forehead into my nose. I shut my eyes at the moment of impact, and stars burst in the darkness. My teeth clicked together. His fingers sank into my shoulders, his grip terrifyingly strong, and he hauled me out of the chair and flung me across the room. I barely had time to open my eyes before the back of my skull collided with the TV table.

"That's my fucking chair." He sat down as I stared, feeling like something in my mind was ripping.

That was the first time in my life my father had hit me.

He turned his eyes from me to the TV. Turned up the volume. Shook the tin I'd been drinking from. Picked up the blue bag, counting.

"You'd better get me some more fucking beers, and all," he said, eyes never leaving the screen. Then he took a deep drink from the can.

I stay late at the office, not wanting to risk bumping into Jenny on the way out. I stop by the shop, pick up the two six packs. Then I grab another two, and a pint of Teachers.

Fuck it.

On the way home, I put the whiskey bottle in my jacket pocket, shoulders hunched against the rain.

When I get back, I open the door and just stand in the doorway, ready to jump back, but this time, the hall is empty. I step in slowly, pushing the door shut with my heel.

I can hear the TV, loud but not deafening. I walk slowly down the hall. The living room door is ajar.

I push it open with my foot, again standing back, but there's no need. He's in his seat. His back is to me, and he doesn't move. I stare at the back of his head. His hair is

black now, sparse and stringy. It clumps. The smell rises off him. Sweet and rancid.

"The fuck you been?"

"Sorry, got caught at work. Here."

I walk over and drop the tins by his side. He looks down at the clank, and I see him start at the size of the bag. I turn to leave, and he grabs me, scary quick. His grip is fierce and I almost cry out, but I don't.

"Grab me one out, would you? Pop the lid for your old man?"

I nod, swallowing fast, not trusting myself to speak. I kneel down, open the bag, grab a can and pull it from the plastic ring, cracking it open. As I do this, he pats me on the shoulder. "You're a good boy. A good son."

The can has suddenly become two, then four, then many. I feel my cheeks dampen as the tears flow. I feel my breath start to hitch.

Then the doorbell rings.

I jerk to my feet, staggering backwards, heart hammering in my chest. I feel him try to grab me, but for once surprise makes me quicker, and I cover the steps back to the lounge door.

"What the fuck, son?"

"I don't know! I dunno, I'll make them go, just..."

"Son..."

"Dad, just please stay quiet. I'll make them go, I swear!"

"Godamnit..."

But I'm already gone, all but running up the hall to the front door, wondering who the hell it could be and what the fuck I'm going to say. I cover the three steps down the hall without thinking of anything. Take a deep breath. Open the door.

She looks beautiful. The night air has brought real colour to her cheeks, sparkle to her brown eyes. She looks nervy, but also determined, angry even. Her hair is still up and there are beads of water gleaming in her fringe.

She takes my breath away. I try and talk anyway.

"Jenny..."

She's smiling, pushing past me into the hall, her coat dripping. "Thank Christ! It's chucking it down."

"Jenny..." Feeling my heart hammering in my chest, breathing heavy.

"I know, I know, I'm sorry, I followed you. Look, I have to talk to you, okay?"

"Jenny..."

"I know, I know, but I just... look, this afternoon, I wanted to say..."

She drifts off, staring at my right hand. I look down at the open tin. The smell of lager hits my nose, and my stomach rolls over, making me feel sick.

"Starting early?"

I look back up at her, with the smell of the beer and the churning in my stomach and a sudden stab of pain behind my eyes. My belly cramps.

"Whatever, look, George, all I wanted to say is I don't give a shit how bad things are with your dad..."

In my peripheral vision, I see the living room door open, slowly, quietly, and I catch my breath. My jaw clenches.

"...that's not what I meant, I meant, I mean..."

She reaches out and grabs my free hand, and I damn near jump out of my skin. My fist tightens around the can. My eyes move involuntarily to her face, and she's smiling, but it's a strained one, sad. I'm paralysed, pain and fear and anger building...

"...I mean we don't have to go out to go out. You don't have to shut me out, just because..."

I open my mouth, finally, to speak, to warn her, but it's too late. He clubs her on the back of the head with a full tin of beer. I have time to watch the white foam spray out in an arc as it hits the wall, then her head follows with a heavy thud. I jump back, and he swings again, there's a loud clunk, and her head thumps off the wall again, harder

this time. She cries out, and I cry out too. I drop the can in my hand, pull the whiskey bottle from my pocket and swing, and it bounces off the back of his head like he's made of concrete. I feel the impact all the way up my arm. He doesn't react at all to my blow, just leans forward and punches her in the side of the head again and again and again, that awful thick, dull clunk each time. I see her eyelids flutter, whites showing, and I scream as he pounds her. Blood from her split scalp imprints on the wallpaper. I swing my own fist over and over, my blows landing on his shoulder, his head, his back, our blows landing in perfect sync, mine on him, his on her, but he doesn't react.

It's like I'm not even there.

The sound of his fist hitting her becomes damp, squishy. Her body has slumped to the floor and he's leant over her, one fist bunched up in the front of her coat, the other still punching her head. Her face now is a blood mask. My own arm shrieks with pain as I keep swinging the bottle.

"George... please..." I can barely make the words out, her slurring is so bad.

I can feel myself screaming, but can't really hear it. I look at her bloody face as I hit him, my arms numb now, losing strength.

Finally he straightens up, letting go of her and stiff-arming me in one fluid movement. I slam into the far wall, head bouncing off. I slide down as he turns and walks back down the hall, into the living room.

I look over at Jenny, and down at my own hands, clenched into fists. At the glass bottle.

Her breathing has become ragged panting, arrhythmic. Her face is a mass of purple and red. One eye is swollen shut; the other is bloody, sightless. I look at the split in her scalp, at the hairline. Where he hit her. Where he...

Where he...

My eyes pull back to the bottle in my fist. I take in the

409

lower edge. The blood beading there. Stark against the dark brown of the bottle's contents. Fresh blood.

My mind replays a sound. The dull clunk as he hit her. As he...

Sitting in the centre of a small clot, right on the edge of the base of the bottle, I see a single blond hair.

I look from the bottle to her ruined face.

I feel something pull, inside my head. It doesn't hurt much.

"George, please. George..."

Everything seems a long way away.

I close my eyes. I can hear her breath start to hitch, becoming moist, bubbly. The sound begins to fade. So does everything else.

ROUND TWELVE
WINNER

ZOMBIE DAD
KIT POWER

ROUND THIRTEEN

RAPE VAN
TIM MILLER

VS

HUSH
DANIEL I. RUSSELL

RAPE VAN
TIM MILLER

The van sped down the empty road as dust kicked up behind it. It was an old cargo van, but Andy used it for road trips. Probably not the safest choice, but it was big enough to carry his friends and their belongings.

"Will you slow down?" his girlfriend, Bridget, barked. "The whole fucking van is shaking!"

"It always shakes. It's old."

"Why won't you trade this in?"

"He loves his rape van too much," Martin said from the back. He and his girlfriend, Chrissy, were lying on an old mattress in the cargo area. With each bump in the road, they bounced off the mattress slightly.

"Will you stop calling it that?" Andy said.

"I thought you were going to fix the radio," Martin said. "It's too fucking boring, and I'm sick of hearing you two cackle at each other."

"I told you, once we get to Austin, I'll have them look at it there." They'd been on the road for several days. They didn't actually have a home. Andy and Bridget lived out of

the van, driving cross country like modern day hippies. They'd picked up Martin and Bridget in Oklahoma and the pair had ridden along with them since. Usually, Andy didn't care for tagalongs, but so far, these two hadn't bothered him too much. It was only a matter of time, though.

They were currently between Austin and Round Rock which consisted of empty fields and back roads. Andy tried to avoid the freeways. There was too much traffic and he liked the scenery.

"Maybe one of you can sing for us if you're bored?" Bridget said.

"Oh, God," Chrissy jumped in. "Don't get him started. He sings in the shower. Makes the dogs howl."

"I do not sing in the shower!" Martin protested.

"Yes, you do! You don't think I can hear you, but the whole neighborhood can hear you!"

"Whatever."

"Aww, look. He's all mad now."

"Hey," Andy said. "Don't let us stop you. If you guys want to get it on back there, be my guest."

Bridget promptly punched him in the arm.

"Ow! What the fuck?"

"You fuckin' perv!"

"You know I'm just messin'."

"Yeah. The fuck you are."

There was a small gas station just ahead. Andy pulled in at one of the pumps and turned off the engine.

"I'm gonna go ahead and top it off while we're here. Anyone needs to use the bathroom or anything, have at it," Andy said as he jumped out. He went inside to find a single attendant working the counter. She was an older woman, looking to be in her fifties. She had on a red vest and was playing on her phone when he walked in.

"Can I help you?" she asked, sleepily.

"Yeah. Forty dollars on pump four."

"All right. Will there be anything else?" she asked as

he handed her the cash. Martin and Chrissy were walking around looking at the snacks. Their food consisted of sodas, chips, and beef jerky. As they sifted through the snacks, an older man came walking out of the back room. He was slightly taller than Andy, also wearing a red vest. He looked outside at the van.

"Did you guys want full service?" he asked.

"Full service?" Andy said.

"You know. I can pump your gas for you, wash your windows. Full service."

"Places still do that?"

"This one does."

"Sure. Go for it."

"All righty." The man headed out to the van as Andy watched. He grabbed a bag of chips and a soda as Martin and Chrissy paid for their food. The woman rang them up as Andy headed outside.

"So where you kids headed?" the old man asked.

"Austin."

"In this thing? Doesn't look very safe. You all riding in this?"

"It's safe enough."

"Better hope you don't get stopped. State troopers out here will think you're running drugs or illegals."

"We'd be driving north if we were doing that, not south."

"Either way."

"Is this part of the full service? Getting hassled?"

"Just making conversation, son. No need to get snippy."

The man finished pumping gas and replaced the nozzle. He grabbed a squeegee and began washing off the windshield when Bridget appeared at the front of the van.

"Well, hey there," she said.

"Hello," the old man said. "You with him I take it?"

"Sure am."

"He always this cheerful?"

"Oh, don't mind him. We been on the road a lot. He gets pissy."

"I can see that." Behind Bridget, Martin and Chrissy climbed back into the van. The old man finished washing the windshield and turned around. He never saw Andy come up behind him until his fist connected. Andy punched the old man right in the nose, knocking him flat on his back. Bridget squealed as the man fell.

"Holy shit! You knocked him out with one punch!"

From inside the van, Chrissy screamed as Martin jumped out.

"What the fuck was that? Why did you do that?" Martin screamed. Chrissy pulled a gun from her purse and shoved it into Martin's face.

"Shut the fuck up and get back inside."

"What? What's going on?"

"Do it!" she yelled.

Martin put his hands up and backed up toward the van and climbed back inside. Andy dragged the old man over and threw him in back, pulling the door shut.

"Go get the old lady," he said. "And make sure there're no cameras."

He stood by and waited. A few minutes later Bridget came walking out with the woman at gunpoint. The old woman reached the van.

"What's going on? Where's Robert?"

"Robert's fine. Get in the van," Andy ordered.

"You robbing us? Just take what you want and go."

"Yeah, it's a robbery. I'm taking both of you, now get in the fucking van!"

The woman climbed in as Andy climbed up after her. Bridget held them all at gunpoint as Andy grabbed a roll of duct tape from under the seat and proceeded to tape everyone's hands behind their backs. He then taped up their feet and pulled the door shut. Bridget got in the driver's seat as they pulled away.

"What is this about, man?" Martin asked.

417

"It's about you shutting the fuck up!" Andy yelled.

"Jesus Christ! Fucking do something, Martin!" Chrissy yelled.

"Do what? We're all taped up. They got a fucking gun!"

They were speeding down the road as Andy looked around.

"You know. I think it's kind of crowded in here. What do you all think?"

"You're right," Martin said. "I think you should just let us go."

"You think so? What do you say, old man?"

"I'd be happy if you let us go."

"Maybe I'll do that." Andy slid the door open as the van sped down the road and dragged the old man into the doorway. "How's this? You want me to let you go?"

"No!"

"Come on! I gotta make some room in here! Maybe I'll let your old lady go. You prefer that?"

"No! Please?"

"Please, what?"

"Just please don't hurt us."

"How about this then?" Andy reached down the back of his pants and pulled out the snubnosed revolver, stuck it in the old man's throat and pulled the trigger. A clump of blood, bone and flesh ripped through the back of his neck as the man gurgled, while Andy let go of his body. The man's body bounced and flopped along the side of the road as the van sped along. Everyone in the van screamed. Even Bridget screamed, but she did so mocking their victims. Andy slid the door shut and looked back at the group.

"There. Now it's a bit roomier in here, don't you think?"

The woman was screaming and crying.

"You killed him! Why? Why?"

"I fucking told you! It was too crowded! Now shut

418

the fuck up or you'll be next!"

He turned and pointed the gun at Martin.

"What did you call this earlier?"

"Call what?"

"My fucking van, numbnuts! What did you call it?"

"Uh...uh rape van?"

"Yes! You called my van...which is pretty much my fucking home, mind you. You called my home a fucking rape van! So, since you think this is a rape van, we better make it live up to its reputation!"

Andy tucked the gun into a pocket behind the passenger seat and unbuttoned his jeans. Chrissy began to scream as Martin started yelling.

"No!" Martin yelled. "Please! Don't hurt her! Don't rape her!"

Andy stopped mid zip and looked up.

"Her? Who said anything about her? My dick is going into your asshole, buddy!"

"What? No! Get me the fuck out of here! Get me out!" Martin began flopping and kicking uncontrollably. Andy pulled his jeans off, exposing his massive erection as he looked at Chrissy.

"You see that shit? He wasn't near that worked up a minute ago when he thought I was about to fuck you."

He looked back at Martin as tears ran down Chrissy's face.

"All right, champ. Let's do this."

Andy reached down and grabbed Martin by the jeans and pulled out a pocket knife. He flipped the blade open and started cutting through Martin's pants. Martin screamed and struggled but was helpless to resist with his hands bound behind his back. Soon, Andy had the pants cut away and sliced off his underwear. He flopped Martin onto his stomach before inserting his erection into Martin's ass. Martin grunted and screamed as Andy began thrusting.

"Look out buddy!" Andy yelled. "I'm going in dry!"

Martin cried and continued grunting as Andy thrust over and over hooting and hollering with each thrust.

"Sorry, pal! I won't give you a reach around! Holy shit! I'm about to blow a load!"

Martin let out a high-pitched squeal as Andy's body tensed while he twitched and grunted. After a minute he stood and pulled his jeans up while pointing at Martin, who was lying there crying.

"Watch it now, wait for it. Wait for it," Andy said. A minute later, shit stained semen dripping white and brown with some blood red mixed in oozed from Martin's butthole. "Haha! There it is! Chocolate cream pie! You wanna eat that shit up, girl?"

"Fuck you!" Chrissy screamed.

"Oh, now. Don't be like that. Gotta wait a few, you know. I'm not a machine! Don't worry. We can still have some fun. Come here, grandma."

He grabbed the older woman and ripped her shirt off. She screamed as he pulled her toward the front of the van by the hair and sat down behind her while holding her up in a sitting position.

"Time for a haircut, Granny." He took out his knife and began cutting just above the back of her neck. She cried out as he sliced through the skin down to the bone, cutting all the way around to the edge of her ears up the sides of her head. She tried pulling away, but he kept a firm grip on her hair. After several minutes, he looked over at Chrissy.

"Now, let's see her new look!" He reached up to the top of her hair and pulled forward. The woman howled in pain as her flesh ripped from the muscle and bone and pulled free of her skull. He continued pulling forward until the flesh was tearing and ripping from her face as he pulled it free of her nose and let the loose skin flop down just below her lips.

"Holy shit! That is trippy as fuck! Bridget! Check this shit out! I ripped her whole fucking face off and she's still

alive!"

"I can't! I'm drivin'!"

"I'll take a picture."

He pulled out his cell phone and held it up as the woman shook and trembled, her face nothing but red muscle and tendons with her eyes bulging. He snapped a photo and put it back into his pocket. The woman muttered something, but he couldn't make it out.

"What was that?"

"Cold," she said. "I cold."

"You're cold? No shit, you're cold! You don't have a fucking face!"

He pushed her and let her fall onto her back. She continued shaking as Chrissy glared at him.

"You're just going to leave her like that?"

"The fuck you want me to do? She'll be dead soon. She's going into shock."

Martin was still moaning, lying on his face as he moved up to his knees. Andy watched as Martin got to his knees and lunged at Andy while letting out a feral growl. Andy stepped to the side and kicked him in the face. Blood and teeth went flying as Martin's jaws snapped shut. He flopped to his side as Andy knelt down.

"Boy, that was fucking stupid. I was going to kill you. But first, you get to watch your girl suck my dick."

Martin lay there with blood dripping from his mouth. Andy grabbed Chrissy by the hair and pulled her to her knees.

"I'll tell you right now, you bite me, bitch, I'll pull every one of your fucking teeth and shove them up your pussy." He took his dick out, which was erect again and slid it into her mouth. She half-ass sucked as she folded her lips in over her teeth while Andy held her by the hair, fucking her face.

"There you go. So how does your boyfriend's shit taste? Fucking good, huh? You're sucking his shit off my dick. That's fuckin' funny!" He thrust faster and faster until

he felt her teeth clamp down around the tip of his cock. He immediately punched her in the nose, breaking her grip and knocking her back. He looked down at the end of his dick. There was some blood but it wasn't too bad. He wouldn't be fucking for a few days.

"Goddammit! I fucking warned you!"

He knelt down over her and pulled the gun from his pants, and using the butt, pistol-whipped her in the face. Bone and cartilage in her face crunched and snapped, as blood splattered his face and shirt. He struck her face over and over. Within minutes, her face was a swollen mess of bone, blood and mushy pulp. There were red bubbles coming out of what Andy thought was her nose, but he wasn't sure. One of her eyeballs appeared to be running down the side of her face.

Next to her, Martin continued crying while still spitting out his own teeth. Andy leaned over to him and took out his knife once again.

"You not had enough, slick? You want some more?" Andy took the knife and thrust it into Martin's asshole. Martin screamed again as Andy twisted the knife back and forth before thrusting it up and down. He pulled it out and wiped off the bloody clumps of skin and Martin's colon from the blade.

"Jesus Christ, dude. You scream worse than your fucking girlfriend did."

Marin had gone completely hysterical at this point, screaming and crying, while mumbling something Andy couldn't understand.

"God, I can't take it anymore," he reached up and cut Martin's throat. Blood sprayed into a small fountain as Martin gagged and twitched before going still. Andy put the knife away and walked up to the front seat.

"You have fun, babe?" Bridget asked.

"You know I did!"

"Good. Next time you'-re driving."

"I know. We take turns. I got it."

"You really make her suck the shit off your dick?"

"Hell, yeah. I wanted it to be cleaned off for you later, but the bitch bit me."

"Awww, you poor thing. I'll kiss it good for you later. Oh, we'll be in Austin in a few minutes."

"Sweet! It will be dark soon too. We'll dump the bodies then and get a hotel. I love you, sugarplum," Andy said.

"I love you too, hunny bunny."

He leaned over and gave her a bloodstained kiss.

HUSH
DANIEL I. RUSSELL

"Sands of time," now there's a popular saying. Grains of sand pouring through the slim neck of an elegant glass timer; each of our lives but an irrelevant speck, slipping through one side to the other, just like all the rest. Yet sand, like the years, gently corrodes and weathers. "Time is the best healer," there's another. Why not combine the two? Time heals by sanding away the sharp edges, leaving only curved, smooth memories.

The director's face. He had short, curly dark hair, fashioned into a trendy mullet prevalent in the eighties, and Hush could remember sniggering behind his hand. The man looked like a race horse. Yet now, trying to remember, those pesky sands of time, he could only see the hair and not the face. He tried to picture the eyes, the nose, the mouth. Only featureless skin resided, time hazing.

Yet, Hush remembered the pain quite clearly.

* * *

"I *hate* this shit, Jobe. I really hate, no, I fucking despise this shit."

"Come on, Mikey. You've been in this business long enough." The younger man grinned, his narrow glasses rising on chubby cheeks. "Ninety percent bullshit. You know that."

Hush groaned and slouched further in the leather armchair.

The company had rented an office on North Las Palmas Avenue, just off the Boulevard. Imported Swedish pine paneled the floor, and high mirrors covered every wall and even the ceiling. Hush didn't know whether to continue the meeting or start working out. The mirrors allowed the director to assess the actors from every angle. *All the better to check out the asses on the nineteen year olds desperate for a break*, laughed the director of Hush's last flick, when he'd recommended the place. *And I've broke enough of them alright!*

"Surely I don't have to be here," said Hush. "I mean, fuck! Isn't De Silva being paid enough? I thought this was his department." He snorted. "*Producer.* I thought they dealt with this shit. What is he producing this morning? A ruptured septum? Until primary photography starts... The script is locked in, the main names cast... why the fuck are we here?"

"Because," said Jobe, stifling a sigh, "you said that this was *your* vision and that you wanted input at every stage of the process."

Hush waved the statement away, "We haven't really started yet. This? This is admin."

Jobe, his eyes having never left his phone since the meeting started, began to furiously tap out a message, dealing with another client. "It's a good look for your first feature. You know this town; word gets around, so better to send the right message at the start. There are enough naysayers not taking this project seriously. Your image is

very important."

"Important to you," grunted Hush. "Keep the parts rolling in. You'd be happy if I played the hero 'til I was in the ground."

Mike J. Hush – born Miko Jan Lahush, a gift from his Slavic mother promptly taken away by his first agent – had made a name for himself as the plucky child actor in the eighties hit *The Fabled Four: The Movie.* His portrayal of a kidnapped villager in the epic sci-fi fantasy had led to better roles, eventually to leads come his mid-twenties. His big action parts would once have been mentioned alongside Stallone, Van Damme... even Seagal, depending on the year.

Now he had made the leap.

"You still haven't told me," he said. "Why the hell are we here?"

"You're meeting the main cast," said Jobe with a sigh, eyes still locked on his phone. Gomez had flashed a nipple at the Globes last night, and the press were going crazy. He was probably checking his bank balance. "Your chance to personally deliver your *vision* before we meet for principles in a week."

"You're joking, right?" asked Hush as a gentle tap sounded at the office door. "I missed out on lunch with Jackie Chan for this?" He rolled his eyes. "He knows a great little Brazilian grill too..."

A timid face poked around the mirrored door: their assistant for the day. Young, blonde, tight miniskirt, and glasses, that while lending her an air of intelligence, just made you want to splash a load over them. Mike had planned on it, but then the girl jumped like a startled rabbit every time he spoke to her. The curse of being a star.

"Excuse me, Mr. Hush, but I have a..." She checked the clipboard she gripped to her chest and pushed her glasses higher up her nose. Adorable! "A Ryder Nash here to see you?"

"Ryder Nash!" Hush spat with a huge grin. "Now

there's a name! Send him in."

The assistant offered a small bow before ducking back out of the room.

Hush sat back in the armchair. "Ryder Nash, eh? The lead! The ex con, the hoodlum for hire, rescuing little Freddy from the clutches of the evil Golden Dragon Gang." He raised an eyebrow to Jobe, who didn't look up from his phone.

The door opened once more, and the assistant ushered inside a boy of around ten and a woman looking around the room in awe, presumably his mother, and a MILF to boot.

"Oh no, here we are." Hush stood and walked around the long table, first shaking hands with the mother. "Good morning. Thank you for coming." He looked down at the boy. "And you must be... Ryder Nash?"

The boy nodded.

"Fantastic," said Hush, shaking hands and returning to his place.

"Ryder is playing the part of Freddy. You'd have known that if you'd come to casting," muttered Jobe. "Or read some of this." He tapped one of the many stacks of paper, files and glossy black and white headshots.

"Alright," said Hush. "Not in front of my young talent, please." He grinned. "Show some professionalism, for fuck's sake."

They ran through the part of Freddy, his background, and how exactly he finds the secret underground layer of the Golden Dragon Gang. Ryder completed some brief readings from the script, mostly pleading on his knees or begging while Hush pretended to tie him up. His mother watched from the corner.

"Well, I for one am happy with the choice casting made," said Hush, making his goodbyes after half an hour. He ruffled Ryder's hair. "Quite an acting talent you have here, Mrs. Nash!"

Daniel I. Russell

"It's actually Narcisse," said the short woman. "My husband is French-Canadian. Raymond's—I mean Ryder's agent suggested we change it."

Hush nodded. "Very interesting. The lad reminds me of a certain young talent from when I was a lad…"

"Culkin?"

"No," spat Hush, jabbing his chest. "Me! Yes… it's invigorating to see the youth chomping at the bit for a part. Most of them are on drugs these days, Mrs. Narcisse. Let me tell you. One young girl I shared a scene with was so high on crack, she… she…"

Hush glanced over her shoulder. Jobe, standing behind, was gesturing for Hush to shut the fuck up. Always trying to protect his clients.

"Perhaps," said Hush, returning his attention to the mother and son, "that's a story best left to another time. Possibly this weekend!" He placed a hand on Ryder's shoulder and gently pulled him closer. "Young man, when I see a talent like yours, it makes one want to nurture it, to trap it in a glass jar, and hold it up to the sun. I've been known to occasionally offer private lessons to such promising young actors, to help hone their skills. Free of charge, of course! Anything we can develop would pay dividends for our little picture. What do you say?"

"Mikey?" said Jobe. "Can I have a word?" He nodded to the side, implying the actor-turned-director to step aside.

Hush smirked. "Excuse me."

He left them in the capable hands of the assistant to confirm upcoming dates, and joined Jobe in the corner, slapping him on the back.

"That kid, man. With him, our lead, the T and A, and my direction, we're making something special."

The agent knocked Hush's hand away. "Are you serious? After what happened last time, are you fucking serious?"

"What?"

428

Jobe grabbed the front of Hush's shirt and pulled him closer. Mrs. Narcisse cast them a curious glance.

"The last time you gave a *private* acting lesson, it cost us thousands just to shut them up and thousands more to keep them quiet. We can't afford to take a hit like that again. If any of this got out..." He shook his head. "As your agent, I have to say that this is a terrible career move, Mikey. The latest one of many. Do not, *do not*, see this boy privately. You don't pull the Hollywood clout anymore to keep this one quiet."

Hush narrowed his eyes. Jobe had been on his back ever since he starred in the low budget remake of *Last of the Mohicans*. Pick the right part, not the right money. Run every decision by him first. Stay away from the child actors. Jobe treated *him* like one of those child actors.

"This is for the movie," Hush said, struggling to keep his voice even. "The kid's good, but his positioning could use some work while he's pleading."

"I bet it could," said Jobe. "Mikey. No."

"You still don't believe me? Jesus, man. I told you nothing happened the last time. The kid was a talentless ham looking to make a quick buck. You've known me years. Think I could do some of the things he said? Look at me. I'm Mike *fucking* Hush. I can get any woman I want in this town. Why the hell would I do...all those other things?" He stared at the boy. Ryder Nash. He had such promise. "Okay, Jobe, you piece of shit. You want to babysit me, fine, but I'm not backing down from this. The movie comes first. Make it official: pay the kid for his time. That will keep the mother sweet. They're Canadian. No one in Canada makes big money; it's too damn cold."

Jobe rolled his eyes. "You're insisting on doing this?"

"It's for the movie, buddy," said Hush, flashing him a grin. "Anything for the movie."

"It won't be at your house again," said his agent, "and *I* need to be there. Just in case..." He took a deep breath. "Just in case this kid decides to try to make a fast buck at

the expense of your reputation."

"Wouldn't be the first time, Jobe. Arrange it before they leave. Oh, and buddy?"

Jobe paused.

"Write the check now. I find actors are more committed once they've been paid."

The director with the black mullet had promised to make Hush a star; hindsight would suggest he'd fulfilled his side of the bargain.

Yet, the young Hush had somehow lost his part in that movie, a shuffling of the cast or a script rewrite had cost him his big break.

He remembered sitting on the sofa at his parents' house, his mother cradling him as she broke the news, tears pouring down her face. They'd never had much money, and through Hush's haze – the pain and fear had ebbed away to a post-nightmare shadow – the guilt rode him hard. Their escape had been promised; an unspoken agreement paid for with confused silence. Now, he'd lost it all.

His father, separate from the unnecessary emotional display on the sofa, sat at the kitchen table, his dinner untouched beside him. In his hands, a sliver of paper. His thumb ran over the zeroes, over and over, while his wife wept, and his TV dinner gradually cooled.

Hush's wall safe sat nestled behind his framed poster of *Speed 4*. The poster was of course signed. By him.

He eased the hinged frame aside, revealing the small, plain metal door behind. The buttons were cold to the touch as he keyed in his passcode: his mother's birthday. The contents were pretty standard: his important documents – passport, various licenses and memberships, and the odd love letter valued enough to escape the fireplace – sat in a folder alongside a few pieces of high-end jewelry, saved for premieres when the paparazzi were

snapping.

Leaning against the back wall of the safe stood a plastic case holding a single CD. He'd been using a usb drive, but a fellow actor had advised him against it. Easier to snap a CD with your bare hands should the need arise.

Hush carried it over to his coffee table and a waiting laptop. He sat on the sofa, removed the CD, and slid it into the drive. Numerous folders appeared on screen containing so many clips he'd never have the time to watch them all. He liked to pick one at random and see what he got; his digital box of chocolates never failed to provide a sweet, delicious treat.

The elite never called or, god forbid, hailed a cab. Some had their own drivers, or at least their preferred company that supplied drivers when needed. Others still, those that had a new supermodel or pop sensation girlfriend, might accidentally drive down the Boulevard in a fresh convertible and complain when they make the cover of *Hello! Daily Showbiz*.

Hush chose to drive himself for this particular jaunt. As the cafes and boutiques flew by, he prayed to the gods of sat nav. The place Jobe had provided was a little way from his usual haunts.

Hush spied a cosy Italian place on the corner of the next intersection, and stopping at a red light, he tried to recall why it looked so familiar. Ah! That's right. He'd had dinner with Casper and his latest girlfriend there a year or two back. No one ate at home in this town, and it became hard to tell the eateries apart after a while. Yes. Casper. A fellow action hero, back in the day. Now he scrapped for parts with the rest of them. Pigs at a trough. Waiting by the phone for the SyFy Channel to call. Hoping they could somehow combine a giant platypus and hamster and needing someone to blow it up in the final scene.

Now, his girlfriend, thought Hush, drumming on the steering wheel. His eyes were on the red light, but he saw

Daniel I. Russell

her face. Young thing. About nineteen with hair the colour of midnight that cascaded down to her shoulders. A touch of Latino in her? There was a bit of *something*. Unfortunately, there hadn't been a bit of Mike Hush in her by the end of the evening. She'd been one of those kid TV stars, Disney Club or some bullshit, kiddy sitcom, when the teenage daughter grows some titties and suddenly dads all over the country are tuning in. Then the network of agents and company heads jump in, launch her pop career, and drop the rest of the cast like rotting corpses. Before you know it, America's favourite daughter is lip-syncing in pigtails and hot pants.

"Yeah," said Hush, pulling away as the light turned green. "That's what everyone wanted to see in the first place."

That Harry Potter chick. The British press had been desperate for a nipple slip or panty flash for years! A snap of her at fifteen polishing Harry's wand would have crashed the internet. They even had a countdown of her Birthday. Many happy returns! You're legal now!

"At the next intersection, turn left," purred his phone.

"I certainly will, you saucy little minx."

A few long stretches and odd turns later, and Hush's phone announced that he'd reached his destination. The area screamed old Hollywood - classy forties art deco style adorned the building. Hush could see it in black and white, a Bogart type smoking in the doorway.

"Things are never so bad they can't be made worse, kid," said Hush with a wink. Chuckling, he climbed out of his car, locked it, and ventured inside the Kasabian Hotel: the neutral ground Jobe had chosen for the acting lesson.

Hush had no problems with his agent's conditions. Jobe was always on his phone. He couldn't possibly be there all the time. Besides, the kid had been paid. He owed Hush for this amazing opportunity.

He was going to make Ryder Nash a star.

* * *

The wizened crone at reception had clearly never seen a movie since silent pictures reigned. Since he was neither Chaplin, Linder, nor Lloyd, she failed to recognise him and resorted to take his name. Jobe had reserved a room. Hush was free to go up there now, but having arrived early, he decided to partake of the bar first. A few bourbons always helped to loosen him up before delivering an acting class. Besides, these old Hollywood establishments off the beaten track, the movie time capsules capturing the bygone decades, held a few golden era faces now and then. Sometimes even the stars liked to go gazing, and these tired bars and hideouts had a way of attracting souls that had fallen off the Hollywood radar. In the shadows cast by the limelight, and while not dead themselves, the ghosts of their careers haunted the backstage.

Through a dingy corridor of peeling wallpaper and worn carpet, Hush passed various closed doors, a staircase of dark, dulled wood, and an ancient elevator of wrought black iron: a squealing cage that reminded Hush of a gibbet for small groups. Beyond that the room opened out into a large ballroom, and a bar that ran the length of the side wall. A few patrons sat nursing drinks on the round tables scattered around, mostly alone or with partners. Hush dumped himself onto a stool facing the barman, and applied his best Jack Nicholson grin.

"God, I'd give anything for a drink. I'd give my god-damned soul just for a glass of beer."

The barman nodded and reached for the chiller full of glasses, pulled one out, and approached the tap.

"No, no," said Hush. "A bourbon please. On the rocks."

The barman frowned, clearly not being paid enough to deal with indecisive assholes, replaced the glass and prepared the drink.

"I'll just set my bourbon and advocaat down right

here," said Hush, still in Nicholson mode, picking up the short glass the moment the barman placed it down.

"Sir would like an advocaat also?"

"For fuck's sake..." Hush growled, flicking a bill onto the bar. "You live in Hollywood. Ain't none of you ever seen a fucking movie?"

The barman stared at him.

"Kubrick's *The Shining*, you big dumb fuck." Hush turned on his stool to survey the room.

Occupying the table closest, a woman toyed with a phone that rested on the stained wood. Manicured nails tapped at the screen, poking from the end of withered digits, reminding Hush of chicken feet scratching in the dirt. A flimsy pale pink garment hung from her skeletal frame, straps resting on wrinkled, atrophied shoulders. Her drinking partner, a younger man with surfer boy golden locks, sat beside her looking bored. His frame towered over hers, lending the table a skew that threatened to topple it over. Still the woman tap-tap-tapped. Aware of being watched, the shriveled crone, perhaps a Hollywood starlet once upon a time, peered up through dry, spider silk hair. A clink of metal stole Hush's attention; he noticed a thick, silver chain clutched in the woman's other hand. He followed its length across the table until it vanished over the edge at the young man's unseen groin. The surfer dude also looked up, giving Hush a polite nod.

Freaks, thought the action star, turning back to the shelves behind the bar. They sported their own Hollywood Walk of Fame: all glittering bottles full of dark spirits.

His only companion leaning on the smooth, elbow-worn bar, sat to his right: an older man in heavy dark clothes, matching beret, and spectacles with thick, black lenses. Like Sartre contemplating his existence, he studied the floating ice cubes in his amber drink, searching for meaning. He glanced at Hush with bloodshot eyes set within an ashen face, born of early German expressionist film. Hell, he looked old enough to have starred.

"Haven't seen you here before," the old man muttered, and scratched the side of his neck with a wickedly hooked nail.

Hush couldn't help but notice the angry welts and bruises looped around the man's throat.

"First time," said Hush with a nervous mile and raised his bourbon. "Surprised I haven't been here before. Such a Hollywood hotspot. Very exclusive." He took a fiery sip. The spirit proved cheap, instantly regretful, and left a sour taste at the back of his throat. Not surprising.

A tickle by his ear caused Hush to swat away the offending bug, only to find the moist flesh of an eager face sniffing his hair. Hush slammed his drink on the bar.

"What the fuck is this?"

The offender stepped back, hands up. Around sixty, the bald man grinned, flashing mostly barren gums, his face glistening with fresh sweat. "I was the next Peckinpah in the seventies, you know." He straightened his miserly suit that reeked of week-old body odour, reaching almost smoky levels in its spicy miasma. "Peckinpah!"

"Touch me again, *Sloth*, and you'll end up like one of his fucking characters."

"Mikey?"

Hush spun on his stool, finding Jobe waiting in the doorway. "Oh, thank Christ." He picked up his glass, downed the remainder of his foul short, and stood, pushing his clammy admirer aside. "Let's go. This place is like *Cocoon* directed by Lars Von Trier."

The room lived up to the high standards set by the rest of the hotel. The glorious California sun was kept at bay by grimy net curtains over a cracked window overlooking the alley. The bedsheets looked almost dusty, and wallpaper had long peeled away from the stained wall in the corner.

"Lovely place," said Hush, collapsing in a chair next to the bed. He'd bought the rest of the cheap bourbon to see him through the afternoon. He took a sip straight from

the open bottle.

"We're not here on vacation," said Jobe. He carried a black briefcase, which he placed on the bed. "We all need places where we can conduct... certain business. No paparazzi, no Hollywood reporters, no requests for autographs. You understand, Mikey."

"Indeed I do, buddy! Hell, I feel kinda bad having to bring a young boy to such a seedy place... but I'll do anything, you know..." He grinned. "I'll do anything for the movie. He should be here any moment."

"Mikey, Mikey, Mikey." Jobe clicked open the clasps on the briefcase, and looked at Hush over his frameless glasses. "Do you really think I would bring a child here? What kind of agent do you think I am? I'm not some... pimp." He sighed. "I told you in the meeting. *No*. It wasn't happening. Not after last time."

Hush sat up straighter in his chair, fingers tightening around the neck of the bottle.

"You might think the Hollywood elite have this safety net; a covert network that protects the stars from the scandals. Well..." The agent opened the briefcase. "You'd be right, but the problem is, Mikey... you aren't Hollywood elite. You haven't been for a very long time."

Who the fuck does this guy think he is?

Hush flung the bottle of bourbon across the room. It flew over Jobe's head and smashed on the wall behind him, adding a brief splash of dark caramel over the yellowed paper.

"Are you mad because of the slur on your career? Or are you pissed that the kid isn't showing up?"

"I'm going to kill you," spat Hush. "The amount of *my* money you take with each part... the cuts here and there. I'd have thought a little more respect would be in order from a sniveling little whelp like you. You're *nobody*." Hush stood from the chair, fists clenched. "I'm the earner; you're just the leech that sucks from every part."

Jobe raised a finger. "I wouldn't, Mikey. I really

wouldn't."

Hush grabbed the agent by the lapels of his suit jacket and slammed him backwards. The men collided with a dresser, shaking the spider-webbed mirror. Jobe, skinny, and probably more concerned about disturbing his $200 haircut, raised his arms around his head rather than fight back. Hush pushed him hard against the wall, not caring. He'd put food on this fucker's table. He was not a celebrity cast off like those losers haunting the bar. He was Mike fucking Hush!

Simian hands grabbed him from behind, sinking into the muscles of his shoulders and casting him back.

Hush tried to hold on to Jobe, his fury directed to a point, that sharp nose, so breakable.

A solid fist to the growing gut stopped Hush in his tracks. He fell to the grimy carpet, wheezing.

One of the two men helped to straighten Jobe up. The agent adjusted his glasses on his sadly unbroken nose, and with his thugs either side, took a steadying breath and looked down at Hush.

"Used to playing the hard man. *Pathetic*. No matter the role, Mikey. No matter how many CGI helicopters you jump out of, or explosions you run in slow motion from… you'll never be a hard man. These gentlemen don't play at anything. As your agent, yes, *still,* I recommend you stay down. Fritz here has been dying to get his hands on you since *Speed 4*. Huge Keanu fan."

The hulking bald man with the tattooed face gave Hush a square boot to the ribs. "You ruin good franchise!"

Jobe smiled. "Easy, Fritz. It was on its last legs after *Cruise Control.*"

Hush rose to all fours but still lay panting against the stinking carpet. "What the fuck? We could…" He drew in a deep breath. It hurt. He wasn't used to hurting, not for a long time. "We could have had… a fucking meeting about this."

"We're doing that now. Gentlemen, keep an eye on

him." The agent approached the briefcase. "I know you fucked that boy, Mikey. You all do it. The drugs, the fetishes, the sick fucking things you privileged whores are into. Yet, as I say, you don't carry the clout anymore. Your last few gigs bombed at the box office. This directing... I don't even know what to call it... this frivolous authenticity you seek? It's about to get canned."

Hush tried to pounce to his feet. In one of his movies, he'd leap up, smash one of the heavies through the mirror, spin kick the other into oblivion, and have Jobe by the throat in seconds. A hard boot on the back of his neck proved once again that life wasn't a movie.

"We go back a long way," Jobe continued. "We've developed quite a trusting relationship and I know you, Mikey, and you were about to repeat past mistakes. Your stature can't quite cover what you were about to do. This presents us with quite the predicament. I can't get the parts for you. You've become quite the liability in certain circles. Actors like... well, you know *who*. You trade with them all the time, but their careers still protect them, Mikey. Yours? Not so much." He crouched down and laid a hand on Hush's shoulder. "You're used to playing the hard man, buddy, and now you are. You're a hard man to sell. That is... unless you know your place in the network."

The agent reached into his jacket and pulled out his cell. He smiled as he tapped away, the bright screen reflected in his lenses.

"What are you doing?" screamed Hush.

"Just making a transaction," said Jobe. "You were right. Actors tend to be more committed after they've been paid. Not that you'll talk." He chuckled and held his cell to Hush's face. "No one ever talks, do they?"

Hush squinted at the numbers on the small screen.

Jobe stood and gestured to the other man. The not Fritz, who wasn't trying to stomp him through the floor spine first.

"Yes?"

438

"Tell them we're ready." He grabbed the briefcase and emptied its contents onto the bed.

Hush focused on a bead of sweat that dawdled down his forehead, only to be absorbed into the warm blindfold.

Playing a part, just playing another part, just a role. A face to be applied; a mask to be cast off once he stepped out of this collapsing old hotel.

Hush screamed as whatever had been crudely shoved inside him dove further still, widening his tested innards. His protests were met by a wheezed grumble, and a moment later, a ball, tasting of noxious cheap plastic, was forced into his mouth and secured by a leather strap about the head. Some of them had wanted him to scream. Each to their own.

Hush bit into the ball, tears squeezing from his hidden eyes. He gripped the top sheet of the bed with fingers and toes, tight rope biting into his wrists and ankles.

Just another role, he repeated to himself again.

They all had their kinks. His had been more traditional in Hollywood circles. The patrons of the Kasabian Hotel however, while cast aside by that old nemesis of time that stole from the glamorous and weathered hard-fought reputations, had a shared fetish. They collected more than just autographs; their bedposts held more stars' names than the Walk of Fame. One particular old dame had taken great pleasure in discussing all her purchases while she sodomised him.

Hush roared as whatever had pummeled him was unceremoniously ripped from his body, exiting with a low, wet pop. He heard a door open, and recognised the thick accent of Fritz, the huge Keanu fan.

"Your time, it is up. We must prepare for next one."

Hush struggled as his unseen lover slowly climbed from the bed, unfastening the gag as they passed. He still had no idea if this one was male or female.

439

"Water," he gasped, the synthetic taste of the ball still on his waxy tongue. "Please."

Fritz laughed. "Big movie star man want drink, yes? Lucky for you. Next customer want to give big movie star man drink. He been holding it in all afternoon, just for you."

Behind the blindfold, Hush closed his eyes. Another one into... *that*.

He'd get through it. This was just a part, playing the victim. It surprised him how easy it had been to slip into character after just a couple of hours of method acting.

Hush heard the clatter of a belt buckle. The actors were on set. Time to start the next scene.

In his head, he clung to a life preserver, and as long as he held that in his mind, he could float through this production. The preserver, round, like a zero. Lots of preservers all lined up in a row. Lots of zeroes. Zeroes that could keep a man afloat in this town.

Hush grit his teeth. He wouldn't say a word.

ROUND THIRTEEN
WINNER

RAPE VAN
TIM MILLER

ROUND WINNERS

LINE DANCING AT HACK HOUSE by Jim Goforth

DEATHDAY WISHES by Toneye Eyenot

BONE AND BREAD by Lex H. Jones

FAMILIAR SCENTS by Jonathan Edward Ondrashek

SIBLING RIVALRY by Matt Hickman

PRANK by Peter Oliver Wonder

SQUIRM by Duncan Ralston

YOU REAP WHAT YOU SOW by Kitty Kane

HAVE A NICE DAY by Michael Noe

CERNUNNOS by Daniel Marc Chant

BROKEN THINGS by Kyle M. Scott

ZOMBIE DAD by Kit Power

RAPE VAN by Tim Miller

SPECIAL AWARDS

GROSSEST STORY
"Familiar Scents," Jonathan Edward Ondrashek

SCARIEST STORY
Tie
"Rape Van," Tim Miller
"Line Dancing at Hack House," Jim Goforth.

WEIRDEST STORY
"Riding the Waves of Luminescent Transdimensional Sea Turtles," Dani Brown

FUNNIEST STORY
"The Throbbing In Thurman," T.s. Woolard

MOST ORIGINAL STORY
"Deathday Wishes," Toneye Blakk

OVERALL WINNERS

BEST US STORY

"Familiar Scents," Jonathan Edward Ondrashek

BEST UK STORY

"Zombie Dad," Kit Power

BEST OVERALL STORY

"Broken Things," Kyle M. Scott.

Disagree with our judges? Have your say at www.shadowworkpublishing.com/VS!

THIS ANTHOLOGY WOULD NOT HAVE BEEN POSSIBLE WITHOUT OUR FANTASTIC JUDGES...

ALAN CONAUGH

JOHN FINNEGAN

KIM MIXON HILL

JOHN RATCLIFF

BRANDY YASSA

AFTERWORD
DAWN CANO

Welcome, dear reader. It's lovely to see you. I sincerely hope you enjoyed the battles between US and UK horror authors, and that this anthology introduced you to some names you've never read before. That's the beauty of a collection like this. Not only do you get to experience new tales from your favorite authors, you also get to taste the offerings of those you've never experienced. An anthology like this benefits the authors who put their heart and soul into their stories by giving them invaluable exposure, and it benefits you, the reader, by helping you find stories that open your mind, spur your imagination, and haunt you at night after you turn out the lights.

One day, several months ago, I was talking to author John Ledger, who happens to work for a small, independent press. We got on the subject of competition anthologies as the press he works for ran several of them in the past. The focus of our conversation somehow shifted to which country produced the best horror – the United States or the United Kingdom. He claimed the US was better, but my opinion differed; I've always preferred

horror that comes out of the UK. One thing led to another, and he suggested a competition anthology, pitting the two countries against one another. With his permission, I took the idea and ran with it, creating the book you've just read.

The original title, *Crossing Lines*, was also John's idea, an idea he graciously let me steal. The title not only refers to crossing borders between the two countries, but also crossing the invisible lines set by horror writers all over the world. The authors asked to participate in this anthology did just that. They crossed lines to bring you everything from literary horror to extreme to bizarro – all the various types of stories a horror reader loves. Some stories were written to make you uncomfortable, some to make you sick, and others were crafted to scare you. A few might have even made you laugh.

Although I am an extreme/splatterpunk horror author in my own right, first and foremost, I am a reader, just like you. I still fangirl over many of the authors in this book, and let me tell you, approaching some of them was one of the most terrifying things I've ever done. If you don't know what I mean, just take a look at the table of contents. Not only have we got the well-known publisher, James Ward Kirk, but Kit Power is in here, as well as Rich Hawkins, Kyle M. Scott, Duncan Ralston, Daniel Marc Chant, Dani Brown, Glenn Rolfe, Thomas Flowers, and...well, you get the point. There are some big names in this book, and asking them to participate was horrifying. Would I do it again? In a heartbeat. These and all the other authors in *Crossing Lines* are some of the most down-to-earth, humble people you could ever meet, and they all deserve our support.

Once the US/UK authors were in place, I realized some very talented people were left out of the mix because they neither lived in the US nor the UK, so I opted to expand the talent pool by adding Australian and Canadian authors. Duncan Ralston (Canada), Toneye Eyenot, Jim

Goforth, and Daniel I. Russell (Australia), all graciously accepted the request to provide stories for this little anthology, and for that I am forever grateful.

The table of contents was finally in place, and I had a firm idea of what I wanted to produce, but because I'd never put together an anthology, I realized I needed some help. I sought out a respected indie press and presented the concept to them, and the owner of that press was enthusiastic about the idea. However, through no fault of our own, the relationship ended as quickly as it began, and I had to again search for someone to help get this book off the ground.

Soon after my relationship with the press dissolved, I was approached by my literary knight in shining armor, Daniel Marc Chant, who is one-third of the *Sinister Horror Company*. He graciously offered to advise me on what needed to be done, took care of the really hard work like formatting the paperback edition, and basically held my hand throughout the entire process. Without his assistance, *Crossing Lines* wouldn't be half the book it is, and may not exist at all. I hope that, should I choose to do this again next year, Daniel will be by my side once again.

Let's move on to what's really important – the charities that benefit from your purchase of this book. Ever since I was a kid, like many of you, I'm sure, I've wanted to help animals. I adopt from the shelters. I donate money and supplies when I'm financially able, which isn't as often as I would like. I always said that if I were to become wealthy, I'd open a shelter of my own.

Sound familiar?

When putting together this anthology, the thought of donating the money to charity was incredibly appealing. As people become more and more aware of the plight of homeless animals, it was a no-brainer for me. Why not make a charity anthology to benefit animals? And so the search for a charity began.

To me, it only made sense that because I had writers

from both the US and the UK submitting stories, that one shelter from each country should reap the rewards of their labor. After researching and contacting multiple shelters in both countries, The Second Chance Center for Animals in Flagstaff, Arizona, was the first organization of choice.

The Second Chance Center for Animals cares for more than 10,000 homeless dogs and cats each year and is funded exclusively through donations. The volunteers work tirelessly to ensure each animal receives the very best care, and an operation of this size needs all the help it can get.

The UK charity of choice is West Wales Poundies. The volunteers at this organization rescue dogs from Welsh council pounds – dogs that have fewer than seven days left to live before they're euthanized. Veterinary care, training, transportation and food are provided until forever homes can be found for these dogs.

In today's world, it's normal to feel overwhelmed and powerless to make a change – to do our part to leave the world a slightly better place than how we found it, and to help those who would otherwise be overlooked. One-hundred-percent of the proceeds of *Crossing Lines* goes to help animals in need, and although it may not be much in the grand scheme of things, at least we're doing something.

On behalf of every author in this book, and on behalf of every animal this anthology helps: thank you. Without you, the readers, projects such as this would be impossible. You offer your time, money and support in equal measure to both your favorite authors and those writers just getting started. You post reviews to encourage others to check out your favorite books. You interact on social media sites, and you tell all your friends. Authors today are a lucky group of people. We have you to support us, and that means more than you will ever know.

Wishing you nothing but peace, joy and love.

Dawn Cano, June 27, 2016

ABOUT THE AUTHORS

Jonathan Edward Ondrashek loves to spew word vomit onto the masses. He's had an array of poetry, reviews, articles, and interviews published in the past decade. His first short story appeared in the anthology *Fifty Shades of Slay*, and his first book in *The Human-Undead War* series debuted in April 2016. He also co-edited the horror anthology *What Goes Around* (KnightWatch Press, June 2016). If he isn't working, reading, or writing, he's probably drinking beer and making his wife regret marrying a lunatic.

Twitter: @jondrashek

Facebook: jonathanondrashek

www.jondrashek.com

Born in Oxford but raised in Massachusetts, **Dani Brown** is the author of *My Lovely Wife*, *Middle Age Rae of Fucking Sunshine*, *Toenails*, and *Welcome to New Edge Hill* out from Morbidbooks. She is also the author of *Dark Roast* and *Reptile* out from JEA. She's the person responsible for the

baby blood bath that is *Stara* out from Jaded Books Publishing. She has written various short stories across a range of publications

When she isn't writing she enjoys knitting, fussing over her cats and contemplating the finer points of raising an army of dingo-mounted chavs. She has an unhealthy obsession with Mayhem's drummer and doesn't trust anyone who claims The Velvet Underground are their favourite band.

Facebook: DaniBrownBooks

Daniel I. Russell has been featured publications such as The Zombie Feed, Pseudopod and Andromeda Spaceways Inflight Magazine. Author of *Samhane, Come Into Darkness, Critique, Mother's Boys, The Collector, Retard,* and *Tricks, Mischief and Mayhem,* Daniel is also the former vice-president of the Australian Horror Writers' Association and was a special guest editor of Midnight Echo. His latest novel, Entertaining Demons, is due for release in 2017 with Apex Publications.

David Owain Hughes is a horror freak! He grew up on ninja, pirate and horror movies from the age of five, which helped rapidly install in him a vivid imagination. When he grows up, he wishes to be a serial killer with a part-time job in women's lingerie... He's had several short stories published in various online magazines and anthologies, along with articles, reviews and interviews. He's written for This Is Horror, Blood Magazine and Horror Geeks Magazine. He's the author of the popular novels *Walled In* (2014) & *Wind-Up Toy* (2016), along with his short story collections *White Walls and Straitjackets* (2015) and *Choice Cuts* (2015).

Facebook: DOHughesAuthor
www.david-owain-hughes.wix.com/horrorwriter
Twitter: @DOHUGHES32

Daniel Marc Chant is an author of strange fiction. His passion for H. P. Lovecraft & the films of John Carpenter inspired him to produce intense, cinematic stories with a sinister edge. Daniel launched his debut, *Burning House*, swiftly following with the Lovecraft-inspired *Maldición*. His most recent book *Mr. Robespierre* has garnered universal praise including Confessions of a Reviewer's Novella of The Year 2015 and a Summer Indie Book Award Nomination 2016. Most recently he has ventured into pulp science fiction with the acclaimed novella *Aimee Bancroft and The Singularity Storm* and veered back to horror with his short story collection *Into Fear*.

Daniel also created *The Black Room Manuscripts*, a popular charity horror anthology, & is a founder of UK independent genre publisher The Sinister Horror Company.

Twitter: @danielmarcchant
Facebook: danielmarcchant
www.danielmarcchant.com

Duncan Ralston was born in Toronto and spent his teens in small-town Ontario. As a "grownup," Duncan lives with his girlfriend and their dog in Toronto, where he writes dark fiction about the things that frighten, sicken, and delight him. In addition to his twisted short stories found in *Gristle & Bone*, the anthologies *Easter Eggs & Bunny Boilers*, *What Goes Around*, *Death By Chocolate*, *Flash Fear*, and the charity anthologies *Bah! Humbug!*, *Burger Van* and *The*

Black Room Manuscripts Vol. 1, he is the author of the novel, *Salvage, Every Part of the Animal* and *WOOM*, an extreme horror Black Cover novella from Matt Shaw Publications.
Facebook: DuncanRalstonFiction
Twitter: @userbits
www.duncanralston.com

Essel Pratt is from Mishawaka, Indiana, a North Central town near the Michigan Border. His prolific writings have graced the pages of multiple publications. He is the Author of *Final Reverie, ABC's of Zombie Friendship*, and many short stories. As a husband, a father, and a pet owner, Essel's responsibilities never end. His means of relieving stress and relaxing equate to sitting in front of his dual screens and writing the tales within the recesses of his mind. His first novel, *Final Reverie* is more fantasy-adventure, but does include elements of horror. His first zombie book, *The ABC's of Zombie Friendship*, attacks the zombie genre from an alternate perspective.

Jim Goforth is a horror author currently based in Holbrook, Australia. Happily married with two kids and a cat, he has been writing tales of horror since the early nineties. He has appeared in *Tales From the Lake Vol. 2, Axes of Evil, Terror Train, Autumn Burning: Dreadtime Stories For the Wicked Soul, Floppy Shoes Apocalypse, Teeming Terrors, Ghosts: An Anthology of Horror From the Beyond, Suburban Secrets: A Neighborhood of Nightmares, Doorway To Death: An Anthology From the Other Side, Easter Eggs and Bunny Boilers, MvF: Death Personified,* and edited volumes 2 and 3 of *Reject for Content (Aberrant Menagerie* and *Vicious Vengeance)*.
Facebook: JimGoforthHorror

Twitter: @Jim_Goforth
www.jimgoforthhorrorauthor.wordpress.com

Kitty Kane, AKA Becky Brown, is an emerging horror writer that hails from the south of England. Kitty is a lifelong, avid reader of horror fiction Although writing has been a pastime that she has indulged in for most of her life, she is currently lined for her first published works as part of several collections for J.Ellington Ashton Press, as well as interest in a forthcoming novella. Her style ranges from more traditional short horror stories to bizarre fiction and poetry. Kitty is also one half of writing duo – Matthew Wolf Kane, alongside another emerging talent, Matt Boultby.

Lex H. Jones is a British cross-genre author, horror fan, and rock music enthusiast who lives in Sheffield. He has written articles for The Gingernuts of Horror and Horrifically Horrifying Horror Blog websites on various subjects covering books, film, video games, and music. When not working on his own writing, Lex also contributes to the proofing and editing process for other authors.

Lex's first published book, *Nick & Abe*, is available for purchase from Amazon, Waterstones, and various other book sellers. The book tells the story of God and the Devil spending a year on Earth as mortal men, to see who has the most to learn about the world they created.

Facebook: LexHJones
Twitter: @LexHJones

Matt Hickman is an avid fan of horror fiction. He spends

a majority of his free time reading books from both established and independent authors. With a diverse knowledge of the genre, he has now tried his hand at writing horror. With the support of his peers, some of which are established writers themselves, he now approaches a new career, one that will see him take horror by storm. He currently resides in Tipton, a small town in the West Midlands with his partner and two children. He travels the width breadth of the UK on a regular basis as a Sales Manager for a construction company. Since his debut release last year he has been featured in numerous short story collections, as well as self-publishing a novella, two novels, and a novel through Matt Shaw Publications.

Twitter: @MatthewHickma13

www.matthickmanauthor.blogspot.co.uk

Hidden in a remote location in California lives a man that responds to the name **Peter Oliver Wonder**. Though little is known about him, several written works that may or may not be fictional have been found featuring a character of the same name. Devilishly handsome, quick witted, and as charming as an asshole can be, Peter has come a long way since his time in the United States Marine Corps. Making friends wherever he goes, there is never a shortage of adventure when he is around. The works that have been penned under this name are full of horror, romance, adventure, and comedy just as every life should be. It is assumed that these works are an attempt at a drug fueled autobiography of sorts. Through these texts, we can learn much about this incredible man.

Salomé Jones is a writer turned editor who enjoys stories

where reality meets the strange and wondrous. Though she can now be found wondering around Europe, her native habitat includes the American Midwest, Northwest, and East Coast. Her favorite place is London, where she often sets her stories.

T.S. Woolard lives in North Carolina with his five Jack Russell terriers. For more of his work, look for *Lovecraft After Dark* by JWK Fiction, *Suburban Secrets 2: Ghosts and Graveyards* by JEA Press, *Horror From the Inside Out* by Whorror House, Siren's Call eZines #17, 18, and 20, and his short story collection, *Solo Circus*.

Michelle Garza is from Arizona. She writes alongside her twin sister, **Melissa Lason**. They have been dubbed **The Sisters of Slaughter**. They write horror, science fiction and dark fantasy. Their work has been featured in *Fresh Meat* by Sinister Grin Press, *Wishful Thinking* by fireside press, *Widowmakers* a benefit anthology of dark fiction and Michelle had a poem included in the *Poetry Showcase Vol. One* put out by the Horror Writer's Association. They have stories soon to be released in anthologies by JEA, including *Rejected for Content 3*, *Fata Arcana* and *Males vs Females*.

Thomas S. Flowers is the published author of several character driven stories of dark fiction. He resides in Houston, Texas, with his wife and daughter. He is published in The Sinister Horror Company's anthology *The Black Room Manuscripts*. His debut novel, *Reinheit*, is published by Shadow Work Publishing, along with *The Incredible Zilch Von Whitstein* and *Apocalypse Meow*. His

military/paranormal thriller books, *The Subdue Series* (*Dwelling, Emerging, Conceiving*) continue from Limitless Publishing. In 2008, he was honorably discharged from the U.S. Army where he served for seven years, with three tours serving in Operation Iraqi Freedom. In 2014, Thomas graduated from University of Houston Clear Lake with a BA in History.

www.machinemean.org

Toneye Eyenot is an author with a long background in the Australian Heavy Music scene. He began writing lyrics back in 1990 and has built a rather large repertoire of songs over the last 25 years. In 2011, he was encouraged to write a novel, which he began in earnest. *The Scarlett Curse* was published by J. Ellington Ashton Press, along with the sequel, *Joshua's Folly*, a werewolf novella, *Blood Moon Big Top*, plus his editorial debut with *Full Moon Slaughter*—a werewolf anthology.

Twitter: @ToneyeEyenot

www.toneyeeyenot.weebly.com

James Ward Kirk Fiction is an independent publishing company specializing in horror, suspense and speculative fiction. We deliver quality fiction, poetry and art at an affordable price. A wide-open approach to fiction makes James Ward Kirk Fiction a publisher to follow. We provide the framework for promoting contributors and their work at the highest possible level. We work with new and established writers. Our number one goal is to provide the highest quality art, professional editing and design for maximum customer impact.

Rich Hawkins hails from deep in the West Country, where a childhood of science fiction and horror films set him on the path to writing his own stories. He credits his love of horror and all things weird to his first viewing of John Carpenter's *The Thing*. His debut novel *The Last Plague* was nominated for a British Fantasy Award for Best Horror Novel in 2015. The sequel, *The Last Outpost*, was released in the autumn of 2015. The final novel in the trilogy, *The Last Soldier*, was released in March 2016.

Glenn Rolfe is an author, singer, songwriter and all around fun loving guy from the haunted woods of New England. He has studied Creative Writing at Southern New Hampshire University, and continues his education in the world of horror by devouring the novels of Stephen King, Jack Ketchum, Hunter Shea, Brian Moreland and many others. He and his wife, Meghan, have three children, Ruby, Ramona, and Axl. He is grateful to be loved despite his weirdness. He is the author of *Blood and Rain*, *The Haunted Halls*, *Chasing Ghosts*, *Boom Town*, *Abram's Bridge*, *Things We Fear*, and the collections, *Out if Range*, *Slush*, and *Where Nightmares Begin*.
www.glennrolfe.com

Kit Power lives in the UK and writes fiction that lurks at the boundaries of the horror, fantasy, and thriller genres, trying to bum a smoke or hitch a ride from the unwary.
In his secret alter ego of Kit Gonzo, he also performs as front man (and occasionally blogs) for death cult and popular beat combo The Disciples Of Gonzo.
www.disciplesofgonzo.com

Michael Noe is a splatterpunk author who lives in Barberton Ohio. Influenced by Richard Laymon, and a variety of horror films, Michael creates dark fiction that is often violent, and filled with gore.

Kevin J. Kennedy is a horror author and publisher from Scotland. He fell in love with the horror world at an early age. In his teens he became an avid reader when he found the work of Richard Laymon. After reading everything Laymon had written Kevin found other authors like Brian Keene, Ray Garton, Edward Lee, Bryan Smith, Jeff Strand, John R. Little, Carlton Mellick and the list goes on. At the age of thirty four Kevin wrote his first short story and it was accepted by Chuck Anderson of Alucard Press for the Fifty Shades of Slay anthology. He hasn't stopped writing since. Kevin lives in a small town in Scotland with his beautiful wife Pamela, his step daughter and two strange little cats.

John Ledger is the author of *Abstract Island*, *Dual Depravity* with Jim Goforth, *Final Review* with Dawn Cano, and has short stories featured in the anthologies *Rejected for Content*, *The Gore Carnival*, *Splat 2*, and many more.

Dawn Cano is the author of several works, including *Final Review* with John Ledger, and *I Am Karma* from Shadow Work Publishing.

ABOUT THE CHARITIES

SECOND CHANCE CENTER FOR ANIMALS

Every dog and cat in Northern Arizona has a home.

Through intervention strategies, targeted rescue, compassionate shelter, responsible adoptions, expert veterinary care, and positive animal training programs, Second Chance Center for Animals exists to save the lives of homeless cats and dogs across Northern Arizona.

http://secondchancecenter.org/

WEST WALES POUNDIES DOG RESCUE

West Wales Poundies Dog Rescue is run by Volunteers committed to rescuing dogs from death row in the Welsh Pounds once they have served their 7 days and are at risk of being PTS (put to sleep).

http://www.westwalespoundies.org.uk/

For more delicious dark fiction, visit
www.shadowworkpublishing.com

Made in the USA
Columbia, SC
16 May 2017